BLA

Jessie Keane's story is one of hardship and struggles against the odds from her teen years onwards. Family tragedy, bankruptcy and mixing with a bad crowd all filled her life.

Her first novel, *Dirty Game*, was published by HarperCollins in 2008. She lives in Southampton.

Also by Jessie Keane

Dirty Game

JESSIE KEANE

Black Widow

HARPER

Harper
An imprint of HarperCollins*Publishers*
77–85 Fulham Palace Road,
Hammersmith, London W6 8JB

www.harpercollins.co.uk

This Production 2011

First published in Great Britain by
HarperCollins 2009

Copyright © Jessie Keane 2009

Jessie Keane asserts the moral right to
be identified as the author of this work

A catalogue record for this book
is available from the British Library

ISBN 978-0-00-790579-9

Set in Sabon by Palimpsest Book Production Ltd
Grangemouth, Stirlingshire

Printed and bound in Great Britain by
Clays Ltd, St Ives plc

Mixed Sources
Product group from well-managed
forests and other controlled sources
www.fsc.org Cert no. SW-COC-001806
© 1996 Forest Stewardship Council

FSC is a non-profit international organisation established to promote the
responsible management of the world's forests. Products carrying the FSC
label are independently certified to assure consumers that they come
from forests that are managed to meet the social, economic and
ecological needs of present and future generations.

Find out more about HarperCollins and the environment at
www.harpercollins.co.uk/green

Acknowledgments

To Louise Marley, great friend and problem fixer, Thea at Phoenix Web Designs, Conan McGale at the Charter Company, and Jane Harvey who always finds the way. Huge thanks to publishing legend Wayne Brookes, to my magnificent agent Judith Murdoch, and to Cliff, who has a lot to put up with.

To Barrie, who would have been so pleased about it all. And to Molly, Charlie and Sherbert, my little writing companions, now flying free.

Prologue

1970

Terror filled Charlie 'The Dip' Foster's world.

Charlie had earned his nickname by being a great 'dipper' – a pickpocket – as a kid. From there he'd graduated with honours to GBH and armed robbery; he'd worked his way up the ranks of the Delaney mob, one of London's finest, until he was Redmond Delaney's right-hand man. So he was no fool. He knew he was up shit creek.

Some heavy faces had brought him to Smithfield meat market and he knew he was in it up to his neck.

They were Carter boys.

For the Cockney Carters and the Irish incomers, the Delaneys, the streets of the East End were a war zone. Always had been, always would be.

They'd snatched him; worked him over. Taken him by surprise.

He'd been at his girl's twenty-first birthday party, key of the door. They'd been bopping the night away; they'd got all amorous and gone outside for a bit of how's-yer-father, and he'd been caught with his trousers down – literally.

So now here he was.

They'd laughed as they put him up here. Hung him up by his jacket collar from a hook while joking about meat being well hung. Then they'd left him here while they stood around chatting. Killing time. *Waiting for something*, he thought. Or somebody.

Charlie was a tough bastard but right now he was scared shitless.

It was the noise. The awful noise of that thing coming down on the wooden block.

Charlie's brain was agile, quick, like his fingers – you didn't get well up in the mobs without having a few brain cells, but now his mind kept faltering. That *noise*.

Thunk!

That thing on wood.

Thunk!

Chopping through flesh and bone.

He tried again to get his hands free from their bindings, but failed. He slumped, exhausted.

He dangled there, limp, fearful, worn out.

And the smell in here. The *stink*.

2

The smell of meat, of death. Pigs' heads surrounded him, the skin flayed from the flesh. Their eyes stared at him blindly. Sides of beef nudged him, smearing him with blood.

The cleaver came down again and a trotter thumped on to the floor.

Thunk!

Oh God help me, he thought.

He knew he'd done bad things. Hurt people. Robbed people. *Bad* things. So perhaps God wasn't listening.

The butcher with the gentle eyes and the blood-stained apron went on chopping patiently away at the meat.

Dead meat, thought Charlie. *That's what I am.*

Sweat was dripping from his chin on to the concrete floor, even though it was cold in here.

Gonna die right here, thought Charlie.

But now the boys who had been slumped around, chatting, straightened up and fell silent.

Something was happening.

Someone had arrived.

Now he could see through his stinging eyes that there was a woman approaching. A tall woman, dressed in black.

Dark straight hair falling on to her shoulders and dark green eyes that were just this side of crazy. A real looker. Black coat. Black leather gloves. *Like the angel of death.*

3

There was a heavy on either side of her. Known faces. Jimmy Bond, he knew that bastard of old. Jimmy was moving off to the left and watching, his eyes going from the woman to Charlie, back and forth, back and forth.

The woman stopped walking several paces away and stared up at Charlie.

He gulped.

'You're Charlie Foster,' the woman said. Her voice was low and husky. 'Are you wondering who I am, Charlie? Or do you know?'

Hanging up here was killing him. His head ached, his shoulders were agony. Charlie gulped again, couldn't speak.

'I'm Annie Carter,' she said.

Fuck it, he thought. *That's it. I'm dead.*

1

Not for the first time, Phil Fibbert wondered what he was doing out in the arse-end of nowhere with the warming Mediterranean sun on his back as he dangled, strapped on, from the top of the telephone pole. It wasn't hot, but this was a tricky job and he was soon sweating and cursing.

'How's it going?' shouted up Blondie from below.

Phil glanced down. His calves quivered with effort as he stood braced on the metal struts. Fucking idiot, he'd only just got up here, how did he *think* it was going? But he bit back a sharp reply. Blondie down there was paying the bills. Plus, the man had mad eyes. There was a funhouse party going on in that guy's head. Best not to upset him.

'Okay,' Phil shouted back.

The girl was down there too, blonde hair, tits

to die for, straining against a tight white T-shirt. She was looking up and shielding her baby blues from the glare with upraised arms. He was on a job with a lunatic and a fucking tart, how sensible was that?

But the money.

He kept his mind on the money.

Phil found an unused pair on the cable. This was a simple REMOB or Remote Observation job. Or Tap and Trace, if you wanted it in layman's terms. He was muscular, squat, powerful, dark haired. His hands were large, dusted with dark hair, the fingers spatulate; but now they worked with the delicacy of a surgeon, fastening on the crocodile clips, setting up the relay. He unravelled the wire and tossed the roll down to Blondie. Then he made his way down the pole, jumping the last four feet and landing in a puff of pink dust. He went to the back of the dirty old van and connected the handset. Then he looked at Blondie.

'Job done,' he said. 'Whatever calls they make, we get to hear them too.'

The tall blond man nodded, satisfied. He looked at the blonde woman. At the dark, muscular man. Their contact had tipped them off, given them the perfect time to strike. That time was *now*.

'Are we ready then?' he asked them, twitching about like always. Couldn't seem to keep still for a moment.

They nodded.

The blond man reached into the back of the van and pulled out three dark wool hoods. Slits for eyes, a slit for a mouth. He dished them out, pulled his own over his bright straight blond hair. Waited until the other two were similarly concealed. The girl was tugging on a shabby old anorak to hide the tits. She zipped it shut, put the hood up, nodded. *Ready.*

'Let the games begin,' said Blondie, and pulled out the gun.

2

Ten seconds before the pool house exploded, everything at the Majorcan *finca* was normal. Later, Annie would distinctly remember that. The bay that encircled their hideaway was silent but for the rush and suck of the turquoise sea against the pink-toned rocks far below. Sparrows were drinking at the edge of the pool.

Normal.

Max's younger brother Jonjo was visiting. Jonjo was sprawled out in bathing trunks on a sunbed, beer belly oiled, torpid in the warming noonday sun. His latest blonde floozy was sprawled beside him in the bottom half of a red bikini. Max was in the heated pool, doing strong overarm laps. Max liked to keep himself fit. Layla was indoors, changing into her swimsuit.

Normal.

Annie would always remember that.

Or as normal as it got, with Jonjo and his blonde – this one was called Jeanette, but there had been so many of them that Annie barely ever registered their names any more – here on a visit. Annie hated Jonjo with a passion, but she never let it show. He treated women like dishrags.

'Feed 'em, fuck 'em, then forget 'em,' was Jonjo's motto.

Annie knew her loathing of Jonjo was mutual. Jonjo hated any woman having any sort of influence on his brother. Most particularly he hated any woman with brains. The Carter boys stood together against the world, and Jonjo saw women – Annie included – as mere embellishments.

Thank God Max had always been different. Max had been her lover, her companion, the father of their daughter. *Layla.* Her little star. Four years old come May, the apple of her father's eye. Their beautiful, dark-haired daughter, whom Max adored. When Annie looked into Layla's face she saw herself there. Her own dark green eyes, not Max's steely blue ones. Her own straight nose and full lips, and even her own cocoa-brown hair; not Max's which was black.

Annie had loved Layla obsessively since the moment the Majorcan midwife had laid her, newborn, in her arms. Born out of wedlock, of course, and that had bothered Annie, but only for Layla's sake.

At that time Max was still married to Ruthie, Annie's sister, although that marriage had been a non-starter. Mostly Annie's fault, of course, and she knew it. So she hadn't complained. But Max had done a wonderful thing for her. He had tracked Ruthie down, got the divorce quickly, and married Annie.

She would never forget it. All right, it had been a quiet affair: no fuss, no bother. But the sentiment of the day, the sheer love she had seen shining in Max's eyes as he placed the wedding ring on her finger, was all that she needed.

It was incredible to think how much time had passed since they'd left England's shores. They'd been here ever since, in this beautiful private place. The days had passed in a happy haze. Dinner at little restaurants in the hills. Visits to Valldemossa to see the monastery up in the silent, blue-hazed mountains. Trips in to Palma to marvel at the cathedral and saunter along the little alleyways and spend too much in the shops and eat lunch on the quay.

They hadn't intended to stay, but stay they had. Annie didn't miss London's grey skies: even in February, as now, the sun shone in Majorca; and Max showed no inclination to get back either.

Soon they would have to think about schooling for Layla, but not yet.

Jonjo visited now and again to let Max know

what was happening with the family firm, and Max seemed content with that. Apart from Jonjo – and of course the blondes – no one disturbed them.

A middle-aged Majorcan couple occupied a little villa up by the gate and tended to their needs. Inez cleaned and cooked, Rufio saw to the pool and the maintenance of the *finca* and took a machete to the date palms every spring to cut their old leaves away and make them look pristine.

All was peace and tranquillity.

But when Jonjo visited, things were different. Then there was tension. On summer nights humming with the song of the cicadas, Jonjo and Max sat out late into the night on the terrace. Tiny lizards clung to the walls above the terrace lights. The air was warm and dense from the heat of the day. They discussed family business, drank San Miguel and smoked cigars, and women were not welcome. Max became cooler, harder. Jonjo whispered in his ear and Max listened. Sometimes his eyes would stray to Annie while he listened to what Jonjo had to say. Annie understood – or she tried to – but some of the blondes rebelled.

Jeanette was the latest blonde. It was cooler now, February, so in the evenings the two men occupied the sitting room instead of the terrace, and talked into the small hours.

'He could be in bed with me; why sit up half

the night talking?' Jeanette complained to Annie one morning. 'We're here for a nice holiday, and half the time he fucking well ignores me.'

Annie hoped Jeanette didn't share that thought with Jonjo, but by lunchtime next day it was obvious the silly bint had. Jeanette was sporting an angry-looking bruise on her right cheekbone, and her expression was sulky.

Jonjo and his blondes, thought Annie with distaste. Annie wore a discreet black swimsuit on the days when it was warm enough to lounge by the pool, but Jeanette seemed intent on going completely nude if she could. Anything to catch Jonjo's attention.

Annie glanced over at Jeanette, lying there with her heavy naked breasts exposed to the warm Mediterranean sun. She'd even asked Annie once if anyone would mind if she slipped the bottom half off.

'Yes,' said Annie coldly. 'I'd mind.'

Jeanette had looked at her and sneered. 'I dunno what you're acting all posh for,' she said. 'I know all about you.'

'Oh yeah? What do you know?' Annie lifted her Ray-Bans and looked at the girl.

Jeanette was a pain in the arse. Yesterday had been great, because she had unexpectedly asked to borrow Rufio's dusty, ugly, rear-engined old Renault to go shopping in Palma. The peace had been wonderful. But now she was *back*. And running off at the mouth, as usual.

'I know you worked as a tart. I know you snatched your own sister's man. You got no cause to act all hoity-toity.'

Annie dropped the Ray-Bans back in place and lay back with a sigh.

'You know nothing and you understand even less,' she said.

'Oh yeah? Well I—'

Annie lifted the Ray-Bans again. Her eyes were dark ice as she stared at the girl. 'You keep that evil trap shut, or I'll have your stupid arse out of here on the next flight,' she hissed.

Jeanette fell silent.

Jonjo and his *fucking* blondes. Jeanette was among the worst of them, dim to a fault and full of meaningless chatter and always flaunting herself, so sometimes Jonjo did take notice of her. After one or two overly flirtatious incidents beside the pool, Annie had had to have a word with him about what she considered to be suitable behaviour in front of a child approaching her fourth birthday. It hadn't endeared her to him, but fuck him. This was her home, hers and Max's, and if he wanted to come here then he would have to follow their rules and keep his dick in his trousers unless he was in the privacy of the bedroom.

On the whole, Jonjo was good with Layla.

He played with her in the pool, chased her around the grounds, made her scream with laughter. Jonjo had a way with kids. Different when they got older, of course. Once Layla hit puberty, Annie knew that Jonjo would treat her as he treated all adult women – with contempt and suspicion.

Still, all was quiet for now. Annie relished the moment. She could hear Layla singing in her bedroom, some silly French song she and Max had been learning together. '*Ma chandelle est morte . . . prête-moi ta lume.*'

Annie felt a surge of pride. She could barely speak a word of Mallorquin, or even Castilian Spanish but, thanks to Max's good ear for languages and the cheerful chatter of Inez, their daughter was going to be multilingual.

Jonjo was snoring like a hog, Jeanette had shut her yap for five minutes, and Max was scything rapidly through the water. Annie watched him as he swam to the edge of the pool and pulled himself out in one lithe movement. He padded over to her, water streaming off his dark-skinned and well-toned body, and bent to kiss her.

'Max!' she complained. He was drenching her with water droplets.

He grinned. 'All right, babes?' he asked, sitting down on the edge of her sunbed.

'You're soaking me,' said Annie, but she was smiling.

He leaned in and kissed her again, deeper and harder. Annie put her arms around his neck.

'Shit, get a *room*,' muttered Jeanette.

Annie ignored her. Max drew back a little and she smiled into his eyes.

'Love you,' he murmured against her mouth.

'Love you too,' whispered Annie.

'Jesus,' groaned Jeanette.

'Coming in?' Max asked Annie.

'Not yet. In a mo.'

He kissed her again and stood up, went to the edge of the pool and dived smoothly in.

I'm married to the hottest man in the world, thought Annie with a happy sigh.

She glanced at her Rolex, a present from her working girls back in the days when she had been Princess Ann, the Mayfair Madam.

A lifetime ago, it seemed now.

A time when she'd got mixed up with the Carter and the Delaney mobs, when she'd run two brothels, one in Limehouse, the other in Mayfair. All gone now; all forgotten. Except when Jonjo called and reminded her of it all. She hated it when Jonjo called.

It was nearly one o'clock. Inez usually called in at twelve-thirty to fix lunch, then she and Rufio took their siesta. She was late, but then the Majorcans were never hot on timekeeping. Everything was *mañana*. Tomorrow, things would get done. Today . . . maybe not.

All was . . . *normal.*
Jonjo snoring.
Layla indoors singing a silly French song.
Max doing laps of the pool.
Normal.
And then Annie's world exploded, and normality was forgotten.

3

Annie woke up by slow degrees. She opened her eyes and saw the blue bowl of the sky above her. A buzzard was circling over the cliffs. There was a smell. Smoke and dust. She lapsed into unconsciousness again. Or was it sleep? Was this a dream?

Again she awoke, and this time it was with a powerful sensation of nausea. Of something wrong. The sun was warm but something was burning. Her eyes hurt, her throat felt as dry as dust. A dream. A *nightmare.*

The third time she came back to herself with a violent urge to vomit. She shot up on the sunbed, leaned over, and was sick. Her head spun. Clutching at the sunbed she lay back again and closed her eyes. There was crackling nearby, like a fire in a grate.

What the fuck's going on? she thought.

She opened her sore eyes and alarm started to take hold. She wasn't in bed. This was daylight, she was lying beside the pool and . . . she fought to clear her jumbled thoughts . . . there was something happening. There had been a bang, then something on her face, and now there was an unpleasant chemical smell in her nostrils and – Jesus – she was going to throw up again.

She vomited again on to the stones of the terrace, then thought: *Layla?*

She had heard Layla indoors singing just before the bang. Sometimes you got hunters up in the wood after rabbits, but this had been different, so much louder. A roll of smoke and dust, a bang louder than any firework, it had hurt her ears and they were ringing with the aftermath of some sort of shockwave. She could hear a dog whimpering nearby.

No. Not a dog, a person.

Layla?

Annie fought her way up into a sitting position, swaying, impelled by the need to get to her daughter *right now*. She felt drunk. Which was almost funny because she had never been drunk in her life. Her mother Connie had been an alcoholic and it had killed her. Annie was happy never to touch the stuff, ever.

She opened her eyes to a scene of horror. Jonjo's sunbed was empty. Jeanette was still there, though.

Jeanette was sitting up and with her head in her hands. The whimpering was coming from Jeanette.

Alarm shot through Annie.

'What's happening?' asked Annie. Her voice came out a croak.

Jeanette dropped her hands. She looked at Annie with eyes wild with terror. She opened her mouth and started to shriek. Annie lurched to her feet, staggered, then righted herself. She plummeted to her knees in front of Jeanette.

'What happened?' she asked again, and her voice was stronger now.

Jeanette's hysterical screams seemed to be echoing around Annie's aching head. She hauled back an arm and slapped the other woman, hard. Then she grabbed her by the shoulders and shook her.

'What happened?' she shouted. 'Is Layla indoors? Is Layla all right?'

Now Jeanette was crying and shuddering.

Christ, thought Annie. She stumbled to her feet and half fell off the terrace and through the door into the sudden cool and semi-darkness of the *finca*'s hallway. The telephone on the hall table tinkled as she passed by. She stopped, looked at it. *What the fuck?* It had never made that sound before. Maybe the blast had damaged the wiring in some way. She picked it up, heard only a normal dial tone. She quickly put it back down again and hurried on. Supporting herself against the walls, she dragged herself to Layla's bedroom, blinking to try to see with eyes that were incredibly sore.

Layla's swimsuit was laid out on her bed beside her teddies and dolls. But the room was in chaos. The stool at the dressing table was thrown on the floor, and a chair had been knocked over, and the dressing table itself was askew, as if it had been pushed.

But the thing was way too heavy for Layla to have moved it.

Where was Layla?

Swallowing bile and a growing panic, Annie lurched into the bathroom, into the master bedroom, into the spare bedroom, the kitchen, then the sitting room.

'Layla!' she yelled, but there was no answer. She ran outside to the back of the *finca* where Layla loved to play; she had a swing there, suspended from one of the palms.

'Layla!' she yelled again, but there was only silence.

Maybe this *was* a nightmare. Please God let it be a nightmare. At any moment Layla would come and jump on the bed and she would wake up and Max would groan beside her and roll over and go back to sleep.

'Layla!'

Nothing. No answer. No sound.

Annie stumbled back outside to the terrace and stepped on something soft. There was a tiny crunch of bones. She looked down. A dead sparrow. Not a mark on it, but it was dead. *The blast*, she thought. The shockwaves had killed it. There had been an explosion. Or had it been merely stunned? Had she just killed the poor damned thing with her weight? Nausea rose again. Her eyes went to the pool house and found nothing there but smouldering wreckage.

Her eyes drifted on.

'Max?'

Her eyes locked on to the body in the pool. A man's body, the skin brown from hours spent in the sun, face-down, floating on the surface. Dark hair on the arms, dark hair on the head – and blood billowing all around it like a crimson halo.

Annie felt the breath leave her body in one horrified, disbelieving rush.

'*Max!*' she screamed, and dived straight into the pool.

Afterwards, Annie couldn't even remember swimming across the pool. One moment she was on the side looking at Max's lifeless body, then she was there beside him.

'*Max!*'

The nightmare was relentless. She rolled him over and he was weightless, lifeless in the water.

21

Max, oh God Max no please don't be dead, please Max . . .

It was Jonjo.

The breath left Annie in a whoosh and she sank and came up spluttering and choking on chlorine and Jonjo's blood. Jonjo's pale blue eyes were wide open, staring blankly at the sky, and between them was an impossibly neat hole, leaking a steady flow of red into the blue water. She flinched away from the body in horror. Glanced at Jeanette, who had seen that it was Jonjo too and was now starting to shriek again.

Where was Max?

Annie felt panic grip her, robbing her of reason. Jonjo was dead. The explosion. Layla, where was Layla? And Max. *Where the fuck was Max?*

Something deadly serious had happened here. A deliberate hit. Max and Jonjo Carter had influential friends but they had bad enemies too. People whose toes they had trod on over turf in London. People who might want to take revenge. Maybe she and Max had been out here lotus-eating for so long that they had dropped their guard. She had to do something. Fuck, she wished Jeanette would shut up.

She looked all around the perimeter of the *finca* and stared up at the rock face looming behind the building. Max could have taken cover up there, if this was a hit. And if this was a hit, they – whoever 'they' might be – could be up there right now, watching, maybe taking aim.

Annie swam swiftly to the side of the pool and hauled herself out. She grabbed Jeanette and yanked her to a standing position.

'Just shut up,' she ordered, and shook the blonde again, hard. 'Shut up. Come inside, come *on*, you silly cow.'

Annie grabbed Jeanette's arm and hauled her indoors. She slammed the door shut and locked it. She went to the back door and quickly locked that too, while Jeanette stood nearly nude, shivering and crying in the hallway. Annie closed all the windows and shutters. Then she bundled Jeanette into the master bedroom, locked the door behind them and shoved her in the direction of the wardrobe.

'Put some clothes on,' said Annie. '*Move*, Jeanette. Come *on*.'

Jeanette was still weeping and wailing. She was just standing there looking at the clothes.

Annie ran over to her. Her heart was pounding, her head was spinning, she wasn't entirely sure she wasn't going to be sick again. She wanted to scream too. *Layla. Max. Where the fuck were they?*

'What did you see out there, Jeanette?' she demanded urgently.

Jeanette just stared at her. *Shock*, thought Annie. *She's in shock.*

23

'Come on. Talk,' she said more gently. If she was ever to get any sense out of the poor bitch, she'd better ease up.

'Men, there were men,' cried Jeanette.

'Go on.' Annie felt herself grow still as she braced herself as if for a fatal impact.

She wanted to hear, but she didn't. Dreaded the details, but she had to know. Christ, she was shivering too now. She wanted to roar and scream at Jeanette, demand every detail; she wanted to *know*. But know what? How terrible would it be, to know what had taken place out there on the terrace? How terrible, to know what had happened to the man she loved so much, to the daughter who was a living, breathing part of her and of him?

'Maybe four of them – I don't know.' A sob burst from Jeanette. Snot and tears ran down her face in rivers. 'It all happened so fast; it was so confusing. They had masks on. They dragged Jonjo off the bed and shot him and threw him in the pool. They put a cloth over your face. I thought they were going to kill me.'

'Max?' asked Annie, thinking: *I'll never survive this, I couldn't live if he was dead . . .*

'They grabbed him.'

'And?'

'They grabbed Layla too.'

Layla.

Annie turned away from Jeanette. Moving like

24

a zombie, she went to the left-hand side of the bed, the side that Max always slept on, and opened the drawer in the bedside cabinet. The first thing she saw was Max's ring. He always took it off when he was in the pool. It was bright yellow gold, with engraved Egyptian cartouches on either side of a square slab of lapis lazuli. She took it out, turned it over. Her eyes suddenly filled with tears.

Max.

She took a breath, blinked, got focused again. She slipped the ring on to her thumb, for comfort, for reassurance; then got back to business. There was a small bunch of keys, and she pocketed them. She pulled out a cloth-wrapped parcel with shaking hands and removed an oilcloth-covered item from within it. Pulled off the oilcloth and sat down hard on the bed as her head spun suddenly and the room tilted and darkened.

Got to get a hold, she thought. *Got to keep thinking.*

But Max. Layla. Someone had them. Fuck it all, someone had *killed* Jonjo.

Come on, Annie. Get a grip. You're still fucking alive. They left you alive.

Annie came back to herself, taking deep breaths. The room steadied. Why had they left her alive? They'd drugged her, left her to find this horror. They'd left Jeanette too, apparently untouched, un-molested. Shit, if they were willing to snatch Max and Layla, if they were willing to plant a bullet hole in poor bloody Jonjo's head, why hadn't they finished the job? Why hadn't they killed her and Jeanette too?

Annie tipped the gun out on to the bed and snatched it up. Christ, she was shaking so hard. She flicked open the chamber, as she had seen Max do. He practised shooting at a target back in the woods sometimes, and he was a crack shot, a brilliant shot, but she was nervous of guns. She'd taken a bullet herself, and that was enough to make anyone wary.

She took out the box of bullets and removed the lid. Started loading the cold, slippery things into the chambers. Tried to, anyway. Her hands were shaking so much she could hardly get the bullets in there. She breathed deep again, steadied herself. Got the bullets in and snapped the chamber closed. Slipped her finger in beside the trigger.

'It's a hair trigger,' she remembered Max saying when he had shown her the gun once. 'You've got to be careful. One squeeze and you've blown someone away. Put the safety catch on once it's loaded.'

Annie had shuddered. She still had the scar from the bullet she'd taken; she didn't want to go shooting anyone. She had seen what guns could do, first-hand.

26

But they could still be here, hiding, waiting. And they had taken Layla. They had taken Max.

Annie clicked on the safety and went over to the wardrobe. Jeanette was still standing there like a spare prick at a wedding. She stared wide-eyed at the gun in Annie's hand.

'We've got to protect ourselves,' said Annie. 'Now come on. Let's get dressed.'

She pulled out tops and jeans for them both and shoved the clothes at Jeanette. 'Put these on.'

Jeanette stood there, clutching the clothes to her and still not moving.

Nearly demented, Annie hissed through gritted teeth: '*Move*, you stupid cow.'

Annie's tone would have galvanized a regiment. Jeanette started to put on the clothes. Annie did the same, yanking on jeans and a blue top. Then the phone started to ring in the hall.

It would be Inez, apologising for being late with the lunch, telling her that she was coming now, *Señora*, she would be five minutes, only five . . . which meant another half an hour. Inez, with no idea that hell had been set loose. Thinking no doubt that the bang of the pool house being blown up was somebody back in the woods, hunting with a shotgun. If she had heard it at all. Inez was a little deaf, and Rufio liked a drink or two; they weren't the brightest kids on the block and that was a fact.

Grabbing Jeanette with one hand and clutching

the gun in the other, Annie went into the hallway and picked up the phone.

'Inez?' Her voice sounded like someone else's. Some dry old woman's. She was breathless with panic and whatever crap they had used to knock her out had affected her voice, made her throat dry and sore.

'Annie Carter.'

Annie dropped the phone. It had been a man's voice, low and mean and Irish. Not Inez. She hauled the damned thing back up by the cord, shaking like a leaf, and clamped it back to her ear.

'Who is it?' Jeanette bleated anxiously.

'Shut up,' said Annie. She took a breath and spoke into the phone. 'Who wants her?'

'No questions.'

Annie was suddenly furious. 'What the fuck have you done with them, you tosser?'

The man was laughing. She'd amused him. She wanted to smash the phone against the wall; she wanted to crawl down inside it and come out the other end and smash this creep to smithereens.

'*Where's my daughter?*' she screamed at him.

'Ah, the girl. I've got her here somewhere.'

'And Max. Where's Max?'

'You mean Max Carter?'

He was toying with her; she could hear laughter in his voice; this was a massive joke to him – her distress, her fear, her horror was meat and drink to him.

'You'll pay for this,' she promised.

'Fine words,' he said.

'He'll make you pay.'

'That would be a neat trick. He's dead.'

Annie sagged against the wall. Her head was thumping with pain now, she was frightened she was going to faint. 'He's not dead,' she said. She couldn't let herself take that in. She couldn't allow herself to believe it, not for an instant. If she did, she was afraid she wouldn't go on. Not even for Layla's sake.

'Oh but he is. We pushed him off a fucking mountain and watched him bounce all the way to the bottom.'

'What is it?' Jeanette was wild-eyed, clutching at Annie's shoulder, almost shaking her. 'What are they saying? Who's dead?'

Annie sank to the floor, unable to hold herself up.

'He's not dead,' she told the man on the end of the phone.

'He's dead.' The voice was harsh. 'Get used to it. I'll phone back in an hour. Be waiting. Oh – and your *staff*, in case you were wondering, are a bit tied up. An hour. Be ready.'

The line went dead.

A bit tied up. What the hell was that supposed to mean? Had these bastards done something to Inez and Rufio? Their smaller villa was up by the

29

gate – maybe they had seen the men coming in and had questioned them? Or had the men come down from the hills behind the property, to maintain the element of surprise?

They had an hour. This bastard was on the other end of a phone, so he wasn't lurking outside.

No, he isn't – but what if he's left someone behind, someone to watch and see what you do?

No matter. She couldn't just sit on her arse for an hour with Jeanette bawling and screaming in her ear. She had to *do* something, or go crazy.

'Did they say Max was dead too?' Jeanette was demanding.

'Yes,' said Annie.

Oh shit, why doesn't the silly bitch just shut up? I don't want to hear that again. Not now, not ever.

'Come on,' Annie said sharply. 'We're going to go and get Inez and Rufio.'

Jeanette looked at her as if she'd gone mad. 'But what about Jonjo?'

'Jonjo's dead for sure. We can see that with our own eyes. Whether we stay or go, there's no help for him.'

Jeanette flinched back as if Annie had slapped her again.

'Jesus,' said Jeanette on a shuddering breath. 'Jonjo said you were a hard bitch, and now I believe it.'

'We can't help Jonjo,' said Annie. 'But we can see that Inez and Rufio are okay.'

Jeanette's eyes were suddenly cold. 'I can see why he hated you,' she said.

'He wasn't my first choice for a brother-in-law either,' said Annie. 'He didn't like any woman close to Max.'

Jeanette's face sagged. 'God, I can't believe he's dead. I can't believe it! Did they really say that Max is gone too?'

Annie felt a surge of hate for Jeanette, but she reined it in. Jeanette might be stupid, she might be a gobby little tart, but she didn't deserve Annie's anger. She regained control of herself with an effort.

'They said so. But we don't know it's true.'

'Oh fuck,' bleated Jeanette, dissolving into tears again. 'It must be true! What would they make it up for?'

Again that almost unstoppable urge to strike out, to stop Jeanette uttering another word. 'I don't know,' said Annie through gritted teeth. 'I don't understand any of this. But we've got . . .' she glanced at her watch. God bless Rolex. Still working, despite the blast, despite the water. '. . . three-quarters of an hour to get up there and back again. It's time enough.'

'But . . . should we go outside?' asked Jeanette fearfully.

'Maybe not. But we're going to, all right? Because if they'd wanted us dead too, then I'm guessing we'd be dead already.'

31

Jeanette nodded dumbly.

'Right. Let's go,' said Annie. 'We're going to keep under cover as much as possible, and we're not going to speak, okay? You're going to follow me, step where I step, and keep your fat mouth shut for a change, got that?'

Another nod.

Annie lifted the gun, slipped off the safety catch, and opened the door on to the poolside terrace. She looked out. The wreckage of the pool house was still smoking. The sun was still shining.

'Jesus *God*,' shrieked Jeanette.

Annie's stomach flinched with fear. All the hairs on the back of her neck stood up.

Jonjo's body was gone.

'All right, shut up. *Shut up!*'

Jeanette was off again, shrieking her head off, signalling their precise whereabouts to anyone who cared to listen. Annie turned in the *finca*'s doorway and whacked her a good one across the face. She was putting them both at risk; it had to be done. Jeanette reeled back and thumped against the wall and was instantly silent. Annie held a finger to her lips and her eyes told Jeanette to shut it, *right now*, or she'd get another one.

Someone was playing mind games with them. Someone had left them alive when they ought to be dead. Someone was here, right here, noting

32

what they were doing, noting their reactions. Perhaps just toying with them until they felt like doing the deed. But perhaps not. Maybe there was a faint grain of hope to be found here, for them and for Layla too.

Annie had to cling to that. She was used to standing alone against the odds. A drunken mother, an absent father, all kinds of rucks after she had betrayed her sister Ruthie, all kinds of battles to be fought. And she had fought them, and somehow she had won through. Where there was life, there was hope.

She put any thought of Max aside with ruthless firmness now. She tucked all that away in a box in her mind marked PRIVATE. She would look in there later. But for now, she was alive, she had a chance. She was not going to throw it away. And there was Layla. She owed it to herself, but more than that she owed it to Max's daughter. If she had to beat this poor dumb idiot to a pulp to shut her up, she'd do it; and Jeanette saw that resolve very clearly in Annie's face.

'We're going to get Inez and Rufio,' said Annie, slowly and clearly, as Jeanette stood there with tears streaming down her bruised face. 'If I hear another sound out of you before we get up there, I'm going to make you pay for it. You got that now?'

Jeanette nodded and swallowed. Annie looked capable of anything. She looked scary.

'You draw attention to us again, I'll just knock you unconscious with this.' Annie held up the gun. 'You'd better believe what I'm saying.'

Jeanette nodded. 'I do,' she said weakly.

'Good. Now let's go. Keep right behind me and keep checking behind us as we go, okay? You see anything, tap my shoulder but say nothing. Got it?'

Another nod.

Annie looked down at Jeanette's feet. *Why* had she put high heels on?

'Take those bloody shoes off, they're too noisy.'

Jeanette kicked off the shoes and held them sheepishly in her hand.

'Shut the door behind us, quietly. Okay?'

Nod.

'Good. Come on then.'

And Annie was off, keeping close to the *finca*'s wall as she skirted the terrace, stepping off and into beds of hibiscus. She paused as she hit the driveway, keeping close to the rocky edge of the drive where they would be concealed from anyone hiding out on the scrubby rock face behind the property.

She looked back at Jeanette, who was nervously looking all around them. That was good. Fear was making her alert. Annie felt fearful herself, and exposed, all her nerves jangling, her skin crawling.

Everything was quiet, only the rising wind in the palms and the faint rush of the sea making

34

any noise at all. At any moment she expected someone to come at them, to finish the job, but she walked on, cat-footed, creeping along the edge of the drive, watching, walking . . . it seemed endless. But finally they were there, stepping on to the back terrace where in summer a huge bougainvillea trailed papery magenta blooms over a rickety pergola. Stepping into deep shade, Annie stopped at the closed blue-painted back door.

Annie was aware that she was wet through with nervous sweat. Runnels of perspiration trickled down between her breasts, and her T-shirt was sticking unpleasantly to her back. She had to keep blinking sweat out of her eyes.

This was stark, consuming terror of a type she had only experienced once before, when Pat Delaney had come after her with mayhem and murder in his twisted mind. It was horrible, making her bowels feel loose, making her want to puke. But if Jeanette saw her losing it, then she would lose it too – and then where would they be? She reached out with a shaking hand and tried the handle. It gave and the door moved inward. She braced herself. Looked back at Jeanette. Jeanette nodded. No one about. Annie brushed the sweat from her stinging eyes with the back of one hand. Found she didn't want to open the door at all. Felt afraid. Horribly, mortally afraid.

She pushed the door open anyway.

4

Inside the little villa it was cool and quiet. They had stepped straight into the kitchen, which was very simple – there was a stone sink, a stout table, an old but clean cooker. Everything was scrubbed, spotless. Inez was a good housekeeper and prided herself on her cleanliness. But to Annie the kitchen looked *too* clean. There was no evidence of lunch preparations on the table, no bread, no cheese, no beer or limoncello, nothing. No sign of activity.

There was always activity around Inez: she liked to keep busy. Layla loved to come up here and make a pest of herself in this little kitchen, and Annie had questioned Inez, was Layla a nuisance to her? But Inez always laughed and said, *No, Señora*. The *bambina* was no trouble at all.

Now there was no Inez bustling about, scolding Rufio with a smile, laying out food, chatting full-tilt in indecipherable Mallorquin, chopping onions and fat red tomatoes grown fresh on the vine by Rufio's own hand. Now there was no activity at all. The *finca* was silent. Annie and Jeanette stepped inside the kitchen, and Jeanette pushed the door closed.

A gust of wind caught it and it banged shut.

Annie gave Jeanette a sharp look. She didn't know what they were going to find in here. They – whoever *they* were – could be lying in wait, ready to spring a nasty surprise on the two women. She didn't want any of their movements signalled ahead.

She crossed the kitchen cautiously to the wide-open parlour door. Here too the furnishings were simple. Polished marble flooring – marble was cheap and plentiful in the Balearics – and a little old couch, a couple of spindle-back chairs, and a scrubbed-clean dining table. But no Inez, no Rufio.

This was starting to give Annie the creeps.

This wasn't normal.

This was anything but normal.

'Where the hell are they?' hissed Jeanette.

Annie held up a finger to her lips and mouthed: *Shut the fuck up, will you?*

Jeanette pulled a face but did as she was told.

Annie carefully opened the door into the hall. It was empty. Holding the gun at the ready, she crossed the hall to the bedroom and pushed the door gently open.

Blowflies swarmed out, and with the flies came the smell. Annie flinched back and Jeanette let out a cry of startled disgust.

Oh God, thought Annie. *No.*

Fighting the urge to gag, she pushed the door wide open and saw what was there. Rufio was tied to the chair, his head flung back, his lifeless eyes staring at the ceiling. Bluebottles swarmed over his face and over the gaping wound that slit him open from neck to crotch. His own blood-stained machete lay discarded on the tiled floor.

The stench of blood hit Annie afresh and she nearly choked. And there was Inez, on the bed . . .

No, she couldn't look any more.

Tied up, she thought. *Your staff are a little tied up.*

What sort of sick bastard could have done a thing like this? They'd been dead for hours, she could see that. For *hours*. While she and the others had been lazing on the terrace, perfectly relaxed, up here this horror had been unfolding, and they had heard nothing, known nothing. Annie's skin crawled to think that the bastards who had done all this had been prowling around, and she had been completely unaware. And now . . . *this*.

She closed the door softly on the grisly scene, but she could still see it in her mind's eye. Her guts still churned and her mind still floundered to take it in.

'Oh *Jesus*,' Jeanette moaned, holding a hand to her throat. 'Who could do that? How could anyone do that? What – what's going to happen to us?'

'Fuck it, is that all you can think about?' Annie rounded on her furiously. 'We're still alive. They're not.'

But they might just be playing with you, said an insidious voice in her head. *Making you really suffer before they strike the killing blow.*

No, Annie told herself. They had Layla. They had Layla and that meant they were willing to negotiate. Didn't it? But . . . it might also mean that they knew what would hurt Annie most, and that would be for Layla to suffer. Inez and Rufio had been tortured. Would these people draw the line at torturing a little girl?

She had to push those thoughts away. She was still alive; she had to dig deep and hold on while there was still hope for Layla. She couldn't afford to give in to despair. She glanced at her watch and her heart seemed to stop dead.

Had they really been that long getting up here, looking around, finding that awful scene? The hour was up. Bang on time, she heard it. The phone was ringing in the main house. And she wasn't there to answer it.

She ran as if her life depended on it. Forgot who could have been watching, hiding, awaiting their

39

opportunity to pounce. She ran and was only dimly aware that the light was going now, that it was growing cooler, that Jeanette had forgotten all that Annie had said about keeping quiet and was bleating along behind her, clacking along in her high heels, silly cow, saying something, babbling and crying, moaning that she wouldn't be left alone up there, that they were never going to get back in time anyway so why try?

But they *had* to try.

Annie thought of nothing except the need to be quick. Quicker than she had ever been in her life. Her heart felt as though it was bursting out of her chest, her legs were on fire. She sprinted on to the terrace, crashed through the *finca*'s door straight into the hallway and her hand was on the phone when it stopped ringing.

'No!' she yelled, and picked it up and flung it against the wall, feeling helpless, stupid, furious. Instantly she regained control. Picked the thing up, listened to the dial tone. Still working. But she had missed the call.

Be there, he had said.

And she hadn't.

Jeanette was still prattling on.

'What will happen? What will they do? Will they hurt Layla? We missed the call, they won't like that.'

'Shut up,' said Annie.

'They won't hurt her, will they? Not a little girl like Layla? They wouldn't do that, would they?'

'Shut up,' repeated Annie, watching the phone, willing it to ring again.

'They won't hurt her,' said Jeanette shakily.

Annie's head shot round and she glared at her. 'I told you, shut up. I can't think with all this yakking going on.'

Annie looked past her at the door, forced herself to think even though her guts were liquid with panic. She'd missed the call. Would they phone back? She took a deep breath. Now she felt really sick. The thought of these people having Layla. She wished Max was here. No hope there, though. No hope at all.

'Shut the door,' she told Jeanette, and Jeanette read her look correctly and quickly obeyed.

But then Annie thought about that and wondered if she was shutting the baddies out, or shutting them *in*, because they could already be here, wasn't that a cold hard fact?

She thought of the quiet way they had moved Jonjo out of the pool, when she and Jeanette had been right here in the *finca*, and they hadn't heard a thing. Four men, wasn't that what Jeanette had said?

Four men wearing masks.

Four dangerous, *deadly* men. They could be in here right now, ready to spring out and do damage.

'They're not going to ring back,' said Jeanette, shaking her head in rising hysteria. She was clutching herself and shivering.

Thank Christ, Jeanette hadn't yet considered they could be shut in here with a clutch of murderers. That would really make her flip.

'They'll ring back,' said Annie, although she also doubted it. 'They've got a bargaining tool. They've got Layla. And maybe they were watching us when we went in to find Inez and Rufio. They'll know where we were and that it was a legitimate delay.'

Legitimate, thought Annie. She was talking as though they were dealing with reasonable people here. Not people who would shoot a man between the eyes, push another off a cliff, snatch a child away from its parents, torture a harmless, good-natured woman like Inez in front of her horrified husband's eyes.

She bit her lip, folded her arms around herself and watched the phone. Along the hallway, the kitchen door was ajar and she could see in there too. It appeared to be empty. She straightened and moved toward it.

'Where are you going?' Jeanette almost shrieked. She was clearly terrified of being left alone.

'Hush,' said Annie, and walked on silent feet along the hallway. Jeanette came mincing and clattering along behind her. Annie stopped and turned and looked at Jeanette.

'For the last time, *take off those fucking shoes,*' she hissed at the girl.

Jeanette quickly kicked off the heels. Annie proceeded into the kitchen. Empty. Silent. Cool and almost dark. There was the larder, though. Big enough for a man to hide in, easily. Annie crossed to the drawer by the sink and pulled out the two large sharp knives she knew were in there. None were missing, and that was good. That was very good.

She handed one of the knives to Jeanette.

'Keep it ready,' she said.

'*Jesus,*' moaned Jeanette, but she took the knife anyway.

Annie held a knife in one hand and the gun in the other and went over to the larder. She nodded to Jeanette to stand aside, then flung the door wide.

Nothing.

Annie leaned against the door and got her breath back. The kitchen was clear. She rechecked the back door lock and the shutters at the tiny window. Left the larder door wide open, so if anyone got in there she'd know about it. Then she ushered Jeanette out of the kitchen and back into the hallway.

'Have you ever used a gun?' Annie asked Jeanette.

Jeanette shook her head, no. She was pale and sweating.

She's cracking up, thought Annie. *She's taken nearly as much as she can take, and she's gonna blow.*

'When that phone rings again, I'm going to answer it and you are going to watch our backs with this.' Annie handed her the gun. It was easier to shoot someone than to knife them. Easier and much more effective, and hey! You could do it at a distance. Triple benefits, no less.

When Annie found herself thinking this way she wondered if she was becoming hysterical too.

'No,' said Jeanette numbly. 'I can't do it.'

'Oh yes you can. Think of what they've just done here. Now hold it steady. That's it. Never point it at me or at your foot or anything bloody mad like that, you got that? That's a hair trigger, it'll go off at the merest pressure. We've checked this end and the kitchen's clear. So all we have to watch is the doors off this end of the hall, and the main door. If anyone opens that main door, or any of the other doors, don't hesitate. Just shoot. Aim for the torso.'

The torso was the biggest and the safest target, that was what Max had always said.

Jeanette was gazing in dumb horror at the gun in one hand, the knife in the other.

Annie grabbed her arm and gave her a little shake.

'Come *on*, Jeanette. You want to get out of this, I need your help. Okay?'

No answer.

Annie gave her another little shake. 'Come on, Jeanette. We can do this. Okay?'

This time Jeanette took a gulp and nodded.

'Good girl.'

The phone started ringing again and Jeanette dropped the gun. The shot was deafening in the enclosed hallway and a bullet thudded into the wall, throwing up a spray of plaster dust.

Nerves jangling, Annie snatched up the phone. 'Hello?'

She looked at Jeanette, who was whimpering and wailing and bending to pick up the gun as if it was going to bite her. As Jeanette straightened, Annie mouthed, *Shut up you fucking idiot* at her. Jeanette fell silent.

'You missed my call.' It was the same voice, unmistakably Irish and low and menacing.

'I didn't mean to,' said Annie, trying to place the accent. *Definitely Southern*, she thought.

'If it ever happens again, the girl will pay.'

Annie swallowed hard. 'It won't happen again.'

'She's a pretty little girl.'

Annie was silent.

'A pretty little dark-haired girl.'

Annie said nothing.

'You haven't asked the question yet,' said the voice.

'What question?'

45

'You have to ask "What do you want?"' he said, and she could hear the smile in his voice; he was enjoying himself here. 'You asked it last time, not this. What's changed?'

'All right,' said Annie. 'What do you want?'

'It's too early to say.'

He was playing with her. This was a game.

'Money? I can get it.'

Could she? She wasn't sure how much Max kept here, but she knew it would be little more than small change. She'd never had to think about money: Max took care of all that. There was no safe here, no cashbox. She felt a shiver of apprehension crawl up her spine.

'I have jewellery,' she said hurriedly when he didn't reply. 'Expensive jewellery. You can have it.'

Now he was laughing, the bastard. Was he the one who had done that to Inez, to poor harmless Rufio?

'Check your jewellery case, you'll find I've already got it.'

Christ! Annie looked at Jeanette and nodded at the gun. Her eyes said, *Keep watch. Like your life depended on it.*

They'd been inside the *finca*, probably when she and Jeanette were up finding that horror in the smaller building. Annie watched Jeanette. The hand holding the gun was shaking and she had tucked the knife into her waistband. She was eyeing the outside door as if a troop of marauders were about to burst through it.

And maybe they were.

'So I'm asking the question,' said Annie. 'What is it that you want?'

'Maybe more than you can deliver,' he said.

'Anything's possible. All you have to do is ask.' Annie's brain was spinning, but she took a deep breath and said it. He wouldn't like it, but what could she do? 'Listen, there's no money here.'

'Don't kid around with me, sweetheart, I don't like it.'

'I'm not kidding. There's no money here.'

'For fuck's *sake!*' he roared. He sounded furious.

'Wait!' Annie started talking fast. She didn't want that anger being directed at Layla. '*Wait*. Just because there's none here doesn't mean I can't get any. I *can*. I can get anything, any amount you want, in London.'

'*Fuck* it,' he said savagely.

Annie flinched.

'Are you bullshitting me?' he demanded. 'Because I warn you—'

'No! I'm not feeding you bullshit. This is the truth, you hear me? You've been in here, in this *finca*, didn't you check? I bet you did. There's no safe here, nothing. But look. My husband owns clubs in London. He has property there, business there; that's where the money is. Give me a chance and I'll get it for you.'

Silence.

'So tell me,' said Annie. 'Tell me what you want, I'll get straight back there and I'll get it for you. It's not a problem.'

She really was going to vomit in a minute, talking to scum like this, trying to persuade him not to just lose it and hurt Layla, trying to persuade him that she could do it, she could come up with the goods.

Could she though?

He was silent again. She was sure he was just going to put the phone down again, leave her dangling in limbo for God alone knew how much longer.

'Come on, talk to me!' she pleaded desperately. 'We can do a deal. You know we can do a deal.'

He was going to put the phone down. There was a silence again, an unnerving silence, and then he said: 'You can get money there? Straight now, no bullshit? Because I warn you . . .'

'It's not bullshit.'

A silence again. A long, long silence, eating into her soul. Then: 'Where will you stay there? Give me the address.'

Annie thought fast. Cursed inwardly. Gave him the address anyway.

'And the phone number.'

She gave him that too.

'Now tell me what you want. Tell me and I'll get it sorted, okay?' said Annie.

'Later. I'll call you again when you're back in London.'

'What?'

'Go back there, I'll get in touch.'

'Wait!' The protest burst out of Annie without thought. Suddenly she knew she couldn't leave the island, couldn't leave Max. Couldn't believe he was dead, and so couldn't leave, couldn't accept any of this. And Layla! Layla was here. She felt sick with fear. She might never see her again if she went back to England and left her here, in the hands of these *animals*. 'No, wait!'

'No?' There was no laughter in his voice now. 'You listen to me, you fucking jumped-up tart. You fly back there tomorrow morning and you don't ask questions or tell me no because I don't like that. You got it?'

Annie took a steadying breath. 'All right.'

'Good. When I get off this phone, you get on it and book a flight out for you and the girl with you. No police, don't even think about that, or your little girl goes right here and now, got that? No more messing about.'

The line went dead.

'What did he say?' asked Jeanette.

Annie took the gun back off her before she shot one or both of them by mistake.

'We're flying back to England tomorrow morning.'

'We can't! What about Layla?'

'We have to,' she told Jeanette. 'They want money, and the money's there.'

But if it wasn't, if she couldn't raise whatever these people wanted, then what the fuck was she going to do? She told herself it had to be there. It *had* to be.

'But tonight! We can't stay here tonight!'

'Yes we can. We're going to barricade ourselves in here, and ship out in the morning, okay?'

'No,' said Jeanette, her voice wobbling all over the place. 'No!' She made a chopping motion with her hand and then lunged across and grabbed the phone. She started to dial with shaking fingers.

'What are you doing?'

'I'm calling the police,' said Jeanette. 'It's what we should have done in the first place. We can't cope with all this, we can't—'

Annie thought of the phone tinkling as she passed by it after the blast. She grabbed it off Jeanette and smashed it back on to the cradle. 'No police,' she said.

Jeanette had finally flipped. She grabbed the phone again. Annie yanked it off her and Jeanette came at her ready for violence. Annie raised the gun and pointed it at Jeanette.

'Back off,' she said.

'What the . . . what the fuck are you *doing*?' yelled Jeanette.

Annie stared at her. The hand on the gun did not waver.

'I'm shooting you dead,' said Annie, 'if you touch that fucking phone again. You silly cow! There could be a tap on this line. The man said no police. If you went ahead and phoned them, they could kill Layla.'

Jeanette stepped back, shaking her head.

'I didn't think . . .' she faltered.

'Well think on *this*, Rebecca of Sunnybrook Farm: if you go near this fucking phone again I swear to you that what little brains you have are going to be decorating this hallway – do you understand me?'

'I understand,' said Jeanette, going pale under her tan.

'Now here's what we're going to do,' said Annie.

What they were going to *do* was this. Phone the airport and book the flights. Make another call, one that Annie thought she would never have to make, one that the kidnappers would find entirely acceptable, so no worries about the line tap there. Then they were going to check out the *finca* from top to bottom.

They did all that, and by then it was nearly dark and the shadows were deepening, making them both jumpy.

'What do we do now?' asked Jeanette, her eyes going in all directions.

Now Annie explained that they were going to barricade themselves into the bedroom with water and a bucket overnight.

'I don't want to stay here,' moaned Jeanette, trailing along behind her like a pathetic baby bird waiting for its mother to feed it. They didn't *have* any food. Annie knew this was an oversight. They should have picked some up when they were up at the little gatehouse. There was nothing in the kitchen here. But who the fuck could have thought about food at a time like that?

'We have to stay here,' said Annie flatly.

'It's horrible. With Jonjo dying out there in the pool, and the servants just up there rotting . . .'

Servants. That was, strictly speaking, what Inez and Rufio had been. But they had also been good friends and helpers, cooks and chauffeurs, life-support almost. And now they were dead. Annie's guts churned at the thought.

'The dead ain't going to hurt anyone,' she said. 'It's the living you have to fear.'

She went on, checking room to room, gun in hand.

Jeanette followed her, thinking that Annie was fucking scary. The woman's child had been snatched and her husband killed, and here she was, ice-cold, ready to shoot anyone who came near.

I'd be in bits if this happened to me, thought Jeanette, not realising that Annie's rigid control was all that stood between her and madness.

Satisfied that the *finca* was clear and secured, Annie filled a large jug with water and grabbed two glass tumblers and a bucket and then ushered Jeanette into the main bedroom, the room she had always shared with Max.

Max.

Heart-wrenching grief gripped her, stifling her as she thought of him. Once more she shook thoughts of him aside, and with Jeanette's help she levered the heavy wooden dresser over the bedroom door.

'What we're going to do is this,' she told the girl, pulling down a suitcase from the top of the wardrobe. 'We're going to take turns sleeping. Two hours on, two hours off. One stands guard, one sleeps.'

Jeanette nodded shakily. 'Okay.'

The windows were barred, the shutters closed, the only door into the room blocked off. Annie assessed the situation. For the moment, they were safe.

Safe, thought Annie. Sure they were safe, unless someone was *really* determined to finally kill them. These people had blown up the pool house, why not blow up the bloody *finca* too? Her ears felt suddenly oversensitized, as if every tiny sound were a threat. She took first watch while Jeanette lay down on the bed, protesting that she would never be able to sleep. Within minutes, she was snoring gently.

Annie sat up in a chair with the gun held ready across her lap. The old building creaked and groaned as it always did, the rafters shrinking and popping after the gentle warmth of the day. Was it that? Or was it someone coming to finish them off?

She didn't know.

She had to hold herself in readiness, just in case. Their plane tickets were booked; Annie had packed a few bits into a suitcase. In the morning they would take Rufio's battered old car and Jeanette would drive them to the airport.

Until then all Annie had to do was wait and think. She knew she wouldn't sleep, although she knew she had to try and rest, to keep strong so that she could cope with all this. So she would try not to think about what could be happening to Layla right now.

She thought instead about Max. Annie Carter, who never weakened, never cried, sat there amid the wreckage of her life and let the grief take hold of her. She let the tears stream unchecked from her eyes, and silently swore that the death of the man she loved would be avenged.

5

The little girl was very afraid as she sat in the damp darkness. She felt very tired, very drowsy. She wondered what had happened to Daddy. They took him away somewhere, she knew that; those bad people took him away. He would never have left her on her own.

She expected Mummy to come and fetch her soon; she had been expecting this for what felt like hours now. Mummy was always watching her carefully, always. She whimpered in the dark, wanting her Mummy so badly.

The men hadn't talked to her. One of them had held something over her nose and that was when she'd started to get really, really sleepy. One of them was small, like a lady, but Layla wasn't sure about that. They wore hoods over their heads and that was scary, like they weren't really people at all.

Layla so wanted someone to talk to. She would have talked to the lady, if she could, even though she had done this nasty thing to Layla. All her dolls and teddies were at home. Now she had no Mummy. No Daddy. Nothing except this horrible place.

When they had dropped her in here and slammed the trap door shut on her, she had been half-awake and had groped her way around her small prison. She found all the walls were dirt: slimy with moisture in places, bone-dry in others. There had been a little daylight left then.

But now it was night and she was cold.

She was able to stand up, although the top of her head touched metal. Metal like waves, like an old tin roof on a hen house. There was a sort of bed in the dirt, so that she could lie down on a rough blanket they had put there for her. They had put a dish of water on the floor; she'd kicked it over by accident when she'd been trying to grope her away around in here. There was some bread too, but it was stale. Like she was an animal.

Layla decided to pretend that she was an animal, someone's pet. She ate the dry bread and licked the bowl clean of what remained of the water. Then she lay down and wrapped herself in the blanket.

Daddy would come back soon. Mummy too. They would never leave her alone like this, with these strange people who didn't speak and who covered their faces.

She was an animal, curled up on her bed and waiting for her owners to come and collect her. She curled up in a ball, rocking herself, hands clasped around her knees. Suddenly, she was asleep.

6

'Fucking hellfire, it *is* you,' said Dolly when she
flung open the front door of her Limehouse knocking
shop and found her old friend Annie Carter and
an unknown blonde standing there. They looked
like someone had kicked the shit out of both of
them. 'Come in, for God's sake.'

Annie stepped into the hall and looked around at
a place that had at one time felt so familiar, but was
now completely changed. The black, wrought-iron
clock shaped like a guitar was gone, so was the
wooden plaque with the matador and the bull. Now
the decor was bang-up-to-the-minute. Now there was
bright orange-patterned wallpaper, the wooden staircase was painted white, and a cane basket chair was
suspended from a hook in the ceiling in the corner.

Where Chris used to sit and greet the punters,
thought Annie.

There was no bouncer there now, but there was

58

a folded newspaper on the chair and an empty mug on the floor beside it.

'We've got a new boy on the door,' said Dolly, seeing Annie's look. 'Ross. He's off on an errand, but he'll be back later.'

Dolly's eyes locked with Annie's.

And then I'll have to tell him you're here, said Dolly's eyes.

Annie nodded. Ross would be another Delaney boy, like Chris the old doorman had been. This was Delaney turf; Dolly paid them protection. The arrival of a prominent Carter family member on their patch couldn't go unannounced.

Annie felt as if she was moving through a dark, unspeakable dream. The familiar was gone, changed, lost forever.

Max, she thought. *Oh Christ – and Layla!*

She looked at Dolly. Dolly had changed too. Once the roughest of street working girls with an attitude to match, Dolly was every inch the madam-in-charge now, in a pink bouclé skirt suit and with her blonde hair immaculately cut and styled. Remembering the rough-edged brass that Dolly had once been, Annie felt even further disconnected from reality. Now Dolly was the embodiment of chic, just like Annie's long-departed Aunt Celia, once the madam here, had been. Dolly even smelled good, of a fragrance Annie instantly identified as Guerlain's Mitsouko.

'You look like death warmed over,' said Dolly, taking Annie's suitcase and leading the way into the kitchen. 'Come and have a cup of tea and tell me what the fuck's happening. I couldn't believe it when I got your call. And who the hell is this?'

'This is Jeanette,' said Annie as they went into the kitchen.

Dolly put the suitcase down, out of the way. She looked at Jeanette.

'She don't say much,' said Dolly.

'We've had a bit of a rough time,' said Annie. Dolly nodded.

'Everything looks different.' Annie peered around the kitchen. Her old table was gone. There was a smoked glass circular table in its place, and snazzy chairs to match, and a big descending taupe-coloured smoked glass light above it. Posh fitted units all around, with oatmeal doors and a wooden trim. Rush matting on the floor.

'Well, it's been a while,' said Dolly, filling the kettle.

She flicked the switch on and turned and looked at Annie, who was sinking down into a chair like an old woman. Jeanette sat down too. Jeanette looked the worst of the two, thought Dolly. Jeanette looked as if someone or something had scared the crap out of her, big time. Annie looked almost grey with exhaustion, but Annie was made of tough stuff. Annie would always bounce back

. . . or would she? Looking at her now, Dolly wondered about that.

'How's business? Good?' asked Annie, her head in her hands.

'Good enough,' said Dolly. She leaned back against the cream-coloured fake marble worktop and crossed her arms over her chest. 'You going to tell me what happened? I couldn't believe it when you called me.'

'I couldn't believe it either,' said Annie.

There had been only brief telephone calls, three or four a year, between the two of them since Annie had left, but they had remained friends.

'Come on, Annie,' said Dolly in sudden exasperation. 'Spill the beans, will you?'

Annie looked at the open door into the hallway. 'Anyone else around?' she asked.

Dolly shook her head. 'We're alone. I made sure we would be, at least for now. So come on. Give.'

Annie sighed and shook her head. 'No, Doll, I'm knackered. I need a bath and a lie-down, then I can think about what's going on.'

Dolly nodded, but she was frowning. This was big trouble – she could smell it. She wasn't exactly over the moon to have Annie Carter here. She didn't want to make waves with the Delaneys. The feud between the Irish Delaneys and the Cockney Carter clans had been raging for years and was still going strong. The Delaney patch was an uncomfortable and maybe dangerous place for Annie Carter, wife of the boss of the Carter clan, to be, but then Annie knew that. The fact that she was here must mean that she had nowhere else to go.

A friend's a friend, thought Dolly. She couldn't turn the poor bint away, now could she?

Annie sat there and the jumble in her brain was as bad as Dolly's, only with more anguish added on.

I could be the only Carter left, she thought. *Max. Jonjo. Both gone. And maybe Layla too.*

Sick despair washed over her again. She just couldn't take any of this in. Not yet. She had to gather herself first, if she could. Then, she'd see.

7

'Your little friend's gone,' said a disembodied female voice.

Annie shot up in the bed, heart hammering, horrors erupting in her brain. She was in a strange bed, in a strange room. A blonde woman was at the window, yanking back the curtains so that Annie winced at the brightness of the new day. A double bay window. A nice room, prettily furnished. The woman with the bubble perm placed a mug of tea on the side table.

Dolly.

Annie clutched her head in her hands as it all came back to her. And with the grim memories came guilt and intense self-hatred. She had slept, deeply and dreamlessly, while her husband lay dead in a rocky gully far away and her daughter was God knew where, in the hands of people who could do her serious harm.

'You were worn out,' said Dolly, sitting down on the side of the bed and staring at her friend with concern. 'I came up last night to see if you wanted anything to eat, and you were spark out. So I let you sleep. This is my room, you remember?'

All Annie knew was that she had fallen on to the bed and literally passed out.

'God, I'm sorry. Where did you sleep?'

'Don't be a silly mare, Annie, there's always a spare bed in a place like this. You can have this room for the time being, no worries.'

'You should have woken me up. Have there been any phone calls? Has anyone asked to speak to me?'

Dolly shook her head.

'There must have been!' Annie burst out in fury.

Dolly kept staring at her. 'Nobody's called. I would have fetched you. But they didn't.'

'Sorry,' mumbled Annie. 'Didn't mean to shout the odds, Doll.'

'That's okay.'

'She's fucked off then?'

'Jean, yeah.'

'Jeanette.'

'Who the hell is she? Not your sort, I'd have thought.'

'One of Jonjo's blondes.'

'Ah. Drink your tea.'

Annie took up the mug with shaking hands and sipped it. The tea was strong, bracing.

'You going to tell me what's been going on?' asked Dolly.

'Nothing's been going on,' said Annie.

Dolly smiled dryly. 'Like fuck,' she said. 'You looked like a ghost when you pitched up here. And you sounded in bits on the phone. You're shaking like a sodding old man now. So what's happened?'

Annie looked straight at Dolly. 'Something horrible, Doll. And now they've got my baby girl.'

'Layla?' All trace of the smile was gone. 'Fucking hell, Annie – *who*, for the love of God?'

'I don't know who,' said Annie. 'They're going to contact me here. That's all I know.'

'Do they want money?'

'Yeah.' Annie tried another sip of the tea but this time it wouldn't get past the lump in her throat. She put the mug aside.

'Have you *got* it?'

Annie shrugged. Anxiety gnawed at her. This was taking her right back to the time when she had been kicked out of home and left to fend for herself. Potless, homeless, abandoned, disgraced, and on the run from the Carter clan. She felt as lost, as hopeless now as she did then. She didn't know squat about Max's financial affairs. There had always been plenty of money, and he had been generous with it, but where it had come from and where he kept it was a mystery to her. She had no money of her own; she'd never needed it while Max was there. But now Max was gone.

'And where is Max?' asked Dolly after a pause.

'I don't know,' said Annie painfully.

'What the fuck do you mean, you don't know? He's your flaming husband, of course you know where he is.'

'He disappeared, Doll. These people phoned me and said they'd killed him.'

Dolly recoiled in shock. 'Jesus, no.'

Annie nodded dumbly. She looked spent, Dolly thought, as if all this had drained the life from her. Dark shadows under her eyes. Her lips parched and cracked. Her skin sallow. This wasn't the polished, controlled woman she knew. This was a beaten stranger. Dolly wondered how *she* would cope with such a bucketload of grief, though. Her kid snatched, her husband topped . . . that was enough to finish anyone, even the strongest.

'You mustn't tell *anyone* that Max is dead,' said Annie. 'I mean it, Doll. No one.'

'You know I won't. What about Jonjo?' asked Dolly. 'Jeanette was with you, so where's Jonjo?'

Annie swallowed and shook her head.

Dolly was silent, gobsmacked.

'Look, I tell you what,' she said at last. 'You get washed and dressed, then we'll think again, okay?'

Annie looked at her. Dolly was the best friend she had ever had, and she knew it. Annie was quite likely bringing trouble to her door, and many another would have turned her away, but not Dolly. She could almost have cried at Dolly's kindness, but she held her emotions in tight check. Dolly would be embarrassed anyway by a display of emotion. She always had been. You'd never get hugs and kisses from Doll, but what you would get was firm support from a genuine ally.

'Thanks, Dolly. Can I borrow something to wear? All I've got in the case is sandals and summer dresses and swimming cossies. Don't ask me why I brought any of it back. I don't think my head was right at the time.'

'Help yourself. Anything you want. Oh, and Annie . . .' Suddenly Dolly looked awkward and anxious. 'I had to phone Redmond Delaney, tell him you're here. Sorry. You're a mate, but I can't be seen to be disrespecting the Delaneys, not on their own turf. I didn't want him just hearing about it from Ross, do you understand? I have to be careful.'

Annie nodded. 'Don't give it another thought, Doll. I know you had to tell Redmond. That goes without saying.'

And Redmond ain't going to be very pleased about it, she thought.

Dolly's tense expression relaxed with relief.

'We'd better get you some breakfast,' she said. 'You come down when you're ready, Annie love. No rush. I'll listen for the phone, don't worry.'

Dolly left the bedroom and closed the door softly behind her. She felt embarrassed at her own inability to help more. All hell was being set loose in the poor bint's life, and she was telling her *not to worry.*

'Doll!'

At Annie's call, she reopened the door and stuck her head around it.

'Yes, Annie love?'

'Does Billy Black still call in?'

'Billy? Of course he does. Every week, regular. He hasn't got many places to go where they'll make him welcome, the poor bastard.'

'When he calls, I want to speak to him.'

'Okay,' said Dolly, and went off downstairs with a troubled mind to see to breakfast for the girls. As she passed the telephone in the hall, it jingled. She looked at it, picked it up, listened to the dial tone. Then she shrugged and put it back down.

When Annie got downstairs, she found Dolly there eating toast and chatting to her 'girls'. There was Darren, a slim blond young man wearing a flamboyant scarf and a yellow shirt, and to her surprise Ellie was there too, dark haired and still pretty, but porked up to double her usual size.

All conversation stopped when Annie opened the door and stood there. She'd borrowed a plain black shift dress from Dolly's wardrobe, some tights and some plain black courts. The shoes pinched, and the dress fitted where it touched, but she didn't give a shit.

'Gordon Bennett, if it ain't Annie Bailey!' said Darren, getting to his feet and coming round to give her a hug of welcome. Christ, he looked as thin as a ghost!

'Carter,' said Annie automatically.

'Gawd yes. I forgot you were playing with the big boys now.' Darren rolled his eyes and kissed her cheek. Camp as a row of pink tents, that was Darren, and she'd always loved his quirky ways.

Annie pulled back and looked at him. He was more than slim – she felt his ribs when she hugged him. And he looked strained.

'Hello Annie,' said Ellie, coming forward for a hug. Annie gave a faint smile, suppressing her amazement at seeing Ellie back here. Dolly had once kicked Ellie out for her backstabbing habits, but here she was again, feet firmly under the table.

Annie hugged her, trying not to think that Darren and Ellie looked like Jack Sprat and his wife, one skinny, one fat, like a comedy double act.

'You're both looking good,' she lied.

She pulled out a spare chair and sat down. She

69

saw a look pass between Darren and Dolly, and Ellie bit her lip as if stifling something.

'Have some toast,' said Dolly, pushing a plate towards her. She poured tea from the pot into a spare mug, and added milk. 'You look like you need a feed-up.'

Annie kept shtoom. If it had been just Darren and Dolly there, she might have spoken now about Layla and Max, but Ellie was sitting there with her ears flapping so it wasn't a good idea. Ellie had always been totally in the pocket of the Delaneys, and this was their manor. There had never been any love lost between the Delaneys and the Carters. And now she was a Carter – maybe the only one left.

Max.

Layla.

Her guts clenched with pain.

Annie stifled her grief and fear and thought instead about the Delaneys. Redmond Delaney and his sister Orla had once been good to her. But she was convinced that all that came to an end the minute Max Carter put a wedding ring on her finger. So in front of Ellie she would keep it quiet. She looked down at her wedding ring now and felt the pain rising up again, nearly choking her.

Max's ring with its bright gold and its solid slab of lapis lazuli was still there on her thumb. It was loose. She'd have to be careful not to lose it. Better to put it on the gold chain Max had given her, along with the gold heart inscribed *Love you forever*, the one she always wore, the one she was wearing around her neck right now.

She picked up a bit of soggy toast and gnawed at it. She had to eat. Couldn't face the idea of food, but she *had* to eat. Had to stay strong. She was no use to Layla in a weakened state. She sipped her tea and forced down the toast, and Dolly nodded her approval.

'I look like shit in that dress,' said Dolly. 'But on you, it's good. I only keep it for funerals.'

Annie's eyes locked with Dolly's as they both remembered when Annie had last seen Dolly wearing the dress. Connie's funeral. Annie's mum, dead of alcohol poisoning, being laid to rest.

'Jesus,' said Dolly, chastened. 'Sorry, Annie. Me and me big gob.'

'It's okay,' said Annie. 'Where's Aretha?'

Aretha had been a star turn in Dolly's whore house. A tall black girl with a damaged past, she had specialized in S & M, punishment chairs, whippings, tying naughty boys up and giving them the whacking they desired.

'She left about a year back, maybe two – didn't I say?' said Dolly. She glanced at Ellie, who turned her full concentration on her breakfast. 'Married Chris.'

'Chris the bouncer?' Annie's jaw dropped. It was

a match that stretched the imagination to its limits, big bald Chris and tall man-eater Aretha.

But then Annie remembered Chris's gentle ways with the ladies, and thought that maybe, after all her trials and tribulations, Aretha had finally found a man who deserved more than to be punished.

She glanced across the table at Ellie. Ellie had had a crush on Chris, she knew. And even now it looked as if the mention of him hooking up with Aretha was causing her pain.

'He's got a job in security now, he's a night guard at Heathrow,' Dolly went on. 'They got a place together, and Aretha still turns a few tricks from home to bring in the dosh.'

Annie nodded. Of course, things moved on. It was a weird feeling to come back here, with everything feeling somehow the same but forever different. Sitting here felt unreal, like a dream. Or maybe a fucking nightmare. People had met, fallen in love, married . . . moved on. Changed. Her life had changed, too. For the worse. Her husband. Her daughter. Her *life*. All changed. All gone. The pain gripped her again and she put the toast down, afraid that she was going to throw up right here, right now.

'Hey – that's my chair,' said a voice behind her.

8

Annie looked up. And up. The woman standing there glaring down at her was over six feet tall and looked like every punter's idea of a dream dominatrix. She had white-blonde hair cut close to her head and weirdly pale, penetrating blue eyes. She had huge tits. She was dressed in a white PVC minidress with cutouts on either side of the waist and a buckle in the centre, teamed with white, thigh-high boots.

She didn't look friendly.

Dolly said quickly: 'Una, this is Annie. Annie – Una.'

'Hi, Una,' said Annie.

'I *said* that's my chair,' said Una.

Annie looked at her. Then she looked curiously at Dolly, who was suddenly faffing around the kitchen fetching another mug, clucking around the place like the Queen of Sheba had put in an appearance. Annie looked at Darren, who looked away. She looked at Ellie, who was watching as if something interesting was about to kick off.

She looked again at Una.

'There's another chair right here,' said Annie, indicating an empty one to her left.

Dolly dropped the tea caddy; it hit the table with a clatter.

'Tea, Una? Or coffee?' she prattled.

'Then *you* fucking well sit in it,' said Una to Annie, ignoring Dolly.

Annie looked at her. It was a long, appraising look. 'Sure,' she said, and moved along to the next seat.

Darren and Ellie exchanged a glance.

Una sat smugly down in the seat Annie had just vacated, sneering sideways at her as Dolly took her breakfast order.

Annie sipped her tea while Dolly fussed around Una.

Fuck it, thought Darren, *that's not the Annie Carter I know.* He caught Ellie's eye. *She's lost it,* said Ellie's look. *Bloody hell. Who'd have thought?*

When breakfast was over, Dolly went off upstairs and Annie caught up with her in the bedroom.

'Doll, can you phone my cousin Kath, tell her I need to see Jimmy Bond?'

'Sure I can.'

'But don't phone from here. Go to the phone box, okay?'

Dolly looked at her. 'Our phone was making a funny noise this morning.'

'What sort of noise?' Annie froze. 'A sort of jingling noise, do you mean?'

'Yeah. That's it.'

'Doll, I think there could be a tap on your phone line. I think these people who've taken Layla tapped the line at the villa, and they might have done the same here.'

Dolly's mouth dropped open, then she closed it. 'Fuck me,' she said. 'I'll use the phone box.'

9

The next day, Billy Black arrived on the doorstep. Annie ushered him into the kitchen and closed the door behind them so that Ross, the hard-eyed young Delaney man on the door, couldn't hear what was said. Ellie and Darren were upstairs with clients; Dolly was sorting the takings in the front room. When they had come face to face in the hall, Ross had given Annie a look that should have turned her to stone, but she ignored it. Una was out – no one knew where and no one dared ask, either, if Annie was any judge.

'Your cousin Kath don't like you,' Dolly had said when she got back from making her calls yesterday.

'So what else is new?' sniffed Annie. Who gave a fuck? The kidnappers hadn't called yet. *That* was Annie's only concern.

'I told her you wanted to speak with Jimmy,

but she put the phone down on me. Twice. Said Annie Carter was nothing to her.'

Good old Kath, thought Annie. *Stupid* and *obstinate, as always*. All right, Annie held her hands up. She'd done wrong, taking Max off her sister Ruthie. But all that was long gone and forgotten. Ruthie had forgiven her. So why not Kath?

Because Kath likes family aggro, thought Annie. *Always did, always will*.

She thought of Kath's face – Kath had never been pretty, but she had these bright eyes that were endlessly curious, gleefully absorbing gossip, gathering grudges like a squirrel hoarding nuts. Kath *loved* a family ruck – or any ruck at all, come to that.

'Did you tell her it was urgent?'

'She didn't give me the chance.'

'Okay, Doll.'

But at least Billy was here.

Billy hadn't changed a bit. Same old raincoat hanging off his thin frame, same old hat on his head, same briefcase clutched against him like it was the bloody Crown Jewels. Same pale face with that vacant look. Same stammer.

The word was that the cord had got wrapped around his neck when he was born, cutting off blood supply to his brain and rendering him . . . well, not simple exactly. But not the brightest nail in the toolbox, for sure. But Billy was devoted to Max. Max had trusted him to do certain undemanding jobs around the manor, and Billy had always had a soft spot for Annie.

'How you been, Billy?' asked Annie, setting a mug of tea in front of him as they sat down at the table.

'F-fine,' he said.

'Still working for the firm?'

'No.' Billy hesitated, forming words. It took a while. 'Not since Jonjo took over.'

Annie nodded. 'But you're still Max's boy, yes?'

'I've always been one of Mr Carter's boys,' said Billy proudly.

Annie knew this was going to be a shock to Billy, but she knew she could trust him to keep his trap shut. She took a breath.

'Max is dead, Billy. And so is Jonjo.'

Billy stared at her.

'Dead?' he repeated blankly.

Annie nodded. She waited for a beat to let that sink in a little. Then she said: 'This is just between you and me for now, Billy. You and me, okay? It mustn't go any further.'

Billy nodded slowly. 'I . . . see.'

'So I'm in charge now. You got that? And there's something I need sorting out, Billy. Urgently.'

'Okay.' He looked bewildered.

'I need my friends around me now.'

'I've always been your friend,' he said, blushing.

'I know you have, Billy. And I appreciate it.'

Annie patted his hand. Poor sod. She'd hated telling him. He'd idolized Max. She reached up around her neck and undid the gold chain. She left the gold heart on it and took off Max's chunky gold ring with the slab of brilliant blue lapis lazuli.

'Do you recognize this, Billy?'

Billy nodded vigorously. 'That's Mr Carter's ring.'

'I want you to get it to Jimmy Bond today – as soon as you leave here, Billy, you understand? Take this ring to him and tell him I need to see him, right now. You got that?'

Billy took the ring and held it reverently in his palm. 'I've got it,' he said, and slipped the ring into his pocket.

'And remember what I said. The thing about Max and Tonjo. That's our secret for now. You got that?'

He nodded.

'Good. Now drink your tea. Time's short.'

10

Billy must have moved like wildfire. Within two hours of his departure, Jimmy Bond was at the door. Ross was ready for him. He knew the Carter boys. He was a Delaney man, of course he knew them.

In particular he knew Jimmy Bond.

Jimmy Bond was a hard-looking bastard. Crewcut pale brown hair. Chippy blue eyes. A chiselled, stern face and a cruel mouth. Immaculately turned out in black coat and sharp suit. All the Carter crowd were snappy dressers. But Ross knew not to be deceived by that. Beneath all the flash, the Carter mob were dangerous. None more so than this one.

'What the fuck do you want?' Ross bulked himself up like a threatened toad so that he filled the front doorway.

Jimmy gave the younger man a look.

'Civility,' he said.

'What?'

'Mrs Carter in?'

Dolly came hurrying down the hall looking flustered. She clocked Jimmy Bond standing on the doorstep in the rain.

'Mr Bond,' she acknowledged him politely. The Carter boys had got them all out of the crap that time when Mad Pat Delaney kicked off, and she hadn't forgotten it. She owed them a lot.

She turned to her stony-faced bouncer. 'Ross, Mr Bond's come to see Annie. Let the man in, for God's sake.'

Ross looked unhappy but he stood back. Jimmy stepped into the hall.

'She's in the kitchen – straight through there,' said Dolly.

Jimmy nodded, stepped around a scowling Ross and went into the kitchen.

He closed the door from the hall into the kitchen behind him and leaned against it. Sitting at the table looking up at him was Annie Carter. There was a moment's thick silence while they stared at one another. Then Jimmy took the ring from his pocket and tossed it to her. Annie caught it deftly, then busied herself putting it back on to the chain around her neck.

'Why don't you take a seat, Jimmy?' she said as she fiddled with the clasp.

81

Jimmy chose a chair and sat down.

Placing himself with his back to a wall, noted Annie. *No doors behind him, and no windows.*

'Nice tan,' said Jimmy.

Annie nodded cautiously. 'Majorca's still warm, even in February,' she said. 'How's Kath?'

'Kath's fine.'

'I tried to get a message to you through her,' said Annie. 'She put the phone down. Twice.'

'Kath bears a grudge.'

'That's ancient history.'

'Not to Kath.'

'You ought to keep your house in order, Jimmy. I wasn't pleased.'

He shrugged.

So that's the way it's going to be, thought Annie.

'Max and Jonjo are busy in Spain, so I'm taking over here.'

Now she got a reaction.

'Bollocks,' he said.

'What?'

'I said bollocks. Max wouldn't hand control over to a skirt.'

'Max *has* handed control over to a skirt. A skirt who happens to be his wife. A Carter, Jimmy. So watch it.'

'*Watch* it? You're having a fucking laugh.' Jimmy sat back and folded his arms.

'Am I laughing?'

'No, but I am.' Jimmy stared at Annie. 'So what's happened?'

'What?' Annie felt her heart leap into her throat. This wasn't going the way she'd planned it, not at all.

She had felt that she owed it to Billy Black to tell him the truth, but she wasn't ready to risk that with Jimmy Bond yet. Tell Jimmy Bond, and all the boys would know. She didn't feel secure enough in her own position at the moment to face that.

'You heard. I want to know what's happened. The truth, not some made-up pile of shit.'

'You're pushing your luck, Jimmy,' said Annie flatly.

'Come off it,' said Jimmy roughly. 'I don't even know you're a Carter, do I? Oh sure, Jonjo said there'd been a wedding, but he wasn't there on the day, was he? He said there was a kid too, but it could have been a bastard Bailey, not a Carter at all, for all he or anyone else knew.'

Annie shot to her feet and leaned across the table, eyes glaring.

'You want to watch your mouth, Jimmy Bond,' she told him. 'My daughter's not a bastard. And Max and I are married. Legal.'

'That's what Ruthie thought,' said Jimmy.

Annie took a breath, tried to calm down. But fuck it. She'd thought that Jimmy would be her ally. She was scared shitless and she needed serious help. But she could see that she wasn't going to get it from him. No way.

'That's in the past,' she said.

'What goes around comes around,' he said, and stood up. He put his meaty fists on the table and leaned in close. Despite herself, Annie found herself leaning back a little. 'I'll see you around, maybe,' he said, his eyes holding hers. 'When you're ready to tell me the truth.'

He walked to the door, not looking back.

Annie sat down with a thump. He was going to walk out. Simple as that. Convinced she was lying. Hadn't Max told her that Jimmy had gypsy roots, that his instincts were always sound? He knew she was lying because she bloody well *was* lying.

'Jimmy,' she said as he placed his hand on the doorknob.

Jimmy half turned and looked at her.

'All right,' she said. 'I'll tell you the truth.'

And so Annie told Jimmy Bond the truth. That there had been a hit. That Jonjo was dead. That Max was dead. That Layla had been snatched. That she had had to come back here to get some cash together and that as yet there had been no word from the kidnappers.

Throughout all this, Jimmy kept quiet. When she'd finished, he pulled out a chair and sat down again, his eyes on her face.

'You're telling the truth,' he said. A statement of fact.

'Of course I bloody am. But no one else can know about this, Jimmy. No one must know Max is dead. Because if they do . . .'

Jimmy nodded. If word got out on the streets that Max was gone, rival gangs would start to move in. He understood that perfectly.

'What if the bastard on the phone spreads the word? No Max, no Jonjo – the manor's wide open,' said Annie anxiously.

'Why should he?' asked Jimmy. 'He wants money. Why would he risk not getting his wedge from you by making trouble on the manor?'

Annie looked at him. He had a point. 'But he's still got my fucking daughter,' she said bitterly.

'Yeah, but he won't hurt her if he wants the dosh. Listen to what I'm saying. He ain't interested in the manor or he'd have done you all over. He just wants the money. If any rumours *do* kick off, we deny everything. And we kill them off at source,' said Jimmy.

'How?'

Jimmy gave a twisted smile.

'Bust a few heads, people start to think twice about opening their mouths,' he told her. 'Trust me, nobody's going to start anything around me. And I'll be quiet as the grave. I'm Max and Jonjo's number one, remember?'

As if you'd let me forget it, thought Annie. *You arrogant git.*

'I'm placing a lot of trust in you,' said Annie. 'More than I'm comfortable with, to be honest, given your connection to Kath and knowing how she feels about me.'

'Kath won't know,' said Jimmy.

'She mustn't,' said Annie. 'Because if she does, family or not, I'd have to have a word. She starts flapping that big mouth of hers and it'll be all over the manor before you can say knife. And then we're fucked.'

'Kath won't know. She knows nothing about the business. Never has, never will.'

Annie nodded. This was the way Max had always conducted his business, too. She recognized an echo of truth in Jimmy's words, because Max's outlook had been much the same. Keep the wife out of it. Keep her in the dark and feed her shit, then she'd be happy.

But was that a good idea? thought Annie. Because look what had happened now. She was adrift in an ocean full of sharks, and Max was fucking nowhere to be found. She had no funds to speak of – unless she found some double-quick. Things were bad. Hard to see how they could get any worse, really. But she had to hold on, keep her head, because while there was a chance she could save Layla – however slim that chance undoubtedly was – then she would have to tough it out.

'So how can I help?' asked Jimmy.

Annie swallowed. 'I'm going to need to find or raise some money, Jimmy. I don't know how much yet.'

Jimmy nodded. 'Max would have some stashed somewhere.'

'Yeah, but where?'

'You've really no idea?'

'None,' said Annie.

'Then we've got a problem.'

We.

Annie felt that *we* was a small victory. If she had Jimmy Bond onside, she had an important ally. Not a friend. Never a friend. Kath had been dripping her poison into his ear for years, telling him what a cheating bitch Annie was, how she had betrayed her own sister, how her own mother had washed her hands of her. So Jimmy would always regard her with suspicion. *But* – and it was a big but – she was also Max Carter's wife.

Or I claim to be, thought Annie soberly. Jimmy was right – she could be lying about all this, up to and including the marriage and the legitimate child. Fair enough, he doubted her. But he had also said *we* have a problem, so she was a little reassured. If she truly was Annie Carter and not plain old Annie Bailey, his wife's slag of a cousin, then Jimmy Bond would at least owe her respect.

Annie looked at him in the thickening silence.

'All suggestions welcome,' she said hopefully.

Jimmy gave a half-smile and stood up. 'I'll think it over,' he said. 'See what I can come up with.'

'What about the clubs? The Palermo? That was always Max's favourite. Maybe he'd have some cash there.'

'Maybe,' Jimmy shrugged.

'Is it still running smooth?' asked Annie. Not that she cared, but she was trying to get him to communicate with her. It was bloody hard going.

'Yeah. Opens lunchtimes too now.'

'Right.'

Annie had to bite her lip to keep back her exasperation. *We don't have time to fuck about,* is what she longed to say. But she stopped herself. She didn't want to start out by trying to push Jimmy Bond into a corner. He was a proud man – Max's best boy – and she had to treat him with respect, too.

'Make it soon,' was all she allowed herself.

'I will,' he said, and left.

She watched him go through the open kitchen doorway, nodding to Dolly as he passed her in the hall and giving the hard man on the door a mocking smile before stepping out on to the path. Ross kicked the door shut behind him.

'Fucking *bastard*,' he muttered, then came along

the hall to the kitchen and handed Annie a note. 'For you,' he said, and went back to his seat by the front door.

Annie looked at Dolly and opened up the folded sheet of paper. The handwriting was forward sloping and almost painfully neat. The note said: *We hope you like your stay, Mrs Carter. Just make it a short one, and there'll be no trouble.*

It was signed *Redmond Delaney.*

Annie pocketed it, her eyes on Ross through the open kitchen doorway. He returned her stare. Dolly, standing between them in the hall, swallowed nervously. And then the telephone started to ring. Annie steeled herself, nerves jangling. The fucking phone had rung a thousand times over the past few days. Always it was clients, or mates of Darren's or Ellie's. Una didn't seem to have any mates, which was no big surprise. But it was never, ever the call Annie was waiting for. She watched Dolly pick up the phone, watched her face go bleached white. Dolly's head turned and she held the phone out to Annie.

'For you,' she said, and Annie's heart froze.

'Hello?' said Annie when she took the phone from Dolly.

Dolly shooed her doorman into the front room and closed the door on him. Then she stood beside Annie in the hall, her face anxious.

'Ah, so you are there,' said the voice.

The same voice again. Irish. Annie hated that voice.

'I'm here.' *I've been here for days*, she thought, but didn't say it. Best not to antagonize him.

'And now you are, what shall we do with you?' he asked, and she could hear it again in his voice, that smile, that loathsome smile.

Annie was gripping the receiver so tightly that her knuckles were white as bone. She relaxed her grip, took a breath. *Calm*, she thought. *Keep calm, think clearly. For Layla.*

'You tell me,' said Annie.

'And what if I don't feel like telling you quite yet?' he said, playing with her, the bastard. A *ding* in the background . . . teacups? Something . . .

'That's your decision,' said Annie, refusing to rise to the bait, refusing to scream and yell and pull her hair like he wanted her to. 'Is Layla all right? Can I speak to her?'

'Yes, and no. In that order.'

'Then how do I know she's still alive?' asked Annie.

'You don't. You have to take my word for it.' *Bastard.*

'I want to do a deal with you,' said Annie.

'You're in no position to be offering deals,' he said.

'Yes I am. And the deal is, me for Layla. Hand Layla over, and take me instead.'

Dolly made a 'for Christ's sake no' gesture. Annie waved her away.

'It's a good deal,' said Annie when there was only silence at the other end. 'It's me you want to torment, isn't it? Or else why am I still alive? You could have killed me in Majorca.'

'There's another reason we could have kept you alive, though,' he said.

We. But of course there was more than one person involved in all this, as Jeanette had told her. To blow up the pool house, kill Max and Jonjo, kill her two friends, snatch Layla, drug her . . . too much, far too much, for one alone to manage.

How many then? wondered Annie. Hadn't Jeanette said four? But then Jeanette was an idiot.

'And what's that?' asked Annie.

'For the dough, dear heart. For the brass, the wonga, the *money.*'

At last.

'How much?' asked Annie. 'Tell me and I'll get it.'

'Ah, now that's something we've yet to decide upon.'

Toying with her again. Playing her. Tormenting her. Annie clutched at her head, which felt as if it was about to burst open. A pulse of pain bloomed behind one eye. *Calm*, she thought. *Calm.*

'So you're going to let me know about that,' she said numbly.

'I dare say. We'll call again in a few days, discuss things further, how's that?'

Annie swallowed her hatred. She wanted to kill him. She *would* kill him, if she ever got the chance.

'Whatever you say,' she said.

'That's right,' said the man. 'Whatever I say goes, right?'

Annie's jaw clenched. 'Right,' she agreed.

'We'll talk again . . .'

'Wait.' She needed to hear Layla's voice. Needed it desperately. 'Let me talk to my daughter.'

'Later,' he said. 'I'll call again on Friday.' And he put the phone down.

'Wait!' shouted Annie, but she was talking to nothing but empty air. With a cry of rage she smashed the receiver back on to its cradle, picked up the phone and flung it hard against the wall.

'You *fucker!*' she yelled.

Dolly stared at her friend, aghast. She had never seen Annie lose it before. Annie stalked off along the hall, turned at the foot of the stairs and walked back, breathing hard. She picked up the phone from the floor, picked up the receiver, listened. Still working. She exhaled sharply.

'Sorry, Doll,' she said.

Annie knew she couldn't go on like this. Waiting powerlessly for that bastard to call again and again; waiting, hoping, and then every time her hopes being dashed and her anxiety increasing. She had, somehow, to reclaim some control.

Oh sure, she thought with black amusement. *And how are you going to do that, smartarse?*

She would concentrate on getting some money together. Work hard at that, and keep strong. Jimmy had rightly said that Max must have a stash somewhere, a secret stash. Maybe more than one. And there were safes at the clubs, weren't there, for the takings. She had to wait until Friday when *he* called again. Why not use that time?

She went out to use a phone box a few streets away. Dolly went with her. They crowded into the little cubicle, out of the rain. Annie dialled Kath and Jimmy's number. Kath answered.

'Kath – Annie,' she said shortly. 'Get hold of Jimmy and tell him to get Tony, Max's driver. I want Max's car at Dolly's place in Limehouse at two o'clock.'

'Who the hell do you think you are, issuing orders?' demanded Kath.

Annie felt a cold, clear rage grip her. Fuck it all, didn't she have enough to contend with, without Kath adding her bit to the mix?

'Kath,' she said icily. 'Now you listen, and listen good, 'cos I ain't about to say this twice. I'm *Mrs Max Carter*. And you'd better cut out the fucking crap. Max isn't here but I am, and I'm taking over for him. You'd better not have a problem with that, Kath. You'd better get your arse in gear and pass the word to Jimmy, *fast*.'

Annie slammed the phone down, breathing hard.

'That's her told,' said Dolly. 'And about time too, the mouthy cow. Where you off to, then?'

'The Palermo. And the Shalimar, and the Blue Parrot.'

Dolly nodded.

Max Carter's three clubs.

Now, with Max gone, they belonged to Annie Carter. And so did his manor.

11

The first thing Vita Byrne saw when she opened the trap door on the disused hen house was a pair of very angry dark green eyes staring up at her.

Shit!

She slammed the door shut.

'For fuck's *sake*,' she said to Danny, her brother, who had just come out from the kitchen and was staring at her. 'You couldn't have given her enough of that stuff, she's awake! You fucking idiot.'

'Hey, how do I know how much to use on a kid?' he demanded. 'I didn't want to give her too much, I didn't want to *kill* her, now did I?'

'I thought she was going to be drugged up. I thought she was going to be *out* of it. And now she's seen my fucking face,' whined Vita.

'Will you shut up? And will you put your fucking hood on, and why didn't you have it on in the first place? That way she wouldn't have seen your stupid face, for God's sake.'

'Don't have a go at *me*,' said Vita. '*You* got the dose wrong.'

'Look, she's a *kid*. I gave her what I thought was enough but not too much 'cos that could have killed her, and that wouldn't be very clever now, would it? She's no fucking use to us dead. What I'm saying is, she won't know you anyway, so will you for the love of God *calm down*?'

'Yeah, it's all very well for you to say calm down, but it wasn't your face she saw, was it?' yelled Vita, getting good and mad and also a bit panicky.

Because for sure the little girl had seen her face. She didn't think Danny was taking that point quite seriously enough.

'She's a little kid,' said Danny with a bored tone in his voice. 'She won't know your face.'

'Yeah, but Da—'

'Shut *up*.' Now Danny was getting mad too. His stupid sister had been about to blurt his name out. A kid might forget a face, but a name might stick in her memory; she might repeat it when she got free – *if* she got free – and then people would come knocking. All of which was a situation Danny Byrne hoped to avoid.

'*Don't* keep telling me to shut up,' said Vita.

Everything about this was upsetting her. It was all too much. She hadn't expected that they were actually going to *kill* people, and she still felt sort of sick to her stomach about that. And most particularly about what Danny had done to the man and the woman in the little villa by the gate. He had seemed to glory in their terror, to get high on it; he had laughed and played in the blood like a kid in a bubble bath. Whenever she thought of it, she felt nauseous and afraid. She'd always known Danny was crazy, but now she thought he was *really* sick in the head, and dangerous.

'Look, no names,' Danny was saying to her. 'We never say names in the girl's hearing, remember? Got that?'

'Yeah, okay,' said Vita sulkily. 'Where's Ph . . . where's he gone, anyway?'

'To hire the boat.'

'Jesus, hasn't he done that yet? I thought this was meant to be a smooth operation.'

'It's smooth,' said Danny.

'Oh sure it's smooth. No boat, and she's seen my face.'

'Will you for fuck's sake *drop that*?' roared Danny.

Vita flinched and fell silent.

'My daddy's going to kick your arse,' said a tearful, furious little voice from inside the hen house.

12

Tony was there at a quarter to two, with Max's beautiful old Mark X Jag all polished up and gleaming. Which was good. Someone was sitting up and taking notice, thought Annie, and not before time. Kath had obviously passed on the message – grudgingly – and Jimmy had acted upon it.

All good.

Not the unqualified support she had hoped for, but the best she was going to get, and that would have to do – for now, at least.

Annie sat in the back of the car and was suddenly overwhelmed by it all. Max's car. She had sat in here nearly five years ago, with the scent of leather all around her like a comfort blanket, the heady smell of luxury, of Max's lemon-scented cologne, with Max right there beside her – a strong, seemingly invincible presence.

Not so invincible though, she thought despairingly.

She looked at the empty space where Max should be. And into her mind, suddenly and starkly, came the image of him being pushed off the side of a mountain: falling, bouncing off rocks, lying crumpled and broken and lifeless at the bottom.

Annie shut her eyes and swallowed sickness. Had they stood and laughed while they killed him? Had he – *oh God no* – had he lain there, fatally injured, suffering, hurting, for hours on end, perhaps days, before he finally died?

She opened her eyes, shuddering, and tried to get hold of herself. She could see Tony's eyes, watching her in the mirror. Max had valued Tony. Tony was built like a fucking outhouse. He was bald and he was ugly and he wore gold hoop earrings with crucifixes dangling off them, but he followed orders to the letter and he was loyal, Max had always said that.

'You all right, Mrs Carter?'

'I'm fine, Tony.'

'Is Mr Carter coming back soon?' asked Tony.

'I dunno, Tony,' said Annie.

So Jimmy had been as good as his word and hadn't told the boys the truth – that Max wasn't going to be coming back, not soon, not ever. Jimmy had kept quiet, as they had agreed he should, and that was good.

All good, thought Annie tiredly as the car glided smoothly through the rain-drenched streets of London's East End. *Oh yeah. Fucking wonderful.* Spring was coming, but today it still looked like winter. She looked out at the grimy terraced houses, the people milling around in the sodden grey streets, the shops, the traffic.

She was back.

But everything was different. Everything had moved on.

Ronnie and Reggie Kray had been banged up a year ago for shooting George Cornell, one of the Richardson boys, in the Blind Beggar, and for doing Jack 'The Hat' McVitie at Blonde Carol's.

Yeah, things had changed.

The Beatles had split up. And Dolly had told her that all through this last winter the maxi-skirt had been favoured by trendy London girls over the chillier mini.

Little changes, big changes. Some bad, some good.

Annie feared that, for her, nothing was ever going to be truly good again.

As Jimmy had told her, the Palermo Lounge was open, the red neon sign shining brightly above the set of red double doors in the sullen daylight. She had brought Max's keys but she didn't need them. It felt odd to just walk in during the day. The Palermo, like Max's other two clubs, had always been very much a *night*club. But today there was a jungle beat going on inside.

There was a man on the door, and Tony introduced her as Mrs Carter. She saw the man's expression change then. Saw the glint of respect that the Carter name commanded.

She went in, Tony dogging her footsteps.

Annie paused and looked at the poster board. Her eyes widened. She glanced at Tony, but Tony was suddenly finding the ceiling of great interest. Annie pushed through another set of double red doors and the beat of the music shot up to deafening levels. She went down the stairs and paused halfway.

The lights in here were dim – Christ, how come no one broke their necks on these stairs coming in here? She looked down and saw about fifteen punters sitting at tables in a fug of cigarette smoke, some clutching drinks bought from the bar at the far side of the room, others just goggling open-mouthed at what was happening on the brightly lit elevated half-circle that passed for a stage.

Above and to both sides of this 'stage' were thick red velvet drapes edged in gold. Annie remembered those drapes. At their apex were the gold letters MC.

Max Carter.

In the centre of the stage, a girl wearing black

pants, bra, suspenders, and stockings was gyrating wildly in time to the music, her huge tits bouncing around like melons in a sack, her blonde hair turned silver by the spotlights. As Annie watched, the girl leered at the watching crowd and reached back, unhooking her bra. The massive tanned breasts jumped free and there was a feeble roar of encouragement from the watching men.

Fuck it all, thought Annie. *Max would hate this. What's happened to this place?*

The girl was parading around now, clutching her breasts – not naked, but brandishing gold nipple tassels – and wiggling them provocatively in the faces of the watchers.

'Get 'em off,' shouted someone.

Annie remembered her Aunt Celia, once proud madam of what was now Dolly's Limehouse brothel, telling her that men didn't like topless dancers wearing tassels.

'If they can't see the nipple, they feel cheated,' Celia had told her. 'To a bloke, a naked tit has to be *completely* naked, or he feels put out.'

No danger of anyone here feeling cheated for long. The girl was now swinging her hips and leaning over the front tables, inviting the front-row watchers to pluck off her tassels.

Annie looked over to the bar as movement there caught her eye. Two girls were loading trays with drinks and gliding off between the tables, wearing tiny black skirts and white waist pinafores. They were topless. They deposited the drinks on the tables, smiling wearily at the punters, dangling their exposed dugs right under the noses of the men. As Annie watched, several of the punters grabbed a quick feel.

For fuck's sake, thought Annie. *It's Tit City in here.*

Jonjo. This was all down to him, she was sure of it. Left to his own devices, he'd installed his own idea of what passed for good entertainment. *Fucking* Jonjo.

'That girl,' she said to Tony, having to shout to make herself heard above the noise, 'on the stage.'

Tony nodded.

'Don't let her leave. I want a word with her.'

Tony nodded.

'I'm going up to the office.'

A punter plucked off a tassel. The crowd cheered. Annie went back up the stairs and passed through the red doors again. She unclipped a rope on which was hung a small sign saying PRIVATE – STAFF ONLY, and clipped it back across when she'd passed through. Then she ascended a smaller staircase. At the top of the flight of stairs she paused before two doors. One she knew was a tiny flat, the other an office. She selected the smallest of the keys on Max's bunch, labelled 'P/Office'. She inserted the key in the lock, but it was already unlocked. She pushed open the door.

There was a naked girl spread-eagled on Max's desk, her legs up around the neck of a man who had his back to Annie. Annie stared at his white spotty buttocks pumping away – his trousers were around his ankles – with first surprise and then distaste. What the *hell?*

The girl spotted her first and let out a small shriek. The man half turned.

'Fucking hell, what do you think you're doing?' he demanded.

Annie's face froze into an icy mask. 'I was under the impression I was coming into my office,' she said coolly. 'Or am I wrong? What is this, a knocking shop now?'

He pulled out of the girl and Annie caught a flash of cunt and another, even less welcome, of a wet, deflating dick. She turned her head away as the girl scrabbled up, snatching clothes off the floor. The man adjusted his clothing and carried on shouting the odds, as if *she* was in the wrong here.

'Look, I don't know who the hell you are, but you'd better get out now or you'll be next over this desk, sister,' he yelled at her.

'Really?'

Annie pulled a hand out of her black coat's capacious pocket and suddenly Max's gun was there. She put the muzzle of the gun flat against the man's forehead and flicked off the safety.

The girl screamed and froze.

'*What the fucking hell* . . . ?' wailed the man, staggering back against the desk, trying to get away from the gun, staring at it cross-eyed in horror.

Annie's eyes were ice.

'Shut your noise,' she said to both of them. The girl fell silent, the man was breathing heavily. 'This is a hair trigger,' she told the man. 'You know about hair triggers?'

The man gave a tiny nod, then groaned and shut his eyes. Sweat was starting to pour out of him. He stank already. Disgusting.

'Good. Now tell me – who the fuck are *you*, arsehole?'

13

'Mrs Carter?' It was Tony, bursting through the door with a struggling blonde in tow. He looked at the girl still trying to get dressed, and the rumpled, white-faced man, and the gun in Annie's hand. 'You okay?'

The white-faced man ran a hand through his thinning blond hair. He looked balefully at Annie, then at Tony.

'Are you telling me this is Max Carter's missus?' he demanded.

'Who is this wanker?' Annie asked Tony, indicating the man.

'Club manager. Lou Morris.'

'Will you get your effing hands *off* me, you great ape,' snarled the blonde with Tony. Then she saw Annie and grew still.

Annie looked around at the assembled company. Five people in Max's office. The last time that had happened, someone had got themselves shot. She flicked the safety back on and pocketed the gun.

'Can we all calm down?' she said smoothly. She crossed the small room and threw open the window. Traffic roared outside and fumes billowed in, but it was better than the stink of stale sex and unwashed bodies.

'You,' she told the girl from the desk, who had gathered up her clothes and was now partly dressed. 'You work here?'

The girl nodded. Bright blue eyes and straight brown hair. She looked terrified. 'I'm a hostess.'

'What's you name?'

'Roberta,' she said.

'Well, Roberta, you never do anything like this again in any of the Carter clubs, you got me?'

Roberta nodded.

A pound note fluttered to the floor and she stooped, blushing, to grab it.

Annie looked at her in disgust.

'And don't sell yourself so damned *cheap*,' she told the girl. 'Go on, get out.'

Roberta hustled past Tony and the blonde.

Annie turned toward Lou and looked at him as if he'd just crawled out from under a rock.

'You're the manager here?'

'That's right,' said Lou with bravado. 'Jonjo Carter hired me last year.'

Annie nodded. 'And I'm firing you this year. That's sort of neat, don't you think?'

'Now wait.' Lou looked outraged. 'Just because I poked one of the girls over the desk?'

'No, because I don't like your face and I don't like your attitude. Now – keys. You're the manager; you've got keys, yes? Hand them over.'

Lou looked at Annie's face. Then at Tony's. The blonde was still, watching.

'Ah, what the fuck, I hated the job anyway,' snarled Lou, rummaging in his jacket pocket and slapping a bunch of keys into Annie's waiting hand. 'But you're gonna be sorry you did this,' he warned, pushing past her and past Tony and the blonde, and stamping off down the stairs.

'See he goes straight off the premises, Tony,' said Annie. 'Don't want him helping himself to the fixtures and fittings, do we?'

Tony pushed the blonde further into the room and followed Lou out through the door, shutting it firmly behind him. Annie shrugged off her coat and went around the desk and sat in Max's high leather chair.

Right here was where she'd been shot. She looked at the wall behind the chair, where the bullet that had passed through her and had imbedded itself. The wall was smooth now, neatly repaired. No trace of that traumatic event remained. But there was still a safe in the corner. She looked at it.

A combination safe. She wondered what was in there, and if it was enough. She doubted it.

She turned back to the blonde and nodded to the chair on the other side of the desk.

'Hiya, Jeanette. Take a seat. We need to have a chat.'

Jeanette looked sulky. She slumped down into the chair and stared at Annie mulishly.

'You didn't even say goodbye,' said Annie coolly. 'And I thought we were such good friends, too.'

'You're joking,' snorted Jeanette.

'That's right,' said Annie. 'I am.'

'So what do you want? I'm supposed to be on again in fifteen minutes.'

'You're not,' said Annie.

'Not what?'

'You're not on again in fifteen minutes. In fact, you're not on again ever, not here.'

'Oh come on!' Jeanette burst out. 'You can't fire me too! I ain't done nothing wrong and you know it. Listen,' she whined, 'I'm just keeping my head down and doing what I'm paid for, that's all. I don't want to know about your business, I don't want to get involved.'

'But you're already involved,' said Annie. 'Remember? You're involved because you were there, right there in Majorca, when it happened. I was out of it; they doped me. But they didn't dope you. So you were conscious all the way through. You saw what happened. And I need to know more about what you saw.'

'I've already told you. Nothing.'

'You said there were four of them . . .'

'Three, four . . . maybe more. I'm not sure.' She shook her head, frowning. She pulled her red robe closer around her. 'It was all so confusing. So fucking frightening. I've never been so scared in my life.' She looked at Annie. 'I thought they were going to *kill* me.'

There was a tap on the door. Tony poked his head around it.

'He's gone, Mrs Carter. Anything else?'

'Yes, Tony. Close up, will you? Send all the punters home, and all the girls and the barmen – we're closed until further notice.' She tossed him the keys. 'Lock up after, will you? Then get the locks changed. Pound to a penny Lou's had a spare set cut, and we don't want any unexpected visitors.'

Tony opened his mouth, then shut it again. The door closed and he was gone. A man of few words, Tony. Annie sort of liked that.

'Now Jeanette,' she said with a chilly smile, 'tell me what happened while I was out of it.'

'I already *told* you,' moaned Jeanette.

'There were four men? Five men? A fucking army? Come on, how many? You were *there*.'

Jeanette nodded wearily. 'Um, I dunno. Maybe

four, maybe three. Two big ones I think, and maybe one small.'

'Small, what? Short?'

'Short . . . um, slight, you know.'

'Slight. What, like a jockey you mean? Short and skinny?'

'Um, I don't know. I was scared to death. I'm not sure.'

'Which one slapped me with the chloroform?'

'God, I dunno.' Jeanette looked away.

'Think.'

'One of the bigger ones. First he . . .' Jeanette's face clouded and she fell silent.

'What? Go on,' said Annie.

Jeanette gulped and her eyes got teary.

'Max had got out of the pool again. I saw him on the other side, he was towelling himself dry, then I saw one of the big ones come up behind him and hit him on the head. He never even saw it coming. He went down like a sack of shit. I was just starting to sit up, then there was another one on our side of the terrace and he slapped that pad on your face and Jonjo started to wake up and then this bloke just turned . . .' Jeanette's face crumpled . . . 'He just turned and shot Jonjo straight between the eyes.'

It was quiet in the office for long moments while Jeanette looked down at her lap. Tears spilled down her cheeks and dripped off her nose.

'I know he wasn't a good man,' she sobbed. 'I know he didn't treat me too well, but they just wiped him out like he was nothing.'

Annie felt her blood run cold, felt despair seize her in its grip all over again. A deliberate, calculated hit. She stood up and closed the window, looking out at the rain, the people scurrying about, the cars moving slowly through the packed streets . . . all these people, with homes to go to, loved ones to see. And what did she have now?

Nothing.

Max was dead.

Layla was God knew where.

She gulped and felt like joining Jeanette and having a bloody good howl. Maybe it would make her feel better, who knew? But she was used to keeping her feelings inside. A loveless upbringing with a drunk of a mother had seen to that.

Dig deep and stand alone.

She hadn't had to stand alone for some time. There had been Max, taking the weight, seeing to her comfort and security; but now he was gone. And she was going to have to learn to stand on her own two feet again – because what was the alternative? Sink into the abyss. Give up the fight.

No fucking way, she thought. *Not while there's still a chance for Layla.*

She turned, leaned against the dusty window

frame. Jeanette had composed herself a little, she saw. Good.

'So which one grabbed Layla?' she asked.

Jeanette scrabbled around for a hankie. She found one in her pocket and honked her nose loudly. She blinked up, red-eyed, at Annie.

'Look, it could have been the little one,' she said. 'I don't know. I heard Layla singing that funny little French song she liked . . .' Jeanette took a faltering breath. 'Poor little cow. I heard her yell, then nothing. The one who'd shot Jonjo and drugged you told me to be quiet or I'd get a bullet too.'

'What did he sound like?'

'Um . . . British, I suppose.'

'Oh come on, you can do better than that.'

'I dunno.'

'Irish? Was he Irish?'

'Um . . . oh fuck it, how should I know? He could have been.' Jeanette was squirming in her seat.

Then maybe he's the one who phones me, thought Annie. *Or maybe not.*

'Did he have any distinguishing marks? Describe his face.'

'I didn't *see* his face. He had a mask on, they all did. And gloves. They were covered right up; I couldn't see anything of them. I saw the one on the other side of the pool grab Max under the arms and drag him off into the bushes, and the one on our side of the pool hauled Jonjo into the pool.'

'Strong man,' said Annie. 'Jonjo was pushing sixteen stone.'

Jeanette nodded. 'He lifted him like a fireman, you know? The fireman's lift thing, over his shoulder, and dumped him in the pool.'

Sixteen stones, dead weight. It would take a very strong man indeed to lift that.

So what do I have? thought Annie. *One small and slender. One big and exceptionally strong. One big and unknown, but he must move like a cat to get up close enough to do Max, because Max was sharp and fast, all instinct and movement and power . . .*

Or he had been, anyway. When he was alive.

That made it three people, not four. But so what? Where did knowing that get her?

Annie turned back to the window and stared up above the rooftops to grey depressing skies. There was no hope, and she had to admit it.

But she couldn't.

'Okay Jeanette, you can go,' she said, not looking round.

Annie heard the door close. Then she looked again at the safe in the corner. It had a combination lock, and she didn't know the code. She wondered who did. Then she let out a sigh, dropped her head on to her chest and closed her eyes in despair.

14

It was all going according to plan. Phil Fibbert had got the boat sorted and they were going to move after dark. Vita had calmed the fuck down after the hood incident: everything was good to go.

Danny was pleased.

He sat out in the late afternoon sun on the terrace and felt that he had everything nicely under control. And then he heard the normally quiet Phil (fucking *boring*, actually) kicking off at Vita in the kitchen, and soon Vita was screaming and yelling so loud that he had to rouse himself and go and see what the *fuck* was going on now.

'What the hell?' he demanded when he got into the cool, dark kitchen.

Phil just stood there, arms folded. *Man could bore for Britain*, thought Danny irritably.

Vita was silent, looking surly.

'Look,' said Phil, indicating the stuff on the table.

There was a bag of groceries. Rolls and fruit and stuff poking out of the top.

Danny frowned.

There was a woman who came in to bring their food, Marietta. They were renting this place in the winding back alleys of Palma from Marietta's husband, Julio, and the deal was, Marietta – who did not speak a word of English, and that was part of the master plan too – came in and cleaned every day, and brought provisions at 9.30 in the morning. So what was all this *new* stuff doing on the table at three in the afternoon?

Also on the table was a fuchsia-pink bag from one of the boutiques. Peeping out from this bag was a pair of Nubuck Majorcan sandals – you saw them everywhere in the shops here, in all colours of the rainbow. These were a bright, clear turquoise – Vita's favourite colour. She often wore it.

'Look, it's no big deal,' said Vita hurriedly, seeing the direction of Danny's eyes. 'I was going stir-crazy cooped up in this place. I got fed up just sitting here painting all day, so I went and got some more food in, and I looked in the shops and went to the flea market on Villalonga, and I had a walk down to the harbour.'

Danny went straight across and slapped her, hard.

Vita reeled back, clutching her cheek.

'Listen, you silly cow, we *stick to the plan.*

Remember the plan? You're getting right up my nose, you really are. The plan is, we stay here. We don't go out flashing the cash about. We don't want no one knowing we're here except Marietta and Julio, and to them we're just tourists, that's all. Marietta brings in the food, she cleans, she fucks off. We don't ever let her go out in the garden, just in case you were going to invite her out on to the terrace for tea and effing cakes, you got that? Oh – and every time you go near the girl you *put your fucking hood on.*'

'All right, I hear you,' mumbled Vita.

'Good. And you.' He turned, glaring, to Phil. 'Don't kick off at my sister, you got that? If you got anything to say, you say it to me.'

'Sure,' said Phil moodily, shrugging and putting his hands in his pockets. *Sure thing, Blondie,* he thought. *Blow it out your arse, Blondie. You fucking maniac.*

'You got the boat sorted? Everything okay?'

'Yeah, it's lined up for eleven,' said Phil, thinking that he for one would be absolutely fucking *delighted* when they got back to England, got their money, and went their separate ways. He could not *wait* to see the back of this crazy pair.

'Okay, we'll clear up at ten and be out of here and down at the harbour by a quarter to eleven – and by the way, Vee, we will be wearing our hoods when we fetch the girl, okay? Then we'll give her a good dose of stuff, blindfold her, and get her on board the boat and that'll be that, okay?'

Vita nodded, one hand nursing her reddened cheek.

'I said *okay?*' repeated Danny.

'Okay,' she said.

15

When Annie got back to Limehouse it was business as usual – punters arriving, punters leaving, Una knocking the living crap out of some poor twisted bastard up there in the back room that Aretha used to occupy. Darren was entertaining a gentleman from the City, Dolly told her over a cup of tea in the kitchen, and Ellie was busy with a chubby-chaser – very popular too, she was.

'It's all hands to the pump, if you'll pardon the expression,' said Dolly, putting her cup down. 'So how's it all going?'

'Oh, peachy,' said Annie. 'My baby girl's been snatched, my husband's been hit, and now I find his clubs have been turned into strip joints.'

'Ah.'

'You knew?'

Dolly shrugged. 'Everyone did, it's no big secret. Jonjo Carter made the changes. No one questions

119

the Carter brothers over what they do. Everyone thought Max knew about it.'

'No,' said Annie positively. 'He couldn't have. He'd have hated it.'

She'd been appalled at what had happened to the Palermo. Then she'd had Tony drive her over to the Shalimar and the Blue Parrot, only to find they'd been given the same down-market treatment.

She'd closed them both up, sacked the managers, got Tony to get the locks changed. Tony had got quieter and quieter as the day had progressed, and finally Annie had asked if there was a problem.

'No,' he'd said, driving through the drizzle and the heavy traffic, his eyes not meeting hers in the mirror.

'No? Only I think there is.'

Tony shrugged.

'Tell me,' said Annie.

'The boys might not like all these changes. That's all.'

Annie sat back. 'You mean Jimmy Bond?'

Jimmy hadn't exactly fallen over himself to welcome her, and that was a fact. Which was a shame, because she knew she badly needed Jimmy onside.

'Him and others,' said Tony diplomatically.

Meaning that where Jimmy led, the others followed, thought Annie.

'Well,' said Annie, 'if Jimmy – or any of the

other boys – have something to say about the alterations I've made, then they can say it to me, can't they?'

Tony had grunted and said no more.

'So you've closed the clubs. Now what?' asked Dolly.

Annie looked at Dolly blankly. 'Meaning?'

'You're not going to leave them shut, are you? Those clubs must have been bringing in a lot of dosh for the Carters.'

Annie sighed and leaned her chin on her hand. Dolly was right. But she'd been outraged at what she'd seen happening to Max's clubs. They'd been his pride and joy, and she had acted on instinct and stepped in. Maybe she shouldn't have. Maybe she would very soon have been glad of that income. But maybe not. When the kidnappers asked her to cough up the money – as soon they must – she was sure that it wouldn't be covered by a couple of big-titted girls twirling their tassels lunchtime and evening.

'I remember those clubs as they were, Doll. Class acts on. Good, respectable punters. The place clean and tidy, the staff happy, the whole thing running smooth.' She pulled a face. 'You ought to see the fucking place now. Sleazy don't cover it. I've run better knocking shops.'

'So what's the plan?'

'For the clubs? I dunno yet.'

'The boys are going to be up in arms.'

'Yeah, Tony told me that.'

'You don't care?'

'Doll – I don't give a flying fuck. I'm just waiting for Friday.'

But before Friday could come around, Jimmy Bond was knocking at the door mob-handed with Steve Taylor and Gary Tooley minding his back. Ross let Jimmy in, and Steve and Gary loitered with insolent ease in the hallway while Jimmy and Annie went into the kitchen.

This time Jimmy was breathing fire. She'd rattled his cage good and proper, and Annie was perversely glad to see him riled. At least he was engaging with her now, not being snide and laughing her off as a 'bit of skirt'.

'What the *fuck* have you been up to?' he demanded when they were alone in the kitchen.

'I beg your pardon?' asked Annie icily.

'You heard me.' Jimmy leaned his gloved hands on the table and loomed over her as she sat there, all innocence. 'You've closed up the clubs. You've had the fucking locks changed. You've fired the staff. You crazy?'

'Nope.' Annie stood up and leaned her fists on the table, too. They were glaring nose to nose. 'And watch your mouth, Jimmy. I told you. I'm taking over.'

'Yeah, sure you are. You know about running clubs, do you?'

'I've run businesses.'

'You've run a high-class whorehouse, and you nearly did time for that, which wasn't very clever, was it?'

Annie bit back an angry reply. She had to get him onside. Somehow.

'Who was in overall charge of the clubs? Who collected the takings from the managers?' she asked.

'I did.'

'Then you know how bad they've got.'

'I know they're making good money,' he retorted.

'How good?'

'Better than they were as nightclubs.'

'I don't believe it.'

'The books don't lie.'

'I want to see them. Who keeps them?'

'I do. You got a problem with that?'

Convenient, thought Annie.

Jimmy took a breath. 'Those acts Max used to hire, they cost a fortune. Strippers are cheap.'

'Jonjo had no right to make these changes without consulting Max.'

'Max must have known.'

'Do you really believe that Max would approve a low-tone operation like that?'

'Who knows what the fuck Max would do? He

123

took off for the sun and left Jonjo in charge of the manor. What did he care?'

Annie heard the resentment in his voice. She looked at him and he dropped his eyes first. 'I want those books here this afternoon,' she said. 'And Jimmy – don't come in here again with half a fucking army, for God's sake. I'm here on sufferance. Redmond Delaney'll only take so much.'

Max had trusted Jimmy, so she had to. Simple logic. She hoped her logic was sound this time. Whatever, she wanted to see those books.

'And do you know the combination on the safe at the Palermo?' she asked him.

There was just the one safe, she had discovered. Nothing at the Blue Parrot and the Shalimar except small cash boxes with bugger all inside.

Jimmy gave her an old-fashioned look. 'Jonjo trusted me with a lot of things, but not with that,' he said.

Fuck it, thought Annie.

'We'll need the locksmith,' she said.

16

Annie awoke with Layla's little body snuggling in against hers. She could feel Layla's silky-soft hair and buried her nose in the back of Layla's neck, where the baby-smell of her was strongest – talc and sweetness. She turned, smiling to herself, and came up against Max's skin – hard, hot, reassuring.

'Annie?'

A female voice.

Max was gone. And that wasn't Inez talking. This voice was pure East End of London. A bit roughened by fags and booze and hard times, but familiar.

Annie opened her eyes and this time came properly awake. Dim light in Dolly's bedroom. Dolly there, smiling down at her like a fond mother, putting a mug of tea on the bedside table. Then it came back to her again, all of it. The pain; the anguish. But instead of howling and screaming with the agony of loss that she was feeling, she sat up. Dolly pulled back the curtains to let in the cold grey English light. The Majorcan villa was a world away.

And – *oh fuck* – it was Friday.

She'd slept very late. What was it with her, all this sleeping? *Escaping from reality*, Annie thought. Funny how she always woke up feeling exhausted, though. All these dreams. Max, falling . . . her reaching for him, but it was too late, far too late. Layla screaming. Annie, alone in a wasteland, no one there except her and a feeling of impending doom. All those *bloody* dreams.

Feeling tired and edgy she washed, dressed in Dolly's black shift dress again, brushed out her hair, dabbed a bit of Dolly's rouge on her cheeks and on her lips and still looked like death – not that it mattered.

She stepped out of the bedroom and on to the landing. Loud voices and laughter drifted up from the front room. Ross was sitting down there in the hall in the corner by the door that Chris had always occupied when she was last here.

Friday. Of course. Lunch party day. Noises from the other bedrooms, someone moaning, someone crying out *yes, yes, yes*. Music, too. Fleetwood Mac playing 'Albatross', fading into older stuff from days gone by – smoky, bluesy

'Mad about the Boy', Etta James's voice dripping with passion.

Annie stood there at the top of the stairs and let it wash over her.

That song said everything she had ever felt about Max. Stupid to have been drawn to him – her sister's husband. Knowing he was dangerous. Knowing he was off limits. Knowing she could not resist his piratical charm, his strength, his masculine allure.

God, I've got to snap out of this, thought Annie.

'What the hell are you looking at?'

Annie looked up. Una, with her white-blonde crew-cut and her pallid blue eyes was standing in the doorway opposite. She was in black leather today. There was a whip in her hand. As Annie watched, a droplet of blood fell from the end of the whip and hit the landing carpet. The droplet expanded, spreading in the thick pile. The door behind Una was ajar and Annie could see a naked man in there, tied to a chair, his shoulders striped red, his head drooping.

A dominatrix didn't get paid, Annie remembered. She was awarded a 'tribute' from the punter when he left. The punter wanted to be abused, debased, humiliated – and the dominatrix happily pandered to his vice, and was amply rewarded for doing so.

'I'm not looking at anything,' said Annie

truthfully. Fuck it, if the punters wanted to be whipped and if Una got her kicks that way, what did she care?

'Good. You want to keep it that way, babes, or you'll be sorry.'

'Right.'

'Only I don't like your attitude.'

Annie looked at her. 'I'm sorry about that,' she said.

'You see? There it is again.' Una came in close. She smelled of sweat and cheap perfume and her eyes were glittery with excitement, ready for a fight. 'Your mouth says all the right words, but your eyes say *fuck you*. You got a real attitude problem, babes, and I don't like it.'

'Duly noted,' said Annie, and turned toward the stairs.

Or she started to. She vaguely saw Una's booted foot come out, but it was too late to step back. She felt herself start to fall, snatched at the banister, but too late. She went head over heels all the way down to the bottom and ended up at Ross's feet with all the wind knocked out of her. She looked back up the stairs as Dolly and Ellie came running to her aid, and there was Una, smirking down at her.

Everything hurt. She'd bumped her head, there was blood coming from a cut above her right eyebrow, her left arm felt wrenched where she'd tried to stop herself falling.

'Fuck it, Annie, what's going on?' asked Dolly, hauling her back to her feet.

Annie looked up at Una, still standing there, gloating.

'Nothing,' she said to Dolly. 'I just tripped, that's all. Careless of me.'

Una's smile broadened. She turned and strolled away, back to her room.

17

It was late afternoon when the call came. The phone had been ringing all day, and every time Annie had tensed, bracing herself for the next horror. All through the long day, she had been in the kitchen, waiting. Wishing she smoked, wishing she drank.

Listening to the revelry of the party going on in the front room, the thumping of feet going up and down the stairs, the laughter, the noises of hot frantic sex going on over her head.

Thinking of what could be happening to Layla. Of what had already happened to Max. And poor bloody Jonjo, who had never liked her. Well, she'd never liked him either. But still.

Driving herself mad.

A few hours later and the party was over, the washing-up done, the bottles cleared away, the takings counted. When the phone rang it was Dolly who picked it up again, and it was for Annie.

'Give us a minute, will you, Ross?' Dolly said quickly, and the bouncer went off into the front room, closing the door behind him. Dolly shut the kitchen door. Only her and Annie were in the hall. Dolly had her hand over the mouthpiece.

Suddenly shaking, Annie took the phone. 'Hello?'

'I said I'd call on Friday,' said the Irish man.

Annie took a breath.

Game on.

'Yeah, you did.'

'And here I am, as good as my word.'

'Yeah.'

'So . . .' He was toying with her again.

'I want to speak to Layla,' said Annie, feeling as if she was about to scream.

'Can't be done right now.'

'Why not?' God, was she hurt? Had they harmed her in some way?

'I told you before, no questions.'

'Sorry.' Annie's heart was thudding sickeningly in her chest. She could barely breathe.

Dig deep, she thought. *Got to dig deep.* 'Listen, think about what I said. We could do a deal. A swap. Hand Layla over and take me instead. Let Layla go and have me.'

There was silence on the other end of the phone, except for that noise again. Teacups, or something. Annie strained to hear it. Maybe it would offer

131

some sort of clue. She was willing to clutch at any straw. But it stopped as soon as it started. She thought that the sound was somehow familiar, but she couldn't bring it to mind. Her brain was in a flat spin.

'Ah, no. The kid's worth more.'

'More money,' said Annie grimly.

'That's it,' he said cheerily. 'Because you'll pay any amount to get her back, ain't that a fact? But who'd pay to get you back? No bastard, I'm thinking.'

Annie swallowed hard. 'Yeah, you're right,' she said.

She had no blood kin who would speak up for her. Ruthie was God knew where, and although they had reached a sort of understanding over Annie's love affair with Max, they hadn't spoken in a long time. Kath despised her. There was no one else. She wondered how he knew that.

'And now we come to it,' he said. 'The money. What we want from you. From the wealthy Carters.'

But I don't know where the fucking wealth is, thought Annie wildly. But she kept quiet. Forced herself to.

'Half a million pounds sterling for the girl. Just that.'

'What?'

'You heard me. I'll phone back next Friday.'

Half a million quid! Annie's ears rang with shock.

'Wait,' she said quickly. 'Wait.'

'That gives you a week to raise it,' he said, rolling right on. 'One week.'

'But wait . . .' *God, why couldn't she think straight?*

'Wait for what?' he snapped.

Annie was shaking her head helplessly. 'I don't think I can raise that sort of money,' she blurted.

Silence.

Silence except for that goddamned *noise* again. What the hell was that noise?

'Well now,' he said. 'That's a pity.'

'Wait.'

'A great pity.' He sounded regretful.

'Just wait. I can raise some, but maybe not that much.'

'Pity. I'll talk to you next Friday. Same time. Enjoy the gift.'

Gift?

She opened her mouth to speak, but he was already gone.

'So what happened? How much do they want?' demanded Dolly as Annie stood there with the phone still in her nerveless hand.

Annie replaced the receiver. 'Too much,' she said, and went into the front parlour and closed the door behind her.

133

Had to *think*.

Half a million quid.

A total impossibility. She looked at the tray of drinks set out on the sideboard. Vodka, gin, whisky. Anything the punters wanted. She took one of the upended glasses and looked at the bottles.

There was a knock on the door and Darren pushed it open and stood there, lounging against the doorframe, arms folded.

'Well, one drink's not going to kill you, now is it, Annie Carter?' he said.

Annie looked back at him. Looked at the empty glass, the bottles. Thought of her mother lying in hospital, yellowed and skinny and dying, because she had to have the fucking booze.

She put the glass down and turned away from the drinks. 'Yeah, but could I stop at one?' she asked him.

'That bad?' asked Darren.

Annie nodded. 'Worse.'

'Dolly told me you've got trouble,' said Darren. 'Did she tell Ellie?'

'What, you afraid she'll tell the Delaneys your business?' Darren shook his head. 'I think Ellie knows which side her bread's buttered by now. And anyway, they know you're here, don't they? Ross must have said. Dolly *had* to say. And didn't the big boss of the Delaneys send you a note?'

Annie let out a heartfelt sigh. Yes, Redmond

knew she was here and for the moment it seemed he was content to let her stay. How long that would last, she didn't know.

'Anyway,' Darren went on, 'you're in tight with the Delaney twins, ain't that right? I heard you used to be big mates with that gang.'

Which was a bit of a joke, really. She'd never even known the eldest Delaney child, Tory, although she had known his brother Pat – to her cost. And Kieron, too. It was true that Redmond Delaney had once done business with her, and Orla his twin had always been polite – almost, but never quite, friendly. A funny pair, those twins. Cold. Red hair and white skin, a perfect, handsome pair, like book ends carved from marble. Hurt too early to ever recover.

Annie thought of Layla, who might be hurt too, abused, ruined for the whole of her life, and the pain and anxiety started to gnaw at her guts again. She folded her arms over her middle, feeling achy and frozen.

'Is this trouble something I can help with?' asked Darren.

Annie looked at him. Good old Darren. He might look like shit, but he was the same. A firm friend; a great listener.

She shook her head.

He indicated the small plaster Dolly had applied over her eye. 'Heard you had a run-in with our Una. And it looks like you came off worse.'

'I'm okay, but things could be better. How about you, Darren?'

'Oh, fine.'

'Liar. You look ill.'

Darren's mouth twisted and his bright blue eyes moved away from Annie's. 'It's nothing,' he shrugged.

'You don't have to tell me if you don't want to,' said Annie.

'Not much to tell.' He went over to the couch and sat down and looked up at her. 'I was in love, you know,' he said.

Annie looked at him. 'With who?' she asked, more gently. Dolly hadn't told her this in any of her phone calls. And if Darren had found someone, why was he still here working as a brass? Ah, but he'd said he *was* in love. Past tense. *Over*.

'No one you know. A punter.' Darren gave the ghost of a chuckle. 'Stupid, falling for a punter. One of my regulars. We just seemed to . . . hit it off, you know. And he didn't seem to care what I was. Which is rare, as you know. Not many men care to associate with us working girls.'

'So what happened? He go off the idea?'

'Nah, nothing like that. We were making plans and everything. He worked in the City doing some funny thing or other with money markets – pork-belly futures or something daft like that – and he said he was going to jack it all in and we would take off together. He was rich. Not too old. Late fortyish. Fair bit older than me, but that has its attractions. We were going to travel the world. See Rome, and Paris, and Venice . . .'

Darren's voice trailed away and he looked at the floor.

'Then he got sick,' he said in a small voice. 'Cancer. Took about a year and a half, and his sister looked after him for the last six months. I visited every week, which she was pretty sniffy about: didn't like the whole gay thing at all. He got pneumonia in the end, I was holding his hand when he died . . .'

Darren swallowed and shook himself and looked up at Annie, eyes bright with tears. 'So that was that, really,' he said.

'Darren, I'm sorry. I didn't know. Dolly never said when she phoned me.' Annie sat down beside him. She put an arm around his stick-thin shoulders. Jesus, it was like hugging a child!

'I asked her not to tell anyone. Didn't want the sympathy vote.'

'I'm sorry,' said Annie helplessly.

'Ah, it don't matter,' said Darren with a sniff and a smile. 'What's that old saying? "Nothing matters very much and in the end nothing matters at all".'

'Wise words. If only we could believe them.'

Annie gave his skeletal shoulder a squeeze. Was this the reason he'd sunk so bloody low, let himself go the way he had? He'd lost the man he loved – just as she had. The loss had hit him like a runaway train – that much was obvious. She had the feeling this wasn't the whole story, but he was upset; she wouldn't push it for now. And she had grief enough of her own to bear without taking on more.

'Come on, Darren,' she said briskly. 'We all get crap sooner or later. What matters is how you deal with it.'

And who am I trying to convince? she thought. *Me, or Darren?*

18

Jimmy Bond had been as good as his word and delivered the accounts books to Annie. Now all she had to do was try and read and understand them, and she'd never kept legitimate accounts in her life.

Annie knew she had a choice. She could sit around and wait, or she could keep busy and stop herself going crazy. No contest. Later that afternoon she snatched the books off Dolly's dressing table, put on her coat, and told Dolly she was off out. She hesitated and then left the gun in Dolly's top drawer.

She'd brought it all through Customs with her, expecting to be stopped, searched, banged up, but no: they'd let her through, and she was glad. Having Max's gun made her feel a little better, a little safer. She told Dolly the gun was there, and Dolly nodded as if this was an everyday occurrence.

'Where are you off to?' asked Dolly. 'In case that bastard phones unexpectedly.'

'To the clubs. And Max's mum's old place.' To search for Max's stash of money. He had to have one somewhere, and she was determined to find it.

'Okay.'

Outside, Tony was reading the paper while sitting patiently behind the wheel. She tapped his window. He wound it down and looked at her without expression.

'We're going to the clubs, Tony. Palermo first.'

Annie got in the back and put the accounts beside her on the seat. She settled back. Tony hadn't started the engine. His eyes were watching her in the rear-view mirror.

'Problem?' she asked.

'You've got a plaster over your eyebrow,' said Tony.

'Ten out of ten for observation.'

'Anyone giving you grief, Mrs Carter?'

Annie held his gaze. 'Fell down the stairs, Tony.'

Tony watched her a moment longer, then he reached over to the glove compartment. He drew out a small cylindrical black item and handed it back to her.

Annie looked at it, mystified.

'You just flick it out. It's a martial arts weapon. It's called a kiyoga,' said Tony.

Annie gave the thing a hefty flick. A spring

appeared, and a steel ball. *Jesus*, she thought. *Whack someone with that, you could kill them.*

'In case you fall down any more stairs,' said Tony.

Annie nodded and looked at the kiyoga. 'Um,' she said.

'Tap the steel ball on a hard surface to close it up again,' said Tony helpfully.

Annie leaned over and tapped the thing on the floor. The spring and the steel ball vanished back inside the thin black tube. Annie straightened and put the lethal little thing in her coat pocket.

'Thanks Tony,' she said.

Tony looked awkward.

'Mr Carter's always been very good to me,' he said, and started the engine.

'Let's call in at Jimmy's place first,' said Annie decisively. 'Time I caught up with our Kath.'

'What the fuck are you doing here?' Kath asked Annie when she opened her front door and found her cousin standing there.

'Just catching up with family,' said Annie, recognizing Kath more by her voice and her bright flinty brown eyes than by any other feature.

She looked beyond Kath and the whining toddler clinging to her leg. The hallway was dusty, dirty, and cluttered. Filth on the carpet, toys and prams littering the hall. A radio was blaring out 'Love

Grows' by Edison Lighthouse somewhere in there, and a baby was crying. Bedlam.

And the state of Kath. Christ, she'd never been a treat to look at but at least she used to make an effort. Annie had never seen anyone change so much in such a short space of time. Kath had never been a beauty, but she'd made the effort, taken trouble with her appearance, and somehow she'd looked good.

Now she looked *bad*.

She'd piled on the weight. Her hair was short now and showing grey at the roots, styled into an unflattering old-lady perm that aged her a good fifteen years. She wore loose dark slacks and a shapeless T-shirt.

Poor bloody Jimmy Bond. And what had Annie said to him? *You ought to keep your house in order*. Where the hell would the poor bastard start in this tip? Well, no one had ever thought Jimmy married Kath for her looks. Maybe for her sparkling personality?

'I suppose you'd better come the fuck in, now you're here,' grunted Kath, turning away from the door to display an arse the size of a small continent.

Maybe not for the sparkling personality, then. Annie trailed in after Kath unwillingly, wondering what fresh domestic disaster she was going to discover.

She soon found out. In the kitchen, the breakfast dishes were still all over the table. There were
dirty nappies on chairs. The draining board and
sink were stacked high with filthy plates. There
was a child bawling its head off in a pram by the
back door. Annie leaned over to look at the crying
infant and the stink of urine and faeces stung her
nose. She touched the baby's bedding and found
it wet. Christ, it was soaking. There ought to have
been a sodding rainbow over the end of the pram.

'This kid's wet through,' she told Kath.

'I'll change her in a minute,' said Kath, shaking
out a ciggie from the packet on the table and
groping around for matches.

It didn't seem to be bothering Kath in the least,
but the baby's wailing was grating on Annie. She
took off her coat and picked up the little girl.

'Where do you keep the clean nappies?' she
asked Kath, clearing a space on the table and laying
the baby on it.

Now the toddler was joining in with the baby's
crying. And Kath was still rummaging around for
matches.

'Kath!' said Annie sharply.

Kath stopped rummaging and looked at her.

'Fuck the matches – get a clean nappy. Now.'

'Christ, you don't change,' said Kath huffily,
but she went off to the airing cupboard and –
miracle of miracles – emerged with a clean, warm

nappy in her hand. Annie pulled off the plastic pants and unfastened the dirty nappy and took it over to the plastic pail by the back door, dunking it in with a grimace of distaste. It was obvious that the poor kid had been lying there like that for hours; no wonder it was screaming the place down.

She turned to see that Kath had shifted herself at last and was desultorily washing her daughter down. Kath dried her, smiling down at the child and making goo-goo noises. Annie handed her the clean nappy and the safety pins. Kath applied talcum powder and then put the clean nappy on the quietening little girl. Better late than never, thought Annie grimly.

She went and looked at the pram. Everything in there was wet and stinking, but it was a fine windy day and things would quickly dry. So she went over to the sink and cleared it, put the plug in, and found a packet of Omo in the cupboard. She ran in hot water and then put the pram's bedding, all of it including the pillow, into the hot soapy water.

'Christ, I never thought you'd turn out to be so domestic,' said Kath, who was now sitting down at the table with the baby rooting away at her breast under her T-shirt. The toddler had stopped whining and was squatting in the far corner on the floor, slapping watercolours on to a sheet of paper.

'This place is disgusting,' said Annie.

Just as well Kath's mother Maureen – Annie's aunt and her mother Connie's sister – had passed over. She had been faultlessly neat about her person and her house. To see her daughter living like this would be a bitter disappointment to her.

'Listen, don't you come around here telling *me* what to do,' said Kath. 'You might be able to boss Jimmy around because he's scared of Max bloody Carter, but it don't wash with me.'

So Jimmy had been as good as his word; he hadn't told Kath what had happened to Max. Annie breathed a sigh of relief.

'What's your name?' Annie asked the toddler, who was now swooshing his paintbrush around in a glass of water. He didn't answer, just got back to his paints.

That noise, thought Annie.

'That's Jimmy Junior,' said Kath with a hint of pride. 'Looks like his dad, don't he?'

The toddler had Jimmy's pale brown hair and vivid blue eyes, it was true. Lucky kid, he looked nothing like Kath at all.

'And this one?'

'This is Maureen, named after Mum,' said Kath with a glimmer of tears. 'Mum passed away last July, and I had Little Mo in August. It seemed fitting to call her after Mum.'

'Yeah. She's lovely,' said Annie.

Dolly had told her all about that. Annie had heard the news of Maureen's death with real sadness and had phoned Kath immediately. Kath had put the phone down on her, so she sent flowers, feeling that she should do more, but knowing that her efforts would not be appreciated. Annie was looking at Jimmy Junior, painting. He dunked his brush in the water again, swooshed it around. Again, the noise. The familiar noise.

The baby had blue eyes and silky light-brown hair too. Lucky baby. Kath fished her out from under the voluminous T-shirt and put the baby on her shoulder to burp her. Mo let out a massive burp and a fart for good measure. Annie's eyes met Kath's, and for a moment Kath was almost smiling at her; then she remembered herself and her face straightened out again.

'So what did you come here for? Really?' Kath demanded irritably.

'I wondered how you were.'

'As you can see, I'm bloody fine.'

Yeah sure, thought Annie. *Everything running just like clockwork, I don't think.*

'You look like you been in the wars,' Kath said, her eyes on Annie's face.

'Fell down the stairs,' said Annie.

'You and Max split up, is that what's really happened?'

Annie tensed. 'Why do you say that?'

146

'Jimmy said you were taking over here and that Jonjo and Max were staying out in the Costas for a bit.' Kath shrugged. 'It just don't seem to fit together, that's all. I know Jonjo and what he's like with women, and he's been running the show here – well, mostly Jimmy has really. Seems unlike Max, that's all. Handing over the reins like he has. Especially to a woman.'

'Max is still in overall charge,' said Annie, wishing this were true. 'He wants me here running things for a while. The clubs, for instance. Things have got sloppy.'

'Christ, I bet you're in your element,' sniffed Kath. 'You always were a bossy cow, giving orders left, right, and centre, snatching your sister's husband.' She looked at Annie with a stern eye. 'Oh yeah, I don't forget. Some of us got long memories.'

'Ruthie and I parted on good terms,' said Annie.

'Like fuck.' Kath snorted. 'She gave up and left the scene, that's all, because she's a nice woman and you're not. It's all about sex with you, Annie Bailey. You wanted Max Carter in bed, and nothing was going to stop you getting him between your legs.'

Annie stood up and put her coat on. 'Has Ruthie been in touch with you?' she asked Kath. She'd been daft to come here. What had she honestly expected, except abuse?

'Sure she has,' said Kath smugly.

Mo was starting up again with the howling. Not to be left out, Jimmy Junior was joining in.

'Can I have her address?'

'No you fucking well can't.'

'Her telephone number then?'

'No. Now bugger off out of my house, Annie Carter.'

What else did I expect but this? Annie wondered. She thought of Jimmy, always neatly turned out, taking pride in his appearance – and the walking shit-heap that was Kath. What would a man like Jimmy do, confronted with this house, this woman, day by day?

She thought she knew.

Annie left and climbed back into the Jag. Tony looked at her in the mirror.

'Palermo, Tony. Please.' She sat back and wearily closed her eyes.

19

Danny had a look of terrible violence about him and it frightened Vita. She had seen him like this before; there was no reasoning with him.

'Well, what did she say?' asked Vita, trying to calm him down.

They were in the kitchen of a shabby two-up two-down on the south coast of England and it was not like Majorca in any way. It was fucking cold for one thing, no central heating, no nothing, and she was shivering the whole time. Venture outside and the wind knocked you flat. The rain was vicious. Waves spumed over the nearby front. All she could do was peer out at grey skies and tossing seas from the upstairs window while she tried to distract herself with her painting-by-numbers.

Not that she was much distracted by it. Not when Danny was like this.

She watched him rifling in a drawer, looking for . . . *oh shit* . . . he pulled out a knife.

'She's not taking this seriously. Can you believe that bitch is trying to pretend she can't raise that much money? Christ, Max Carter owns half the East End. No, I've got to send her something. Something to convince her I mean business.'

He had that demented look in his eye again.

Vita could feel the bile rising in her stomach, the fear squeezing her guts. She knew Danny had a dark side. Look at what he'd done to the Majorcan couple. Even as a kid he'd been crazy. At eight years old he had strangled his pet rabbit, killed it, and laughed when she ran off crying.

Phil Fibbert, sitting at the kitchen table, was sipping tea and watching all this going on. His eye caught Vita's. She gave him a look that said: *Listen, can't you do something? Help me out here? Calm him down?*

Phil carried on placidly sipping his tea and buried his head in the paper he was pretending to read. He had already decided that Danny Byrne was mad as a box of frogs. And there was no way he was going to try reasoning with him when he had a fucking great knife in his hand.

'What you going to do?' Vita asked Danny.

'Send the bitch a little souvenir,' he said, and went to the cellar door. He threw it open, flicked on the light at the top of the stairs, and hurried off down to where Layla passed her drugged-up days on a little put-you-up folding bed.

Phil looked up and his eyes met Vita's again. Then he went back to the paper, and his tea.

Shuddering, Vita left the room. She edged past the open cellar door and went back upstairs. She didn't want to hear or see what was happening.

20

Arnie McFay had been having a good night down at his local snooker hall: he was on a roll and feeling fine. Out with his mates. Having a laugh and a few pints. Everything was good. Stripping off his black leather bomber jacket with ARNIE picked out in studs on the back, he prepared to win a few frames and then the game, pocket the dosh, and roll on home to the old lady.

'That fucking peacock Arnie,' his friends always laughed.

Arnie was a character: everyone said so. He was dark and good looking and prone to being pursued by short-skirted dollies wearing tight tops, white heels, and love bites. One slapper had chased him all through Woolworth's and her boyfriend had got a bit narked. Finally the boyfriend had tracked him down to this very place, where he was propping up the bar with his pals and had said: 'Are you Arnie?'

'Me? No,' said Arnie – with his fucking name picked out in studs on the back of his jacket.

Oh, how his mates had laughed.

Before the skin and hair started flying, that was.

But that had been before the Carter mob moved in and kept the peace, squashing such incidents before they even started. Lolly Dean the owner now paid a good wodge over every week, and this was a decent place. Fights were a dim memory. Dim like Arnie, his friends joshed him.

The trouble with Arnie was he always bent the rules. Couldn't resist it. Loved to throw the dice in the air and see how they fell. Loved to take risks. Loved to live on the edge.

So tonight he was on a roll, a real diamond of a roll. He was playing this dickhead from across town who couldn't use a cue to save his life, so why not make things a little more interesting? He laid down fifty quid and so did Dickhead.

Only maybe the man wasn't such a dickhead after all.

Because suddenly Dickhead's form seemed to come good; he was potting them all over the place and Arnie was standing there with his mouth open, catching flies. His mates were wincing and smirking. Poor Arnie, he'd fallen for one of the oldest scams in the book. You played like a two year old, let the other boys see what a complete cunt you were at the game, and you waited for them to take the bait. Then you turned out to be county champion.

Arnie had swallowed the bait whole. Had invited Dickhead to play a game, and what about a wager on the side?

Dickhead had reluctantly agreed.

And Arnie had been neatly stitched up.

He felt the anger burn him as his mates stood at the bar, snorting with laughter into their pints at what an arsehole he'd been made to look. All Dickhead's mates were sniggering down the other end and Dickhead was potting the black. He'd wiped the table with Arnie.

'Nice,' said Dickhead, his hand reaching for the hundred-quid prize.

But Arnie whipped out his cue and rapped Dickhead's knuckles.

'Nah, that's not fair. Best of three. Let's say best of three,' said Arnie.

All his mates held their breath.

'I've had enough excitement for one night.' Dickhead pushed the cue aside. 'One game was the deal, and one game we had.'

'I still think we ought to do best of three,' persisted Arnie. His face was smiling but his eyes were cold. He didn't like being made to look a prick.

'Sorry,' said Dickhead.

'Never mind, Arnie, come and have a pint,' said

Col, one of Arnie's mates, feeling nervous on his pal's behalf.

Not that there would be any trouble. The Carter boys were sitting in the corner . . . or they had been. Col straightened, feeling a little twinge of unease. He looked up and down the bar but all he could see was that gawky mare Deirdre polishing glasses behind the bar and eyeing the punters. Deirdre was a lovely girl but no looker. She was tall with big feet that played her up so she had to wear orthopaedic shoes.

'Christ,' he'd teased her on more than one occasion, 'with feet that size you'd be better off wearing the fucking shoe boxes.'

Oh yes, how they'd laughed at *that* one. But nothing seemed very funny right now. No Lolly, no Carter boys. Nothing, in fact, between silly Arnie and a good kicking, because he was in the wrong, as usual, but the dopy cunt was still pushing his luck all the way.

Col was looking at Deirdre, whose face was suddenly rigid with horror. Behind her in the bar mirror he saw the chair coming, and ducked. The chair crashed into the mirror and knocked half a ton of bottles about like skittles. The noise was deafening. Col turned and saw Arnie on the floor, with Dickhead using Arnie's stomach for football practice.

Silly bastard, thought Col.

All Dickhead's mates had gathered around to cheer Dickhead on.

Col looked down at Arnie as Dickhead transferred his attention to Arnie's head. It was too late for Arnie, but Col gave his mates the nod and they waded in. Right or wrong, a mate was a mate, after all.

But where the fuck were the Carter boys?

Deirdre was screaming her stupid head off and yanking down the metal grilles over the bar. The other punters were scattering for the door. As Col doled out a punch to someone's chin, he saw the club doors swing open and spotted Greg, one of the Carter boys, getting it in the neck even worse out there in the car park than they were in here. There was a big gang at work here tonight. He realized that as he lay on the floor next to what remained of Arnie.

Silly bastard, he thought again, and then Col passed out.

21

'It's started,' said Jimmy Bond.

Annie sat at the kitchen table next day and looked up at him as he stood leaning over her, gloved fists on the table. She had the nightclub books spread out before her and she'd been deep in thought jotting down figures when Ross had reluctantly let Jimmy in. Depressing thoughts like, strippers probably *do* pay better than class acts. Black thoughts like, my child is missing and my husband is dead. Killing thoughts like, *why am I bothering with this?* Despairing thoughts like, where the fuck did Max keep his money?

'What's started?' she asked him wearily. 'And when's that bloody locksmith showing up, are you on that?'

She had to get that safe open. Had to know what was inside.

Half a million?

She knew she couldn't get that lucky.

'Yeah, I'm on it, I told you. There was trouble down Lolly's billiard hall last night. Someone kept our boys busy out the front while they trashed the place.'

Annie's attention sharpened. 'Anyone hurt?'

'One of the regulars got brain damage – he's in a fucking coma. Couple of others hospitalized. And Lolly's hitting the roof. Asking why did he pay protection to the Carters when they didn't actually *protect* him.'

Annie sat back. 'The Delaneys?'

Jimmy sat down, exhaling sharply. He glanced sideways at the closed kitchen door and lowered his voice a notch.

'Fucking sure,' he said. 'Word on the street is that Jonjo and Max are long gone, so they're chancing their arm, trying to muscle in.'

'Where were our boys?'

'They jumped them first when they were out front.'

Oh Jesus, thought Annie. She threw down the pencil and rubbed her eyes.

'Get some of the boys round there,' she said. 'Make good any repairs. Replace anything broken. Double up on security for the foreseeable future. Apologize to Lolly, but don't make a big thing of it.'

'He was talking about a discount,' said Jimmy.

'He's having a laugh,' said Annie. 'That's not open to discussion. Make sure he understands that. Make sure he knows that this was a one-off. It won't happen again.'

Jimmy nodded. He didn't look happy, but at least he was agreeing with her and that was a fucking miracle.

'You look like shit,' said Jimmy.

'I've had better times,' said Annie. She looked at him. 'I went to see Kath yesterday.'

'She told me,' said Jimmy.

'Not exactly a warm welcome, I have to say.'

'Were you expecting one?'

I was expecting some respect at least.' Annie's voice was sharper.

'For what? Kath still thinks you're the cow that stole her own sister's husband. She has family loyalties, you can't blame her for that.'

'*I'm* family,' Annie reminded him.

'Not to Kath.'

'You can't steal a grown man, Jimmy,' said Annie.

'Some women can,' said Jimmy reflectively. 'They creep right in and make off with the silver right under your nose. Ruthie never stood a chance against you, and you knew it.'

Annie's cheeks burned. 'I'm not proud of that,' she said.

'No? Only you seem pretty bloody full of your-self, coming back here and giving orders. You're fucking shameless.'

'I'm doing what I have to do.' *And how dare he talk to her like this?*

'Yeah? Well that don't include going round to mine and laying the law down to Kath.'

'The place is a tip,' said Annie angrily. 'The kids are filthy. Kath looks like a bag lady. Can you honestly say you're happy with a setup like that?'

A muscle was working in Jimmy's jaw. 'That's my business,' he said, 'not yours. I don't want you going round there, clear?'

Annie drew a breath. 'I was extending the hand of friendship,' she said more calmly.

'Well, you're lucky she didn't bite the fucker off.'

'I want Ruthie's number,' said Annie. 'Kath's got it. So you can get it too.'

'I'll see what I can do,' said Jimmy, standing up.

'Have a word with her, Jimmy. I'm serious.'

'I *said*, I'll see what I can do.'

'Good.' Annie picked up the pencil again as Jimmy approached the closed door into the hall. 'And Jimmy?'

'What?' He paused.

'Hit two of the Delaney halls.' Annie pulled the books back toward her. She didn't look up. 'Hit them hard.'

22

'He fancies you,' said Dolly, strolling into the kitchen when Jimmy was gone.

'What?' Annie looked up blankly.

'That Jimmy Bond. Fancies you rotten.'

'Doll, you're going mad.'

'I'm *telling* you.' Dolly put the kettle on and spooned tea into the pot. Then she turned and looked at Annie. 'Trust your Aunt Dolly, she knows what's what. Actually he's quite tasty.'

'I couldn't be less interested, Dolly,' said Annie, scribbling away again. Then she paused. 'You know, I bet he's got a girl tucked away somewhere. He's a creature of habit, Jimmy Bond. He wouldn't play around, exactly. He'd have one woman in a flat somewhere, nice and discreet, well out of Kath's way.'

'He'd rather have you, out of Kath's way.' Dolly poured the boiling water into the teapot. 'Don't pay any attention to all that macho bullshit posturing. You're tough and that's winding him up, but it's also turning him on.'

'Well he isn't *going* to have me, out of Kath's way. I told you, I'm not interested.'

'Max Carter would be a hard act to follow, that's for sure,' said Dolly, putting two mugs, milk, sugar, and teapot on to a small tray and bringing it over to the table.

She sat down and looked at Annie squarely. 'And you've got to be careful, in your position,' she said.

Annie put down the pencil and looked at Dolly. 'Meaning?'

'Meaning you're like the Virgin Queen. You got to be above all that. Above reproach. Spotless and aloof. Can't be seen to be mixing with the *hoi polloi*, now can one?'

Annie almost smiled as Dolly put on a posh voice for that last bit.

'Only you've got a bit of a position to consider, ain't that so?' Dolly stirred the pot thoughtfully.

Annie watched the movement, heard the noise. A little like the noise she kept hearing over the phone. Familiar, but forgotten . . . or was it? Somewhere at the back of her mind, a horrible suspicion was starting to form.

'If someone got close to you,' continued Dolly, 'they'd . . . well, they'd sort of be in charge then, wouldn't they? The Queen's consort. The manor's wide open – but for you standing there like the prize in a coconut shy. No Max or Jonjo in the way, just you. A woman. And you know how these men rate women. And if you got involved with someone – someone like Jimmy Bond, for instance . . .'

'Who's married to my cousin, with two kids,' Annie reminded her.

'Like he'd give a shit. You'd be really tempting to a man like Jimmy Bond. From what you say, his wife's turned into her granny as soon as she's got him up the aisle – and I wish I had a sodding quid for every time I've seen *that* happen – and you're all that's left of the Carter clan and you're a looker into the bargain. Wish I had those legs . . .' Dolly sighed as she considered her own shapely but short pins. 'Let's face it, when God handed out legs, I was behind the frigging door.'

'Is this going somewhere?' asked Annie politely, quietly fuming at Dolly's lack of tact. What did she care about men? She was Max's wife.

No, she thought painfully. *Max's widow*.

With the thought came the horrible pain of it again.

'Yeah, it is.' Dolly poured the tea. She flicked a glance at Annie and her eyes were serious now. 'Just watch your step, okay?'

'Meaning what?'

'Meaning watch yourself with him. He'd be on you like a shot given half the chance, and I don't think you want to open up *that* can of worms.'

Annie splashed milk into her mug. 'I don't want to open up any can of worms at all, Doll,' she told her friend sadly. 'I don't want another man. Why the hell would I? The only man I ever loved is dead. Anyone else would be second best.'

23

Next day they were sitting around the kitchen table again, Annie and Dolly and Darren and Ellie – no Una, she was upstairs with a punter. All mates together, just like the old days.

Only nothing's like the old days, thought Annie. *My husband's dead. My kid's gone. My life's in bits. Everything's tainted.* She was looking through the morning paper, turning the pages, not really taking any of it in. Nixon was attacking the communists in Cambodia, someone had tried to assassinate Makarios in Greece, John Wayne had won Best Actor at the Oscars for *True Grit*. None of it meant a damned thing to her. Ellie was spilling toast crumbs over the table as she devoured her breakfast, and Dolly was looking at Ellie as a mother would look at a difficult child.

Annie had questioned Dolly about Ellie's surprise return to the fold, and Dolly had said: 'I felt sorry for the silly tart, all right? I know she's a bit two-faced . . .'

'A *bit*?'

'But don't everyone deserve a second chance in life?'

So here they all were, together again.

'When I was on the game I wouldn't kiss a client,' Dolly was telling Ellie, who was apparently having problems in that direction. 'If he looked like Elvis and fucked like a weasel, I still wouldn't kiss him. Kissing's too intimate. But occasionally a punter insists. And if it's a choice between throwing a screaming fit and exchanging one small kiss, then I always went for the kiss – even though I didn't want to.'

Ellie screwed up her pudgy face.

'Yeah, but a lot of my clients are *old*. Let me tell you, there's no bigger turnoff than kissing an old man with rattling dentures and bad breath.'

They all shuddered.

'Then don't do it,' shrugged Darren. 'Explain beforehand – nicely – that mouth-to-mouth is off-limits, anything else is fair game. Although I don't see it myself. If you're prepared to give some ugly old fart a blow job, why draw the line at a kiss?'

Annie looked at Ellie, who was diving into the biscuit tin again. Annie glanced at Dolly, whose expression said it all. They'd both seen this before with seasoned brasses, and they both knew what it meant.

The fact was, boffing strangers all day and half the night required a variety of coping mechanisms. Quite a few prostitutes took a bath or shower after every client, and that was okay, personal hygiene was always a good thing. Rules were rules. The punters might come in here drunk, disorderly, smelly, but the troops had to be fragrant to a fault.

Which was *fine*, up to a point. But Ellie had reached that point – in fact she had passed it about a mile back down the road.

'Caught her in the loo scrubbing herself *down there*,' Dolly had confided to Annie earlier in the day. 'With a flaming nailbrush. And she's had the bleach bottle out after she's washed, scouring the sink and the bath. How long before she starts thinking it's a good idea to use the bleach to clean herself off? I'm telling you, she's not right.'

It was the beginning of the end of tarting for Ellie, and they both knew it.

'That's why she's getting so bloody fat,' Dolly had told Annie. 'Can't cope with it all any more. Comfort eating.'

Annie almost envied Ellie that. She couldn't comfort eat. She could barely eat at all. Just waking up every day was a renewal of the pain she was suffering. She'd lost the love of her life, lost him forever. And maybe Layla too, who could say?

Dolly kept forcing toast and egg down her, but she felt sick every single day, creased up with anxiety and a feeling of utter helplessness. She was in the hands of the kidnappers, totally. She had no power over what happened next, hard as she found that to accept.

'Maybe you should take a break, Ellie love,' suggested Dolly. 'A couple of weeks down Southend would do you the world of good.'

But Ellie was looking mulish. 'I'll think about it,' she said.

From above them came the sound of someone letting out little yelps of either pain or delight.

'Jesus, I really think Una enjoys her job too much,' said Darren, staring up at the ceiling.

And there's poor Ellie, not enjoying it at all, thought Annie.

'Something's come for you,' said Ross, poking his head around the kitchen door and looking coldly at Annie. She wasn't on his Christmas card list, that was for sure, and his expression whenever he looked at her said so loud and clear. But for as long as Redmond Delaney said it was okay for her to be here, he'd just have to swallow it.

'For me?' Annie repeated stupidly. But no one would send her anything. 'Can't be.'

Ross was holding out a small white box, four inches by four, a couple of inches deep.

'It was on the doorstep.' Ross shrugged. 'It wasn't

posted, but I didn't see anyone leave it there. Just stepped outside for a fag and there it was. Look, it's got your name on it.'

Everyone in the kitchen was silent and still. Ross was right. In block capitals on top of the box was written ANNIE CARTER.

Enjoy the gift.

Annie jumped to her feet and barged past Ross and out into the hallway. She flung open the front door, ran down the path and stood gasping in the street, looking left and right. Didn't know who or what she was looking for, but someone had brought the box here, had placed it right on the doorstep while they were all inside, unaware. But she could see nothing suspicious. Just people, walking the dog, pushing prams, parking cars, the odd one or two looking at her, at this dark-haired woman all dressed in black, with distress and madness written all over her face.

Nothing.

Annie took a shaky breath and went back inside. Ross had returned to his chair by the door. She walked straight past him and into the kitchen, shutting the door behind her. Dolly, Ellie, and Darren were still there, and there was the little white box in the middle of the table. They looked at it, then at her.

Annie felt her head begin to pound. Her hands started to shake.

Enjoy the gift.

Oh Jesus God.

She sat back down. Looked at her friends. Looked at the box.

'What the fuck is it?' asked Dolly.

Annie couldn't work enough spit into her mouth to answer. She stared at the box. ANNIE CARTER.

'Well, open it,' said Ellie.

Annie took a breath. So simple. *Open it.* Easy enough, but for the moment she felt too scared to even touch the thing.

Dig deep, she thought. *Got to dig deep.*

Annie reached out in the dead silence of the kitchen and touched the thick cardboard. She grasped the lid; it wasn't stuck down. It was nice and easy to open.

'Go on for fuck's sake,' said Darren, clutching both hands to his chest.

Annie removed the lid.

Inside, on a bed of cotton wool, was a child's finger.

24

'The bitch should have got her present. She'll toe the line now,' said Danny confidently, his eyes jumping wildly between Vita and Phil.

Vita was sitting pale and shaken at the kitchen table again, head down. Right now she couldn't even *look* at her brother.

Phil was quiet, pretending to read the paper when really he felt as if he was going to vomit.

Really, he was shocked. When he'd gotten into this deal it hadn't included harming kids. He looked up at Blondie. Danny. *Fucking lunatic*, he thought.

'You got something to say?' demanded Danny.

'To you? No.' Phil got back to his pretend reading, a muscle flexing in his jaw.

'Good. Get your arse off that fucking chair then and get going.'

Phil closed his paper. He looked across at Danny. He looked at the gun on the table between them.

Danny's eyes were challenging. *You think you're hard enough, fast enough? Try it.*

Phil stood up.

'Fine,' he said, and left the room.

Vita's head was hung low, as if she was waiting for a storm to break. She looked at the painting laid out on the table. Ducks. Painting by numbers. Her brush was in a cup of water, she was going to do the Mandarin drake's head next, and that colour was almost red, almost like blood. She felt her stomach start to roll.

Painting by numbers! Christ!

Vita had seen the kit and brought it along, thinking that the kid would be amused by it, but she'd ended up painting the thing instead, to stave off madness. The kid was hardly ever awake enough to do anything, anyway. Getting absorbed in the painting stopped her from thinking too much about the plight of the little girl in the cellar. They'd had to drug Layla Carter when they'd snatched her, and they'd had to keep on drugging her, keeping her out of it on the stuff, and that was good, Vita thought, that was very good. Because then she wouldn't have really *felt* it, would she, what Danny had done to her?

That was what Vita had to tell herself. That way she could deal with this. She wondered all over again why she'd got involved with any of this. For the money? But she didn't much care

172

about the money, not really. No, it was mostly because Danny had told her to go along with it, and she had gone along with pretty much anything Danny had told her to, ever since the cradle.

But now something in her rebelled. Hurting a kid. And what he'd done to that Majorcan couple. And she couldn't forget that the kid had seen *her* face, not Danny's, not Phil's. *Hers*.

'She's not eating much,' she said to Danny.

Danny shrugged and sat down, pulling the paper closer.

He neither knew nor cared how much a kid that age ate.

'Do you really think you should have done that?' asked Vita quietly.

Danny looked up from the paper.

Vita quailed.

'I mean, damaged the goods,' she said quickly, in case he went off on one. 'What if she gets an infection or something?'

'If you do your part of the job right, she'll be okay.'

Vita felt the dry heaves start in her throat again. The kid had been spark out of it when Danny had done *that* – she couldn't even name it in her head – and afterwards he had told Vita to fetch the Dettol and bandages he'd brought along with them, he thought of everything, Danny, mad as he was, *crazy* as he was, he never dropped a stitch.

He had shown his sister how to hold the kid's arm up to stop the bleeding, had shown her how to clean the wound, the *stump*, and bandage it up. Because it was Danny – and because she had never, ever, said no to Danny – she did it, but she had gagged all the way through and afterwards she had gone into the loo and vomited up her breakfast.

She had started to wonder what damage it would do the kid, the way Danny kept her drugged up all the time. Even when Layla was conscious, when she ate – and how little she ate, just a tiny amount, was that normal? – she was in a daze, not quite with it, poor little cow.

But Vita knew the drugs were necessary. Otherwise, Layla would probably start screaming her head off, they would have to gag her, and she'd still make a noise, and they couldn't risk that. Not in the hen house behind the little place in Palma, because there were other people living close by, and Marietta coming and going. Not on the boat either, because Phil had carried her aboard in a large canvas holdall that Danny had slashed here and there to make air holes.

The fishermen on board didn't ask questions. Probably thought they were transporting drugs, and they'd been paid well, what did they care?

But no, it was Layla, it was a little kid drugged to fuck, unconscious. And now Vita was really worrying about it all. Would all this really not harm the kid? Would she really recover?

And now they were back in England. It was all building up to some sort of horrible crescendo, and she was full of fear, wondering where this mad scheme – which had seemed so easy, so simple, to start with – was going to end.

Danny was hopping to his feet again, all restless energy.

'Get packed up,' he told her. 'We're off up to the Smoke tonight.'

He left the room.

Vita sat there, looking at the ducks in the half-finished painting. Then her eyes strayed to Danny's gun, just lying there on the table, and she thought of Layla, who would probably always suffer the after-effects of all that crap Danny had been dosing the poor little bitch with; Layla, who had seen her face.

25

Annie thought she would never stop being sick. She was crouched over the toilet bowl heaving her guts up and Dolly was there, stroking her hair, making soothing noises. Even when there was nothing left to bring up, still she was heaving and gasping, her innards rebelling at the outrage.

Layla's finger.

They'd cut off her baby's finger, and placed it on the front doorstep and walked away.

Bastards.

How could they do that? How could anyone torture a child that way?

Of course it had been Dolly who had stayed calm, stoic to the last. Annie had screamed her head off when she saw it. Ellie had cringed back in disgust. Darren had turned milk-white and looked as though he might faint. Then Annie had fled the room, blundered into the loo and been sick.

Dolly had searched desperately for something to say, *anything*, that would help Annie's pain.

'Look, it means she's alive at least. They're trying to throw a scare into you, that's all.'

'*That's all?*' Annie straightened, tore off a strip of toilet paper and wiped her mouth and stared at Dolly. 'I tell you what, Doll – they've fucking well succeeded.'

And the finger didn't mean Layla was still alive, she thought. *Of course it didn't. They could have hacked it off after they'd killed her. They could post back her baby girl to her bit by bit to prod her into raising the cash, only to reveal at the end that Layla had been dead all along.*

'What the fuck am I going to do?' she asked Dolly wildly.

Dolly flushed the loo and let out a sigh. 'I wish I knew, Annie love. I really do.'

Annie stood up shakily and rested her head against the cool tiles on the wall.

'I need help,' she moaned. 'I can't handle this.'

'Yes you can. You can handle any damned thing.'

Annie was shaking her head, her hair hanging in rat-tails around her ashen face.

'No. I can't. I need help. Get hold of Billy. Tell him to get Jimmy Bond to meet me at the Palermo and to bring the locksmith. We're getting that fucking safe open.'

*　*　*

Jimmy didn't bring the locksmith to the Palermo. He brought a tall, ginger-haired man with a potbelly and a long, hawkish face, carrying a Gladstone bag.

'What the fuck's this?' she demanded when they came into the office and the ginger-haired one promptly pulled out a stethoscope.

Tony had driven her over to the Palermo, and she had twitched around the office for an hour waiting for Jimmy and the locksmith to show, and now he *hadn't* brought the locksmith, and she was hopping mad with Jimmy Bond's lack of co-operation, lack of respect, lack of giving a *fuck* about what happened to her and to her daughter.

'*Jimmy* . . .' she started in, furious.

'This is Ginge,' said Jimmy. 'I didn't think the locksmith was a good idea. We don't know what's in there and we don't want the general public knowing our business, do we? Ginge is safer, he's one of our own, he's good on combination locks. Go to it, Ginge.'

Ginge knelt down by the safe, pulled on a pair of thin cotton gloves, put the stethoscope in his ears and attached it to the metal beside the dial on the safe.

'*Jimmy*,' said Annie. 'For God's sake can we hurry this up?'

Ginge half turned and held a finger to his lips. *Fuck it all.*

Annie sat down at the desk and waited. Jimmy stood there, hands in coat pockets, waiting too.

After ten minutes, Annie stood up.

'For fuck's *sake*,' she said, and left the room.

She went downstairs, went into the deserted club, walked around. Seeing nothing. Her footsteps echoed around the place. She walked around because she couldn't sit still. Couldn't rest.

Suddenly she grabbed a chair and flung it across the dance floor. Then another. Then another. Then she stopped, panting, the blood singing in her ears, her heart thudding, her hands shaking so badly she wondered if she was about to collapse.

I'm cracking up, she thought. *I'm losing it. And I can't afford to do that*.

She drew a deep breath. Tried to steady herself, get a grip. But her mind was full of Layla.

All she could see in her mind's eye was Layla's finger. All she could imagination was Layla's suffering.

All she *wanted* was the blood of these people who had hurt her baby.

She put the chairs straight again. Sat down. Gathered herself. After twenty minutes had passed she went back upstairs to the office.

Ginge was turning the dial and listening to the tumblers clicking over on the mechanism. Jimmy was perched on the edge of the desk. She sat down again in the big leather chair. Another five minutes passed.

Then there was a distinct *click* and Ginge swung the safe door open.

He drew back, repacking his stethoscope into his Gladstone bag, tucking away his gloves. He didn't look inside the safe. He nodded to Annie, shook Jimmy's hand briefly, accepted an envelope from him – no doubt an envelope stuffed with cash – and trotted off down the stairs.

They heard the club's outer door swing open, then close.

They looked at each other.

Annie stood up and went over to the open safe door. She knelt and pushed it open wide, hoping against hope. She looked back at Jimmy Bond, and he came and had a look too. She held her breath, and looked inside.

Annie's heart plummeted to her boots.

The safe was empty.

By three that afternoon, Annie was sitting in Dolly's kitchen, looking at the closed box in the centre of the table. She'd brought Jimmy back here, put the box there on the table, told him to take a seat.

'So what's going on?' he asked, sitting down opposite Annie. He looked at the box. 'What's that?'

'Take a look,' said Annie.

She was calmer now. For two hours she had raged and vomited and screeched like a wounded animal, and then she had discovered that the Palermo's safe was empty and raged about *that*, but now she was calmer. Calm as sheet ice with a wild river crashing beneath it. Holding in her fear, her hatred, her despair beneath a cool shell. Occasionally a shudder racked her guts, made her stop and hold her breath and wonder if she was about to die. Despair, disbelief, grief, and rage would sweep over her like a vicious tide. But she held that in too.

Jimmy shrugged and reached for the box.

'I didn't tell you, we did two of the Delaney places last night,' he told her.

'Right,' said Annie flatly.

'What the *fuck* . . . !' Jimmy had casually opened the box and just as quickly he now flung it down.

The finger rolled out on to the table, the nail like a small delicate shell, the flesh pale blue with one frayed end. You could see the bone in the centre of the digit. The stained cotton wool had come out too, and there was a piece of paper. Annie had already seen it, read it. Now Jimmy looked at her, then picked up the little note. It said in block capitals: *ENJOY THE GIFT. CATCH UP WITH YOU A MONTH ON FRIDAY.*

'Someone left that on the doorstep,' said Annie.

'Fucking hell,' said Jimmy.

'I need help with this, Jimmy. They're asking for big money, and somehow I've got to find it.

181

There was fuck-all in the safe, so I'm going to have to look elsewhere.'

Jimmy sat back. 'How big?'

'Half a million.'

'Jeez.'

'I thought of selling the clubs,' said Annie.

'You can't do that.'

Annie's mouth twisted in a ghost of a smile. She looked at the severed finger on the table. So tiny.

'I can do whatever the fuck I like, Jimmy. Remember? I'm Annie Carter. Max Carter's wife.' *Widow*, she amended to herself. 'But even if I sold the clubs, even if that's possible and I don't think it *is*, because there must be legalities involved, and where the fuck would I find the paperwork for that? And anyway it wouldn't be anywhere near enough. So what's the point?'

'So what's the plan?'

The plan, since she didn't know where Max had his wealth stashed and had very little of her own, was simple – she was going to have to get out there with her begging bowl.

'Max had friends,' she said to Jimmy. 'Powerful friends. *Rich* friends. I can remember when the clubs were heaving with celebrities and minor royals and members of Parliament, all Max's friends.'

Jimmy snorted.

'You really think any of those bastards would

help you out of a corner? You got another think coming.'

'He was in tight with the Americans. They came over and they were doing regular business with Max, he was protecting their venues up West. They were *tight*.'

Jimmy shook his head.

'You don't go cap in hand to those people,' he said. 'You'll be in debt to them forever.'

Annie's eyes were glittering with purpose as she stared across the table at him.

'They're letting me sweat for a month. Playing with me. Taunting me. Sending me bits of my baby girl. Okay. So we've got time. Time enough to contact the Barolli family and ask for help. Maybe use the clubs for security. Queenie's old place too.'

Queenie was Max's mother, long dead. Killed, it was always said, by the Delaney mob in a hit that had been a step too far. Queenie's death had sparked a gang war. Annie would never forget it.

Jimmy was shaking his head.

'You don't know what you're suggesting,' he told her.

'Yeah,' said Annie. 'I do.'

'No you *don't*.' Jimmy thumped the table. The finger jumped. Annie flinched visibly. Muttering 'for fuck's sake', he picked it up gingerly and placed it back in its box, putting the cotton wool and the note in too, and replacing the lid.

Then he sat back and looked at Annie.

'You think this is a bad thing?' Jimmy indicated the box. 'This is *nothing*. This is *nothing* to what the Barolli family would do if you ever tried to shaft them on a deal, I'm telling you. These people are *Mafia*. Once you're in debt to them, you're fucked.'

Annie nodded. Then she stood up, rested her fists on the table, and looked first at the box with its pathetic, fragile contents, and then directly at Jimmy. Jimmy thought she looked, in that moment, crazy. Totally freaked. Capable of anything.

'Look at me, Jimmy,' she told him. 'Two good friends of mine have been hit. My brother-in-law has been hit. My husband too. And now someone is sending me bits of *my daughter*, my own *flesh and blood*, Jimmy. Now tell me.' She leaned in closer. 'Do you seriously think I give a monkey's fuck about what happens to me? Do you seriously think I'm afraid of doing business with the Barollis?'

Now she was laughing, and he wondered if she really had gone mad, whether all this had finally made her crack wide open. Suddenly she stopped laughing and her eyes skewered him where he sat.

'*Look* at me, Jimmy. I'm dead already, dead and buried. All I want now is for Layla to be safe. Beyond that, who gives a shit?'

'I can't okay this,' said Jimmy.

184

Annie fumbled at the chain around her neck, couldn't find the clasp because her fingers were shaking too much. She grabbed the chain and pulled it, breaking it. Max's ring fell on to the table and lay beside the pitiful little white box containing his daughter's finger. Annie grabbed the ring and flung it at Jimmy Bond.

'You think I need your approval? Think again. You get your arse out of here *right now*,' she ordered, 'and tell Constantine Barolli I want a meet and that it's urgent, like life or death, you got that? *Now!*'

26

With Jimmy gone, there was nothing for Annie to do. Seething and restless, she took the box, gold locket, and broken chain upstairs to Dolly's bedroom. Dolly had let her stay in here, refusing all Annie's offers to move into one of the other rooms, or even to kip down on the sofa in the front parlour.

'Stay where you are,' Dolly had told her. 'You've got enough on your plate as it is, you might as well be comfortable.'

Annie went in, shutting the door behind her, keeping the world out. She lay on the bed with the little box on her chest, and wondered what sort of animals she was dealing with here. Wondered what Layla had suffered, and what she was suffering now.

Maddened, groaning at the images that were crashing about in her brain, she turned her head into the pillow and curled up into a ball and screwed her eyes shut, trying to block it out.

But she couldn't.

Because Layla didn't have that luxury.

And if Layla was suffering, then she was suffering too.

Got to get a grip. For Layla.

But there was a horror movie running in her brain and she was caught up in it, unable to get free.

A living nightmare.

Annie sat up. Couldn't rest. Couldn't even think. Had to do something. Walk, or yell, or *something*.

She picked up the box with shaking hands. Looked at it, and at the broken chain, the fallen heart. *Love you forever*, the inscription said. Max had bought it for her. *Love you forever.*

Her life was officially in the toilet. She felt the beginnings of a scream building at the back of her throat. Turning, she swept the brush set from the top of the dresser with one hard swipe. Dolly's treasured silver-backed brush set.

Shit, she thought, and instantly fell to her knees and scrabbled about. The brush and comb were okay, but the mirror, had she broken the hand mirror? That was seven years' bad luck. Her heart was in her mouth; she felt sick with panic now.

No. It was still in one piece.

Dimly aware that tears of terror and despair were slipping down her face, she carefully picked up the brush set and placed it with trembling fingers back on on the dresser.

Sorry, Doll.

She looked in the large dressing-table mirror. Saw her own haggard reflection there and barely recognized herself. Angrily, she brushed the tears away, picked up one of Dolly's lippies from the dresser and quickly rubbed some colour into her cheeks and applied it to her mouth.

She looked again at her reflection.

Better, she thought. *Not a fucking mark on me.*

She raised a mirthless smile at the woman in the mirror. Then she went back to the bed and sat down. Gently, she opened the box.

Careful not to disturb its gruesome contents, she tucked the broken chain and the gold heart in beside Layla's finger. Then she slipped the box into her pocket, pushed her hair back out of her eyes, and took a breath. Stood up. Went to the door. Opened it and went out on to the landing, closing the door softly behind her.

'Fuck, not you again,' said Una, wandering past wearing her white PVC outfit and trailing her feral scent of cheap perfume and stale sweat. 'Thought you'd be gone by now.'

Annie turned and stared at her. Una was six and a half feet tall in her four-inch heels, staring straight back with her weirdly pale blue eyes, the pupils dilated.

Druggie, thought Annie.

Annie suddenly felt very calm. 'No, you lucked out,' she said. 'I'm still here.'

Una stopped walking. 'You see, there it is again. That *attitude*.' Una turned and came back to where Annie stood near the top of the stairs.

Una leaned in very close to Annie's face. *Not* a pleasant experience.

Annie locked eyes with the bigger woman, aware that there was movement along the landing, near Darren's room. Ellie had come out to see what was going on, and Darren now followed.

'Annie's upset,' Darren said too loudly to Una, nerves making his voice harsh. 'She's had bad news about her daughter, Una, go easy . . .'

Una turned her head and looked at Darren. He fell silent.

'She don't know the meaning of bad news yet,' said Una. 'But if she keeps up with this *attitude* of hers, she's going to find out.'

Darren looked uncomfortable. Ellie was silent, watching.

Trust Ellie not to put herself in harm's way for a friend, thought Annie.

In the end, all you had was yourself. Hadn't she learned that over the years? You had to fight your corner. You had to dig deep, and stand alone.

Una's head turned back and her eyes were on

Annie again. Her face was close to Annie's. *Trying to intimidate me*, thought Annie, almost amused.

Annie's brow hit Una square in the nose and the blonde reeled back, blood spurting out. She slammed up against the wall and then tried to turn to the side, clutching at the top banister, hand slipping, blinded by sudden and unexpected pain.

Into Annie's brain came Max's words: '*If you get in a fight, finish it. Don't stop until they're down and no longer a danger to you. Get them down, and make sure they* stay *down.*'

Annie brought Tony's kiyoga up out of her pocket in a high arc, whacking Una's shoulder, knocking her off balance. Una tumbled backwards and shot down the stairs, end over end, coming to rest at the bottom. Ross stood there, open-mouthed, looking down at the toppled blonde.

He looked up.

Annie came down the stairs like the wrath of God and threw herself on to the squirming woman's chest. She gave Una a hard smack on the side of the face with the kiyoga and felt the woman's screams reverberate around the house. Then she grabbed her waistcoat and shook her violently, cracking Una's head on the floor, before she spoke.

'Now listen,' said Annie as Darren and Ellie came pounding down the stairs and stopped near to where the toppled Una lay sprawled beneath her.

Annie gave the woman another vicious shake.

'You've broken my fucking *nose* . . .' burbled Una, blood and tears all over her face.

'I'll break your fucking *neck* next time,' Annie promised her. 'Now, are you listening? Nod if you are, or are you so spaced out you don't understand me? Because if you don't, I'll spell it out r-e-a-l-l-y s-l-o-w-l-y for you.'

Una nodded, wincing.

'Good. Now listen. You got another single word you want to say to me, you write me a fucking letter, okay? You don't talk to me, not a *single word*. You got that, you cheeky cow? You keep out of my way, that's all you need to do, and we'll get along just fine. And you don't give my friends a hard time or you'll be very sorry. You watch your behaviour with them, you got that? Nod yes, you still with me?'

Annie gave Una another shake.

'Now you show Dolly respect,' Annie went on. 'She's the boss here, not you. You remember that and act accordingly. Got it?'

Una groaned.

'*Got* it?' Annie gave her another shake.

'All right, I got it,' Una moaned.

'I hear any more trouble coming from you and you're out that door and walking the streets. So you keep a really low profile now and everything will be just fine. Yes?'

A shake.

'Yes,' mumbled Una.

'See, now was that so hard?' Annie dropped the waistcoat and Una's head thumped back on to the floor.

Annie stood up and looked at Ross.

'Help her get cleaned up,' she said, and walked off into the front room and shut the door behind her.

Darren and Ellie looked at the groaning and bleeding Una, who was being dragged upright by Ross. Then they glanced at each other.

'See that?' said Darren. 'Told you she still had it.'

27

Jimmy Bond was back two days later. He found Annie in the kitchen and she went straight to work.

'So, what's the news with Barolli?' she asked urgently.

'That's what I came here to talk about.'

'Okay, so talk.'

Jimmy sat down and stared at her across the table.

'This is a dangerous thing you're thinking of doing,' he said carefully.

Annie shot out an exasperated breath.

'Jimmy, we've had this conversation.'

'Yeah, but Annie—'

'It's Mrs Carter to you,' Annie pointed out coldly.

'Sodding hell. All right. Mrs Carter. Look, if you let Constantine Barolli know Max is dead, there's every chance that fucker's going to move in on us. On the manor.'

Annie stared at him. 'I won't do that,' she told him firmly. 'I'll tell the Barollis that Max had to take off, do some business.'

Jimmy was shaking his head.

'You ain't got a fucking clue, have you? You really don't know what you're playing around with here,' he warned.

'I know they're the only ones with this sort of cash at their disposal,' said Annie irritably. 'What else is there to know?'

Jimmy suddenly lost it and thumped the table. '*Look*, for Christ's sake. They'll kill her anyway. Whatever you do, they'll kill her anyway. But you know that already, don't you?'

Annie went white.

'No, *you* listen. You think I'd do this off the top of my head, like a whim or something? Wrong. Constantine Barolli and Max were friends and business associates. The Barollis have big money. I need big money. End of conversation.' Annie jumped to her feet, throwing back the chair. It toppled. She leaned back against the worktop, breathing hard, furious. She looked at Jimmy still sitting there and suddenly she knew. 'You haven't been to see him, have you? You haven't given him Max's ring. *Have you?*'

Jimmy's eyes were on the table. He said nothing.

Annie nodded slowly.

'Okay, give it back to me. Give it back *right now*.'

Jimmy looked up at her face. Then he reached into his pocket and drew out Max's ring and placed it on the table.

'Now fuck off,' said Annie.

Jimmy went, brushing past Dolly in the hall.

Annie was setting her chair back up, grim-faced, when Dolly came into the kitchen and closed the hall door behind her. Dolly took in the room at a glance and then went to put the kettle on.

Annie picked up Max's ring, clutched it tightly in her fist.

Oh God, Max, help me will you? She thought desperately. *Help me do the right thing. Help me save Layla.*

'Hey, what the fuck did you do to Una?' Dolly asked brightly. 'Darren told me Ross had to take her into Casualty yesterday. Darren and Ellie were like little kids who saw Santa Claus. They said you beat the crap out of her.' Dolly turned and looked at Annie. 'And now here she is today, creeping around like a church mouse with two fabulous shiners on her ugly mug, being all polite and helpful. What happened?'

'I had a word with her,' shrugged Annie.

'Ah.' Dolly rummaged in the cupboard for tea, put a couple of spoonfuls into the teapot and then added boiling water.

Annie turned and looked at what she was doing.

That noise again.

'Tea?' offered Dolly.

Annie turned away, shaking her head.

'Got to go out, Doll. Bit of business.'

Annie huddled into the black coat and hurried along the pavement toward Max's car. *Her* car now. A gust of cold wind caught her, making her eyes water. She missed the warm sun of the Med. Spring was coming here, but not fast enough. Above the crowded buildings and the hurrying people the skies were grey and full of rain – the light was going, soon it would be evening. People would be tucked up warm indoors with their families, huddling together against the night.

But not me, thought Annie. *My family's gone.*

Now she was back here, alone, her husband dead, gone from her forever, trying to save her daughter's life – haunted by the constant feeling that she was failing in her task. She knew she had to get over that feeling, quash it somehow. To fear failure was to invite it to come calling. She had to stay positive, somehow. To hope for the best.

But I fear the worst, that hopeless voice inside her cried out.

She put her head down against the buffeting wind and hurried out into the road. Tony saw her coming and got out from behind the wheel and opened the rear passenger door for her. Annie looked up, gave him a nod, and then he came charging toward her and knocked her backwards.

What the fuck? thought Annie angrily.

They cannoned into a parked car. Annie took the brunt of the impact. Tony's huge weight knocked all the wind out of her. She was aware of a jumble of things. Losing her footing, slipping to her knee, a crack of pain – another pain to add to all the others, she thought dimly. A blare of horns, headlights blinding her, then Tony hauling her upright and grabbing her shoulders and looking at her.

'You all right, Mrs Carter?' he gasped.

Annie nodded. Couldn't get her breath.

'Sure?'

'Fine,' Annie managed.

'That fucking car nearly had you. Didn't you see it?'

Annie shook her head. Straightened. Checked herself over. Her tights were laddered. Yeah, she was okay. Shaken, but okay.

'He pulled out down the road. Came straight at you, revving up fast. Would have knocked you flat if I hadn't seen him coming.'

Annie looked up the road to where the car had shot off around the corner with a mad squeal of tyres. Long gone now, of course.

'Did you catch the number plate? Did you recognize the driver?' she asked.

Tony was shaking his head.

'No, Mrs Carter. Sorry.'

'Don't be sorry, Tone. You did good.'

Better than good. You saved my damned life, she thought. If Tony hadn't spotted her coming across the road and got out of the car to open the door for her, he wouldn't have seen the car coming. And she had been distracted, worried, head down, not thinking . . . *not thinking that anyone would try to kill her*.

She was shaking slightly with the shock now. Realizing that she could have been mincemeat. Realizing that someone had tried to take her out. Not a nice feeling. And who the hell would want to do that?

She didn't have a clue.

Tony escorted her back over the road to the Jag and settled her into the back, closing the door gently as if she was a precious package, safely retrieved.

God bless Tony, thought Annie. What would have happened to Layla if anything had happened to her?

But Jimmy thought Layla was dead meat anyway.

Annie shivered and huddled down. She had the box in one pocket, Max's ring in the other, and she clung tightly to both for reassurance. Tony restarted the engine and the big car purred into life. The heater blasted out hot air, reviving her.

'Where to, Mrs Carter?' asked Tony.

'Do you know the Barolli house in Holland Park, Tony?'

'Yeah, I do. Mr Barolli's over here at the moment to give his daughter away. She's marrying a stock-broker or something like that.'

Annie closed her eyes, feeling the aftermath of the shock she'd just had, feeling suddenly that she might even cry. Would she ever see Layla grow up, get married, have children of her own? She squashed the sudden weakness and her eyes met Tony's in the rear-view mirror.

'Take me to the Barolli house, Tony,' she said.

Tony looked at her doubtfully. 'Is Mr Barolli expecting you, Mrs Carter? Has Jimmy okayed this?'

Annie sighed wearily. She didn't know what the hell Jonjo had been up to, but it was clear that Jimmy had for some time felt that he was running things – and so had all the boys.

But then Jonjo would have been off screwing blondes, not taking care of business, she thought. Max shouldn't have trusted him. But then, didn't you always trust family? Weren't you supposed to be able to do that?

'Yeah,' she told Tony. She didn't feel strong enough right now to argue the toss. 'Mr Barolli's expecting me. And Jimmy okayed it.'

Her soul was never going to get to heaven,

wasn't that what her mother Connie had always told her? It was bad to lie, she was a *wicked* girl. Maybe that was it – maybe this was what they called karma, payback for what she'd done to poor Ruthie. Annie had lost Max and her child had been taken from her. Maybe she deserved all this shit. Certainly there had never been any hope of Annie achieving her mother's approval – all that had been reserved for her good sister Ruthie. Not for Black Sheep Annie.

Yeah, a black sheep, she thought as the Jaguar slid smoothly through the streets.

Now, of course, a black widow.

28

Annie's first thought when they got to the Barolli residence was that she'd made a huge mistake in coming here. There were swarms of people wearing expensive clothes and buttonholes unloading from limos and taxis and going in through the front door. She clocked two obvious faces checking invites.

Fuck it, she thought. The wedding was today. And it looked as if the reception was going on *chez* Barolli.

'You didn't tell me the wedding was today,' she told Tony in frustration.

Tony shrugged.

'I didn't know, Mrs Carter.'

Annie thought it over. But not for long. She was too hyped up to just turn around and go home. Home! Well, back to Dolly's place anyway. Her home was gone, along with her life.

'Wait for me, Tony,' she told him, and got out, slamming the door behind her.

This time she was careful; she looked left and right before hurrying across the road. She shuddered again as she thought of what could have happened. Had someone really intended to knock her down? Other people, people dressed up to the nines in their wedding finery, were ambling along the path up to the big house in front of her, chattering and laughing, making her grind her teeth at their slowness.

It gave her time, though, to look up at the house. It was just as big as Max's Surrey place. It was a red-brick William and Mary mansion, beautifully proportioned and standing full-square. As she edged toward the pillared doorway and the big men in black suits, she saw the lollipop bay trees placed on either side of the vast doorway, decorated with pink and cream satin ribbons.

Moving along with the crowds, she slowly ascended the six big curving marble steps leading up to the front door. Chamber music, refined and gentle and soothing, drifted out from the open doorway along with a gust of warm air.

Finally she was on the top step.

Now the people right in front of her were wandering off inside, into a palatial and opulently lit hallway, taking champagne from a silver tray held out by a waitress. And one of the men in black was holding out his hand for her invitation.

'I don't have an invite,' said Annie, pulling herself up to her full height. 'I've got urgent business with Mr Barolli.'

There was a roar of laughter from inside. The taller of the two heavies was regarding her with gently quizzical eyes.

'Mr Barolli is busy today. Family business. His daughter's wedding.'

'Still, I need to see him. It's urgent. Or I wouldn't bother him, believe me.'

The two men exchanged a look, then the one she was talking to shook his head and reached past her to take the invitation card from the next guest.

'I have to see him,' she said, as the guests around her looked at her curiously.

Annie suddenly realized what a strange picture she must present. All in black, with her hair uncombed and no make-up on her face. More suitably attired for a funeral than a wedding.

Should have thought this through, she berated herself.

'I have to see him. Please,' she said more urgently.

Guests were moving past her, their eyes on this strange woman with her desperate ashen face and her weird black clothing.

The two heavies no longer seemed to be hearing her.

'Seen enough?' Annie snapped at one woman wearing a huge pink-feathered hat. The woman quickly looked away.

One of the heavies moved in and gently clasped Annie's arm.

'Look,' he said. 'Come back tomorrow. Or phone.'

Annie shook her head. 'I need to see Mr Barolli,' she reiterated.

'Well, perhaps Mr Barolli don't need to see you. Not today, anyway.'

'Tell him I'm here, will you?'

'Please go away.' He gently clasped her arm.

'Look, it's all right,' said Annie. Another minute and he'd be hustling her down the steps and off the premises. She had to convince him she wasn't trouble.

But she knew that's exactly what she looked like. Unhinged. Disarrayed. *Crazy.*

'It's okay, it's okay,' said Annie, pulling her arm free. 'I'm not here to make trouble. I just need to see him. Look, I'll wait.'

She went over to the far edge of the top step and sat down on it.

'I'll wait, okay?' she said hopefully.

Fortunately they were busy or they'd have kicked her arse straight off that step and down the others, she was sure of that. They went back to attending to the invited guests, who continued to file past Annie and gawp at her curiously. Annie tried to ignore them.

She just sat there, waiting.

She was still there when the last of the guests had gone in, and the heavies went inside too, closing the door on the laughter, the music, the warmth.

Annie sat there and shivered.

Along the road, as the light started to go, she could see Tony sitting in the Jag, watching her with anxious eyes.

He thinks I've lost it, thought Annie. *How long before he trots off to the nearest phone box and calls Jimmy and tells him I've flipped?*

It was almost dark now. Two big lights came on over the porch, and moths started to do their suicidal dance around them. Annie could faintly hear the music going on, the laughter, the clink of glasses.

Time passed.

After what she guessed was about an hour – she wasn't wearing a watch – one of the heavies opened the door and stared out at her, then shut the door again.

Time went on. She couldn't see Tony behind the Jag's wheel any more, and she hoped he hadn't gone and found a phone box; she hoped he wasn't talking to Jimmy at this minute; she hoped and prayed the pair of them weren't going to come and grab her and move her on as if she was a drunken old bag lady. That would be embarrassing.

Her buttocks were numb from sitting on the step. She was stiff. She was aching.

More time passed.

It was full dark when she stood up creakily. Had to either fuck off or bang on the door. Couldn't decide which. *Time to shit or get off the pot*, she thought, and approached the door, her fist raised.

The door opened.

The blast of light, heat, and noise made her blink.

'All right, what's your name?' asked one of the heavies, looming in the doorway.

'Carter,' said Annie, swallowing her surprise. 'Annie Carter. Max Carter's w—' *Widow. She'd nearly said widow. Maybe she really* was *losing it.* 'Wife. I'm Annie Carter, Max Carter's wife.'

'Wait.'

'No! Hold on.' Annie brought Max's ring out of her pocket. 'Show him this, will you?'

The man nodded and took the ring. The door closed again.

Annie stood there, staring at her reflection in the highly polished navy blue paintwork of the door.

Now, of course, he wouldn't see her anyway,

she thought in dreary exhaustion. And what the hell would she say to him if she saw him? Hey, lend me half a million? Help me out here? Her mind felt numb and woolly, not her own. It was no good. Jimmy was right, Layla was dead meat and here she was, kidding herself that she could save the day. Save her daughter. Rescue a situation that was already too far beyond her control.

She turned and walked down the steps.

Give it up, you silly cow.

And then the door opened behind her, and light flooded out. She blinked as she looked back up the steps, at the man who was standing there in the open doorway.

'Mr Barolli will see you now,' he said.

29

The noise and the hot crush of bodies inside nearly defeated her. She stumbled after the hulking shape of the heavy as he cut a swathe through the glittering crowds beneath huge, brilliantly lit chandeliers. The place was massive, she took in that much. A huge curving staircase, swathed with more ribbons . . . hundreds of candles, all alight with a golden glow that warmed the happy scene . . . massive arrangements of white lilies in glass bowls.

In the midst of all this grandeur, Annie felt shabby, insignificant, badly out of place. But she had a job to do here, so she followed him even though she was stiff and aching and almost out of hope.

The man paused at a set of double doors and knocked.

'Come,' Annie heard from within.

The man opened the door, gave her a nod. She slipped inside.

Into quiet and warmth. A man's study, lined with books, two large worn tan leather Chesterfield couches set out on either side of a fire that was burning brightly, fending off the chill of the spring night. At the far end of the room there was a big desk, a golden banker's light there spreading a gentle glow.

The door closed behind her and a man rose from behind the desk and came forward, extending a hand, palm down.

What, does he expect me to kiss his hand? Ain't that what people do when they meet a Mafia don?

She had no intention of doing that.

'Mrs Carter? I'm Constantine Barolli. Come and sit down.' His accent was pure New York.

Her first sight of Constantine Barolli shocked her. She had expected an old man, heavy in body and grave in manner. But he was younger than she had supposed he would be – early forties, she guessed given that he had an adult daughter getting married. He looked fit, tall, streamlined, with broad shoulders and narrow hips. The silver-grey suit he wore was beautifully cut, and he even smelled good. Annie caught a fragrant whiff of Acqua di Parma cologne as he came close. He had a thick head of silver-grey hair, darker brows and a tanned, intelligent face with stunningly clear blue eyes.

Annie walked forward over costly rugs and sat

in the chair on her side of the desk. The soft tan leather creaked as she sat down. Max's ring was in the centre of the desk, beside an empty crystal brandy glass.

'Drink, Mrs Carter?' he offered, sitting down behind the desk.

Annie shook her head.

He reached for the decanter and poured a snifter for himself.

He had big hands, she noticed. But it was his eyes that really caught her attention. They were deep-set, penetrating, searching her face. *Mafia*, she thought, and shuddered. These were dangerous people. People that not even someone with gangland connections on this side of the pond should mix with. She remembered all Jimmy's warning words and thought: *What the fuck am I doing here?*

But she knew.

This was Last-Chance Saloon.

There was nowhere else for her to go, nothing else for her to do. *Desperate times called for desperate measures*. But still, she shivered at her own boldness and wondered if this was a terminally stupid move.

'What can I do for you, Mrs Carter?' he asked. He had a low voice, calm, unhurried. 'I apologize for keeping you waiting today,' he went on, surprising her. 'It's not every day a daughter gets married.'

'Congratulations,' said Annie automatically.

He shrugged and spread his hands in a gesture that was pure Italian. *No*, thought Annie, *Sicilian*.

'He wouldn't have been my choice, but then, who would? Who would ever be good enough for a father's little girl?'

It was a rhetorical question. Annie sat silent, thinking of her own little girl, wounded now, perhaps irreparably damaged by what had happened to her.

'So tell me what I can do for you,' said Constantine again.

Oh nothing much, thought Annie. *Lend me half a million. Save my daughter. Bring my husband back. Turn back the clock. Make it all go away.*

'I heard there was some trouble on Max's turf,' said Constantine when she didn't speak. 'At one of the venues.'

Jesus, already the word was spreading. And wasn't Jimmy Bond supposed to be keeping a lid on things?

'I heard two of the Delaney venues had trouble too.'

'I ordered that,' said Annie, her eyes moving nervously away from that laser-like gaze.

'It don't pay to let these things go uncorrected,' he agreed, sipping brandy. 'You're sure . . . ?' He held up the brandy balloon.

Annie shook her head.

'What is it you want then? Backup?'

'No. We can handle our own affairs pretty well.'
*Just in case you're thinking of moving in like Jimmy
says you are.*

'Max abroad?' asked Constantine.

'Jonjo and Max had some urgent business to take
care of,' lied Annie smoothly. 'I can't reach them.'

'And I guess you're in charge now?'

'I'm in charge now.'

I'm a wreck and I'm in charge . . .

'Only the word on the street says Jimmy Bond's
running the show.'

Annie shook her head. 'Then the word's wrong.
Jimmy has stood in, sure. But now I'm back to
take over. That's what Max wanted.'

'So the problem is . . . ?' he prompted.

'I have to raise some money fast. A lot of money.'

He nodded again. 'For what?'

And here was where she could either go on lying
her head off or appeal to his better nature.
Supposing he had one, which she doubted. With
unsteady fingers she took the little box out of her
pocket and opened it. She took out the broken
chain and the heart, slipped those back into her
pocket. Then leaving the box open, she placed it
in the centre of the desk, beside Max's ring.

'You have a daughter who's getting married
today, Mr Barolli,' said Annie. 'I have one who's
missing a finger.'

The silence in the room was almost choking. Annie swallowed and felt sick all over again, looking at Layla's lifeless finger on its little bed of grubby cotton wool. A roar of happy laughter went up from outside in the hall, and she flinched.

Constantine was still looking at the finger.

Why don't he say something? she thought in frustration. *Is he that cold-hearted, to sit there looking at a child's finger and feel precisely nothing?*

Next thing his wife would be in here, asking why he was neglecting his guests. Maybe she ought to have gone away, tried again tomorrow. She was getting nowhere here.

I'm sorry,' she said stiffly, standing up and reaching for the box. 'This wasn't a good day to call, was it?'

Constantine was still staring at the box and its pitiful contents. He reached out a hand and caught hers before she could pick it up. His hand was hot. Hers was freezing cold.

'Wait.' His eyes rose to her face. 'You can't come in here, show me *this* and just go. Tell me what the fuck's happened.'

Annie swallowed hard. 'Layla – my daughter – was snatched in Majorca,' Annie said. 'She could be there or in England now, we don't know.'

'Max don't know about this?'

'No.'

'You can't get in touch with him?'

'No.'

'And now these people want money?'

Annie nodded.

'You refused?' He nodded toward the finger.

'I didn't refuse. It just threw me, how much they were asking for.'

'And that was?'

'Half a million pounds sterling. I said I couldn't raise that sort of money . . .'

'That true?'

'Of course it's true!'

'And that's why you're here. To ask me for this money?'

'I know you were a business associate of Max's.'

'Were?'

'*Are.*' Annie clutched at her brow. 'I don't have access to that sort of money and I can't contact Max about it.' She hesitated. 'Look, I have three clubs and a house.'

'No.' Constantine put the brandy glass down on the desk. 'You don't. *Max* has three clubs and a house. Unless of course he's dead, in which case, as his widow, *you* would own them. You got the title deeds?'

'I'll get them.' *But they're in Max's name, of course. And I don't have a fucking clue where they might be.*

'So you don't.' Constantine was silent for a beat. 'Is Max dead, Mrs Carter? Because without a body

I believe it's five months before he can be legally declared dead and his estate would then, and only then, pass to you.'

Annie felt sick again. His cold assessment of her situation was just too painfully accurate. All she was doing was tying herself in more knots. There was no way out of this situation. Layla was lost. She got shakily to her feet.

'I'm sorry to have wasted your time,' she said stiffly, reaching for the box.

Again he caught her wrist.

'Hold on. Now come on. Level with me. Is he dead? Is that it?' asked Constantine.

'No, he's alive. He's not free to help at the moment, that's all.' *They'll take over the manor*, Jimmy had warned her. This was a huge mistake.

Constantine's eyes were steady on hers. 'Is there a deadline on this?'

'A month last Friday,' said Annie.

'Then we have time. Okay, so why pay up? There's an alternative.'

'Such as?'

'Find them.'

'And how the hell are we supposed to do that?'

'It's worth a shot. Have your people tried?'

'No.' Annie shook her head firmly. 'The kidnappers told me no police, no funny business. If they even suspect we're looking, they could kill her. Could you let go? You're hurting my wrist.'

He let her go.

Annie repacked the little box as Constantine Barolli came around the desk. He held out Max's ring to her as she pocketed the box.

'Thanks,' said Annie, glancing up at him. She took the ring.

'We'll start looking,' he said.

'No,' said Annie.

'Time may be shorter than you think. Any chance is worth taking.'

Annie looked at him, shook her head in confusion. 'No. I don't know. I'm not sure.'

She had come for the money, that was all. Now she had an offer of something more, something riskier for Layla. And yet there could be a chance here. He was right. A chance to get Layla out whole, or at least alive. Not dead.

'Do you have any idea how many people were involved in taking her?' he asked.

Annie looked at him and gave up. She told him what Jeanette had told her about the gang. It wasn't much.

'The address of the villa,' he said.

She told him. He wrote it down.

'Give me a description of Layla.'

She described Layla. He wrote that down too.

'How do I reach you, Mrs Carter?' he asked.

'You don't,' said Annie with a firm shake of the head. 'I think they had a tap on the phone line in

Majorca, and I think they've done that here too. So no phone calls to where I'm staying. Sorry.'

'All right.'

'Have someone pass a message to my boy Billy Black. He drinks at The Grapes in Bow.'

Constantine nodded. 'No problem. To be doubly sure we're safe, I'll use the code.'

'What code?'

'Caesar's code,' he said. 'It's over two thousand years old. Each letter of the alphabet becomes a number, and you add three. So A is one, plus three, which equals four, B is two, plus three, that's five, and so on. You got that?'

Annie nodded. Then she looked at him and spoke from the heart.

'Layla's life could depend on this,' she said. 'For Christ's sake be careful.'

'You got it,' said Constantine Barolli, and held out his hand, palm down.

Annie looked at his face and she almost believed what he was saying. Her eyes dropped to his hand.

And here we go again, she thought. *He expects me to kiss his damned hand. It's like having an audience with the Pope!*

Something in her rebelled.

Annie extended her own hand and shook his briefly. Constantine Barolli looked at her with an expression of mild amusement.

'I'll be in touch,' he said.

Jessie Keane

Annie nodded and left the room, feeling that she had somehow made a pact with the devil.

When she'd gone, Constantine stood there for a long moment staring at the closed door. Then he went back to the desk, picked up the phone, and dialled. It was quickly answered.

'Nico?' he said after a beat. 'Got a job for you.'

30

Tony was waiting in the car, patient and enduring as always. She was suddenly very thankful for Tony. It was dark outside now, dark and cold. She huddled into the back seat and absorbed the warmth of the car's interior.

Tony was good. He didn't ask how the meet with Constantine Barolli had gone, and she was grateful for that. She wouldn't have known how to answer anyway. Talking to Constantine Barolli had been like entering a foreign land. In the sumptuous Holland Park house the overwhelming aura had been one of great riches, extreme comfort.

Yeah, and they say crime don't pay, she thought sourly.

She reminded herself that Constantine Barolli was a crook of the highest order, cunning as a fox. Wasn't that what they called him on the streets of London and New York, the silver fox? Now she could see why. She was hoping that a man with Barolli's clout could somehow turn the odds in Layla's favour, magic up a good result.

Impossible.

In her heart, she knew that her baby girl was lost, gone from her forever.

And maybe that's what I deserve, thought Annie painfully.

After all, she'd done some pretty bad things, things she wasn't proud of. She thought of Ruthie, her lovely trusting sister. She'd stolen her sister's man from right under her bloody nose, and she had walked carelessly on the dark side of life – she had even colluded in murder. She *deserved* to suffer, that was it.

But still she couldn't give up. She knew she was beaten, she knew it was all for nothing, but she *could not give up*. Not while there was even the smallest chance that Layla could still be alive.

'Where to, Mrs Carter?' asked Tony as he moved the car smoothly off into the flow of traffic.

There's a block of apartments in Mayfair, on the corner of Oxford Street and Park Lane. Let's go there.'

But what the hell for? she wondered the instant she'd said it.

She knew what for. She was revisiting her old life, the life where she had been in control, where things had never been easy but at least they hadn't ripped her guts out and left her to die slowly inside. She was trying to reassure herself, to tell herself that all was not lost – even when she knew that it was.

They were passing Hyde Park, the car zipping along smoothly.

Max's car.

Is he dead? Constantine Barolli had asked her, his hand on her wrist.

She hoped he hadn't felt her pulse leap with the lie.

Now they were cruising past Park Lane, into Piccadilly, and then they were there, and the block of flats looked just the same. Tony eased the car into the side of the road.

Nothing had changed. She had lived here with Max as his mistress, and she had been so happy. Rapturously, first-love happy. There were lights on in the apartment; someone else was living there now. Annie wondered if human feelings sank into the bricks of old buildings, if other people could feel the happiness of past generations . . . but if that was so, then what about Dolly's place? There had been plenty of sex there and plenty of laughter – but there had been other things too. Worse things. Pat Delaney meeting his Maker. Poor little Eddie, Max's youngest brother, too . . . but she didn't want to think about that.

Tony waited behind the wheel, the motor idling.

'You know Upper Brook Street, Tony?' she asked at last.

'Yep. I do.'

'Let's go there.'

It wasn't far. Back along Park Lane, passing the glitzy hotels, then the car swung right and she was back in her old life again.

This place was luxurious too. But the memories she had made here had not been like those she had made in Mayfair with Max. These memories were of a successful business, a high-class brothel. Peers of the Realm and MPs and City gents had flocked here to see Madam Annie's classy girls. But then it had all gone sour. It was here that she had been arrested. Here that Kieron Delaney, pampered brat of the rival Delaney gang, had tried to force himself on her . . .

'That's enough, Tony. Let's get home.'

Or what passed for it.

'No, wait.' Annie straightened. 'You know Max's mother, Queenie, you know where she used to live? Max never sold the house, did he?'

Tony shook his head.

'I know it,' he said. His eyes moved sideways, away from hers, in the mirror. 'It might not be convenient tonight though, Mrs Carter.'

Annie stared at his face curiously.

'Convenient for who?' she asked.

'It's just that the boys meet there sometimes . . .'

'Ah. And they're meeting there tonight? Well

good. Come on then, Tony. Let's take a look at the old place.'

Tony glanced at her face in the rear-view mirror. He sighed, then pointed the car toward the meaner streets of the East End.

Annie had never been inside Queenie Carter's home. She knew Max and the boys used to meet there – they still met there even after Queenie was dead – but she had never stepped inside. She had never even met Queenie. Her sister Ruthie had. Ruthie, as Max's prospective bride, had been taken to Sunday tea with the imperious woman and had declared herself to be 'scared shitless' throughout. Which had to be true, because Ruthie rarely swore, but she had come back home from the meeting in a real lather.

'She's horrible,' Ruthie had told Annie. 'Really scary.'

But Max had adored his mother.

Had Queenie lived, Annie doubted that she would have found favour with the old woman, either. At least Ruthie had been sweet natured and biddable, which must have been what Queenie wanted in a daughter-in-law. But Annie was strong-headed, opinionated – too much, she felt, like Queenie herself. They would have clashed. That much was certain.

There were people still arriving when Tony stopped the car. Dark shapes passing beneath the streetlights, disappearing into the doorway.

'Coming then, Tone?' Annie was out of the door but then stopped dead, remembering what had happened last time she hurried across a street.

But the road was quiet.

Tony got out and locked the car and followed her over the road.

He knocked and the door opened to reveal a rat-faced little man holding a cigar. Rat Face's jaw dropped when he saw Tony standing there with a woman in tow.

'What the fucking hell . . . ?' asked Rat Face. 'Who's this, Tony?'

'This is your boss,' said Annie, pushing forward and into the hallway. 'Shut the door, will you? It's freezing out there tonight.'

'This is Jackie,' said Tony to Annie. To Jackie he said: 'Watch your mouth. This is Mrs Carter.'

The faces of the men seated around the big table in the back room upstairs were so comically startled by her appearance that Annie almost had to stifle a laugh. Jimmy Bond was there, at the head of the table. He looked not just startled but badly put out. There were a couple of others she recognized. Gary Tooley was there: lanky, blond and – by all accounts – vicious. And Steven Taylor, a squat and powerfully built man with mud-coloured eyes and a permanent five o'clock shadow on his chin. If Jimmy was Max's most trusted lieutenant, these two were tough sergeants-at-arms. Hard men. Handy men. Men who were not to be trifled with.

'Hi Jimmy,' said Annie brightly, unbuttoning her coat. 'Introduce me to all these nice gentlemen, why don't you?'

Jimmy looked as though he was about to blow a gasket, but he swallowed it and stood up.

'Boys, this is Max's wife.'

'Who is taking over, as of now,' said Annie, smiling tightly.

'Yeah,' said Jimmy. 'Annie—'

'*Mrs Carter*,' Annie reminded him sharply, still smiling.

'Mrs Carter,' said Jimmy with heavy irony. 'This is Steve, this is Gary . . .'

'Yeah, I remember you two,' said Annie.

They nodded, looking at her as though she'd just landed from Mars. 'This is Deaf Derek, and this is Benny. This is Jackie Tulliver . . .' The cigar-smoking little Rat Face nodded, all the while looking at her as if she'd crawled out from some place beyond his understanding.

The welcome was distinctly underwhelming, but Annie was determined to remain unfazed.

'Thanks for the intros, Jimmy,' she said, walking straight to the head of the table. Tony followed.

As Jimmy stood there with his mouth open, Annie slipped into his chair. Tony took up station behind her, arms folded, looming over the assembled company.

'Take a seat, Jimmy,' said Annie, looking at the frozen faces around the table. 'Nice to see you, boys. I suppose Jimmy's already told you what's going on. Max is doing some business with Jonjo in the Med, so I'm taking over here.'

With a face like thunder, Jimmy sat down in a vacant chair near the bottom of the table.

'Now,' said Annie. 'Let's talk business, shall we?'

Two hours later the boys picked up their coats and started to leave. Annie still sat at the head of the table, sweating with nerves but outwardly cool as ice. Aware that these were serious hard nuts and that she badly needed them on her side.

But she did hold one ace.

She was Max's wife.

Max had once *owned* this manor. He had been feared and respected here. Oh, she knew the Bill were trying to clamp down on the gangs, but they were a long way off succeeding in clearing the streets just at the moment. So the Carter name still had a lot of clout.

As a Carter wife, she had to be accorded respect. Any other woman coming in off the street would be given very short shrift; Max's boys would laugh in her face. But she was *Mrs Carter*, and that counted for something. Thank God.

Even so, she could see they were sceptical. Even so, they had looked at her at first as if she must be having a laugh. *A woman, in charge?*

Get used to it, boys, she thought.

And actually it hadn't gone too badly. After that first sticky half an hour, they had started to tell her what was happening out there on the manor. That the arcades and parlours were turning over trade nicely, that there had been trouble here and there, like that little fracas at Lolly's place, but that had been the Delaney mob trying to edge in while Jonjo was away. They had jumped on that hard, hit two cunting Delaney sites like a ton of effing bricks . . .

'Any trouble since then?'

Steve shook his head.

So all was well. Or sort of.

When they had all gone and Jimmy was wandering out after them, Annie called him back.

'Tony, can you wait outside in the car?' asked Annie.

Tony nodded, and went.

Jimmy sat down and leaned nonchalantly back in his chair. He looked at Annie.

'All right,' he said. 'What?'

'How many sets of keys to this place?' she asked.

'*Why* are you so obsessed with locking things up?'

Oh, maybe because I've had nearly everything I thought I owned snatched away from me, thought Annie.

Aloud she said: 'Just answer the question, Jimmy.'

'Okay. Jonjo had a set, and so did Max. I've got a set too. No one else.'

Annie nodded. So she might find a key on Max's key ring, the one she had brought with her from Majorca.

'Okay. Get another two cut, will you?'

'Fine. Listen, the boys ain't happy about you shutting up the clubs.'

'I know.' Annie paused. 'Tell me again who collects from where, Jimmy.'

Jimmy went through it all. Laid it out. There were twelve people involved in collecting for the firm. Jimmy named each of them, and which of the arcades, brothels, car showrooms, and shops each individual was responsible for. All monies were passed to Jimmy Bond, and he passed the cash on to Jonjo.

Annie listened intently.

'And you personally collected the monies from the three clubs?'

'Yeah, I did.'

'So where are they?'

'Where is what?'

'The monies you've collected from the clubs. And from all the other venues.'

Jimmy shrugged. 'Sitting in Jonjo's bank account, I suppose. Or Max's.'

'Yeah, but what about last month's?'

228

'What?'

'Jonjo's been away for at least a month, in fact nearly two, so you've collected about two months' worth of takings – from the clubs and from all the other venues – that haven't been passed on to him.'

Jimmy's face reddened. 'Are you accusing me of something?' he asked.

Annie eyed him curiously. 'No, Jimmy. I'm asking what you've done with two months' takings.'

She knew it would be a sizeable sum, in the thousands.

'Stashed safe at home,' he said coldly. 'What, do you want me to hand that over too?'

'Yeah, that would be good,' said Annie sweetly. She was getting a bit fucking fed up with Jimmy Bond and his attitude. 'And any future monies too. Every week. As Jonjo's not here, they come to me.'

Jimmy Bond was in a stinking mood by the time he parked his cream and blue Mark 11 Zodiac outside his house. By the time he walked through the front door his mood had degenerated even more. Annie fucking Carter had kept him at Queenie's, turning the place inside out in case Max or Jonjo kept cash hidden there. They'd come up with nothing.

And now he was home.

Home. What a bloody laugh.

It was late and still the fucking kids were screaming and bawling. He tripped over a kiddy car and a mini chair in the messy, dusty hallway, and was cursing Kath up hill and down dale by the time he got through to the kitchen.

In here, it was worse.

What exactly does the dirty cow do all day? he wondered. *Anyone would think she had six fucking kids, not two.*

She was sitting there at the kitchen table nursing the baby, a fag in her free hand sending up a ribbon of smoke. Jimmy Junior was whining for something and hanging on to her knees, grizzling to himself.

For fuck's sake! Shouldn't the kids be in bed by now?

'What you got to eat?' Jimmy asked, taking off his coat.

He looked around for a clean surface to lay it on but there was nowhere. Muttering under his breath, he went back into the hall, barking his shins on all the crap on the floor, and hung the coat up on a rack that was bursting with stuff. Everywhere in this sodding house was bursting with stuff. Open a cupboard and a ton of shit fell out on you. Open a drawer and you couldn't close it again. He hated it.

'I been looking after your kids all day, in case you ain't noticed,' Kath yelled after him. 'I ain't had time to think about cooking.'

Jimmy went upstairs. Even the bedrooms were stuffed with crap – bottles and sponges and spiders' webs and dust balls. He went into their bedroom and straight over to the loose bit of carpet beside the window, yanking it back. He lifted the board and took the cash out and sat on the bed, wrinkling his nose at the dirty, mildewy smell of the sheets. He counted up the cash. Then he frowned. Then he counted again.

Jimmy stuffed the cash in his trouser pocket, replaced the board, and kicked the carpet back into place. He went downstairs, into the kitchen.

'It's not very fucking easy, you know, just stuck here all day with these two howling and screaming,' Kath was whining loudly at him in her high-pitched and bloody irritating voice.

Jimmy didn't pause in his pace. He hauled back and slapped her right across her fat chops, then gave her another one, then another.

Jimmy Junior started to shriek. The baby, knocked loose from the teat, joined in. *Happy fucking families*, thought Jimmy in rage. He gave Kath another slap and she cowered down in the seat, no longer giving him earache.

Well, that was good.

'What is it?' she screamed, trying to cover her head with her upraised arm. 'What did I do?'

Jimmy hit her again. Blood flew, spattering over the dirty floor as his signet ring caught her brow.

Fucking fat useless cow, thought Jimmy. The kids were going apeshit now. *How the fuck did I ever get tucked up with a slag like her?*

Jimmy grabbed a handful of his wife's hair and pulled her head back and yelled full in her face: 'You been in my money?'

Kath's face froze in fear and denial.

'No! No, I—'

'Don't lie to me!' He shook her head about, to emphasize his point. 'That money ain't yours, I keep telling you. You don't touch it. It belongs to the firm. Hear me? You. Don't. Touch. It. Ever.'

Kath tried to nod, tears and blood running down her face.

Jimmy released her.

'I just wanted to buy some nice bits for the kids,' sobbed Kath.

'You want bits for the kids, you ask *me*. You don't go in there and help yourself, you got me?'

'Yeah. Okay.'

She'd taken out five hundred pounds. *Five hundred pounds.* But then Annie Carter wouldn't notice a damned thing, why was he worrying? And even if she did – and she wouldn't, he was sure of that – then he could always say that it had been Kath, the silly cow, and Kath was her family; she wouldn't begrudge the kids a few bits, now would she?

Had Jonjo been here, it would have been a very

different picture. Jonjo would have noticed straight away and there would have been hell to pay. And Max always kept a tight eye on the books, too. Rob Max, and you'd only ever do it the once.

But that was then, and this was now. Max and Jonjo were history.

She won't notice, he thought, and started to relax a bit.

'Right,' he said, feeling calmer. 'Stick a steak on, and I'll have some chips with it.'

Kath nodded tearfully.

The kids kept right on shrieking.

'And for Christ's sake shut them *up*, will you?' he roared.

Jimmy shook his head in disgust. Kath wanted shagging with the rough end of a pineapple, the lazy, ugly mare. *He* certainly wasn't going to shag her, that was for sure. He went to the fridge. He took out a beer and got the bottle opener from the drawer and went into the front room, kicking the door shut behind him. He turned on the telly to drown out all the noise.

Happy fucking families!

It would all be okay.

Annie Carter wouldn't notice.

After all, she hadn't noticed what he'd already milked from the clubs.

31

They'd gone to the villa up near Deia, looked at the wreckage of the pool house, stood around by the pool, just soaking it up, taking it all in. First, they stopped in at the little villa by the gate to see what was inside.

'Phew,' said the one in charge, a big friendly-looking bear of a man. He put his hand over his nose and mouth as he stood in the bedroom door. 'Not pretty, uh?'

His colleagues agreed that no, this was not a pretty sight.

They went off down to Palma.

The word had gone out.

There had been a kidnapping at a Majorcan villa, three people or possibly four involved. Maybe two, three men and one who might or might not be a woman, who the fuck knew just yet?

But they were going to find out.

People were doing door-to-door in Sóller and Manacor and Felanitx and in Palma, covering all the bases. Questions were asked and leads were pursued and sometimes – just occasionally – they got a result.

Marietta and Julio Degas were lying peacefully upstairs in bed one night when someone broke their front door down. Suddenly chaos filled the house as men surged up the stairs, big hooded men with knives and machetes.

Marietta screamed, '*Madre de Dios!*'

Julio started up, and was shoved back down on to the bed. The men switched the light on; it glared harshly on the bemused couple. They blinked, trembled, stared. Wondered what the hell was going to happen to them.

'Money? You want money?' asked Julio in hasty Castilian Spanish. 'It's in the drawer over there, right there.'

No one made a move toward the drawer. Five masked men stared down at the trembling couple on the bed.

'You been renting out the place next door?' asked one of them in English, and instantly the one beside him translated.

Julio hesitated. The angry blond Englishman had told him not to say a word about their transaction, had said that they wanted only to be private and not be bothered by anyone, so he was not to discuss the fact that they were there, not with anyone. He had paid handsomely, too. Julio was a man of honour, and he had given his word.

One of the men moved forward and clubbed him around the ear with the handle of the machete. Marietta screamed again, then started to sob. Julio cringed in pain as blood began to pour from his scalp.

'Answer the fucking question,' said one in English.

It was repeated in Spanish.

Julio answered. He told them about the two men, the woman.

'A child? Was there a child, a little girl? Dark hair, green eyes?'

They both shook their head. What name had the people given?

Philips.

Which meant nothing.

'Describe these people,' said the one in charge, and Julio did, in detail.

'What about the child?'

No. No child. Neither of them had seen a child, what were they talking about, a child? And anyway the people were gone, they'd paid for a fortnight and they'd left at night, not saying where they were going. The big one, the dark one, he was a nice quiet man and he called in and paid them.

The blond man was not so nice. Nervy. Aggressive. And the blonde woman never spoke, she seemed afraid to.

'You've no idea where they've gone?'

Both of them shook their head fearfully.

'Fuck it,' said the one who spoke in English.

'The nice one asked who to see about a boat,' said Marietta suddenly in faltering English. He *had* been nice, the dark-haired one; he always thanked her politely for the food and drink she delivered to them every morning.

The men listened. But no child, they asked again. You're sure, no child?

The couple in the bed shook their heads.

No. They'd just moved in and then out again with their luggage. Big bags, nothing else.

Big bags.

The men looked at each other.

How big? they asked.

Very big bags.

The men piled back down the stairs and out through the front door and away. Marietta started sobbing with relief. Julio was bleeding like a pig. They clung to each other. Julio's eyes strayed over to the drawer. Marietta's followed. The men hadn't even touched the money.

32

Vita was getting worried. They were in a little terraced house now down by the Albert Docks. No one knew who they were and no one gave a fuck. Danny had told her this, before going out and not saying where he was going. Phil had gone out too, saying he was going mad cooped up in here all the time, and now, wouldn't you fucking well *know* it, the girl had come out of her drug-induced stupor. At first she'd whimpered but now she was crying. Loudly.

For fuck's sake.

Danny just never seemed to get that dose right.

Vita ignored it for as long as she could. They'd put the girl in the smaller of the two bedrooms. Danny had taken the other one, and Phil had slept on the sofa downstairs, and Vita was supposed to sleep in with the girl, make sure she was okay.

Which was not at all okay with Vita.

'You don't like it, tough,' said Danny, and that should have been the end of *that* debate.

But Vita had whined on about it, so eventually it was agreed that Vita would sleep in Danny's room on the floor, in their one dirty old sleeping bag, while Danny took the bed.

Vita could live with that. Anything to avoid being alone with the girl.

Vita felt sick about the whole thing now. It was creasing her up to even look at the girl during the day; if she had to spend the night in there with her she'd go berserk.

She wanted out, but she didn't dare say so to Danny. Danny was fully committed to this gig now. He'd done Max Carter and Jonjo Carter too, and the hired help up at the little villa by the gate, and he'd cut up the girl just a bit, make her doting mama pay up and not give him any more lip.

Annie Carter was their cash cow. Danny had explained that very carefully to his sister. The cash cow was the one who would pay them any amount of money he cared to mention, just to get the kid back.

Because Annie Carter was the cash cow, because they *knew* the Carters were rolling in loot – shit, they owned half the East End – Danny had gone in hard with half a mill, but then the silly cash cow had quibbled and he'd had to cut the girl. Her fault, not his.

Vita didn't like to think about that. But Layla's wound – she thought of it as Layla's wound but it was really Layla's *disfigurement*, who was she kidding? – was healing well, she was getting no pain with it. Vita was always careful to change the bandages, keep the . . . the *stump* clean, and it all looked okay. Hideous, but okay. Only the girl sat there and looked at her as if she was a monster every time she went near her.

And maybe that's what she was, going along with a thing like this. A monster.

It must be frightening for the kid, all these people around her with their faces covered up. You had to feel sorry for the little girl: it wasn't her fault she was in this predicament. Not Vita's fault, either, really. All Danny's idea, as usual. She'd gone along with it, her big brother, of course she had. Danny was usually right about everything, anyway.

But this time – for the first time ever – Vita wondered about that.

She put her hood on and went upstairs. Phil had fitted a bolt on the outside of the bedroom door, and Vita slid it back and went into the small bedroom. Layla was sitting up on the edge of the bed, kicking her feet and crying.

'Hey babes, what's up?' asked Vita, going over to her and sitting down.

'I want Mummy.'

'She's busy right now.' Christ, hadn't she said

this a thousand times? When would the kid shut up about her fucking mummy? 'Soon you'll be back with her.'

'When?'

'Very soon. You hungry, peanut?'

Layla bit her lip. There were tears and snot all over her face. She nodded. 'I don't like it here,' she whined.

Me neither kid, thought Vita.

Layla looked up at the hooded face.

'Your eyes are blue,' she said.

Vita quickly stood up.

Oh great, she thought. *She's seen my face and now she even knows what colour my eyes are. Wonderful!*

And how come it was always her who had to fetch and carry for the kid, while the two men just sat around downstairs reading papers and drinking beer? How come when *she'd* gone walkabout in Palma there'd been a riot, but when they went out – like now – she was expected to say nothing and just sit here, as usual, clutching the shitty end of the stick?

She left Layla and went downstairs to the kitchen. She got out a tin of beans and the can-opener and again the gun caught her eye just lying there on the kitchen table. Why'd Danny leave the damned thing lying about like that, in full view? She looked at it. Thought again about Layla seeing her face in the hen house, and now commenting on the colour of her eyes. She turned away from the gun and opened the cupboard to find a pot for the beans, and then the front door opened and something small shot past the corner of her eye and a man said 'Hey!' very loudly, and a child screamed.

Really *screamed*.

Vita ran out into the hallway and found Danny there with Layla squirming and kicking in his arms, his hand over her mouth, his eyes blazing with fury as he rounded on Vita.

'For fuck's sake!' he roared. 'What the fuck you doing, you stupid bitch? She nearly ran straight past me.'

The bolt, thought Vita. *Forgot to shoot the damned bolt on the bedroom door.*

'Sorry, I'm sorry,' she gabbled.

'*Sorry?* For fuck's sake, will you get a hold of yourself? We nearly lost her then, what are you, crazy?'

Maybe she was crazy. Vita felt that she was going seriously *mental* with the stress of all this.

'It's all right, she didn't get out, no one saw her, no harm done,' she said hurriedly.

'She screamed the bloody place down.'

'Yeah, but there's no one about. It's okay.'

But Danny was not to be appeased.

'We'll move on tonight,' he said, and carried

242

Layla back up the stairs. 'Can't take any chances. Next time make sure you *bolt the fucking door*, okay?' he shouted down at her.

'Okay,' said Vita faintly, thinking that the kid had seen Danny's face too now, and that things were not looking at all good for Layla.

Oh Jesus, she really wanted *out* of this.

33

Annie got up next day and found an orgy going on down in the hallway. *Friday*, she thought.

This morning she'd awoken to the same old nightmare. Clinging to those blissful moments before full awakening, when she still had a home, a husband, a child, the cold reality of being awake, properly awake, sent her groaning and reeling all over again.

She knew she'd grown soft.

She'd grown accustomed to having Max there, making all the decisions, covering all the bases . . . yes, she'd grown soft.

And slack.

And lazy.

She'd been happily playing the little woman, and now it had landed her in the crap right up to her neck.

Once she had stalked about, made her way in

the world fearlessly because she'd had to. But her luxurious life with Max had eroded her strength. Now she had to learn to stand alone again, to conquer her fear and somehow, *somehow*, make her way through all this.

But she felt as if someone had pulled all the props of her world away, and left her to slowly keel over into the dust.

She was dead in the water. And she knew it.

And – oh fuck – it was Friday again. Party day. And somebody was having a noisy orgasm in the hall.

People were amazingly perverse. That was the simple fact that had always astonished Annie. Working girls were used to being asked to meet a stunning variety of requirements from clients. Granted, some wanted a simple screw, but most did not.

'They can get that at home,' Dolly always said.

No, prostitutes were more often asked to perform things wives would never stoop to. Like talking, for instance. Some men didn't want sex, they only wanted to talk about all their problems, all the stuff they couldn't tell their mates or their wives. Work problems, health concerns, that sort of thing. The men who *did* want sex usually wanted sex that was out of the ordinary. Like anal. Like being pissed on: the 'golden rainer' syndrome. Like being tied up, whipped, fucked with a variety of implements, beer bottles even . . . oh, the laughs they'd all had over the kitchen table.

For Ellie, though, the laughs were over. Annie walked into the kitchen and there Ellie was, telling Dolly all about her woes.

'If I can't face working as a prossie no more, what's going to happen to me?' Ellie was asking tearfully. 'This is my home. You and Darren are my friends. But if I can't pull my weight, I'm sunk, right?'

Dolly had seen this coming for weeks. She glanced at Annie and her eyes said, *See? Didn't I tell you?*

'I know,' she said, patting Ellie's hand.

'What the fuck am I gonna do, Doll?' wailed Ellie, burying her face in her hands.

Oh, the Delaneys will see you right, thought Dolly. Ellie had been a Delaney snitch for years. Poor bloody Ellie, she'd had very few chances in life and a rotten background, no wonder she'd grown up not knowing right from wrong. Right, to Dolly, was never grassing on your friends. But she knew Ellie had done that, time and again, to ingratiate herself with the Delaney clan. You just had to know that Ellie could turn either way, and be careful.

'It'll all work out,' said Dolly.

But truthfully Dolly felt that nothing was

working out any more. Look at all the shit that was coming Annie's way. The poor cow was up against it big time. And how much longer before the Delaneys decided enough was enough, and told Dolly to get rid? Darren was not himself. Ellie was throwing a wobbly. Una had settled down a bit since Annie had marked her card, but just having her in the house caused an atmosphere.

Still, Friday was payday. Plenty of punters in, plus a few spare girls because she was running short of workable staff. Plenty of drink taken, plenty of nibbles consumed. Plenty of action all over the house, and at the end of it a good-sized wedge of cash, so Dolly couldn't complain. Whoever said life was going to be easy, anyway?

'So what's the big man like?' she asked Annie as they sat there later in the afternoon, sharing a cup of tea.

'Barolli?' Annie got a mental image of silver hair, laser-sharp blue eyes. 'Rich. Which is all that matters.'

'Yeah, but what's he *like*?'

'Like someone who enjoys throwing his weight about. And having everyone kissing his arse.'

'I'm surprised you got in to see him at all,' said Dolly.

'Didn't think I was going to,' said Annie. 'I waited outside for hours. His daughter was getting married.'

'So you picked a bad time.'

'The worst. But he says he's going to help.'

'With the cash.'

'He didn't say a definite yes or no on that,' said Annie. 'He said he was going to have his people look for Layla.'

'Is that a good idea?'

'I don't think so.'

'But he's going to do it.'

'Look, he's calling the shots. I have to trust him to do the right thing.'

'I hope you know what you're doing.'

'Doll.' Annie looked at her friend in exasperation. 'Do I *look* like I know what I'm doing? I have no idea what those bastards have done to her,' said Annie, her voice cracking with strain. 'If Constantine Barolli thinks he can help, then sod it – I'll let him help.'

Dolly nodded, her heart wrenching for Annie's pain. There was nothing she could do about Layla being missing, but what she could do was offer a little distraction.

'Tomorrow we'll go up West,' she said. 'You got cash?'

Jimmy had delivered a couple of thousand quid to her this afternoon, so yeah, she had cash. No inclination to spend it on frivolities, though. None whatsoever.

'I dunno, Doll. I'm not in the mood.'

'Come on, girl,' said Dolly bracingly. 'I'm not taking no for an answer.'

And so there they were next day, trawling the posh shops. It occurred to Annie that the last time she and Dolly had done this, their situations had been reversed. She had been the one in charge, Madam Annie, and Dolly had been a rough, mouthy brass with no dress sense and hair like fuse wire.

But now Dolly had assumed the mantle of Madam, and Annie had put her right on turning herself out as a Madam should. Neatly groomed. Coiffed to the nines. Altogether in control.

'Got one or two things lined up,' said Dolly in high excitement as their cab whizzed across town.

'Like what?' Not that Annie cared. She guessed that this was depression, this hopeless, useless feeling of not being able to swim out of the shit.

'Wait and see,' said Dolly.

Dolly took her into one of the boutiques and kitted her out with several ravishingly well-cut shift dresses and a jacket and a coat. All black.

'Let's face it, black's your colour,' said Dolly.

And it suits my mood, thought Annie.

Then they shopped for underwear, and tights. Then make-up.

'You look bloody washed out. That tan's faded and you're looking sallow,' said Dolly.

'Thanks, Doll,' said Annie dryly.

The overpainted woman behind the counter agreed, and sold Annie a fistful of products including mascaras, eye shadow, eye pencil, tinted moisturiser, loose translucent powder – and pillar-box-red lipstick.

'You can take a red that strong,' said the girl through her mask of thick foundation. 'With those dark eyes and that dark hair, you can get away with a dramatic statement.'

And then it was off to Vidal Sassoon's to get a new hairdo – or that was Dolly's plan. In fact Annie would not be budged on this. She agreed to having a couple of inches trimmed off the length, taking it back up to the shoulders, and she had a blow dry that left it gleaming.

'Bloody lovely,' said Dolly, satisfied as she tipped the stylist and the boy who had done the shampooing. 'Now for tea, I've got it all organized.'

And they hailed another cab and bombed off up Piccadilly to the Ritz.

'Fucking hell, Doll,' muttered Annie as they piled out of the cab.

'We need cheering up,' said Dolly, leading the way inside. 'Well, you do for sure. You've got a face on you like a smacked arse.'

Annie pulled a worse face at Dolly's back as they went into the circular red-carpeted reception area.

But maybe this was what she needed. As they

were guided to their table in the Palm Court, all pink and gold, so beautiful, so soothing with the little band playing away in one corner and black-clad waiters moving smoothly between the tables, Annie actually did find herself relaxing slightly for the first time in weeks.

'Have you seen these sandwiches they do? Little fingers of bread with these lovely dainty fillings . . . and the cakes and scones . . . it's lovely, I love it here,' said Dolly, looking like a child on her birthday.

'Who is this treat for, you or me?' asked Annie wryly.

'Both of us,' said Dolly. 'Fuck it, we deserve it.'

Dolly ordered champagne, and when it came and the waiter poured them each a glass, Dolly clinked her flute to Annie's.

'What are we toasting?' asked Annie with a sigh. 'What have we got to toast?'

'Being alive,' said Dolly 'Drink the fuck up, Annie Carter. Even you can get a glass of champers down your neck, it's weak as gnat's piss. Look, we're still here. We've come through storms before, and we'll get through them again. To us!'

Dolly was right – it was a lovely treat. They ate egg and cress fingers and smoked salmon rounds and miniature scones with cream, tiny chocolate profiteroles, and fancy cakes, all washed down with champagne and the finest tea

Annie had tasted in years. She folded a few chocolate truffles into a napkin and slipped them into
her bag. All around them the other guests were
chatting and smiling. Everyone looked so happy,
so relaxed.

Another world, she thought.

And then with a sharp stab of surprise she saw
him, on the other side of the room.

Constantine Barolli. The silver fox.

He was with a beautiful, brittle-looking dark-
haired woman of middle years, and two men in
their very early twenties, one blond, one dark. As
Annie saw him, he looked up and across at her.
She looked away.

'Who's that?' asked Dolly.

'Who?'

'That man over there who's staring at you.'

'That's Constantine Barolli.'

Dolly looked at him assessingly. 'He's still staring,'
she told Annie.

'So?'

'Just saying,' said Dolly with a shrug, pouring
them both more champagne. 'Tell you what, girl
– you could do with some of that.'

'Some of what?'

Dolly nodded in Constantine's direction and
gave him a toothy grin. He raised his glass.

'Some of *that*,' said Dolly. 'He's dishy.'

Annie stared at her, aghast.

'You've changed your fucking tune,' she said sharply. 'Whatever happened to the Virgin Queen?'

'Ah, that was different. We're not talking about men on the make here. We're talking about someone who's on your own level.'

'Dolly – I'm married. And so's he. So shut the fuck up, will you?'

Shit, Dolly could be so insensitive – particularly when she'd been on the sauce.

Weak as gnat's piss my arse, she thought. The champagne had gone straight to Dolly's head. Straight to her *gob*, too.

'You're widowed,' Dolly reminded her. 'I'm sorry as hell about that fact, but face it, you are. Get used to it.'

'I said shut *up*,' said Annie through gritted teeth.

She glanced back at Barolli. Dolly was right, he was still looking, and now so were the rest of his party.

She took another reluctant swig of champagne, but now it tasted sour. Her baby girl had been snatched, and she was here, living the high life; and so for that matter was Constantine fucking Barolli, and wasn't he supposed to be looking for Layla? Wasn't he supposed to be helping her out here, not staring at her and making her feel so damned uncomfortable?

'Come on, Dolly. Get the bill and let's go, shall we?'

253

Annie stood up, gathering her bag, summoning the waiter.

'Blimey, where's the fire?' grumbled Dolly, slipping the man some money and a sizeable tip.

'Where we off to now then? Back to the ranch?' asked Dolly as they surged out past the doorman, who tipped his hat.

'Can we call in on Kath and the kids?' asked Annie.

'We can do anything we fucking well like,' said Dolly, who was definitely more than a little drunk.

They hailed a cab and very soon they were pulling up outside Kath's place.

Kath opened the door holding the baby and stared with hostility at Annie, then at Dolly.

Annie stared back in surprise, seeing the bruise over Kath's eye, the cut that looked as if it was healing.

'What the hell happened to you?' she asked, shocked.

'Tripped on the stairs,' said Kath, her eyes sliding away from Annie's. Jimmy Junior was hanging on her grubby skirts, grizzling again. Always grizzling, that kid.

Annie stared at her.

'What you looking at? I tripped on the kid's skate on the stairs, okay? Like you care.'

Annie shook her head, exasperated. 'Of course

I care, Kath. We're family. We grew up together, didn't we?'

'Yeah, we did. And so did Ruthie, remember her?'

'I remember her,' said Annie. 'If you'd give me her number I'd get in touch with her. Are you going to ask us in, then?'

'You can come in if you want,' shrugged Kath, turning and walking back up the hall to the kitchen.

Annie stepped in and followed, and so did Dolly.

'Bloody hellfire,' said Dolly when she saw the mess in the place. When she got to the kitchen, she looked around in disbelief. 'Dirty *mare*,' she hissed out under her breath.

It looked exactly as it had when Annie had last seen it. Dirty pots and pans and cups and saucers piled up in the sink and on the draining board. The floor filthy, unscrubbed. Everywhere mess and disorder. And Kath in the middle of it, fat and sheet-white, flopping down on to a chair beside the table.

'Go and do your colouring,' she snapped at Jimmy Junior.

The child wandered off to his corner with the paints and sheets of paper. Annie followed him over and knelt down beside him. He looked at her with suspicion.

'Got a present for you,' she said, and pulled out the napkin. She placed it on the sheet of paper he was colouring in. He looked at the napkin, looked at her.

'Are you a bad lady?' he asked. 'Mum says you're a bad lady.'

'Jimmy!' Kath's voice was like a whip. Jimmy Junior flinched.

'I'm not a bad lady, Jimmy,' said Annie, almost amused. 'Have a look,' she said, indicating the folded napkin with a tilt of her head.

Jimmy Junior opened up the napkin and looked at the chocolates inside.

'They're for you,' said Annie.

A big unaffected grin spread itself over Jimmy Junior's face. He picked up one of the chocolates and put it in his mouth.

'Nice?' asked Anne.

He nodded, chewing.

'I don't like him having too many sweets,' said Kath in a masterly piece of irony.

'What, you eat all the bastards yourself, do you?' asked Dolly.

'Who's your fucking friend?' Kath asked Annie, glaring at Dolly.

'This is Dolly.'

'Well tell her to mind her mouth if she wants to keep hold of her dentures,' snapped Kath.

'Charming as well as lovely,' commented Dolly. Dolly, with her habit of calling a spade a spade, was not helping.

'Could you wait outside for a bit, Doll?' asked Annie. 'I won't be long.'

'Glad to,' said Dolly, and turned on her heel and left.

Annie stood up. Jimmy Junior was totally absorbed in eating the chocolates, his expression rapturous. Annie went over and looked down at Kath.

'Is that true? Did you really trip on the stairs? Jimmy didn't hit you, did he?'

'Course not,' snorted Kath, but her eyes were on the floor.

'Are you going to let me have Ruthie's number, Kath?'

'Might do, if I can find it.'

Which was a definite softening, Annie felt. It was better than 'fuck off', anyway.

'I'm going to have Jimmy send one of the cleaners who used to do the clubs round, Kath. Give you a hand with the place.'

Now Kath did look up.

'I don't want your fucking handouts, Lady Muck,' she said.

'It ain't a handout, you berk,' said Annie. 'You're my cousin and you're drowning here. You can't cope, any fool can see it. So take some help and don't be so fucking stubborn.'

'Well . . .' Kath's eyes slid around the room.

'Just try it. If you don't get on, tell me or tell Jimmy, we'll send someone else.'

'I'm sick of people looking down their noses at me,' said Kath as the baby started to wriggle and cry.

'Then how about not giving them reason to?' asked Annie.

'Easy for you to say,' pouted Kath.

'I know you must miss your mum,' said Annie.

'What, like you miss yours? You couldn't wait for Auntie Connie to croak and be out the way, could you, you cow?'

Well, Rome wasn't built in a day, thought Annie. Kath had softened a little, but there was still a hell of a long way to go.

But she was persistent. She would keep on pushing. It was her speciality.

Annie glanced over at Jimmy Junior. He had finished the chocolates and was back at his painting, sloshing water around in a glass with his paintbrush.

The noise again.

Tantalizing. Teasing.

She went outside and got back into the car with Dolly.

Kath hating her . . . Little Jimmy's delight with her gift of chocolates . . . then the painting . . . the brush in the water . . . *that noise* . . . and the Irish voice on the phone, southern Irish just like . . .

'Jesus!' Annie sat bolt upright.

'What the fuck?' demanded Dolly as Annie clutched hard at her arm. 'Ow.'

'Dolly, I know who's behind it.'
'What?'
'The hit. The hit in Majorca.'
'Well, *who* for the love of God?'
Annie took a breath.
Had to be.
Couldn't be anyone else.
She looked at Dolly.
'Kieron Delaney,' she said.

34

Kieron Delaney had come back to haunt her. Annie was sure of it. He had been obsessed with her, and she had been mad to believe that he would just let it go, forget it, move on. No. That wasn't his style. Because even when she had been deeply involved with Max, he had been incapable of taking a hint and buggering off.

Of course she had been fooled by him at first.

She had seen him as the odd one out of the Delaney clan, the only one not involved in the dirty game of gangland thuggery, murder, and crime. He had been an artist, a talented painter. *That* was the noise she could hear down the phone – the swoosh of a brush being dipped into water, swirled around. *Kieron Delaney.* She had believed him to be gentle and trustworthy.

She had been a bloody fool.

Max had warned her.

And she had ignored his warnings.

Which meant, of course, that Kieron Delaney's escalating obsession with her had been fed by hope as well as desire.

She remembered too that he had pitched up at dinner with his sister Orla and his brother Redmond and behaved to Annie as if everything was perfectly normal when he had already decided that he was going to kill Max.

That time, he had failed.

This time, he had succeeded.

'I think he's in Spain,' Orla had told her not long after that. 'The light's good, you know – for the painting.'

Oh yes – the painting. That had been the clue. Kieron had painted her in oils when she was strapped for cash. He had done the odd water-colour study of her too, high up in his attic studio in Shepherd's Bush, and she remembered now the swoosh of the brush as he dipped it in water, the paints swirling into muddy brown as they mixed together. That was the noise she remembered. That was the noise she kept hearing on the phone when the Irish kidnapper called.

Southern Irish, like Kieron, like Redmond and Orla, like the whole of that demented family. Despite the hardness of the man's tone, his voice still held the lyrical, almost musical cadences that were so distinctive. The ranks of the Delaneys were dense with bruisers from the south of Ireland. Those such as Charlie Foster, a Londoner born and bred, were the exception rather than the rule.

Yeah, but then shit always floats to the top, thought Annie.

It wasn't too big a leap to see that it was a *Delaney* man on the phone to her, not Kieron himself because she would know his voice. Christ, she would never forget it. But she could see him there, in her mind's eye, listening in the background, laughing at her, thinking that she was suffering and that he was glad.

Kieron *fucking* Delaney.

He was there, right there in the background, listening in, perhaps smiling as she went mad with distress. Paying her back for rejecting him. Making her *suffer*.

Maybe Kieron had still been in Spain when Annie and Max moved into their secluded villa on Majorca. Perhaps he had got wind that they were there, had tracked them down, had plotted and schemed to finish the job this time, to kill Max, his rival for Annie's affections, but to let her live. To let her endure the agony of grief over the loss of her husband, to know the anguish of having her daughter taken from her.

Men who feared powerful women wanted to 'put them in their place' – to control them by violence or the fear of it. And wasn't Kieron controlling her now? Wasn't she dangling on a string here, doing the bidding of the mysterious 'kidnappers', being hounded, tormented – yes, controlled. Waiting and wondering, hoping against hope that Layla could be saved?

She could be dead already.

Annie knew it.

An eye for an eye, a tooth for a tooth.

Wasn't that what the Bible said?

She dropped Dolly off, telling her to get word to Jimmy, and then went on over to Queenie's old house.

An hour later she was sitting in Max's chair at the head of the table in the upstairs room. It was cold in the house, which was empty but for a bed in one room, this table and chairs in another. No carpets, only curtains. A bare, empty shell. Max should have sold it years ago.

She heard the key in the front door, heard the heavy tread of a man in the hall downstairs. Footsteps coming up the stairs. Suddenly Jimmy Bond appeared in the doorway.

'What's going on?' he asked her, coming into the room and pulling out a chair.

'I popped in to see Kath today,' said Annie.

'Oh?' Now he looked wary.

'Bad accident she had,' said Annie. 'Marked her face up a bit, poor thing.'

'Yeah.'

'Walking into a door, for God's sake,' said Annie jovially. 'She'll have to take more water with it, won't she?'

'Yeah, she's a clumsy mare,' said Jimmy with a smile that smacked of relief. 'Could have been holding the baby, too. Could have dropped the poor little fucker on her head.'

'Or did she walk into a door?' Annie's face was thoughtful. 'Have I got that right, Jimmy? Is that what happened?'

The wariness was back in his eyes.

'I think so,' he said slowly. 'Wasn't it? I've been busy – ain't had much time to chat to her.'

'Well, accidents happen, don't they?' said Annie, her eyes hard on his. She knew damned well now that he'd been using Kath as a punchbag. 'We'll just have to make sure they don't in future.'

'Yeah,' said Jimmy, looking uncomfortable.

'Send one of the club cleaners round to help her out a couple of times a week,' said Annie. 'It's a lot to cope with on your own, two little kids.'

He said nothing.

And why the fuck didn't you think of that yourself, you selfish bastard? wondered Annie angrily. *Couldn't you see the state she was getting into? Or didn't you even care?*

Men! He'd been quick enough to knock her up, but after that he'd clearly lost interest. *Got something going on elsewhere*, she thought. She was very sure about that now. He had some little tart secreted somewhere living in style, while his own wife struggled on in that pigsty.

'So what did you want to see me about?' he asked, pointedly changing the subject.

Yeah, you don't like this line of conversation, do you?

'I want to see Billy Black. Oh yeah – and there's something else. There's a Delaney involvement in this.'

'What?'

'You heard. I think Kieron Delaney's involved.'

'You're crazy,' said Jimmy.

'Crazy or not, I'm fucking well fed up with letting these bastards call the tune, so this is what we're going to do,' said Annie, and told him the plan.

Jimmy Bond stared at her. 'Have you gone fucking mad?' he asked.

'Nope, I'm sane as you are,' shot back Annie. 'I need a bargaining tool.'

'You have,' said Jimmy, nodding dazedly. 'You've gone bloody nuts.'

'Just do it, Jimmy.'

'You'll start a fucking war,' said Jimmy.

Annie stared at him; Jimmy thought she looked mad as a cut snake.

'It's already war,' said Annie flatly. 'It was war the day they killed Max and Jonjo and decided to abduct my little girl. From that point on, it was war.'

'You're fucking crazy,' said Jimmy.

'Yeah, could be. But at least I'm fighting back now.'

Fighting back felt good.

And this time, she was fighting fire with fire.

An eye for an eye, a tooth for a tooth.

35

Jimmy wasn't happy, but for now he was following orders. So Billy Black called two hours later and found Annie still there in the cold, abandoned house.

'Who is it?' she asked as Billy knocked at the door.

'It's Billy, Mrs Carter.'

Annie opened the door. Billy took off his hat, smoothed down his greasy, thinning hair.

Annie led the way upstairs, Billy following silently behind.

He hovered just inside the door as Annie sat down at the head of the table.

'Come in and sit down,' said Annie. 'Any news yet?' she asked.

Billy stared at her. It was like pulling teeth, but Annie waited patiently. If you tried to hurry Billy's thought processes along, he just got muddled and took even longer.

'Has Constantine Barolli been in touch at all?' she asked hopefully.

Billy shook his head.

Fuck it! Hadn't the damned man said he'd sort it? What a load of horseshit. Well, it just went to show. You had to shift for yourself in this world: no one was going to help you. Or, if they did, they'd want a heavy payback in return.

'There's something I want you to do for me, Billy,' said Annie.

Billy looked at her, all attention. Anything his beautiful Annie wanted was perfectly all right with him. He'd always adored her. He still did. He was so pleased she was back. Sorry that she was having trouble, of course. That went without saying. Sad that Max hadn't come back with her, although he certainly didn't miss Jonjo, who had always mocked him mercilessly.

'I want you to tail Jimmy Bond,' said Annie. It had been playing on her mind, the idea that Jimmy was making a fool out of Kath. One way or another now, she wanted to know the truth, because Kath was her kin and she wasn't going to let a prick like Jimmy Bond take the piss out of her.

Billy stared at her, open-mouthed with surprise. 'Jimmy . . . Bond?' he queried.

'That's right.'

'Why?'

Annie told him what she wanted to find out. Billy blushed a bit, and chewed his lip.

'Will you do it?' she asked.

He nodded. 'Yes.'

'And you're sure Mr Barolli hasn't been in touch at all? It's very important, Billy. Vitally important.'

'No. He hasn't been in touch.'

That fly bastard, thought Annie. *Men! All talk and no fucking do.*

'The minute you hear word from him, come straight to me, Billy. All right?'

Billy nodded vigorously.

'That's all now, Billy. Thanks for coming.'

And he backed out of the room as though she was the Queen, and loped off down the stairs and out through the front door, closing it softly behind him.

I'm surrounded by fucking idiots, she thought. It wasn't a comforting thought at all.

She got back to Dolly's place an hour later. Everything was normal, quiet. Darren was upstairs resting. Una was with a client. Ellie was tidying up in the front room.

'She's finished with the game,' said Dolly as she and Annie sat at the kitchen table.

'Can't face it at all now. And I'm not about to force her. So I'm a girl short.' Dolly sipped her tea. 'Well, actually, maybe I'm not. Had a word with Aretha, she'd like to do a couple of days a week and Chris has no objections.'

Aretha had been the brothel's dominatrix before Una got the job. She had married Chris the ex-doorman, much to everyone's surprise, because they had all thought Ellie would nab him.

'But then you'll have two S & M specialists, and who'll manage the older clients?' asked Annie.

'I know. It's just a stopgap. Aretha's mellowed, anyway.' Dolly gave a wry smile. 'Jesus, next to Una she's a fucking saint. Una's a nasty piece of work. I thought she was okay when I first took her on: she was on her best behaviour at the start. Then she started chucking her weight about and, to be honest, she's pretty bloody scary. You want to watch her, you know. I'm serious . . . You heard anything from Barolli yet?'

'No word.'

'Well it's early days.'

'We're running out of time,' said Annie. 'He might be able to find her; he might not. Who knows if he's even got people looking?' She ran a hand through her hair and briefly closed her eyes as desperation ate into her again. 'I need to get the money in place one way or another. Either with his help or without it.'

'Yeah, but if he's telling the truth and they find Layla, then you won't have to worry about the money.'

'Fat chance. There's no word. And how the fuck is he going to find her, Doll? Through a bloody psychic?'

'We've got to hope for the best,' said Dolly.

'Yeah.' Annie let out a breath. 'So what's Ellie going to do now? Is she stopping or going?'

'Going?' Dolly looked at Annie. 'She's got nowhere to go, poor cow. I suppose she could pick up a job with the Delaneys, God knows she's been a good servant to them over the years. But I dunno. For the moment she's doing a bit of cleaning for me and that's about it. I'm a bit pissed off about it, really. Her room could take a proper nice brass who could manage our old codgers and some of the younger clients too. But for the moment all I've got is Ellie, taking up space and fiddling around with the fucking dusting.'

'Does she do a good job on the cleaning?'

'Oh yeah. She does well. Seems to like polishing things, making them all shiny. I told you she'd started on the hand-washing business, didn't I? – she was getting proper manic about it, and that's a really bad sign in a brass, as you know.'

Annie did know.

'Do you think she'd do a bit of cleaning over at my cousin Kath's place?'

Dolly pulled a face. 'You'd need a fumigator, not a cleaner, in that dump.'

'It'd keep Ellie busy, make her feel she's doing something worth while.'

'I'll have a word with her, see what she thinks.'

Ross poked his head around the kitchen door. 'That nutter Billy Black's here,' he said sneeringly, and opened the door wide.

Blimey, that was quick, thought Annie. But Billy was diligent when it came to following Carter orders, she knew that. Now she would find out the real dirt on Jimmy Bond.

Billy came in, taking off his hat, and surprised her.

'I've got news, Mrs Carter,' he said. 'From Mr Barolli.'

Annie gulped, her heart kicking into a gallop. Dolly stood up.

'I've got things to do,' she said. 'You shout me if you need me, Annie.'

'No, Doll, stay,' said Annie. 'I need you now.'

'Then you got me,' said Dolly, and sat back down. 'Come on, Billy, take a seat. Cup of tea?'

Billy shook his head. He was staring cow-eyed at Annie.

'One of Mr Barolli's people told me that he's been making enquiries,' he began.

'And?'

'And so far there's no real news.'

Fucking arseholes! Now Annie was truly irritated

and exasperated. He'd sent Billy here to tell her *that*?

'Is that all?' she demanded.

Billy shook his head.

Annie took a steadying breath. You couldn't hurry Billy. *Slowly, slowly*, she told herself.

'What else then, Billy?' she asked.

'Mr Barolli wants a meet,' said Billy. 'With you, Mrs Carter. He wants more details. That's what his man said.'

Annie stamped down on her exasperation.

'All right. When and where?'

'At his house in Holland Park. Three o'clock today.'

Where was she going with this? She didn't know. In her aching heart Annie felt that this was just another dead end, just another false hope. But any avenue had to be pursued. Any avenue at all.

'All right,' she said. 'You had any luck with Jimmy yet?'

'No, Mrs Carter,' said Billy.

'Okay, keep on it. And you can tell Mr Barolli's man when you see him that I'll be there.'

36

'Tell me anything you know about Constantine Barolli,' Annie said to Tony as he drove her over to Holland Park.

Tony shrugged. The gold cross on his earring glittered and his bald head gleamed in the dim light as he glanced back at her. 'Well . . . he's got Sicilian roots,' he said.

'I know that,' said Annie. Although Constantine didn't have anything other than a New York accent, she had noticed that his gestures gave away his true heritage: they were pure Latin.

'There was some sort of big Mafia cleanup out there,' Tony went on as he wove his way through the traffic. 'Word I heard was, Barolli's grandpa was a big don, the head of the family. Someone took out his son, Vito, who was a *capo*, a made man. Vito was Constantine's father. And – I don't know if any of this is true; it's just word on the

street, you understand? – the grandfather sent
Constantine over to New York to stay with part
of the family there, where it was safer. That's where
Barolli grew up. When he was twenty, he got
married. About the same time, his mother – she
was American, not Sicilian – and his brother got
hit back in the old country by one of the other
families. You know he's got the hair, the silver
hair?'

'Yeah?' Annie had wondered about that –
Constantine was only in his early forties, but his
hair was not so much silver as *white*.

'It used to be black. Black like Mr Carter's, you
know? They say that when he heard about their
deaths, his hair turned that way overnight. Can
you believe that?'

Annie had heard of this sort of thing happening
before. 'Yeah, maybe.'

'And his grandpa died of a broken heart, they
say.' Tony's eyes met Annie's in the mirror. 'Do
you believe that, Mrs Carter? That a person could
actually die of a broken heart?'

Oh yes. Annie believed that all right.

She nodded.

They passed the rest of the journey in silence.

The Holland Park house was quiet today, all the
wedding festivities over and the pink ribbons and
bows gone. Annie eyed the place as Tony parked

the Jag outside. Tony then walked her up the immaculately clean path, although she didn't ask him to.

Taking no chances, thought Annie wearily. Someone had tried to run her down the other day and now Tony's guard was up. He knocked at the door. One of the heavies she recognized from her last visit opened it and looked at Tony, then at her.

'I've got an appointment with Mr Constantine Barolli,' said Annie.

'This is Mrs Carter,' said Tony, eyeballing the man on the door.

But this time she didn't have to sit on the front step and wait until Barolli felt she had waited long enough. This time the door was opened wide.

'Mr Barolli is expecting you, Mrs Carter,' said the man politely.

'Wait in the car, Tony,' said Annie as she was ushered inside.

The same hallway. It looked bigger today, being empty. Still the same lush marbled floor, the huge sweep of the highly polished staircase, the chandeliers dazzlingly alight. All was quiet now. All was peaceful.

The man led her across to the double doors of the study.

So here she was again. Wasting time, she was sure of it. There was no way anyone could find

Layla. She was probably dead already. Annie had to face that, had to *force* herself to acknowledge that cold hard fact.

Her heart clenched and her stomach churned as she thought again of what had already been done to her darling little daughter. Dolly had taken Layla's finger in its little white box and tucked it into the back of the freezer compartment in the fridge. She had shown Annie where it was, had told her that it would keep better in there.

As opposed to rotting out in the air, thought Annie. *Left out, Layla's finger would go bad, decompose . . . ashes to ashes, dust to dust . . .*

Dolly hadn't pointed that out to her, at least. She hadn't needed to. Annie knew. A picture of the finger rotting had crowded into her mind anyway, making her feel sick to her stomach, reminding her vividly of what had happened to Rufio and Inez. There couldn't be anything left of them now in that heat. Poor bastards. Their only crime was to be in the wrong place at the wrong time.

The man knocked at the door.

'Come!' The same voice, American, confident, *macho*.

The man opened the door. 'Mrs Carter to see you, Boss,' he said, and stood back to let Annie in.

Annie stepped inside the study. In full daylight it still looked very much a man's room. A big desk. Leather Chesterfields. Rows of books. You'd swear a lawyer was the sole occupant of this room. Not a mafioso.

The door closed behind her. Constantine Barolli stood up behind the desk and moved smoothly around it, his hand outstretched, palm down.

Annie walked forward.

Again with the hand, she thought in bitter amusement.

He seriously thinks I'm going to kiss it, she thought.

Annie took off her glove and shook hands firmly. His grip was firm, neither crushing nor limp – a neutral, businesslike grip.

'Good afternoon, Mr Barolli,' she said, looking directly into his startling blue eyes. She released his hand.

'Mrs Carter, it's a pleasure,' he replied, and she could see that little flicker of amusement around his mouth again at her refusal to kowtow to him.

'Take a seat,' he said, and moved back behind the desk again.

Annie took a seat on this side of the desk and waited. She could be patient, calm, whatever was required of her in any given situation.

Dig deep and stand alone, she thought.

She was aware that Constantine Barolli was giving her a discreet once-over and was grimly pleased that Dolly had made her shape up despite all her troubles. She knew she looked good today.

She had forced herself to make an effort, to take trouble with her hair and her make-up. She was wearing an elegant black scoop-necked shift dress beneath a beautifully cut black cashmere coat. A luminous string of pearls glimmered at her throat, pearl studs winked in her ears. She was drenched in Femme de Rochas and wearing killer suede courts and black gloves cut from leather soft as silk. She knew she looked good.

And she was prepared to admit that Constantine Barolli looked good too. Only to herself, though. She was the wife of Max Carter and deep down she still ached for him.

But he's dead, whispered that insidious voice in her head.

Suddenly she felt like crying.

It came over her time and again, the stark realization of it all.

Sometimes she could pretend that nothing had happened. And then it would crash in upon her like a tidal wave. Layla snatched. Jonjo shot. Rufio and Inez, her dear friends, butchered. Max . . . *Max*. Her husband. Thrown down a mountain, disposed of like a piece of rubbish.

But it was weak to cry.

She couldn't afford to show weakness here, she knew that.

She took a deep breath. He was watching her. *The silver fox.*

66*Jessie Keane*

In daylight he was even more imposing. Thick, light grey hair; light grey suit. Tanned face that was . . . yes, she could admit this to herself too . . . *very attractive*. More than handsome. A man at the height of his powers, intellectually and physically. Watching her as though she was of interest. Watching her as though she was a woman who was appealing, right now, right here, to him.

'I hear that you want more information,' she said, trying to get her wandering mind back on track.

'Yeah. I'm sorry. We didn't have much time to talk when you called.'

'My fault. I didn't realize there was a family occasion going on.'

'What I want to know is the sequence of events. Everything that happened, step by step. Anything you can think of, anything you can remember.'

Annie took a breath and cautiously started in. She told him about the pool house exploding. About being drugged. Coming to and finding Jeanette still there, Layla gone. She added the lie that Max and Jonjo had taken off the day before on business.

'Where, on business?' Constantine Barolli asked.

Annie shrugged and lied again: 'I don't know. They didn't say. Max never discussed business with me, but he said he'd be gone months rather than weeks.'

Constantine Barolli sat quietly, listening as she ran through a carefully edited version of events.

Edited or not, by the end of it Annie felt that she had relived the whole ghastly experience. She was pale and sweating.

'Have a drink of this,' said Barolli, pouring water from a decanter into two glasses. 'Or would you like something stronger? Brandy?'

Annie shook her head. She sipped at the water and forced herself to breathe deeply and steadily. Tried to convince herself that she was here in Barolli's plush, comfortable study and not in the living hell that her mind had conjured up.

'It must have been shocking for you,' said Barolli after a pause.

'Yeah,' she agreed, thinking that it had been far more shocking than he would ever know. She thought of Jonjo, floating dead in the pool. And Max – one moment there, the next gone for good. She would never see him again. Never again know how it felt to be held in his arms.

'And now your child's in danger.'

'Yeah.' Annie unbuttoned her coat. God, she felt so hot.

A wave of sickness hit her. She swallowed and the room faded to black.

She came to with Barolli's hand on the back of her neck; he was holding her head down between her legs. Instantly she tried to straighten, and immediately he took his hand away. She leaned back in the chair and closed her eyes. The room reeled. She groaned.

'Sorry,' she gasped out.

'Don't be sorry.'

'I'll be fine,' Annie said stiffly.

Fuck it. Going through it all again had been too much. It was still too raw, too painful. She made a gargantuan effort and got a grip on herself. She opened her eyes. Breathed deeply.

'I'm okay now,' she told him.

She looked at him. He was crouched down in front of her, smoothing back her hair from her face, gazing at her in concern. A hot wave of embarrassment engulfed her. She'd made a fool of herself in front of Constantine Barolli again. It was getting to be a habit.

Last time she'd been here she'd sat out on the front step like some demented vagrant and been a talking point for all the wedding guests filing past her. But this time was even worse. This time she had actually *fainted* in his study.

At least I didn't throw up all over his fancy suit, she thought. It was a miracle that she hadn't.

'You're sure you're all right?' he asked.

'Perfectly,' said Annie coolly.

She'd amused him again. She could see it on his face.

Damnit, what did I have to go and do that for? Annie wondered in irritation.

She stood up, annoyed with herself, furious with him.

He stood up too.

They were close. Constantine Barolli was looking directly into her eyes.

'Max is dead, right?' he said.

Annie stared at him in total shock. Then she stepped back, away from him, her eyes moving away from his.

Constantine grabbed her arms and pulled her back. Annie stared at him from inches away, startled, wrong-footed.

'That's the truth, yeah?'

'No,' said Annie.

'Look, let's cut to the chase here. My people have seen the villa, they can read the signs. And I know Max. If he was alive he'd be here, ripping up the entire country and everyone in it to get his daughter back. Shall I tell you what they think, what *I* think? Max died that day, and Jonjo too, on the very day your daughter was snatched. They didn't go *anywhere* on business.'

Annie shook her head. 'Look, Max don't know Layla's missing,' she said desperately. 'There was no way I could get in touch with him.'

Constantine looked into her eyes. 'Liar,' he said.

He let her go and went back around the desk and sat down.

Annie dragged a hand through her hair. She

hadn't bargained on this. Still, she put both fists on his desk and leaned in.

'Look,' she said. 'I need that money. Can you get it, or not?'

Constantine looked at her. 'Half a million pounds sterling,' he said.

'Yes.'

'That's a lot of money, Mrs Carter.'

'I know that. All I want from you is a straight answer. Can you get it, or not?'

'That depends,' said Constantine.

'On what, exactly?' asked Annie.

And so Constantine Barolli told her the deal, and Annie stood there in a daze and listened to what he was saying. Finally, she picked up her gloves, rebuttoned her coat, and left the room – slamming the door shut behind her.

'Ah – hello,' said the man she walked straight into as she was crossing the hall for the front door. She just wanted to get *out* of here.

She paused. 'Sorry,' she said automatically.

Then she looked at him.

It was the dark-haired young man from the restaurant. Annie hadn't liked the look of him at a distance. Close up, he was no more appealing. He was the sort of slimy lounge-lizard type she would go a very long way to avoid, always smiling but ready to plant a knife straight

between your shoulder blades when you turned
your back.

'We haven't been introduced. I'm Lucco Barolli.
You know my father, I believe?'

He was taking her hand. For a minute, Annie
thought the oily git was going to kiss it. There was
something repugnant about Lucco Barolli, something glutinous and unpleasant. *He looks as if he'd
like to drag me off to a dark corner and kick the
crap out of me*, thought Annie with a shudder. His
hand felt wet and soft, disgusting. It was hard to
believe that this *object* was Constantine's son.

'I'm Annie Carter,' she said reluctantly.

'You were here on Saturday, in a meeting with
my father,' said Julio. 'I saw you. And then at the
Ritz . . . we seem to keep coming across each other,
don't we?'

'You don't look like your father,' said Annie.

You look like a snake-oil salesman, she added
to herself.

'Everyone says that.' His smile showed perfect
white teeth but didn't reach his black, black eyes.
'Alberto – my brother – looks like him. He was
with us at the Ritz, you remember? Cara, my sister
– she's just got married – she looks like my father
too. But I look like my mother, everyone says so.
Dark. Latin. A little like you. In fact –' he drew
back and eyed her, assessing – 'you're very like my
mother. *Very* like her.'

285

'She's a very attractive woman,' said Annie, unsure where this conversation was leading. A neutral compliment to the woman she had seen with Constantine's group at the Ritz seemed the safest path. She just wanted to get out of here, but his soft, clammy hand was still holding hers and she couldn't jerk it away without seeming rude . . .

Lucco laughed. It was a distinctly chilling sound.

'Ah, no. You think Aunt Gina's my mother. No, no. Gina's my father's sister. My mother Maria is dead.'

His eyes were suddenly flat, unreadable, as they stared into hers.

'I'm sorry,' she said.

'She died five years ago. And of course my father is devoted to her memory,' said Lucco. '*Utterly* devoted.'

The little fucker's warning me off, realized Annie.

'Of course he is,' said Annie stiffly.

This time she didn't care if she was being rude or not. She didn't give a stuff. She wrenched her hand free.

His eyes sharpened on hers, but she kept staring right back at him.

'Nice meeting you,' said Annie, and swept past him to the front door.

'And you,' he called after her, rather too loudly. 'Likewise.'

37

'So what the fuck happened?' asked Dolly when she got back to Limehouse.

'It's like sticking your hand in a pit full of scorpions,' said Annie, collapsing into a chair in the kitchen and kicking off her heels.

And did she want to do that again?

Simple answer – *no*.

Constantine Barolli could stuff his half a million quid. He could stuff his empty promises about looking for Layla, too. Annie knew she was on her own. She was going to have to go to Plan B.

Whatever the fuck Plan B was.

She sank her head into her hands. 'Christ, Doll, I need a drink,' she moaned.

'I'll put the kettle on.'

'Thanks, Doll.'

'Jimmy been back yet?' asked Annie.

'Nope.'

'Darren and Ellie out?'

'Darren's at the doctor's,' said Dolly. 'Feeling a bit below par, poor kid.'

'He don't look well.'

'Keeps having blackouts. Bit anaemic, maybe.'

'And where's Ellie?'

'Over at your cousin Kath's place, cleaning it up.' Dolly slapped three spoonfuls of tea into the pot and pulled a face. 'Jumped at the chance to do something different like we thought she would – but, my God, I wouldn't wish that fucking dirty hole on my worst enemy. Sorry, I know she's your family, but it's true, ain't it? Don't know how she'll get on there. Probably never want to go back again if I'm any judge.'

'I told Jimmy to get a couple of the club cleaners on the job,' said Annie, taking off her coat and gloves. 'Don't think he bothered, though. He don't seem to take a blind bit of notice of anything I say.'

Which couldn't go on. Annie knew it. Jimmy was going to have to be pulled back into line. Trouble was, she didn't have a clue how to do it at the moment. She didn't have a clue about anything much at all.

'Una behaving herself?' she asked.

'Yep. Can't last. Keep your eye on her. She don't seem the type to take a pasting lying down. She's a brooder, that one.'

Like Lucco, thought Annie.

She thought back to their encounter in the hall at Constantine's. Yes, she'd definitely been warned off. Tony had told her that Constantine and Maria had married when they were both just twenty, then had the three children in quick succession. They had remained together until Maria's death five years ago. Lucco didn't want his dear daddy taking any interest in a woman who looked like dear dead mummy, and Annie knew why. If Constantine remarried, if he fathered another child, then Lucco would see that child as competition – possibly for his father's affection, definitely for his father's position and his money.

He needn't worry, thought Annie sourly.

A liaison with Constantine Barolli was the last thing on her mind.

She thought back, to the shocking thing he had said to her. Still couldn't believe it.

'Penny for them?' Dolly sat down beside Annie and started pouring the tea.

Annie looked at her, startled. 'What?'

'You're miles away.'

'Oh, nothing.' Annie gave a tight smile.

'Did something happen at the Barolli place?'

'What? No. Nothing.'

'Is he going to help then? With the money?'

'No. I don't think he is.'

'But I thought he was a friend of Max's. Well,

at least a business associate. I thought they were tight together.'

Annie shrugged and sipped her tea.

She had sworn to herself that she would do anything, *anything*, to get her daughter back safe.

But not this, she thought. *I can't do this.*

Because Constantine Barolli wanted her in bed.

He'd stated that fact, calmly, clearly, shocking her rigid, making her run for the hills. But how far could she *really* run? Layla's safe return, the money, *everything* hinged on her compliance.

But she just couldn't do it.

So then. Plan B.

And then Jimmy Bond came in, and sat down at the kitchen table across from Annie, and looked at her.

'It's done,' he said. 'We've got him. Shall we go? We'll take my car.'

It was time to stand up and be counted. Annie gathered up her coat and gloves.

'I'll see you later, Doll,' she told Dolly.

Dolly just nodded. She didn't know what was going on and she didn't want to know either. It was better to be left in ignorance.

38

Charlie 'The Dip' Foster was Redmond Delaney's right hand, and right now Charlie knew he was done for.

Some heavy faces had brought him to Smithfield meat market and he knew he was in *big* trouble.

They'd snatched him, worked him over. Taken him completely by surprise.

He'd been at a party at his girlfriend's house, her twenty-first birthday. They'd gone outside for a bit of how's your father and he'd been caught with his trousers down – literally.

So now here he was.

They'd laughed as they'd hung him up here, joking about meat being well hung. Then they'd left him here for an hour, just left him dangling.

He was a tough bastard but right now he was scared shitless.

It was the noise. The awful noise of that thing

coming down on the wooden block. His brain was agile, you didn't get to be well up in the mob without having a few brain cells rattling around in your head, but now his brain kept faltering. That *noise*.

Thunk!

That thing on wood.

Thunk!

Chopping through flesh and bone.

He tried again to get his hands loose from their bindings, but again he failed. He slumped again, exhausted.

They'd hung him up from one of the meat hooks by the back of his jacket collar, laughing as they lifted him up there. The smell had hit him first. The smell of meat, of death. Pigs' heads surrounded him, the skin flayed from the flesh. Their eyes stared at him sightlessly. Sides of beef nudged against him.

The cleaver came down again and a trotter thumped on to the floor.

Thunk!

Oh God help me, he thought. *Please help me*.

But then he knew he'd done bad things. Hurt people. Robbed. Bad things. So perhaps God wasn't listening. Perhaps he was turning a deaf ear.

The butcher with the gentle eyes and the blood-stained apron went on chopping away patiently at the meat.

And now Charlie could see through his stinging eyes that there was a woman approaching.

A woman in black.

All black.

Dark hair and eyes that were just this side of crazy. Black coat. Black leather gloves.

A heavy on either side of her. Known faces. Jimmy Bond, he knew that bastard all too well, moving off to one side and watching, his eyes going from the woman to Charlie, back and forth, back and forth.

The woman stopped several paces away and stared steadily up at Charlie.

He gulped.

'You're Charlie Foster,' the woman said. Her voice was low. 'Are you wondering who I am, Charlie? Or do you know?'

'I don't know,' said Charlie with an effort. Hanging up here was killing him. His head ached, his shoulders were agony.

'I'm Annie Carter.'

Fuck it, thought Charlie. Carter was a name he hadn't wanted to hear, not here, not now.

'And you're the Delaneys' main man,' said Annie. 'Got a question for you, Charlie. Think carefully before you answer.'

Charlie nodded.

'Where is Kieron Delaney?'

'I don't know,' said Charlie.

Jimmy came over, slipping something on to his hand. He suddenly gut-punched Charlie with a brass knuckle-duster. All the air came out of Charlie in a whoop.

'Think again,' said Annie.

Charlie was struggling to get his breath back. He was gasping like a fish out of water.

'Jesus, I don't know,' groaned Charlie, his face screwed up in pain.

Panic blurred his thoughts. His brain felt like mush.

'Come on, Charlie. You can do better than that. Just tell me where Kieron Delaney is and you can go.'

'I don't *know* where he is,' said Charlie. 'If I knew, I'd tell you.'

'I think you *do* know, Charlie. And you'd better tell me.'

'I don't. I don't know,' babbled Charlie.

An eye for an eye, thought Annie.

She nodded to Jimmy.

Jimmy nodded to the boys. They manhandled him back down on to the concrete floor. His legs sagged under him. He was shaking. Urine trickled down his thighs. They held him up between them.

'Put him here,' said the butcher, indicating the block.

Charlie started to scream.

39

Ten minutes later, Annie went outside and was sick into the gutter. Being sick, feeling sick, repulsed, disgusted, was becoming a way of life. For the first time, she seriously wondered if she had the balls for this.

An eye for an eye, a tooth for a tooth.

All very well to think it, say it – but to do it? That was another thing altogether. Layla had lost her finger and her freedom and Annie had craved revenge for that. So Charlie had lost a finger too. However, he still hadn't given away Kieron Delaney's whereabouts. And he wouldn't. Charlie was tough. Scared shitless, yes – but hard as nails. He wouldn't squeal.

'Should we go on?' Jimmy had asked her after the butcher had done the job on Charlie.

She'd shaken her head, disgusted with herself, that desperation had driven her to this. She'd walked out.

Oh yes – and then she'd been sick. Sick as a cowardly dog in the gutter.

Sick like the feeble woman she was. Max wouldn't have been sick. Neither would Constantine Barolli. They would have severed Charlie's digits themselves and then carried right on until he blabbed or died. She knew it.

But she'd done what she had to do. She'd sent a clear message to the Delaneys that they crossed her at their peril. And she wasn't finished yet – not by a long shot.

'You happy now?' Jimmy said, coming out and finding her, apparently composed, waiting by the car.

'Oh, I'm fucking ecstatic,' said Annie coldly.

'There'll be trouble over this,' said Jimmy.

Annie looked at him. For fuck's sake! He was meant to be on her side; he was meant to be her right-hand man. And all she was getting from him was aggro.

'There's already trouble,' she told him. 'I'm unhappy. And when I'm unhappy, you'd better watch out.' She turned away from him and got into the car. Jimmy drove her back to Limehouse in silence and then sped off without a word.

40

It was Friday – party day again. The weeks were speeding past. There were three new girls in, entertaining the punters in the front room. Music drifted out, not too loud of course – had to keep the neighbours in mind. The door from the hall was wide open and Ross was at his station beside the door.

As she passed the open front room door, Annie saw the drinks set out, and the nibbles, and the low, intimate lighting in there. One of the girls was straddling an older punter in an armchair, bouncing up and down. He looked too old to take the strain. Annie hoped she didn't kill the poor old sod: a stiff on the premises would be awkward.

But then, she thought wryly, *it wouldn't be the first time it had happened.*

Two of the girls – pretty, fresh-looking young girls – were kneeling on the carpet giving two punters blow jobs on the sofa. The two men were chatting about the state of their share margins as the girls gave them head. They could have been in the boardroom. They looked the type.

There were rapturous noises coming from upstairs, and the fainter sound of a whip whacking on flesh. *Una.*

Dolly emerged from the kitchen, closing the door carefully behind her. She beckoned to Annie.

'Billy's here,' she hissed. 'He says he's got news for you. Christ, he does pick his moments, don't he?'

Annie hurried into the kitchen, closing the door on the sounds of revelry behind her. Billy Black was there, sitting at the kitchen table, his hat in his hand, his briefcase clutched on his lap, a cup of tea steaming in front of him.

He looked up as she came in, and blushed.

'Hello Billy,' said Annie, and sat down at the table. She looked across at him. 'Dolly says you've got news. Have you found out something?'

Billy nodded and haltingly told her what he had discovered. That he had an address. It hadn't been easy and it hadn't been quick. The quarry had been cagey, taking careful steps, but Billy prided himself on his persistence and it had certainly paid off. He'd found that this was a long-standing arrangement, not an overnight wonder. The quarry had been back and back and back for more.

Annie stood up.

'Right,' she said. 'Come on, Billy.'

Tony was waiting in the car, reading the paper. Senator Kennedy was on the front page and there was trouble in Sudan and Ethiopia. Same old, same old. Annie tapped on the window and he wound it down and looked at her expectantly, and at Billy standing there at her side like a spare part.

'We've got an address to go to, it's not far. Billy's going to direct you.'

Tony nodded and put his newspaper aside. Billy got in the front passenger seat, Annie in the back.

Stammering and halting, Billy directed Tony through the streets until they wound up at a small row of terraces with a neat and tidy air about them. Tony got out and opened the door for Annie. Billy came around the car. They stood on the pavement and looked up at the house in question.

'That's his old Zodiac over there,' said Annie. She'd clocked the registration number when he'd driven her back from Smithfield meat market, and the colour was distinctive: it was definitely the right one. She looked at Billy. 'Make yourself scarce now, Billy. Can you get back home from here?'

'Course I can,' he mumbled, and shambled off along the road.

She didn't want Billy taking any heat because he'd helped her with this.

'Okay, Tone,' she said, bracing herself for this. 'Let's go.'

41

So the kidnappers were not in Palma any more. There had been talk about a boat, so perhaps the scum had already left the island? But *talk* of a boat didn't mean they'd actually got on one, did it? Constantine Barolli's boys had done door-to-door and that had proved worth while. Now they concentrated on taxis, car rentals, and the bars and, yes, the *boats* in and around Palma's harbour to find the route out that the kidnappers had taken. They drew a blank on the taxis and the car-hire firms – nothing on those names, nothing on those descriptions, not a damned thing. Then they started on the bars, talking to bartenders, owners, waitresses.

In one of the last they tried they spoke to two waitresses who said that on the night in question, a Wednesday, they hadn't been working, but Talitha, another waitress, had, and her boyfriend

was a fisherman who had a boat with his father
and – guess what? – sometimes they did little jobs
here and there; not fishing, little jobs, did they
know the sort of thing?

Oh yes, the men laughed, they knew the sort
of thing.

And where did Talitha live? the men asked. Oh,
we couldn't tell you *that*, giggled the girls, and the
men said, oh but you *could*, and smiled, and flashed
enough money that the girls managed to overcome
their scruples towards their colleague's privacy.

It was a very slim chance, but they were used
to pursuing slim chances now.

42

The girl was gorgeous. Blonde, Afro-style hair. Big tits, pink nipples you could hang your hat on. Tiny waist, real womanly hips. *Not* a natural blonde, which was a bit of a disappointment. Reddish bush. But still – luscious. She was the sort who'd run to fat in later life, but he wouldn't be boffing her in later life, so who gave a fuck? And she had too much chat, but then that was women for you, thought Jimmy Bond as he lay in the afterglow of a stupendous sex session.

One of many stupendous sex sessions.

He felt like a tiger in the sack with this girl.

Oh, he'd had other girls since he'd walked up the aisle with Kath. Silly cow got up the duff on their honeymoon – fucking rubber had burst – and after that it was all downhill. First with the morning sickness, then the not wanting sex in case it hurt the kid, then on and on and on, nag, nag, nag, until he'd just tuned her out. When they'd first been married he could have eaten her; now he wished he fucking well had.

He'd been hanging out at the Blue Parrot the night she'd dropped the first sprog, and down the billiard hall with the lads when she dropped the second. By then he knew the drill. Kath was a dirty cow, let the house go all to fuck, and he was fastidious by nature, he hated mess. So what else could he do but look elsewhere for his pleasures?

'Was that the doorbell?' his bed-mate asked, rolling against him and giving him the equivalent of a full body massage.

Jimmy felt himself getting excited all over again. Christ, she was a handful. He clutched at the big breasts, rolling them around in his hands. *Luscious*, he thought. Yeah, that really summed her up. And of course there was another little bonus involved in shagging this particular girl. It turned him on every time he thought about it, and he was thinking about it now.

'You're awful,' she groaned happily, arching her back and moaning. Then she stiffened. 'That *was* the doorbell. Just a tick, sweetheart, I'll have a look, see who it is.'

And she was gone.

Fuck it, thought Jimmy. It would be some frigging door-to-door salesman, trying to get her to buy brushes or cunting encyclopaedias.

'Leave it. They'll go away,' he said lazily.

But she was peeking out through the nets, looking down. Jimmy stretched and yawned and thought *what an arse* as he watched her standing there in the buff. He thought of who else had admired that arse and lay there feeling like a king.

Only trouble was, the Queen had come back, and that was a bit of a downer.

He frowned.

Annie fucking Carter.

The King is dead, he thought. *Long Live the Queen.*

Wasn't that what they always said? He'd heard it somewhere, and he'd rolled it around in his head many times over the years he'd worked the Carter patch. His version had recently changed, however. His version now said: Max Carter the King is dead, and Jonjo the King's brother is dead too, and the new King was going to be him – Jimmy Bond. King of the hill; top of the whole bastard heap.

Only so far it hadn't worked out that way.

Annie fucking Carter.

She seemed to have nine lives, like a cat. She'd been shot in the chest, and lived. Had been set upon by Pat Delaney – and he knew hard men, real faces, who had walked in terror of Mad Pat Delaney and his drugged-up benders. But she'd survived that too.

Couldn't seem to kill the bitch for love nor money.

That fucking skirt had stormed back into the manor like a whirlwind, dishing out orders, and Jimmy was not used to taking orders, not any more. It had suited him down to the ground, Max out in the sun, Jonjo flitting back and forth between the manor and Majorca and not caring too much what was going on. He had taken charge. Now, he was used to *being* in charge. And he didn't like it one little bit that he wasn't King any more.

Of course, he could play it smart, get in good with the Queen. She was certainly tasty, in that stuck-up, 'how dare you think about touching me?' way she had. It was sort of challenging with a woman like that, breaking down the reserve, *penetrating* (and here he congratulated himself on making a really good pun) that thick layer of ice . . . But he didn't like bossy women. And Christ, she was bossy.

Needs a good stiff talking-to, he thought, feeling his erection tenting the bed sheet as he thought about doing just that. *That would sort her out. And I could be just the man to do it. And then I'd be King – because she'd be the Queen, but I'd make sure she took a back seat, left me in charge . . .*

'Shit!' yelped the girl.

She snatched up her robe from the floor.

Jimmy looked at her in surprise, disturbed from a pleasant reverie in which he was master of Annie Carter, master of the whole effing *manor*.

'What?' he asked irritably. He wished she'd stop arsing about and come back to bed. He'd got himself all worked up thinking about how he was going to bring Annie Carter to heel, and he was annoyed that the girl was faffing around the room now, checking her hair in the dressing-table mirror, shuffling into her slippers, telling him to *get up*.

'What the fuck for?' Jimmy asked, sitting up in bed, getting pretty angry now.

If it was her mother calling round again, he was going to give the stroppy old bint a piece of his mind.

The girl was nearly hopping from one foot to another.

'For Christ's sake, Jimmy, get *up*. It's *her*. It's Annie bloody Carter.'

43

'They're in. But they're not answering,' said Annie. She had seen the curtains twitch upstairs.

Jimmy certainly hadn't wasted any time. Straight back from the meat market, straight into bed. Maybe violence gave him a hard on. Annie stood there, still feeling sick, but determined.

Tony rang the bell again.

They waited. And waited.

Finally Annie said: 'Can you get this door open, Tony?'

Tony snorted.

'I could get that door open with the cheeks of my arse.' He paused. 'Pardon my language, Mrs Carter.'

'Okay, open it.'

Tony opened the door with a shoulder charge. It popped back, shattering the lock, and whacked against the inside wall. There was a girl with a blonde Afro halfway down the stairs, frozen in action in a pink dressing gown and slippers. She was holding her head in her hands and looking at her wrecked door in horror.

'For fuck's *sake*,' she complained. 'I was just coming.'

'Hiya Jeanette,' said Annie with a bright smile. 'Long time no see. I like the new hairdo.'

Jimmy Bond appeared at the top of the stairs, pulling his shirt on.

'And Jimmy!' said Annie. 'This is cosy. Well, you going to ask us in?'

They stood around in the kitchen. A nice kitchen too. All the latest units. They'd passed the front room on the way in here: that was nice too. Beautifully decorated, neat. Very nice. Money had been spent. Lots of it. Jeanette didn't offer tea. The silence was ominous.

Annie waited.

'Would you like me to wait in the car, Mrs Carter?' asked Tony.

Annie glanced across at him, leaning against the worktop. Tony looked awkward. Jimmy Bond was a well-respected Carter boss. It was obvious that Tony felt bad about busting in on him like this. And Jimmy wouldn't forget that Tony had witnessed his embarrassment today.

'Yeah, if you'd like to,' she said.

Tony was out of there like a dose of salts. Leaving the three of them, Jeanette fiddling with her hair, Annie quietly waiting, Jimmy with arms folded, scowling at the floor.

'How long you two been an item?' she asked the pair of them.

Jimmy opened his mouth.

'A couple of months,' said Jeanette the motor mouth. 'Jimmy bought me this place, wasn't that good of him?'

'For God's sake, why don't you ever learn to button that fat mouth of yours?' snapped Jimmy.

Jeanette flinched back, flushing, eyes wide.

Oh, so she hasn't had any of the rough stuff yet, thought Annie. *That was a surprise to her.*

'But not too long ago you were with Jonjo, in Majorca,' said Annie.

Jeanette looked sulkily at the floor.

'Yeah, I know, But he wasn't very nice to me. He used to, you know, get rough sometimes.'

Poor old Jeanette.

How long before Jimmy, who was now flavour of the month, began to 'get rough' too? They were still in the honeymoon period. Jimmy beat up on his wife; sooner or later he was going to beat up on his girlfriend too. Annie guessed that Jimmy's good behaviour wouldn't last beyond a year.

She looked at Jimmy.

'Jonjo couldn't have known about this,' she said.

He shrugged. 'He didn't.'

Because he'd have cut your balls out with a blunt carving knife if he had.

'I take it Kath don't know either?' Annie enquired. 'You remember Kath – my cousin? Your wife? The mother of your two children?'

'Hey, don't start on me,' snapped Jimmy, stabbing with his finger. 'You know what she's like. She's a filthy bitch and she's frigid as a nun.'

'She's had two children and she's lost her mother. She's had it hard.'

'No, *I've* had it hard. You don't know what it's like, having to go back to that fucking tip every night, the kids crying, Kath sat there stuffing her face and bleating on about what a struggle her life is.'

'For God's sake Jimmy – Kath's life *is* a struggle. And since you probably ain't bothered to get her any help, I've sent one of the girls over from Dolly's place to help her get the place cleaned up,' said Annie.

Jimmy looked as if he was about to burst a blood vessel. 'You had no right to do that,' he said.

'I had every right. She's family, and she's drowning.' Annie looked at him and her eyes were hard. 'Plus, she's very accident-prone. Keeps walking into doors. Or tripping on the stairs. Or something.'

Jimmy went even redder. 'I don't want you sending people into my home to spy on me,' he shouted suddenly. 'I know what you're doing.'

'I'm helping Kath,' said Annie. 'That's all.'

'No you're not. You're snooping around, seeing what you can find. How did you find *this* place, eh? I know. I was followed, right?'

'Jimmy, you can't be surprised I want to know what you're up to,' said Annie. 'You've been anything but straight with me. For instance, you *knew* about what had happened to Max and Jonjo when we first spoke about it, because Jeanette must have told you. Jeanette usually tells everyone everything, don't you Jeanette?'

Jeanette just stood there, open-mouthed.

'So you knew they'd been hit. You knew, but you made me jump through hoops anyway. Why, Jimmy? For fun? Because you're a fucking sadist?'

'Look.' Jimmy made an effort and got himself back under control. 'I'm entitled to a private life.'

'You're not entitled to treat a member of my family like a fool. Your loyalty should be to her and to the firm. Right now, *I* am the firm. Don't make me question your loyalty again. I want this finished, Jimmy. Kath's your wife – start treating her like it.'

Annie left the room. She went out of the shattered front door and got into the car and sat there, fuming. She was up against a whole shitload of grief. And the one person she was supposed to be able to depend on most, Max's number one man, was proving to be nothing but fucking trouble.

She leaned her head back against the leather upholstery and closed her eyes. She was getting nowhere. Time was slipping past, and she was getting *nowhere*. Snatching Charlie Foster, Jimmy's opposite number on the Delaney firm, had proved nothing except that she had no stomach for torturing people. And there could be repercussions – Redmond and Orla Delaney would not take an attack on a Delaney boy lightly. There could be trouble.

Everywhere she looked, there was trouble. And she was still no closer to getting Layla back alive.

Time.

Time was her enemy.

Time was running out *fast*.

'Where to, Mrs Carter?' asked Tony, starting the car.

'Limehouse,' she said.

I need help, she thought.

Well, it had been offered.

Oh yes – but at a price.

When they got back to the Limehouse brothel, Dolly had news.

Aretha was back in the saddle, doing three days a week.

Ellie was disgusted with Kath's place, but she was cutting through the dirt downstairs like a good 'un, even though Kath had made it clear she didn't want any favours off 'Annie fucking Carter'.

Una and Aretha had – predictably – hated each other on sight.

Darren was off sick again.

'What – again?' Annie asked, worried about him. 'What's up with him Doll – really? He looks damned rough and he don't seem to be getting any better.'

'Don't ask,' said Dolly grimly.

Oh yes – and Billy had dropped by to say that Constantine Barolli wanted another meet with her.

44

It was getting dark by the time they got over to
Holland Park. Tony drove steadily and smoothly
through the traffic while Annie twitched with
impatience in the back.

*This could be it. The breakthrough. He might
have news of Layla's whereabouts. Soon, very soon,
she might hold her daughter in her arms again.*

But it was dangerous to hope too much. Because
it could be bad news, not good.

It could be the *worst* news.

Layla could be dead.

Annie refused to believe that. She could not
allow herself to even think that for a second. Layla
was *alive*. She had to be.

She was ushered inside the palatial house by the
same doorman.

'Mrs Carter, please come in.'

The big man ushered her across the empty,

cavernous hallway and into Constantine Barolli's study.

Third time lucky, maybe, she thought as the doorman knocked on the study door and she was summoned inside.

'Mrs Carter.' Constantine Barolli came around the desk, hand outstretched, palm down. Charming, authoritative, strikingly handsome.

And he knows it, Annie thought. And *again* with the fucking hand, and she still wasn't going to kiss it.

She shook his hand firmly and once more Constantine seemed to be suppressing a smile.

'Is there any news?' she asked, getting straight down to business. 'Or haven't you even bothered to start looking?'

Constantine looked at her.

'Take a seat, Mrs Carter,' he said, and went back around the desk. The light was growing dim as he started to speak. Annie listened and put everything else to the back of her mind, including the shocking thing he had said to her on her last visit here.

Constantine Barolli told her that in fact he *had* bothered. He had bothered quite a bit.

'Yeah?' Annie looked at him sourly.

'Yes,' he said. Then he told her about the *bother* he'd been to.

The word had gone out, he told her. A little girl

315

with dark hair and eyes had been snatched in Majorca. This girl was Max Carter's daughter. The word had gone out in Majorca, Ibiza, Minorca, and mainland Spain, and throughout France and the UK, too. The word was: say nothing, keep watch, report back.

In bars and snooker halls and working men's clubs and discos and restaurants, in Salvation Army hostels and on newsstands and anywhere else the word could be carried, it was delivered, seeping into the minds of the people who heard it, dripping like rainwater on to rock, moving down through layers until it reached the substrata, the basest levels.

Working girls heard about it as they shivered on the streets. Doormen hovering in the neon-lit doorways of strip joints passed the word on. Say nothing, keep watch, report back. Truckers stopping at greasy spoons were passed the word, taxi drivers met on their stands outside airports and in the high streets, and they passed it on to co-workers.

Everyone wanted to find this girl. This was an opportunity not to be missed. A chance to do a favour not only for the New York Mafia don, Constantine Barolli, but also for his London associates, the Carters. They would be effusive in their thanks and generous in their rewards to whomever helped with this, and that help was needed *fast*.

Speed was necessary here: Constantine had made that very clear.

Everyone wanted to find the girl.

And the people who'd taken her.

Three people, they knew that now.

One slim and slight blonde woman, big breasts, blue eyes. Annie thought this was the one who had bodily snatched Layla: it tallied with what Jeanette had told her.

One big, dark-haired, dark-eyed, squat, powerful. Maybe a telephone engineer who had the knowledge to tap lines.

One tall, restless, straight blond hair, crazy eyes. *This one could be Kieron Delaney*, Annie thought. Fast enough to get up close to Max and take him by surprise, because in a fair fight Kieron wouldn't have stood a chance against Max and he knew it.

In Palma they had used the name of Philips, claiming to be a married couple and a brother on holiday together. But none of the three had worn a wedding ring, and they had not seemed like people on holiday. They were edgy, nervous. No one had yet seen the girl with these three people, who had rented a place in Palma from Marietta and Julio Degas. But there had been mention of a faint noise, maybe a child crying, heard once and never explained. And when the three adults had left that place, the big dark-haired one was carrying a large holdall, big enough to hold a child.

The word had spread like lightning, conducted by word of mouth: Constantine Barolli wanted this little girl, Layla Carter, found and delivered safely home to her mother. The person or persons who did him this favour, whatever their contribution, however small, however large, would be paid back a thousand-fold for their efforts.

Constantine filled Annie in on all this and, when he stopped speaking, Annie nodded, a bit dazed by the scope of it. But reassured too. If anyone could help here with this, it was Barolli. Despite all her misgivings, despite the fact that she knew she was out of her depth here, she knew she'd come to the right man. She'd doubted him, but now look – he'd surprised her. He'd got the whole thing moving.

'Soon, hopefully, we'll get more news,' said Constantine.

He reached out and switched on the yellow banker's light on the desk, illuminating them both in a soft glow as dusk crept further in, lengthening shadows.

'Thank you,' said Annie. It nearly choked her to say it, because she had been *convinced* that he was just screwing around, just kicking his heels and wasting time until she was desperate enough to fall into line with his demands.

Constantine shrugged.

'We've started the ball rolling, that's all. Within

two weeks I have to go back to New York. Business. But before then I hope we'll see a breakthrough.'

That soon, thought Annie.

Suddenly her heart was in her mouth. Suddenly she was shaking. She might, she really might, get Layla back.

But if they were carrying her around in a holdall, she must be gagged, restrained, surely? Or drugged.

Oh Jesus.

'You're not going to faint again, are you?'

'No.' Annie shook her head, trying not to smile, trying not to just whoop with joy or maybe even cry her bloody eyes out. 'It's just . . . I can't believe it.'

'Hey – no guarantees,' he warned. 'You know, I've thought about this a lot. And I think to these people the money's a bonus, but maybe they also want to see you squirm. My guess is someone's got their eye on you, Mrs Carter. They're watching you.'

Annie sighed. 'I don't know. I don't even care. I just want to get my daughter back – that's all.'

He nodded. 'I heard there's been trouble. A Delaney man hurt. Rumours, you know.'

Annie looked at him blankly.

'There's always rumours, Mr Barolli,' she said.

He nodded. 'Do you suspect Delaney involvement in this?'

319

Annie shrugged. 'The Carters and the Delaneys are old enemies.'

'Sure. But go easy. These things escalate. You pick up a brick, they pick up a knife, you pick up a gun, they throw a grenade. And so on. You know how it goes. Things can turn ugly.'

He looked at her. Annie said nothing.

Constantine sighed and went on: 'Maybe we can turn this thing around now, get a good result. There's hope.'

And before I had none, thought Annie. She owed Constantine Barolli, big time. But then, he had already pointed that out to her the last time they'd met.

These people always want payment, Jimmy Bond had told her. *They don't ever do favours for nothing.*

But then, she knew what Constantine Barolli wanted. He'd made it very plain.

It wasn't the Carter clubs.

It wasn't Queenie's old house.

It wasn't, as Jimmy Bond had feared, the entire manor.

It was *her*.

And she wasn't sure she could bring herself to give him that.

Constantine rose, closed the curtains on the encroaching darkness of night. Suddenly the study was cosy, comfortable. Then he came around the desk and stood there looking down at her.

Their eyes locked.

Constantine Barolli extended his hand, palm down.

'Now, Mrs Carter,' said Constantine, his blue eyes holding hers. 'Kiss my hand.'

Well, she'd known this was coming. She knew there would be a price to pay. And now was the time that she was expected to pay it.

'Mr Barolli,' she said candidly, 'I haven't seen any real results yet. When I see results, maybe I'll consider paying the price for those results.'

Constantine looked down at her. Then he laughed.

'Mrs Carter, you have a lot of nerve, and I admire that. But my patience has its limits.'

Annie looked at him. Looked at his hand, still outstretched to her.

What the hell, she thought. *For Layla*.

She clasped his fingers and brought his hand closer to her face. Inclined her head slightly. Looked at the ring on his index finger. A thick band of gold, set with a scattering of small, perfect diamonds that glinted as the light caught them. She could smell his cologne – Acqua di Parma. Classic, fresh . . . *arousing*.

Surprised at that, Annie started to draw away, but his fingers had closed around hers and she was swiftly pulled to her feet. She staggered slightly, caught unawares, and found herself being held tightly against Constantine Barolli's chest.

She felt his breath, warm and sweet-scented on her cheek, and quickly turned her head away.

'Now my lips,' he said.

'Let go of me,' she said, alarmed, shaken.

'Mrs Carter, this was always part of the deal. As I told you the last time we met.'

Annie turned her head and glared at him.

'I can't,' she said. And it was the truth.

She was Max's wife. *Max's.* Everything in her fought against this. Yes, she had known it would be expected. Logically, she had even begun to accept that this would be the case. She had known from the very first meeting that Constantine Barolli had been drawn to her. His wife had been dark haired and dark eyed and so was she. Probably – like Max – he had always been turned on by brunettes. He was doing her a favour – and she was expected to return it.

All perfectly logical and reasonable.

But emotionally, impossible.

Constantine took hold of her chin and turned her head toward his. Annie's eyes met his, obstinate, panicked.

'He's dead,' said Constantine.

'No.'

'Yes. You didn't tell me the truth about what happened in Majorca. You told me Max and Jonjo were in Spain on business, and I'm telling you they're not. For one thing, we tried to find them, and you know what? We can't. For another, there was a lot of blood on both sides of the pool. And brain matter too. Now – these people didn't hurt you, and they didn't hurt the girl with you. And Layla was indoors. Do you see where I'm going with this?'

All right, she'd lied to him. Big fucking deal. In every other way that mattered for the sake of finding Layla, she had told him the truth.

'He's alive,' she said.

'He's dead. I told you. If Max was alive he'd be here. He'd be tearing this whole country and half of Europe apart to find his child.'

'He can't be here.'

'No he can't. Because he's dead. All right, don't admit it to me. Even if all the evidence points to that. Don't admit it to anyone else. But at least admit it to yourself.'

Annie stared at him.

'Is that what you did, when your wife died?'

He paused. She had surprised him. 'Yes. Exactly.'

'I'm like her,' said Annie.

He looked at her curiously. 'Who told you that?'

'Your son. Lucco. In fact, he warned me off last time I came here.'

Constantine paused for another beat, digesting this.

'You still haven't done it, Mrs Carter,' he said.

'What?' She wished he'd let her go. Wouldn't admit that it felt good, being held in his arms. Warm and secure. A safe place.

Safe!

Constantine Barolli was anything but safe. He was a big-time crook. And she was Max's wife.

His widow, you mean, said the voice in her head.

'You haven't kissed my lips.'

A kiss. Would it really hurt?

Betraying Max, thought Annie, *that's what it was. Not just a kiss.*

But then, Max was dead.

There, she was admitting it to herself. Max was *dead*.

And Constantine Barolli wanted her. She could feel how much he wanted her.

'Think of this,' said Constantine, 'as therapy for a broken heart.'

Annie shrugged, feigning nonchalance. Convincing nobody, not even herself.

'If he's dead – and that's only your say-so – then what makes you think I'm sorry? We could have been at each other's throats night and day. I might be glad he's gone.'

Constantine stared at her so long that she had to look away.

'You're not glad he's gone,' he said quietly.

'Every time I look at you, I can see your heart is broken.'

Smooth, charming bastard, she thought. That was one thing Constantine Barolli had in bucket-loads – charm.

'One kiss,' said Constantine.

One kiss and I'm out of here, she thought.

He was taller than Max. She was tall, too, but even in heels she had to stand on tiptoe to reach his mouth. Steeling herself, she put her lips against his. Kissed him. Then instantly pulled back – or as far back as she could get, because his arms were around her, pulling her in closer, closer.

And now he was kissing her. His hand slid up her back, clasping her neck, holding her head still and now this was a real, full-bodied kiss. His tongue was in her mouth. He was holding her tight against him. Annie felt stifled, delirious, unreal. This couldn't be happening. She was betraying Max. She was being kissed by Constantine Barolli. And then the door opened and Lucco's voice was cutting through the moment like ice, saving her – thank God – from further embarrassment, from her own stupid animal urges.

'Oh . . . I'm sorry, Papa – I thought you were alone.' Lucco paused, taking in the spectacle of his father in a passionate clinch with a woman. 'I hope I'm not interrupting anything?'

45

It was dark when Tony pulled up outside Dolly's place. He walked Annie to the door, glancing left and right. Someone had tried to kill her and he was being extra cautious.

'I won't need you again tonight, Tony. Thanks,' she said, as Ross opened the door to her, outlining her in yellow light from the hall.

Tony did the right-left glance thing again, planted a hand on her back and gently but firmly pushed her inside. 'Don't stand about in doorways, Mrs Carter,' he said. 'Too visible.'

And he pulled the door quickly closed behind her.

Ross went off to the kitchen and for a moment she was alone in the hall. She leaned back against the front door, her mind in total turmoil. Was she glad Lucco had interrupted them, or disappointed? She couldn't believe that she had actually been kissing Constantine Barolli.

She pushed a shaky hand nervously through her hair, trying to collect her tumbling thoughts, trying to regain what little composure she had left.

'*Fuck* it,' she said savagely under her breath, closing her eyes, thumping the door with her fist in anguish.

What was happening to her? Her husband was barely cold, her daughter was in danger, yet there she'd been kissing another man. Was she going completely off her head?

Dolly was coming along the hall as Annie started to unbutton her coat. She froze at the look on Dolly's face.

'What's up, Doll?' she asked.

'Mr Delaney's in the front room. He says he's come to see you.'

Annie stopped taking off her coat. Checked her pockets. The kiyoga in one, the gun in the other. She slipped one hand in her pocket and grasped the gun. *Kieron fucking Delaney.* At last. This time, given half a chance, she would finish this for good. She would put him down like the mad dog he was.

She thought of Layla's finger.

Max, dead.

Jonjo, shot between the eyes.

Rufio and Inez, butchered.

Now it's your turn, you bastard, she thought. But then she paused. No. She mustn't act in haste.

He might be here to review terms for Layla's return. She had to slow down, to think, to talk . . . but later, given the merest chance, she would kill him. She swore she would do that.

'It's okay, Doll,' she said, sounding surprisingly calm even to her own ears. 'I'll talk to him.'

And she went into the front room and closed the door behind her.

She leaned against it and looked at the man standing there.

It wasn't Kieron Delaney. It was *Redmond*, his older brother. Orla's twin and the boss of the Delaney mob.

Redmond!

Once her friend. Cool and red haired and immaculate in black coat, black leather gloves, black suit, and shoes. Just the same as always. Emotional as a block of stone. Pale green eyes watching her through a fringe of reddish-blond lashes. Tall and slender and warm as an icicle. Not a bruiser like his dead brothers Tory and Pat. A thinker, and all the more dangerous for that. A cold, bloodless ruler.

Her hand closed over the gun in her pocket.

He had his hand in his coat pocket too.

'Mr Delaney,' said Annie with a nod. Her heart was thumping.

The head of the Delaney clan was standing here in Dolly's front room, confronting the head of the

Carter clan. But they were on *his* patch, not Annie's. He looked very cool, very confident. As always.

'We haven't seen each other in some while,' he said. 'Orla sends her regards.'

'That's kind of her.' Was he going to just shoot her? Would she have time to shoot back, before she died?

And what would happen to Layla then?

He was staring at her, his eyes intent, his expression regretful. 'But sadly this is not a social call,' he said.

'Oh?' Annie's mouth was dry.

'I have a reputation to protect, Mrs Carter.'

'I understand that.'

The pale eyes stared into hers. 'Do you? Good. Because I've been very fair, wouldn't you say? I allowed you to be here, and said nothing. As a matter of courtesy, because we were once business associates, I allowed that. But it seems that now you are taking advantage of my generosity, Mrs Carter. You will understand that I cannot be seen to do nothing when my right-hand man is abused. That would indicate weakness on my part, and that might lead on to trouble.'

Annie nodded. His voice was just as she remembered when she used to take his weekly phone calls. The same musical Irish lilt, sounding so calm, so assured, but now promising mayhem.

He was going to kill her. Shoot her dead where she stood.

She knew it now.

She wondered why she didn't care more. Maybe she was just tired of the struggle. Trying to save Layla. Mourning Max. Attempting the impossible in winning over Max's boys. Trying not to admit to herself that she was going to sleep with Constantine Barolli to get her daughter back. Wondering how she could bring herself to do that, hating herself because she had relished his kisses, felt desired, felt *wanted*, and that feeling had been good. And would poisonous Lucco stand aside and watch his position within his father's firm rendered unstable? Would he risk letting his dead mother be usurped by another woman?

Dig deep and stand alone, she thought.

That was what she had always done.

But she was tired now, tired of finding another iota of strength to carry on, tired of standing alone against the world. It was strange to her now, doing that. Her love for Max had made her weak.

Redmond Delaney looked into her eyes.

Silence settled between them.

'We never involve the police, do we, Mrs Carter?' he said quietly. 'We always take care of our own business.'

'Yeah,' said Annie. 'That's true.'

What the hell, she thought. *Constantine was*

right. He warned me this could happen. And now, do I care? Not much.

'I did say I hoped your visit here would be a short one, didn't I, Mrs Carter?' said Redmond. 'In my note. You did *get* my note?'

'I got it,' said Annie.

'And yet here you are – still.'

'I won't stay much longer.'

'No,' he said. 'You won't.'

Annie nodded. *Get on with it*, she thought.

'And now I have business that I have to take care of and regrettably it involves you,' he said.

Annie wondered why she couldn't just shoot. The gun was in her hand, Max's hair-trigger gun; it was loaded; she was ready to deal out death at a moment's notice.

Redmond would shoot first, and this time she would die. No recovery, no hope of redemption this time. Just blackness, just death.

I'll be with Max.

And soon with Layla too.

But Layla wasn't dead yet. That jolted Annie. Layla had had no chance to even live her life. She was so young, everything ahead of her. She ought to grow up into a beauty, perhaps marry, have children of her own. But if Annie died, she knew that Layla was finished, her story unwritten.

Something in Annie choked at that. She couldn't accept it.

Her life had become intolerably hard, but she had to live – for Layla.

Her hand tightened on the trigger, and she gently released the safety catch. But then Redmond took his hands out of his pockets.

Her hand grew still.

'Redmond,' said Annie.

'Yes?'

'There's something I have to ask you.'

He nodded. 'Go on.'

Annie swallowed. She took her hands out of her pockets too. 'Where's Kieron?' she asked.

Redmond's long, pale face twitched briefly with amusement.

'You don't change – Mrs Carter,' he said.

'So I'm told. So where is he?'

Redmond was silent a moment, watching her face. Then he said: 'He's in the graveyard, Mrs Carter. Kieron's dead.'

46

'That's a lie,' said Annie.

'I assure you, it's the truth.'

'I don't believe you,' said Annie, her eyes searching his face, looking for signs of a lie. 'Until I see his rotting *corpse*, I won't believe you.'

'You think he's snatched your child, don't you? Oh yes, I know about that. I've heard the rumours. But think again, Mrs Carter.' Redmond's smile was bleak. 'My younger brother is dead. Dead and buried and beyond hurting anyone any more.'

Annie looked at him, open-mouthed.

It *had* to be Kieron who was doing this to her.

If not Kieron, then who? Who could possibly hate her so much as to cause her such torment?

But she looked at Redmond's face and saw that he was telling the truth.

'When did he die?' she asked numbly.

'Two years ago. In Spain. He was painting in Andalusia. He cut himself when he was sharpening a pencil, isn't that silly? He had surgical scalpels to do it with, obtained through a friend of the family who worked as a nurse. Cut his finger, didn't get treatment, developed blood poisoning, and died. All perfectly accidental and entirely preventable. By the time we got to hear about it, he'd been dead for a fortnight.'

And you're even cold-blooded about that, thought Annie.

'Did you see the body?'

'Mrs Carter, of course I didn't. Two weeks after the event, in that heat? It wouldn't have been a pretty sight.'

'The grave, then?'

'Yes, I saw the grave. And I can tell you exactly where it is.'

'He *can't* be dead!' she burst out.

'That's what Orla said,' Redmond told her. 'She was wrong, Mrs Carter, and so are you. Kieron is dead.'

'No . . .' Annie was shaking her head.

It couldn't be true. She had been so sure it was Kieron behind all this. It *had* to be Kieron. Redmond was just protecting him . . .

But then she looked at Redmond again. Saw the truth written in his face. Saw the sorrow behind the blank coldness of those pale eyes.

He'd lost all his brothers now. Only had his sister left.

Kieron Delaney was dead.

Someone else was doing this to her.

But who?

'I'm really sorry about this, Mrs Carter,' said Redmond, and walked towards her.

So this was it.

The end of the road.

Annie tensed as Redmond came closer, but she didn't touch the gun again or even the kiyoga. She waited to see what he was going to do. Maybe slit her open with one of Kieron's scalpels. Maybe throttle her with his bare hands.

Redmond came up to the door and stood right there in front of her, inches away.

'I really do regret this, Mrs Carter,' he said, and reached past her and opened the door. 'Finish your business, and don't take too long. I want you out of here,' he said, and then he was gone, closing the door gently behind him.

She was still in one piece.

Annie slumped against the wall. She heard him going softly along the hall, heard the front door open and close. For a moment there was silence, then Dolly threw the front room door open and looked wildly round it. She saw Annie standing there and put a hand to her chest.

'Fuck! You're all right.'

Annie nodded. Couldn't get a single word out. *Kieron Delaney was dead.*

And what the fuck did Redmond mean by what he'd said? Yes, she was still alive, and he was going to let her finish her business here. But her stomach was doing somersaults; she felt sick with apprehension.

She put a hand to her mouth to stifle a groan of horror at what she might now have unleashed. *I was wrong. Oh Jesus, I was wrong*, she thought, half crazed with the realization of it.

She had made a huge mistake. Misread the signs. Fastened in her panic and despair on answers that were hopelessly misguided. There would be blood spilled over this. Redmond Delaney had something planned. Something bad.

47

Next morning they were all around the kitchen table having breakfast – Ellie, Darren, Dolly, and Annie; no Una, thank God. Then Aretha breezed in like a chic black tornado, her hair in a huge Afro, a tan Afghan coat swirling around her, a purple feather boa wrapped around her neck, her six-foot frame hoisted even further upwards by three-inch platform soles.

'Hey, girlfriend,' she greeted Annie with a grin.

Annie stood up and was enveloped in a bear hug. Aretha took her shoulders and pushed her back and looked at her face.

'You look like shit, Annie Carter,' she said frankly.

'You, on the other hand, look bloody great,' said Annie.

Aretha was right. She *did* look like shit. Felt like it too. She was in a state of terror and bewilderment so bad since seeing Redmond that she wondered if all this was going to drive her completely mad.

'I get by,' said Aretha modestly, giving her a high-five.

Nodding at her other friends, she took off her coat, revealing skin-tight denim hot pants and a tie-dyed cheesecloth shirt. Dolly poured her a mug of tea and Annie sat back down, budging up to make room for Aretha.

'So, you still in the biz then?' Aretha asked Annie.

'Nope. Going straight. How's Chris?'

'Oh, he cool,' said Aretha.

'Yeah, but is he cool about *this?*' asked Annie, trying to take an interest. 'You coming back to work and everything?'

'I tol' you, he cool. No worries.'

Annie glanced across at Ellie, who was diving into the biscuits again, her chubby face suffused with angry colour. Darren looked down in the dumps, too. He looked really ill and it worried her. She turned her attention back to Aretha. Aretha's presence here might rattle Ellie's cage, but it would also give this place a much-needed shot of exuberance.

'Well, that's good,' said Annie.

'I've got something to tell you that's not so good,' said Ellie.

'Oh?'

'Your horrible cow of a cousin kicked me out.'

'What, Kath?'

'How many cousins you got? Yeah, Kath. Your dirty-bitch-mother-from-hell cousin. Those poor kids.'

'So what happened?' Annie asked, feeling a surge of anger at her description of Kath – but it was accurate. Ellie was only telling it like it was, annoying though it was to hear.

'Told you,' said Ellie past a mouthful of biscuit. 'She kicked me out cold. I was just minding my own business and going up to start doing the bedrooms – I ain't been up there yet, had my hands full downstairs, I can tell you – and she went apeshit. She said to get out and not bother coming back. Said she didn't want me poking around among her private things, it gave her the creeps. I ask you. I was getting sick of it anyway, working there,' said Ellie. 'I mean, the place is a tip. I don't mind a bit of mess, but that place is something else. And she was always following me around the place while I cleaned, too. Actually, I never saw the upstairs at all. I wasn't sorry when she told me to clear off.'

'Well,' said Annie. 'At least you tried.'

'I certainly did,' said Ellie, giving Aretha a smug glance, as if she'd just got a commendation off teacher. Then she looked at Annie. 'I was sort of thinking, maybe you've got something going for me at the Carter clubs?'

Annie shook her head. 'The clubs are shut.'

'Yeah, but you could reopen them,' said Ellie.

'Not right now,' said Annie.

Christ, didn't she have enough to think about without that?

And open them as *what?* Jimmy was right about one thing: the old-style clubs that Max had favoured were no longer in fashion. Strip joints were the new thing. And discotheques. Not classy nightclubs. Those were going to the wall every day. She knew that. Yeah, Jimmy was right. But right *now,* she didn't have the strength or the inclination to tackle the problem.

'Come on,' wheedled Ellie. 'We could all help. It'd be us against the world again. The four musketeers.'

'Except there's five of us,' pointed out Darren, nodding at Aretha as he sat there chewing a hangnail, shoulders hunched as if against the cold. It was toasty warm in the kitchen.

'Don't split hairs – we could do it,' pouted Ellie.

'Annie don't want to do it,' said Dolly, giving Ellie a warning look. 'She's got a shitload of problems already, don't talk rubbish, Ellie.'

Ellie's expression was sulky. 'It was just a thought.'

'An' a good one,' said Aretha. 'But maybe not right now.'

'Who asked you?' snapped Ellie.

Aretha shrugged amiably. 'Just sayin'.'

'How you getting on with Una?' Annie asked her, tactfully changing the subject.

She knew Ellie was needled by Aretha coming back here to work. Dolly had said there might be one or two minor ructions about it, because Aretha had what Ellie had always wanted – a good steady husband in Chris, a home, a proper life, maybe even soon a baby. It offended Ellie that Aretha was coming back here to get pin money and a few thrills when she had all that Ellie desired. But Annie thought that if Ellie pushed her luck too far with the sharp comments, then Aretha's legendary good nature might reach the edge of its endurance. And, when that happened, she would without doubt kick Ellie straight up the puss.

Aretha rolled her eyes at mention of Una. 'Oh, she just a *barrel* of laughs that one. Sashays around the place like she own it. Don't you worry, I got her number. An' from what I hear, you have too, Annie girl. Knocked her showy white behind all down the stairs, I heard. Wish I'd seen that. Good goin', sister.'

The doorbell rang.

'First punter of the day,' said Dolly, standing up and stretching. 'Come along, troops, time to shake a leg.'

*   *   *

341

A week on Friday, the kidnappers would be expecting Annie to pick up the phone and say yes, she had the money.

Today was Wednesday.

Annie's guts churned as she lay on Dolly's big comfy bed that afternoon, listening to the sounds of sex all around her in the other rooms. The moans, the shrieks, the bouncing bed springs.

A week on Friday.

In just over a week, she was going to have to perform a miracle. Produce the money. That huge amount of money. Or risk losing Layla's life. Constantine still hadn't said a definite yes or no to that, and she knew what he was waiting for. For her to succumb, to agree to his demands.

She listened to the sounds of sex. Couldn't help it. The sighs, the groans, the secret shared laughter . . . she'd had all that and more with Max. He had been a wonderful lover: rough, passionate, vigorous.

She thought of Constantine Barolli, and into her mind came the treacherous images that she'd been fighting off since she had last seen him. What would he be like as a lover? She knew he would be different to Max. Subtler, she thought. Slower. More sensuous. Very different.

She turned over, beat at the pillow, tried to get comfortable, tried not to feel the ache of it, the soft siren pull of sex.

If the people who were looking for Layla actually found her, would Constantine tell her, or would he withhold the information until his demands were met?

Annie rolled over, hugging herself. She was supposed to be resting, but she couldn't. She was churning around at night, exhausted during the day. Dolly had suggested she take a nap in the afternoon, but she couldn't sleep. Just couldn't. The tension of it all was getting to her, gnawing away at her remaining shreds of composure.

She buried her head in the pillow and thought: *What the fuck am I going to do?*

And the answer came back, loud and clear. *Whatever you have to, to get Layla back alive.*

48

Constantine Barolli was at his desk when the call came in.

'We've got a line on something,' said a male voice.

'Go on.'

'The other woman who was there when the kid was snatched. Nasty background she's got.'

'Yeah?'

'Oh yeah. A brother and two sisters, records for GBH, smash and grab, demanding money with menaces. One of them's called Vita; she was in Palma the day before the hit at the villa with another blonde woman, she bounced a cheque on a pair of shoes, the shop owner was *very* annoyed.'

'Okay, I want to know all about this family, where they are, what they're doing, *capisce?*'

'You got it.'

The line went dead.

49

Max was knocking on the door. A soft, insistent knocking, wanting to come in, to know what the fuck she was playing at, considering sleeping with another man when she was his, absolutely and completely his. Hadn't he always told her so? Hadn't she said she'd loved him forever?

Knock, knock, knock.

But the thing was this. If Max was her husband, her *one true love*, then how could she be lying here now thinking about Constantine Barolli? Thinking about how it had felt to be held by him, how it was to be kissed by him. Thinking that if that little rat Lucco hadn't interrupted them, then she could have betrayed Max, trashed her wedding vows, right then and there.

Knock, knock, knock.

It was Max at the door. Furious with her, of

course, because he would know, Max always knew everything . . . but wasn't Max dead?

A shiver coursed through her body and the erotic images faded. Her and Constantine, twined together like snakes in a broad, warm bed. Suddenly all that was gone, and instead there was a nightmare image in her brain. *The Monkey's Paw.* One bleak Christmas – all her childhood Christmases had been bleak – her drunken mother Connie had sat Annie and her sister Ruthie down and said she was going to tell them a ghost story.

It was Christmas Eve, it was traditional, she told them. She was a little drunker than usual. It was Christmas, she was alone bringing up two kids, their father had fucked off long since. Times were hard. So she drank a little more, keep the cold out. Medicinal purposes only, ha ha. She sat them down and read them the story.

It was a chilling tale, about a son horribly injured and killed in an accident, and a grieving mother who had a magical monkey's paw which would grant her three wishes – and she wished to have her son back. Of course she did. In the middle of the night, there came the knocking. Her son was there. He had come back to her, fresh from the grave, mangled, inhuman, rotting . . . as Max was coming back to Annie now.

Knock, knock, knock.

With a sense of impending doom, she was leaving the bed. She reached for the door, and it swung wide . . .

Suddenly she was wide awake. Bolt upright in the bed, her hand clamped to her mouth to stifle a scream of horror. She was sweating with terror. *Oh Jesus no*, she thought helplessly, screwing her eyes tight shut and then opening them wide. It was dark. It was . . . night. She'd fallen asleep at last, and . . . oh shit . . . it had only been a dream. A horrible fucking dream.

Knock, knock, knock.

This time she did cry out.

Someone really *was* knocking.

She'd heard it, there, for real – not dreamed, not imagined.

She saw a slit of light appear under the bedroom door. Outside, a car door slammed, and an engine roared away into the night. The landing light went on. Someone else had heard it too. Shaking, Annie threw back the covers and swung her legs to the floor. The cold night air hit her overheated skin, making her shiver. Voices out there now, nervous voices, worried voices. Someone was going downstairs.

Don't answer it, thought Annie, the dream still winding its foul tendrils around her brain.

She snatched up Dolly's robe from the floor, scrabbled around, found the light switch, blinked against the sudden glare. Looked at the little clock on the dresser. It was two thirty in the morning. Dolly had let her sleep right through. She stood up, slipped the robe on, belted it. Went over to the door and flung it wide.

Dolly was going down the stairs. Darren was watching her from the landing in his pyjama bottoms, no top.

Christ, he's skinny, thought Annie. *You could play a sodding tune on those ribs.*

Ellie was just coming out of her room, belting her robe around her bulky middle, yawning. She looked at Annie, at Darren, at Dolly descending the stairs.

No Una. The place could be firebombed and Una wouldn't wake. Too stoned, probably.

'Dolly!' Annie hissed it. Dolly froze on the bottom stair and glanced back up at her. Dolly looked pale, worried.

'Wait,' said Annie, and went back into Dolly's room.

She got the gun out of the knicker drawer and went out on to the landing and down the stairs to where Dolly stood.

Dolly looked at the gun, wide-eyed, then at Annie's face.

'Who the hell can it be?' Dolly whispered.

Knock, knock, knock.

They both flinched back, staring at the door.

348

'I don't know,' whispered Annie. 'But we've got to be careful.'

Ross had left at one o'clock, after close of business. No help there. The front door was securely locked, chained; it was solid. But there was a letter box, through which people could put post – or burning rags. She thought of Tony's words at Jeanette's equally solid-looking door: 'I could get that door open with the cheeks of my arse.' She thought too of Redmond Delaney's visit, his almost sorrowful face as he told her that something would have to be done about her actions. Something bad.

Knock, knock, knock.

And then they heard a long, spine-chilling, agonized moan.

They froze.

Annie looked at Dolly and Dolly looked at her. Dolly swallowed hard. There was someone out there, someone *hurt.*

Or was there?

Was it just a blind, to entice them to throw the door open, to admit whatever trouble was lurking out there in the shadows of the night?

'Who the hell is it?' bleated Ellie from the top of the stairs, hugging Darren.

Annie shushed her.

She moved to one side of the door, and hauled Dolly after her. If someone was going to blast the door with a shotgun, they would have been standing right in line. Not clever.

Knock, knock, knock.

Annie licked her dry lips. Her heart felt as if it was going to burst right out of her chest, it was beating so hard. She flicked off the safety catch and held the gun at the ready.

'Who is it?' she shouted at the door.

The moan again. Just that. No answer.

Annie yanked back the bolts, undid the chain, braced herself, held the gun at the ready. She threw the door wide open – and Billy Black fell at her feet.

It was what was left of Billy, anyway. What tumbled into the hall was no longer a human being. It was a tangle of arms and legs and clothes, all bathed in blood. But the face was Billy's.

'Oh Jesus, oh Jesus, oh Jesus,' Dolly was saying over and over again, one hand clutching her midriff, the other half over her mouth. She looked as if she was going to be sick.

Ellie was screaming.

Annie stood, dumbstruck, horrified, at what lay at her feet. She could not believe what had been done to him. Could not take it in.

Because of me. Her mind seemed to flinch at the thought.

Redmond Delaney, standing in the front room talking to her, full of regret but saying he had to act, had to be *seen* to act, or there would be trouble and he wouldn't have that. Cold, efficient Redmond Delaney. Needing to strike at Annie in a decisive way. Needing to hit hardest where it would hurt her the most. Regretting it, naturally. But doing it anyway.

And who was her staunchest ally, the one Carter boy who would walk the streets for her tirelessly, doing her business, fetching and carrying for her? Why, Billy of course. Billy who had for years been allowed safe passage around the Delaney manor because Redmond Delaney had decreed it. Now that decree had been violently revoked.

Billy moaned and rolled over, lying there like a parcel that had come unwrapped. There was a frayed bit of rope still tied around his waist and she thought she knew what they'd done to him. He'd been dragged through the streets behind a car, his clothes dissolving into tatters, his skin flaying from his poor broken body. Annie felt herself starting to gag, but she forced it back when she saw that his eyes were open. They were open and they were looking at her.

She put the gun down and knelt beside Billy. The blood was still seeping from him, very slowly, where once it must have gushed. Blood soaked the hem of Dolly's robe. His eyes were still open, looking at her but already taking on a milky glaze.

I did this, she thought, and somewhere inside

her she howled with grief and rage at what had happened to this poor soul who worshipped her. But she smiled down at him, trying desperately to hide the shock.

'Hello Billy,' she said, and stroked his bloody cheek. The flesh was cold. Already, it was cold. She felt her smile falter, but pasted it back on.

His lips moved. He was trying to say something. Annie put her head down closer to Billy's, looked in sorrow at the long, thin, vacant face, the soft brown eyes that only ever wanted to please her.

'You're going to be all right, Billy,' she said. 'Everything's going to be all right.'

Which was a useless lie, but if it gave him some comfort, why not?

His mouth was moving again. The pool of blood was spreading, enveloping Annie's knees, the robe soaking it up like a sponge, seeping into the long thin rug that ran the length of the hall.

Annie was aware of Dolly moving, stepping towards the phone to get an ambulance, but she looked up and shook her head firmly. Dolly stopped moving. Ellie stopped screaming. They were silent now, watching Billy.

His mouth moved. His eyes never left Annie's face. He tried again.

'My . . . beautiful . . . Annie,' he managed to mumble at last.

And then Billy Black quietly died.

50

Annie called Tony, who picked up the phone, barely able to speak through his tiredness.

'H'lo?' he grunted.

'It's me. Can you come over? One of the customers is playing up and we need a hand, he's made a bit of a mess of the place. You might need a van instead of the car, take the rubbish away.' Her voice broke then and she swallowed hard. *Sorry Billy,* she thought. 'Um . . . bring one of the boys with you.'

She didn't wait for a reply. Tony would come. And if the phone was tapped – as she now firmly believed it was – then nothing out of the ordinary would be recorded. Just an unruly customer. Not a dead body, a body that had been dragged through the London streets behind a Delaney car, then dumped on Dolly's doorstep.

Annie sat in the kitchen later and thought of

that, of how he must have suffered, and thought of the Delaneys with a black and bitter hatred in her heart.

Hadn't Max told her that the Delaneys were vipers, never to be trusted? Yes, he had. And he was right. She had once felt sorry for Orla Delaney, and Redmond her twin had once been Annie's business partner. But now the battle lines were clearly drawn.

She was a Carter.

They were Delaneys.

It was war.

Time drifted on. Ellie and Darren came gingerly down the stairs and hurried into the kitchen, stepping around the horror in the hallway. Tony arrived with ugly monkey-faced little Jackie Tulliver. They stared in disbelief at what awaited them.

'What the *fuck*?' Tony gasped, forgetting his language in front of Annie and going a bit pale around the gills as he stared down at Billy's corpse.

'Shit,' said Jackie Tulliver. He pulled a face as he realized his shoes were sticking to the doorstep – sticking to the blood that had seeped out of Billy.

'You've got to get him out of here,' said Annie, and she told them where she wanted Billy taken.

Tony was nodding, pulling on his gloves, telling Jackie to do the same.

'We'll sort it out, Mrs Carter,' said Tony.

Dolly went out to the kitchen and Annie went

upstairs to clean up. She had a quick bath, lying there in the hot water and still shaking, still shivering, looking at the gun on the loo seat and thinking that she would like to shoot the bastard who had committed such an act of hideous violence against Billy.

But then she remembered Constantine Barolli's words of warning. *You pick up a gun, they pick up a grenade . . . things get out of hand, Mrs Carter. Be careful.*

She hadn't been careful enough. She'd been so busy panicking over Layla's safety that she had blundered badly and had cost Billy his life. It was a bitter pill to swallow, but she knew she was responsible. Even that fucker Jimmy Bond had warned her.

She put the gun back in Dolly's drawer, got dressed, and took the ruined dressing gown downstairs with her. She paused on the top stair.

Billy's body was gone. The front door was closed.

All that showed something hideous had happened was the wet gloss on what could be seen of the hall tiles, where they had cleaned away Billy's blood. The long strip of carpet down the centre of the hall was pristine clean, too.

Shuddering, she went down into the kitchen. Dolly, Ellie, and Darren were sitting around the table, passing around a half-empty brandy bottle.

Annie stuffed the robe into the washing machine, added powder, switched it on. Then she filled the kettle, got out a mug and the tea caddy.

'That poor bastard,' said Dolly.

Annie turned and glared at her. '*Yes*, Dolly. I know.'

Dolly looked taken aback. 'I'm just saying.'

'Well don't, okay. Shit, give me some of that brandy, will you?'

Annie went over to the table, poured brandy into a spare glass and knocked it back in one. Then she went bright red, coughed and clutched at her throat.

'Jesus, how can you drink this stuff?' she wheezed, grimacing.

'Easily, right now,' snapped Dolly. 'I don't know what the hell's happening, Annie, but I don't bloody like it. Jesus Christ, I hope never to see anything like that ever again.'

'Here's to that,' said Darren weakly, raising his glass with trembling hands and taking a long swallow.

Ellie still looked deathly pale. Annie thought she had probably been sick. Ellie was staring at Annie. So was Darren. So was Dolly.

'For Christ's sake, will you all stop looking at me like that?' yelled Annie.

'Guilty conscience?' asked Dolly.

'*What?*'

'Come on Annie. We didn't come over on the last banana boat,' said Dolly. 'This is gang stuff. Somebody done Billy because he's your lapdog. Or he was. Poor little sod. I tell you, I don't like the way all this is going.'

'And what am I supposed to do about that?' demanded Annie. 'I'm floundering here, Doll. Ask me where I am and I'll tell you: I'm up shit creek without a paddle. My daughter's in the hands of maniacs and I'm getting bits of her sent to me. Now Billy's copped it. You think I'm happy with any of this? Think again.'

'Will the pair of you just stop shouting?' whined Ellie, clutching her head. 'It's bad enough seeing that – that – in the hall, but why argue about it? What good does that do?'

Darren nodded. 'Ellie's right. It's not Annie's fault.'

'No? I don't know so much,' said Dolly, who had now got up a full head of steam and wasn't about to be stopped from delivering her opinion. She looked at Annie. 'Fuck it, Annie, I don't mind helping out, but when it comes to having people fucking *die* on my doorstep, I have to start drawing the line.'

'So what are you saying? You want me to leave?' asked Annie.

Dolly drew a breath and blew out hard.

'I don't know,' she said. 'That's the truth, I don't

bloody know. But we were getting along just fine until you showed up, and now it's all starting again. The Delaneys always left us alone before. Took their protection money and kept the fuck out of it. Which was fine. But now this! Redmond Delaney was in here a few days ago talking to you and when he'd finished you looked like he'd scared the crap out of you good and proper. I don't mind jokes but I don't like sodding pantomimes Annie. I'm not a fool. Not by a long shot.'

Annie sat down at the table, her tea forgotten. If Dolly was turning against her, she was sunk. She'd lost Billy. A shudder heaved through her. She'd lost Max. Lost Layla. Now was she going to lose Dolly too? Dolly, her dearest friend?

'What do you want me to do, Doll?' she asked more quietly. 'You want me to go?'

Dolly hesitated, looking at Annie's face. Darren and Ellie were watching anxiously.

'No,' said Dolly at last. 'Christ, what sort of friend would I be if I turfed you out of here when you're in this much trouble? No, I don't want you to go. And anyway, how the hell could you – those rotten bastards reach you here, don't they? You can't go, and you shouldn't go either. I want you to stay.'

And Dolly reached out and patted Annie's hand.

No hearts and flowers, not from Dolly. But Annie felt reassured. It was a small thing, but it was something precious, to have Dolly's support even when Dolly wasn't sure about the wisdom of giving it.

Next day they heard about it on the radio. A dead body had been dumped outside the local hospital and the police had no comment to make until they had traced the victim's relatives, but it looked like a gangland killing, they said, and beyond that they had no further comment to make.

Poor old Billy.

Annie was tormented by the thought of his miserable life. She knew his mother was a rough, dirty old cow because Max had told her so. She knew about Billy's succession of live-in 'uncles'. Knew that his mother knocked him about, despised him because he was a bit simple. Which was nothing more than the truth. Billy had been a bit odd, but he had been loyal to Max all his life, and to Annie too.

Rest in peace, Billy love, she thought, and felt choked up all over again, and wondered where the hell she went from here.

She sat in the kitchen staring at the wall while Dolly and the 'girls' got on with the business of the day. It was Friday again. And in a week's time, exactly a week, the kidnappers would phone again; and if she hadn't found Layla by then, or secured the money by then, Layla was as good as dead.

What to do?

She sank her head into her hands and tried to think straight, but her brain was darting here and there and getting nowhere. She felt trapped.

All around her, again, there were the sounds of sex. Laughter, whisperings, bangings, cries of pleasure and cries of pain.

What scared her was this: there were times when she tried to call Max's face to mind and she couldn't do it. Black hair, dark skin, a hook of a nose, fierce eyes that could become gentler, smokier, when he held her and loved her.

Which he never would again. She mourned him bitterly, mourned their lost love.

Now she was in trouble and having the worst time of her life, feeling adrift, needing someone to lean on because she had become used to having a man making decisions, taking control: *that* was why she was feeling a tug of attraction to Constantine Barolli; that was the only reason.

She told herself that, over and over. Trouble was, she didn't really believe it.

Someone was having an orgasm upstairs.

She stood up, went through to the hallway, past the open door of the front room wherein the revellers waltzed semi-nude to Dana's sugar-sweet voice singing the Eurovision winner, *All Kinds of Everything*. Ross looked up at her expectantly as she took her coat off the rack and quickly put it on.

'Going out,' she said, and scribbled her name in the book. Everyone had to sign in and out, for security. Christ knows they needed it. Now, more than ever.

'Fine,' said Ross.

Annie gratefully left the building. As she walked down the path she saw how thorough a job Tony and Jackie had done of cleaning up during the small hours. Not a speck of blood anywhere. But Annie could still smell it; it seemed to have permeated her soul, the scent of Billy's blood pooling around her as he lay dying.

She quickened her step. The spring sun was shining, glinting off the highly polished bonnet of the black Jag parked at the pavement. The trees were budding. Nature was renewing herself all over again. She tapped on the window and Tony lowered his paper and wound down the window.

'Going over to Kath's,' she said, and got in the back and felt momentarily safe as she sank back on plush polished leather upholstery. The big engine purred into life. Tony, without fuss, steered the car out into the traffic.

Safe!

Annie sneered at the very thought.

She wasn't safe. She wasn't safe to be let out on her own. She had made bad – *disastrous* – decisions and she loathed herself for that. But she had to quash that feeling. Had to get over it, keep functioning, keep the faith. For Layla, if for nothing else.

After all, what else was left to her now?

51

When they busted in on Talitha in her cheap, tatty flat, the waitress was alone and terrified, pleading her innocence.

'I don't know anything about any men or a woman with a kid. How the hell would I know that? I just wait on tables, that's all.'

'A tall thin blond man and a big-busted, blonde woman. The other one has dark hair – he's big, powerfully built. All English and English-speaking. No?'

Talitha looked up at the huge men gathered around her as she lay cringing on the bed. Huge men with guns, knives, pick handles. Christ, if she knew *anything*, she'd tell them. She shook her head violently.

'You've got to believe me. I don't know anything about these people.'

They believed her.

They knocked her around a little, but she was scared already, scared enough to talk, and she said nothing more that was of any help except that she had a boyfriend who was a fisherman, his father owned a boat called the *Fiebre*, but he would never do anything like this; would never have anything to do with people who had kidnapped a child.

Which wasn't much help, really. So – maybe a dead end.

They left Talitha there, bruised and sobbing.

They went down to the harbour and started talking to the sailors, the fishermen, just hanging around shooting the breeze, buying some *pescado*, chatting, being friendly but also saying, *do you know anything about this?* Three people – two men and a woman. Plus a child.

It took just a week, and it turned out that Talitha's boyfriend was in the frame. The *Fiebre* was owned by a father and son who fished the waters around the island. The *Fiebre* had gone out late at night about a week ago, not at the usual time but an hour later – the fishermen had noticed this. Three people had got on board: yes, two men and a girl. One tall thin blond man, one with dark hair, stocky, powerful. A pretty blonde woman. The *Fiebre* had not come back until three days later.

And the child? There must have been a child?

The fishermen stood around and shook their grizzled heads in unison.

'No. No child,' said one with a swift shake of the head, and his words were instantly translated into English. The one in charge looked at the little man, at his sun-weathered skin and crinkled brown eyes, and in an instant the air of camaraderie was gone. He moved in close to the small fisherman and spoke low, his eyes cold.

'My friend, think hard. A child. *Think*.'

The fisherman gulped. His friends all shuffled uneasily, wondering if there was going to be bad trouble now, whether they should intervene, and thinking probably not. It didn't look safe with these men. One moment, they had been so friendly. Now, the pretence was gone. They looked like killers.

'I . . . I can't think,' mumbled the fisherman, his eyes suddenly wild, wishing to placate, to help, if only to save himself from violence.

'We can help with that,' said one of the men, the one who was translating from Spanish to English. His eyes skewered the little fisherman. 'We got things we can do, help you concentrate.'

'I told you, I can't think of anything else,' said the fisherman desperately. 'I didn't see no child.'

'Not good enough, my friend,' said the one in charge regretfully. 'Nowhere *near* good enough.' He stepped in even closer to the cringing little man.

'The dark-haired one was carrying a big bag,' said one of his friends hurriedly.

The one in charge stopped moving. *The bag again*, he thought.

'How big?' he asked. He spread his arms. 'So big? This big?'

The man who had spoken nodded. '*Very* big, *sí*, like that.'

The one in charge looked around at his men.

'Big enough to hold a small child,' he said.

They nodded. This bore out what Marietta had told them.

'And the *Fiebre*'s coming back when?' asked the one in charge.

'Tonight,' said the fisherman, and his friends all agreed, *sí*, tonight, with a palpable air of relief, of disaster closely averted.

'Hey, that's good.' The one in charge was smiling. Suddenly he was the big genial bear of a man again, everyone's friend.

He paid the fishermen handsomely and bought them many glasses of *hierbas secas*, the island's herb and aniseed liqueur, and *sangría*, in one of the bars. Then he and his men settled down by the quay to wait for the *Fiebre*'s return.

She came in on the morning tide, a medium-sized fishing vessel looking the worse for wear, but serviceable. Big winches on the back, nets in a mess on the deck, one younger man jumping on to the dock to tie her up, the older one steering her in.

'Hey, we got us a result,' said one of the waiting men, straightening, flexing his stiffened limbs as the *Fiebre* approached. His colleagues followed.

They grabbed the small lithe young one as soon as the boat was secured, but the older one surprised them – this was his son, after all – when he saw what was happening and put the engines hard astern. The engines screamed in protest as the vessel tried to drag half the dock away with her. Two of the men jumped quickly on board.

'Hey, stop fooling around. Switch it off,' said one of the men, and it was translated. The older fisherman ignored this, so one of the men gave him a warning cuff around the face.

'We *said*, turn it *off*.'

The grey old fisherman was cupping his lined and now bruised face in his hands. He took another look at them and switched it off.

The men bundled the youngster back on board. Both fishermen were dark-skinned and small by European standards, as most of the islanders were. They threw the youngster into the wheelhouse along with his father and advanced on the pair of them. The pair started shouting and screaming.

'*Shut up!*' yelled the one in charge. He drew his hand out of his pocket and suddenly he was pointing a gun at the older one's head. The older one looked at it as if his eyes were going to pop straight out on stalks.

The fishermen fell silent.

'Ask them,' he said to the man who stood beside him.

The man asked them in Castilian Spanish if they had just shipped two men and a woman and a large holdall over to England.

No, they said, shaking their heads.

The one in charge whacked the older fisherman hard around the head with the pistol. He fell back against the wheel, and the younger one surged forward.

'Don't be silly,' advised the one in charge, swinging the gun in his direction. The young one stepped back.

'Ask them again,' said the one in charge, and stepped coolly forward and kneed the youngster in the groin. He collapsed, groaning and retching, to the wheelhouse floor. 'And tell them no more games.'

The other man asked them.

They said nothing, absorbed in their various ills.

The one in charge stepped forward and raised the gun and hit the younger one in the nose, shattering it. Blood flew, spattering the wheelhouse floor. Then he stepped forcefully on the older one's balls.

The older one yelped and then started talking. He was told to empty his pockets, and this he did.

'*Lots* of pesetas,' said the leader of the men, looking around at his companions with a grin.

'Hey, if I knew fishing paid this well, I'd get me a boat too, wouldn't you?'

They nodded agreement.

'So what's he saying?'

'He's saying his balls hurt.'

'That's too bad. But at least he's still *got* balls: that's a plus. Tell him that.'

The message was relayed. The older fisherman looked sick with terror.

'Now, did he take these people to England? Ask him. And tell him that he'd better not try anything fancy. We want the truth. We don't want to cut off his family jewels, but we will if we have to. Tell him.'

The translator relayed all this. The fisherman looked sicker all the time. Then he started talking, very quickly.

The translator grinned, looked at the one in charge, and nodded.

52

'Jesus Christ, Kath, look at the state of you,' said Annie when Kath opened the door to her.

Kath had sprouted more bruises. Her jaw was yellow, and there were finger-sized black bruises on the forearm that was holding the yelling baby against the front of her grubby, overstretched T-shirt.

'I don't want you round here,' said Kath, and her eyes darted left and right as if Jimmy might somehow be watching, and taking note.

'Tough. I'm here,' said Annie, and pushed on into the hallway. Jimmy Junior ran up to her, smiling, remembering the chocolates. 'Hiya, Tiger,' she said, and bent and tickled him. He laughed in delight. Annie thought of Layla, and her guts clenched in pain.

She straightened and turned to Kath as Jimmy Junior ran into the kitchen.

'What happened to your face? And your arm?' she asked.

Kath kicked the door closed and brushed past Annie. 'I tripped on the stairs,' she said, not looking Annie in the eye.

'Again? Okay. Right,' said Annie with a sigh. 'Ellie says you've sacked her.'

Annie followed Kath's wide beam into the kitchen and looked around. Slightly better this time, thanks to Ellie. But it was hardly the Ideal sodding Home Exhibition. The sink was still full of crocks, for a start. And the floor needed mopping. Kath sat down at the kitchen table and fastened the baby on to the teat. Then she glared at Annie.

'I didn't ask you to send people snooping around here,' she said. Her chin wobbled. 'You got me in bother with Jimmy.'

Annie shrugged off her coat, went over to the sink and squirted washing-up liquid into the bowl, then ran some water. But it was stone cold.

'The immersion's not on,' said Kath.

'So how'd you wash the kids today? Not in cold water?' Annie went over to the door Kath indicated, and flicked the switch down. Then she filled the kettle and stuck it on the stove to heat up.

'Haven't got around to much yet,' said Kath.

Annie felt a stab of anger at her cousin. It was nearly two o'clock in the afternoon, and the kids hadn't even been washed yet. Here was Kath – and oh yes, Annie could see the poor cow was up against it, what with losing her mother and being married to that prize prick Jimmy Bond – but here she was with two beautiful kids, and she wasn't even looking after them properly.

If I had Layla right now, I'd be treating her like a princess, she thought miserably. When she had first held Layla, bloody and squawling after her birth, she had known the meaning of complete and utter love. Oh, she had loved Max. She had loved him with a passion that had never ceased to surprise her. But Layla had come from her, was a *part* of her. When she was separated from Layla, she ached to be with her. When Layla suffered, she suffered too.

She was suffering now.

And Kath was here, with her two wonderful children, neglecting them.

All right, she could understand that Kath felt depressed. Christ, she certainly wasn't having a ball being married to Jimmy. And she'd been so closely connected to her mother that Maureen's death had come as a horrible blow to her.

But still, she had her kids. And wasn't that worth making the effort for?

Annie certainly thought it was.

The kettle whistled and she turned off the gas and poured the hot water into the bowl. She found rubber gloves under the sink and started on the washing-up.

'Christ, Annie Carter the domestic type,' sneered Kath, watching as Jimmy Junior picked up the tea towel and held his hands up to Annie. She handed him down a saucer, and he started to dry it with enthusiasm, his brow knitted in concentration.

Lovely kid, thought Annie. Jimmy Junior! She was sure it was Jimmy's idea to call his son by his own name, the bigheaded bastard. Didn't Kath deserve a say?

Angrily, Annie plunged her hands into the sink and cut a swathe through the washing-up. It helped to do something constructive, even if it was only a small thing. It helped her rage at Billy's death, helped her grief, helped her confusion.

She'd shut the clubs, when according to the books they were good paying concerns. She'd lost people their jobs, their livelihoods. Wrong.

She'd made such a bloody hash of everything, she knew that.

She had heard that stupid noise on the phone and jumped to the wrong conclusion. Half hysterical with distress, beyond reason, she had pinned all her suspicions – which had been totally wrong – on Kieron Delaney.

She'd moved in on Charlie and incurred Redmond's wrath – *so* wrong.

And now Billy was dead.

Full house.

And what had she got right in this whole sorry

mess? Nothing, yet. But she had to keep at it. There was nothing else she could do. She knew she'd grown soft and slack, had come to rely on Max too much. Now, somehow, she had to conquer her doubts, get a grip on herself, and be self-reliant again, the way she used to be.

It was going to be hard, and she knew it.

If you were up against it, you had to take responsibility, make decisions.

Sometimes, they were the wrong ones.

Oh, and how she knew that.

But you had to keep going. Keep your eye on the goal.

Jimmy Junior was tugging at her dress and she was staring out of the window, sudsy water dripping from her hands. *Away with the fairies again.*

She passed him down a sandwich plate. Kath was talking.

'What?' Annie asked.

'Jimmy told me Billy Black got hit,' said Kath.

Annie felt the stem of a glass snap in her hand. There was sharp pain and then blood spurted.

'Damn,' she said. 'Got any plasters, Kath?'

Kath nodded towards one of the kitchen cabinets. Annie held the tea towel around the cut on her finger and scrabbled about with the packet of plasters. She got one out, stuck it over the cut.

'You all right?' asked Kath as Annie sat down at the kitchen table.

Annie looked at her in surprise. Kath was watching her nervously, as though she might flip at any moment.

'Yeah,' said Annie on a sigh. 'I'm fine, Kath.'

There was a brief silence, broken only by the baby's noisy suckling.

'It's rotten, losing someone,' said Kath, her eyes on the baby's head as she stroked the downy hair.

'Yeah,' said Annie. Jimmy Junior ran over to her and gave her the dried plate with a big beaming smile on his face. 'Thanks, Tiger. That's nice.' She looked at Kath. 'You must miss your mum something awful.'

'Yeah.' Kath didn't look up but a fat tear rolled down her cheek and plopped on to the baby's head.

'It gets easier,' said Annie. 'Don't it?'

Christ, I really hope it gets easier, she thought.

Kath looked up. 'S'pose so,' she sniffed. 'Look, no offence. But I don't want you coming round here any more, and I don't want that bloody Ellie here either, poking around. Jimmy don't like it.'

'Okay, Kath. I understand,' she said. She stood up and put her coat on. No point staying where she wasn't wanted. Best to get on, do what she had to do. She was halfway out the hall door when Kath said: 'I'm sorry you lost Billy. On top of everything else.'

Annie paused and looked back at her cousin. Kath looked awkward.

'And I'm sorry about this business with Layla,' said Kath haltingly. 'Jimmy told me someone's snatched her. I'm sorry.'

Annie stood there, thinking that Jimmy had obviously been mouthing off more than he should have been, but *also* thinking, miracles would never cease. Kath was being almost nice to her.

'Thanks, Kath,' she said, and she went on out through the front door, closing it softly behind her.

Tony was waiting in the car. Reading the paper again. Jesus, Tony read a *lot* of papers. Annie sneaked a quick peek. The Israelis and Syrians were fighting again.

Thank God for Tony, thought Annie.

'Where to, Mrs Carter?' he asked as she got in the back.

Annie braced herself. She'd had an idea, maybe a stupid one, but what did she have to lose now?

'Constantine Barolli's place,' she said.

53

Barolli was on the phone when Annie was shown in. She sat down in her usual chair and looked at this man who she knew had his fingers in all manner of extortion rackets. And new things, too: things that the London gangs weren't much into yet. Things like legitimate business loans, offered at better interest rates than the banks. So long as the retailer paid up promptly, all was well. If a retailer defaulted, the Barolli firm claimed the business, asset-stripped it, and sold it on. Which wasn't that dissimilar from the banks, really. Only the banks didn't break your legs if you complained about their business methods.

'Sorry about that,' said Constantine, putting the phone down at last.

'That's okay,' said Annie. 'Is there any news of Layla?'

'Not yet. Be patient.' He sat back, looked at her.

Annie clasped her hands together and stifled the

impulse to launch herself at him in fury. For fuck's sake! *When* was there going to be news of Layla? There was less than a week to go now. Desperation boiled in her, but she was determined not to show it. He would use it against her, she knew he would.

'I heard our mutual contact had a mishap,' he said.

Annie's fists clenched in her lap, the nails digging into her palms.

'He's dead,' she said flatly, staring at him with cold, emotionless eyes. 'If you can call being dead a mishap, then yeah, he has.'

'I'm sorry.'

'Yeah.'

At least he's not saying 'I told you so', thought Annie. There was that to be thankful for. If he knew more details, if he knew how big a hash she'd made of things, he didn't say so.

'How do I get in touch with you now?' asked Constantine.

'Through my driver, Tony,' said Annie. *And please God don't let anything happen to Tony because of me.*

'Good.' Constantine stood up, went to the window behind his desk, lifted the blinds and glanced out. He turned back to Annie.

'I've been thinking about your problem, Mrs Carter,' he said, putting his hands in his pockets and leaning back against the wall.

'Oh?'

'You know, it puzzles me. Why ask for such a large sum? Half a million! That's a great deal of money. And why give you so long to raise it?'

'Perhaps they've given me so long to raise it precisely because it is so large a sum,' said Annie.

'Maybe. But why not pitch it lower – say, half of that? Then it would be a safer bet, yeah? In their shoes, that's what I'd do. The mark should be able to raise that, even if it was a struggle . . . and then no need for this long wait for the money. Little fish are sweet, Mrs Carter. So you know what I think about this?'

'No,' said Annie.

'I still think that whoever is doing this is doing it not only to get the money, but to hurt you too.'

'Do you think they expect me to fail to raise it?' she asked. God knew she had her doubts about her own ability to come up with the goods. The doubts were increasing all the time, and now she felt almost at screaming pitch.

Constantine shook his head.

'No, they know you'll raise it, one way or another. You're a mother; you'll raise it. But they're in no hurry to get it, and that makes me suspect that the big buzz here is all about twisting your tail. So the question we should be asking is – who hates you enough to do that?'

Annie stared at him. *The silver fox.* She looked away.

'I thought it was Kieron Delaney, but Kieron Delaney is dead,' she said. 'He had a . . . a sort of obsession with me. I was sure it was him, but Redmond Delaney says it's not possible.'

'And you believe him?'

'Yeah,' said Annie. 'Funnily enough, I do.'

'I heard you shut all three of the Carter clubs.'

'That's right.'

'Why? If you need to raise money to get your daughter back, why close a profitable business?'

'Because those clubs had been turned into tacky hellholes, that's why. And we both know that the money I'm losing through the clubs won't cover a fraction of what these people want from me.' Annie clutched at her head. It was pounding. She looked up at him. 'There's really no news? None at all?'

Constantine's blue eyes stared into hers. 'Nothing concrete yet.'

'Or are you just saying that to string me along?'

'We're following leads.'

'All right, then. The money. Loan me the money. Right now. So I've got it in place.'

'What?'

Annie jumped to her feet. Suddenly she couldn't just sit there and pretend to be cool any more. Time was running out fast. There was less than a week to go. *Less than one week!* They couldn't let this thing go right to the wire. If there was no news now, then the money had to be there very soon.

'You heard me.' Annie planted both fists on the desk and glared at him. 'You make business loans. The banks won't lend me fuck-all. But you could. A legitimate business loan, Mr Barolli. From you to me. All signed and sealed. All perfectly above board. You loan me the money and—'

'And what?' Constantine pushed himself away from the wall. 'You've closed down the only means of income you have and, Mrs Carter, loans have to be repaid.'

'I know that.'

'Plus there's the *slight* problem that you don't own the clubs, your husband does . . .'

'I have Max's permission to act as necessary, always.' She was in limbo and she knew it, tangled up in a web of lies.

'He's been in touch then?'

'No,' said Annie. 'He hasn't.'

'No,' said Constantine. 'Thought not.'

'He's alive,' said Annie, but it was a lie. She knew it. He knew it. She was fooling nobody.

'He's dead. Everything points to that.'

Annie took a deep breath.

'Look,' she said. 'The point is that I'm here and Max is not. So *I* closed the clubs because I was unhappy with the way they were being run, and *I* am going to reopen them and run them at a profit. So *you* can give me a business loan, and if I default on any of the payments then you can beat me over the head, anything, only *give me the fucking loan.*'

Constantine didn't even blink. He looked up at her with the same blank impassivity he always displayed. Then he said: 'No.'

'*What?*'

'I said no. You know my terms, Mrs Carter. I don't particularly want to extend a business loan to you. You know I have a more personal arrangement in mind. I'll come up with the goods when *you* come up with the goods.'

Annie closed her eyes briefly. She slumped back into the chair and then stared at him.

'You bastard,' she said flatly.

'Yep, I guess that's true.'

'You utter, fucking *bastard*.' Now she was shaking with rage, incandescent with it. 'Don't you have any feeling? Don't you have any *conscience?*'

'An upright prick has no conscience, Mrs Carter. As I'm sure you know.' Constantine's mouth tilted in a slight smile. 'And, incidentally, the last person who spoke to me like that was my mother, and I didn't much like it. I still don't. I suggest you stop right there.'

Annie jumped to her feet. 'And I suggest you

stuff it up your *arse*,' she yelled. 'You can *shove* your personal arrangement.'

And she stormed from the room, crossed the empty hall, and went out of the front door and on to the steps. Once outside, she stopped. Breathing hard, she hesitated. Because she had no choice. No choice at all.

She went back inside and crossed the hall and opened the study door and went back in, closing it behind her. She looked at Constantine, sitting there patiently behind his desk.

'You gonna tell me to shove my personal arrangement again, Mrs Carter?' he asked.

Annie gulped down a calming breath and finally shook her head.

'No, I'm not going to say that.'

He looked at her curiously.

'What, then?'

Annie thought: *Here we go.*

'I'm going to ask you if you've got a key for this door. People seem to keep bursting in on us.'

Constantine stood up, came around the desk, walked over to where she stood. He took a small key out of his jacket pocket, put it in the lock and turned it.

Oh fuck it Max, I'm sorry. Forgive me for this.

Constantine drew closer, staring at her face.

'What?' she asked nervously.

'Nothing.'

'No, what is it?'

'I'm just wondering if any woman can be worth half a million pounds,' said Constantine.

Probably not, thought Annie.

'You remember the art exhibition in Jermyn Street? Kieron Delaney had painted a nude of you. I was there.'

'I know. I saw you.' Annie remembered that occasion very well. Constantine had been there with his family, and she had instantly noticed him: a stunningly handsome man, glossy and polished as only wealthy American men ever were.

'Kieron Delaney was all over you like a cheap suit. And Max came in and there was a fight. Even Redmond Delaney was treating you respectfully, and I don't think he has much time for women on the whole. I know all about the bad blood between the Carters and the Delaneys, and that was a factor, but Kieron Delaney and Max were mostly fighting over you. I could see that. And you know what? I could see why.'

'Why?' Annie asked, dry-mouthed.

'Because you're something else, Mrs Carter. Something different.'

'You don't have to flatter me to get me into bed, Mr Barolli. It's a done deal.'

'It's not flattery. It's a fact.'

'Whatever – it's not needed,' said Annie coldly.

Constantine smiled a little at that. 'I think you're going to be a very tough nut to crack.'

Annie shook her head. 'No, I'll be easy. That's the deal, right? I'm easy and you pay. But first I want to know one thing.'

'And that is . . . ?'

'When do I get the money?'

'Straight down to business. Money for sex, very direct. I like that.'

Annie felt herself colour up. She knew he was alluding to her past.

'I've never been on the game, Mr Barolli, whatever you may have heard or read in the press.'

'The Mayfair Madam,' said Constantine thoughtfully.

'Yeah, note the word "Madam". I ran the show, I wasn't a performer.'

'Were there other men? Kieron Delaney?'

'No.' Although Max had always thought there was something between the two of them. His endless jealous suspicions had driven her crazy; they were groundless.

'And, before Max . . . ?'

'No.'

Constantine drew back a little, his expression sceptical, his mouth curving in a cynical smile. 'A one-man woman?'

'Excuse me, is that even remotely bloody funny? And you haven't answered my question.'

'You get your money when I'm satisfied, Mrs Carter – but certainly by Friday. Of course, if I'm *not* satisfied . . .'

'You will be,' said Annie quickly, feeling sick at heart, cursing the evil, miserable bastards who had pushed her into this corner.

He looked around. 'On the couch over there would be good.'

He indicated one of the big tan leather Chesterfields. Annie walked over to it as if she was about to be shot. So this was it. Down to business. But now it was here, now she was actually going to have to *do* it, she wasn't sure she could.

Constantine saw her hesitation.

'Let me take your coat,' he said, and he slipped it off her shoulders.

Annie stiffened.

He was standing so close to her, right behind her. Only Max had ever done that.

Now he was pushing her hair to one side, and she felt with absolute panic his hands moving at the back of her neck, felt him grasp the zip on the back of her dress and pull it down.

This is the deal, she told herself firmly. Her teeth were gritted so hard she felt her jaw start to ache.

Constantine pushed the dress from her shoulders and it fell to the floor.

She was wearing a black bra, black panties,

stockings, suspender belt. And her high-heeled shoes and supple leather gloves. She made to pull them off.

'No – keep the gloves on,' said Constantine. 'And the shoes.'

Annie stood there, not knowing what to do next, feeling like a stupid virgin, feeling as if she was going to really freak in a second. Jesus, what if he was kinky? What if he was into rough stuff or something like that? She wasn't Aretha. She couldn't deal with this. She was *Max's wife*.

'Lie down on the couch, Mrs Carter,' said Constantine.

Oh God. This was it.

Annie sat down on the couch, the cold leather striking the undersides of her thighs and making her shiver. She glanced up, and Constantine was shrugging off his jacket, undoing his tie, unbuttoning his shirt.

Oh shit.

She looked down at the expensive rug beneath her feet. Braced herself. Swung her legs up on to the couch and lay back, eyes closed. If she watched him undress then she really would have an attack of the screaming abdabs and she knew it.

She couldn't open her eyes. She just couldn't do it. No. She'd let him get on with it, a couple of minutes and it would all be over, he'd be happy and she'd be on her road to the half-million-pound payout. She just had to stop thinking about Max, with his dark hair and swarthy skin and his hooked nose . . . fuck it, and here she was thinking about Max again, and this was a totally inappropriate time to do it.

She was about to allow a stranger to fuck her for money.

'Mrs Carter,' Constantine said softly against her ear.

'What?' asked Annie, her eyes tight shut.

'Mrs Carter, I don't have any appetite for rape. You want to call this off?'

Now Annie opened her eyes. Jesus, no, she couldn't let that happen. She couldn't call it off. She couldn't allow him to find her anything less than appealing. For Layla.

Constantine was half-smiling down at her. He had taken his shirt off and she could feel the masculine heat coming off him, warming her even though she did not want to be warmed. He had curls of crisp hair on his broad and well-muscled chest. His all-American tan didn't stop at his neck. She brought her eyes hastily back up to his face.

'No, I'm all right.'

Shattered, brokenhearted, devastated, but all right.

'Good,' he said, and bent his head and kissed her. Then he drew back.

Annie opened her eyes and looked at his face, very close to hers. He was frowning.

She swallowed nervously. 'What?' she asked. 'What is it?'

'Nothing. It's nothing,' he said, and bent his head and kissed her again. Deeper this time, a proper, hot-blooded, tongues-and-everything kiss.

Oh Jesus, thought Annie.

Then he stopped again.

She opened her eyes. He was still frowning, staring down at her.

Suddenly Constantine pulled back. He got off the couch, stood up and began yanking his clothes on.

'What the . . . ?' Annie sat up, staring at him. He zipped up his trousers and turned to face her.

She took a gulp of air and tried again. 'Did I do something wrong? Something you didn't like?'

His face was closed, unreadable. 'No. Nothing.' He was putting on his shirt, buttoning it closed, tucking the tails in.

'Wait!'

Now Annie jumped to her feet, running her hands through her hair in desperation, her eyes wild with alarm as she saw him withdrawing from her. Layla's life depended on her doing this. She *had* to do this.

'Tell me what I did,' she babbled, trying to speak

calmly, but panic was making her voice come out all wrong. 'Just tell me, I won't do it again.'

'You didn't do anything wrong,' said Constantine, slipping on his jacket.

But he looked angry. *Furious.*

She couldn't afford to let him be furious.

'Look, you said you wanted this,' she said breathlessly, trying to sound reasonable, trying to coax him back to her somehow.

He stopped tying his tie and looked at her.

'I did,' he said, thinking that she was beautiful, that she was everything any man could want in a woman, that he'd wanted her fiercely ever since she'd first walked into his study. So fiercely that he'd lost all pretence of finesse and issued what amounted to a very indecent proposal indeed. So fiercely that he'd misjudged her and – worse – himself. He knew he'd blown his chances with her, right out of the water. He'd been a bloody fool.

And now here he was – feeling lower than a snake's belly, knowing that he was the world's biggest son of a bitch because in her despair she had agreed to this mad scheme, had agreed to fucking well *prostitute* herself, to save her child.

He knew he was no saint. He'd grown up fast the hard way, running numbers in Queens, dealing with scum, seeing what desperation could do to people. And now he could see what it was doing to her, and he didn't like it one little bit.

'So here it is,' said Annie, her voice shaking with the effort of remaining calm. 'You wanted this, you got it. Come on. Take what you want, take *anything*, I don't care.'

Constantine just stood there, looking at her for long moments. *But I do*, he thought.

He'd believed he could handle this. Mentally and physically. But his mind, his *conscience*, was telling him otherwise, and now his body was telling him the same thing. *He just couldn't do it*.

He turned away from her, back towards the desk. 'Go away,' he said. 'Go home.'

Annie ran forward and grabbed his arm, forcing him to stop, to look at her.

'You can't do this,' she said furiously. 'For fuck's sake, listen to me! You *can't*.'

Constantine coolly removed her hand from his arm. 'I can do anything I want, Mrs Carter. Now get the hell out of here.'

Annie stood there, defeated. It was no good. It was finished. Moving like a sleepwalker, she gathered up her clothes, dressed as fast as she could. He unlocked the door – still ignoring her. When she left, he said nothing.

When Constantine heard the front door close behind her, he picked up the phone, ran a hand through his hair, let out a heartfelt sigh.

Hey, he thought angrily, *what's the deal here? Am I finally going soft or some-fucking-thing?*

When the phone was answered, his voice was calm, rock steady.

'I want that girl back with her mother,' he told the man on the other end of the phone. 'What's the hold-up?'

'We're doing everything we can, you know that,' said Nico.

'Do more. Break some heads. Do whatever it takes.'

'Hey, you got it.'

'I mean it, Nico. Step it up a gear.'

'Will do, Boss.'

And in the meantime, he would get the cash together for Friday. Just in case Nico failed.

54

Annie got back to Dolly's place an hour later, feeling like there was no hope left in the world, none whatsoever.

Now she had another thing to add to the list of things she didn't have the bottle for. She was cursing herself for her stupidity. She had behaved more like a frightened virgin than an experienced woman of the world and she hated herself for it. She was sure that her stupid behaviour had put him off – after all, what normal man wanted to feel that he was having to *force* himself on a woman?

She should have behaved like an adult about the whole thing. It was a bit of business, that was all. She should have kept her nerve. But now look. Because of her, Layla had no hope of salvation at all. Her daughter would die because she still didn't have the cash, and that was because she couldn't bring herself to sleep with Constantine.

Disgusted with herself, she went into the kitchen after saying a curt goodnight to Tony. Darren, Ellie, Aretha and her husband, man-mountain Chris, were all around the table, laughing and joking and drinking tea being poured out by Dolly. They were all enjoying their weekend.

'Hi, Annie, come on in, don't stand there in the hall with your mouth open,' said Dolly.

She reluctantly complied. She really wanted to crawl off into the hole that Dolly's bedroom had become and be alone with her misery. But everyone was around the table making a huge effort, trying to cheer her up even though they knew it was damned near impossible, and she was standing there like Banquo's bloody ghost at the feast.

Annie pasted a smile on her face and went in, closing the hall door behind her.

No Una, thank God. Una didn't do friendly gatherings, she just did intimidation. Chris pulled out a chair for her and a slice of cake was placed in front of her. Annie nearly gagged at the thought of even taking a mouthful.

'Long time no see, Annie,' said Chris. 'Aretha told me you're having some trouble. If there's anything . . . ?'

'No.' Annie sat down and he sat too. 'There's nothing you can do.'

Nothing anyone can do, except me. And like a

prize idiot I wouldn't do it, she berated herself furiously. *And now that option's gone.*

Christ, she'd made herself look like such a twat. It was her fault that Constantine had pulled back. All she'd had to do was be seductive. She was a woman, for Christ's sake, how hard could it have been?

Everything was her fault.

For Dolly's sake she nibbled at the cake, although she really felt like throwing up, like screaming, like crying her fucking eyes out. The happy chatter was going on all around her, and there she was in the middle of it all, feeling that she was in a dark and terrible place, lonely and afraid.

Her friends were concerned, but they couldn't help. There was no prospect of help coming from any quarter. It could only have come from herself, when she did something that seemed to her to be a betrayal of all that she had once held dear. But now that ship had sailed.

She tuned into the conversation, if only to distract herself from the horror story she was living in right now, and was immediately plunged back into it.

'Told Chris about Billy,' said Dolly.

'Oh.' Annie gulped. The thought of Billy lying in a bloodied heap was still so raw in her mind.

'Some sick bastards around,' said Chris solemnly.

Annie and Dolly exchanged a look. It wasn't

the only horrendous thing that had happened here. Annie thought of the death of Max's brother, and the night when Pat Delaney had come at her, intending murder.

'The funeral's Monday,' said Dolly, her eyes still on Annie's face. 'I'm going, if you want to come along . . . ?'

She didn't want to go. The very last thing in the world Annie wanted was to stand at Billy's graveside. But she knew she must pay her respects; say that final, awful goodbye.

Monday! Five days then until Friday, five days during which Layla's fate would be decided once and for all.

Oh shit, she thought.

'Yeah. I'll come,' she said.

Dolly nodded her approval and raised her cup of tea. 'Let's give a toast to Billy Black,' she said.

Everyone raised theirs too. 'To Billy,' they mumbled, and drank.

And then, thank God, Dolly dropped that subject and started talking to Chris about what a good doorman he'd been, and that he ought to go back to it.

'You really think he should do that?' Aretha asked hopefully. She hated Chris working the graveyard shift night in, night out.

'Not a chance,' said Chris. 'I'd rather get back in the ring than be a doorman again.'

Chris had relished his time in the boxing ring, but you had to know when enough was enough or you'd end up punchy, fucked-up for life. Annie looked at him. He was no oil painting, even though he'd quit the ring a long time ago. Chris was bald, with a matching set of cauliflower ears and a nose to make a plastic surgeon weep. But it was his manner that appealed. He was hard but fair with men, kind and considerate with women. A regular gentleman. No wonder Aretha had married him before someone else snapped him up. No wonder Ellie still looked at him that way.

'It's easy money,' said Ross, their current doorman, who had come to stand in the open kitchen doorway. He didn't even look at Annie, and since Redmond's visit had not addressed a single civil word to her.

Fuck him, she thought.

'Being a doorman's a piece of piss,' Ross said to Chris.

Dolly looked at Ross. 'Oh yeah? Am I paying you too much?'

Ross grinned. 'You know what I mean, Doll. Not much trouble. *Easy* money.'

Ellie was diving into the cake, shooting furtive glances at Chris.

Still got the hots for him, thought Annie. *Poor cow.*

Annie glanced at Aretha – stunning, black, not

a spare pound on her. *Stiff* competition. Ellie was well outgunned.

The doorbell rang and Ross went back into the hall, closing the kitchen door behind him.

'Yeah, but you liked it here, didn't you?' said Darren to Chris. 'We've always had a good bunch of girls here.' He gave a coy smile and suddenly Darren was like he used to be, not the sickly-looking individual he had become. 'And boys of course.'

Chris nodded. 'It was good. But security work's easier.'

'Yeah, but permanent nights.' Aretha pulled a face. 'Girl gets lonely.'

'Yeah, but good pay. No hassle.'

This sounded like a conversation the two of them had had many times before. Chris was happy in his job; Aretha was feeling bored and neglected and that was why she had come back to work at Dolly's. Not that Chris seemed to mind too much. He knew the woman he was getting; he was clearly under no illusions about his exotic-looking wife.

'Think I told you,' said Dolly to Annie, 'Chris does nights at the trading estate at Heathrow.'

Did you? Annie couldn't remember. Her brain was befuddled by all the shit being heaped on her day by day.

'What, looking after stuff before it's shipped abroad?' asked Annie, trying to take an interest.

'Yeah, that's it. We get big consignments in. *Huge* amounts of stuff.'

'And real good stuff too,' Aretha looked across at Annie with eyes alight with simple girlish greed. 'Gold sometimes. Real bars of gold. What they called? Ingots. Ingots of gold.'

There was a chorus of wows and sighs from around the table.

Chris was smiling and shaking his head. 'That's rare,' he said, looking fondly across at Aretha. 'They store it sometimes at Heathrow and then transport it to Gatwick; it's usually headed for banks and businesses in Hong Kong. But mostly we just get the dosh coming through.'

'Yeah, but it's dosh by the *bucketload*,' said Aretha excitedly. 'More money than you can count, I heard.'

'Yeah, you heard,' said Chris, smiling across at her.

Suddenly Annie felt as though she'd been punched in the chest. Her breathing had shut down. She looked at Chris. She worked some spittle into her mouth and managed to get the words out.

'How much are we talking here? A few thousand? Half a mill?'

Chris shook his head. 'Couple of million's the usual amount. Sometimes more.'

Sometimes more.

But she only needed half a million pounds.

She thought of Constantine Barolli. She had nearly sold her soul to him, in order to get her hands on the cash to rescue Layla. But now maybe she wouldn't have to. Maybe Chris had just given her the get-out clause she needed. A couple of million pounds, sitting in a depot at Heathrow Airport.

'And that sort of amount's there now? Right now?' she asked.

Chris looked at her. Nodded.

'We could take it,' she said suddenly, surprising herself.

Everyone looked at her.

'Oh sure,' said Chris, thinking she was joking.

He turned away and chatted to Dolly, but his eyes kept whipping back to Annie's, as if to say: *Did you mean that? Are you crazy?*

Annie meant it all right.

She was a desperate woman.

Her eyes told him so.

55

It was impossible, of course. When she thought about it later, when she got Chris on his own and got the full details, when she really thought it through and tried to make sense of it, she knew it was madness. Talking about hitting a secure depot and running off with the cash – what a joke. She couldn't risk a jail term. She'd stood in the dock once before and only Max pulling strings had got her out of a very sticky situation that time.

This time there was no Max to tug her arse out of the mire at the last minute.

This time, she would go down for sure.

If she got caught.

But maybe she wouldn't.

On the other hand – maybe she would.

The idea of the heist kept plaguing her, even though she knew it was crazy. She had the boys, Max's boys: they'd been out on the rob and on the heavy game – their term for armed robbery – many times before, and Max with them. They were handy men, hard men, and they would know how to tackle a job like this; they would know where to get experts in to assist, what the snags would be, what could go wrong.

She had to face that. *Anything* could go wrong. But they had the advantage of an insider, and her years with Max had taught her that inside knowledge, inside help, was key to a good job. But would Chris co-operate? He'd looked at her dubiously when she had sounded him out. Chris liked a quiet, orderly life. And if he did the job with Max's boys he would have to get out of the country afterwards, which he wasn't keen on, or face a lengthy jail term, which he was even *less* keen on, and anyway, how would Aretha like any of *those* apples?

No. It was impossible.

Even though Chris had agreed – reluctantly – to talk it through again, it was impossible.

There were so many things against them. For example, what if the money was marked in some way? What if for some reason the full amount wasn't there, and she was left with all the shit from the heist but still without the huge amount of cash she'd need to pacify the kidnappers?

It bothered her all through the rest of the weekend and, when Monday dawned, she was no further forward. Chris had said the cash came in on Wednesdays, which gave them about a day and a half to put the wheels in motion, and she knew that wasn't time enough. Sometimes a job could take weeks, even months, of meticulous planning: she knew that. To go in hastily, without thinking everything through, without making precise plans, was suicide.

Madness.

And she was only considering it because she couldn't face the alternative she was now thinking about. The alternative could start a gang war the like of which hadn't been seen since Spot and Hill in the Fifties – she could hand the Carter manor and everything in it over to Redmond Delaney.

It had crossed her mind in the dead cold hours of early morning. To save Layla, she might be forced to do that.

But she didn't want to. She resisted it with every iota of strength she had left. Because, if she did that, all that Max had worked for would be gone. And, besides, Redmond *fucking* Delaney was the reason she was going to Billy's funeral today. He had ordered Billy's death and she knew it. And how the fuck was she, a Carter to her bones, going to face doing business with the hated Delaneys?

Yeah, sure it was Redmond's fault, whispered that voice in her head. *No way it was yours, right?*

She was still mulling it all over when Tony drove

Dolly and her over to the church for Billy's funeral. Mulling it over – and getting precisely bloody nowhere.

'I'm glad we've got a chance for a private word,' said Dolly as the Jag glided through the grey streets of the East End.

'Oh?' Annie looked at her. Dolly was looking at the back of Tony's head. She glanced back at Annie. 'You can say anything in front of Tony,' Annie told her. 'He's sound.'

Dolly let out a sigh. 'Well, it's not good news,' she said.

'Come on then, out with it.' Annie gave the ghost of a smile. 'I'm used to bad news by now, Doll, or ain't you noticed?'

'It's Darren, Annie,' said Dolly, and Annie was shocked to see tears start in Dolly's eyes.

'What is it?' she asked, her heart sinking.

'He ain't been too good for quite a while,' said Dolly, gulping and scrabbling around in her bag for a hankie. 'Fuck, we ain't even *got* to the funeral yet and I'm blubbing already.'

'I could see he wasn't right when I first came back,' said Annie. 'He said he'd lost his boyfriend. Well, more than a boyfriend. He was in love with the man, and he died.'

Dolly nodded and dabbed at her eyes. 'That's right. The fucker went and died and at first Darren was really upset, wouldn't eat, went downhill . . .

but then, time passed, and I thought, he'll perk up soon. Only he didn't. He kept going down and finally I persuaded him to get off to the doc's and find out what the hell was wrong. And he did.'

'You told me about the blackouts. He said he was having some tests done,' said Annie.

'Yeah, and the results came back.'

Annie looked at her, wondering what the hell she was about to say.

'Well, go on. Spit it out.'

'It's a wasting disease. Got a big long fancy name, but the specialist said in layman's terms it's MS. Basically he's getting weaker and weaker and he's going to end up in a fucking *wheelchair*.'

Dolly choked on the last word and turned tear-filled blue eyes to her friend.

'Oh shit, Doll.' Annie stared at her in horror. Darren had been handed a slow, lingering death sentence.

'I went to see the doc with him. Wanted to hear it for myself. We said I was his big sister and, you know what? I've always felt like that.' Dolly paused and drew breath. 'Poor bloody Darren. He's going down and he's not going to come back up again. The doctor said to expect serious organ damage, confusion, disability . . . death.'

And now the car was pulling in through the church gates, and they had Billy's funeral to get through.

* * *

It was hellish, of course.

Tony stayed in the car. Annie had sent flowers, red roses: she thought Billy would have liked that. Doll sent pink lilies. Max's boys were there to show their respect for one of their own. Billy's Mum was there, hugely fat and hobbling on a stick, with a man in braces and a cheap jacket and baggy trousers. One of Billy's 'uncles', Annie guessed. One of the succession of men who had passed through his mum's life.

Because Billy was a well-known face around the Carter manor, a fair slice of the populace had turned out, despite the showery weather, to see him on his way. Annie felt guilt gnawing away at her all through the service.

Who was she kidding?

Redmond Delaney may have ordered Billy done, but it was her fault he'd gone that far. If she hadn't come back here, Billy would still be alive today, walking around the Carter manor and going to Dolly's Limehouse parlour on Delaney turf while Redmond and his mob cheerfully turned a blind eye.

There came the awful moment when they had to file past Billy's nearest and dearest, his mum and the uncle, no brothers, no sisters. Poor bastard. Dolly was in front, shaking Hilda Black's hand, patting it, saying what a lovely service it had been, the vicar had done Billy proud.

Then it was Annie's turn.

She clasped Hilda's podgy hand. 'I'm sorry,' she said, dry-mouthed, hating this. 'He was a good friend to me.'

Nothing could have prepared her for what happened next.

Hilda went bright red and drew her head back. Then, like a snake shooting venom, she spat full in Annie's face.

Everyone stood frozen in shock.

'*You!*' she hissed. 'If it wasn't for you, my boy would still be alive today! I don't know how you've got the fucking *nerve* to come here.'

Annie recoiled in horror and disgust.

'Mrs Black . . .' she began, groping in her bag for a hankie to wipe Hilda's spittle from her face.

But Hilda was on a roll.

'He was doing some jobs for you, you evil cow. He told me so. He was pleased as punch because you were back. He was always soft on you, the dopy little git. And now look where he's ended up, look what's happened! They dragged him through the streets and killed him, and it's all because of you.'

'I'm sorry,' whispered Annie, riven with guilt.

Hilda was only telling the truth. But God, it hurt. 'I'm so sorry,' she said.

Hilda spat again, hitting her straight in the face.

'Now what you gonna do about *that?*' yelled

Hilda in fury. 'You gonna get me done too, like poor little Billy? Ain't that what you people do, when you're answered back to?'

Annie looked along the silent line of watchers and her eye caught that of Jimmy Bond. He was standing there, and on his face was a faint look of satisfaction. The bastard. He should be rushing over here, telling Hilda what for, to watch her mouth and remember who she was talking to.

But no.

The fucker was *pleased* she was being slapped down.

She looked at the other boys. Ugly little Jackie Tulliver, lanky, evil-eyed Gary, and squat, powerful Steve. All spruced up in their Sunday best. They looked at Jimmy, then at her, then away, shuffling their feet awkwardly.

Annie got the message.

The boys looked to Jimmy for leadership, not her. Jimmy was doing nothing to defend her, so neither were they. It was loud and clear. She got the hankie out and wiped her face.

There was silence all around her. Avid faces, watching, waiting. This was *Mrs Max Carter* being disrespected, and no one was doing a fucking thing about it. It would be the talk of the manor within the hour.

'Come on, we ought to go,' said Dolly, looking uncomfortable as she tugged at Annie's arm.

Then there was movement behind Annie. Suddenly Tony was there, pushing through the crowds. He stopped at the graveside and stared at Hilda Black as if she was shit on his shoe.

'You want to watch your step,' he told her roughly, and she shrank back. 'This is Mrs Carter you're talking to. You just remember that.'

The latest 'uncle' standing beside Hilda Black started puffing himself up and Tony gave him a look.

It was enough.

The man stepped back, looking at the ground.

Annie looked around at all the faces there. Jimmy Bond was gone. Everyone else seemed embarrassed by the scene being played out in front of them. The vicar had said his piece and was gone. Didn't want to get involved.

Annie stepped back. 'I'm sorry,' she said to Hilda Black. 'I'm truly sorry for your loss.'

Hilda Black looked at her with bitter loathing.

Then Annie turned, with Dolly on one side of her and Tony on the other, and walked away.

56

Jimmy Bond was waiting for them back at the car, leaning against it with arms folded, looking smug.

Annie stiffened when she saw him.

Her right-hand man. Yeah. Very funny.

'Wait for me in the car, will you Doll? You too, Tony,' she said. She looked straight at Jimmy.

'I want a word with you,' she said.

He pushed himself away from the car and followed as Annie walked off along the gravel pathway. It was starting to rain again, and the sky was gunmetal grey above the fresh lime-green budding on the trees around the graveyard.

'Well,' he said, falling into step beside her and pulling up his coat collar, 'you bollocksed that up good and proper.'

Annie shot him a glance. 'Yeah, and thanks for your support,' she said, her voice dripping sarcasm. 'There was I thinking you were on my side, too.'

Jimmy stopped walking and stared at her.

'You really are bloody shot away, ain't you?' he remarked. 'I *told* you what would happen if you started stirring things up by working Charlie over. I *warned* you that the shit would start to fly, but would you listen? No. And now I suppose you're in deep shit with the Barolli clan and you want me to get you out of *that* pile of crap too.'

Annie stopped walking. She stepped in and stared hard at Jimmy.

'It must be marvellous to be so fucking clever, Jimmy,' she said coolly. 'Only you see, it ain't your kid who's in the hands of villains, it's mine. *My daughter*, my flesh and blood. She's all I have left now Max is gone . . . are you hearing me, Jimmy?'

'Oh, I've heard you. I've heard a lot these past weeks and I don't like the sound of none of it. You're a fucking loose cannon. You're causing trouble with the Delaneys, you're upsetting the boys, and closing the clubs, and fuck knows what will happen to them now. You've gone cap in hand to the sodding *Mafia* – Christ knows what sort of shit-storm that's going to set off in our direction.'

'Jimmy.'

'What?'

'Just *shut the fuck up*, will you? I'm getting tired of listening to you whining on. All it boils down to is the fact that you don't like me being here at all. Fact is, Jimmy, I think you wish I'd got hit too when Max and Jonjo did, and that would have solved all your problems for you.'

Annie was breathing hard with fury and staring balefully at him. Jimmy was saying nothing.

'Yeah, that's it, isn't it? You could have taken the manor straight over. Run the clubs into the ground and picked over the rest, grabbed all the money and lived like a lord.' She thought with fury of the cosy set-up he already had with Jeanette, all paid for – she was sure – with the firm's money, *her* money. 'And then – oh dear – *I* show up. Ruined all your plans, didn't I? It was all real sweet, then I come around and want things done my way, not yours. Well, it's time you realized certain things, Jimmy. Time you got with it. The big news is this: I'm in charge – not you.'

Jimmy looked at her, his face tense with anger. 'Finished?' he asked.

'Oh no.' Annie gave a tight, furious smile. 'Not by a long shot. Listen up. You've been having a fine old time of it. Having the whole manor at your beck and call. Having Kath waiting on you at home, looking after your kids, shit-scared of you, the poor mare, and Jeanette tucked up in your love nest for a little afternoon delight on tap whenever you wanted it. You thinking all the time that what Kath don't know won't hurt her . . . But what if she *did* know, Jimmy? What if things got said somehow or other, and Kath suddenly started to see the light? She's not alone any more, Jimmy. *I'm* here. I'd help her walk away from you. I'd pack her sodding suitcase myself. And what about the rest of the boys?'

'What the fuck are you talking about?' asked Jimmy roughly, but she could see he was rattled. Kath was no loss to him but the kids were, she could see that.

'What would they think of a man who beats up women, Jimmy?' Annie paused, seemed to ponder. 'I think I know. I think they'd say he was a yellow-bellied fucking *coward*, and I don't think they'd take many orders from a man like that.'

Jimmy's face had flushed brick red while she talked. 'You threatening me?' he spluttered.

'Just stating facts,' shrugged Annie. 'See, I don't think Jeanette's the maternal type, do you? Can't see her looking after your two kids part time when Kath kicks you out. Maybe she'd let you see the kids, but I sort of doubt it. It's a shame; I think you really love those kids too. But then, I can't really see Jeanette playing happy families at the weekends, wiping up baby sick and playing with Jimmy Junior while you're off down the dog track looking for another little blonde with a twinkle in her eye . . . I dunno, Jimmy, your whole, well-ordered world could come crashing down if someone was to say a word in the wrong place to poor old Kath.'

'You want to be careful,' said Jimmy, looming over her with rage flashing in his eyes.

'Careful? Me?' Annie gave an ironic bark of laughter. Then her face grew stony. 'Get real, Jimmy. I'm beyond being careful. I'm hanging out over a cliff with sharks trying to snap my arse in half, or ain't you noticed? You really think that I'd quibble about blowing the whistle on you?'

Jimmy was breathing hard. 'You vicious cow,' he said flatly.

'Yeah, you got that right. You remember that, Jimmy, and next time you see anyone disrespecting me, you fucking well shift yourself and *do something about it*.'

Annie turned on her heel and walked back to the car. After a few paces she paused and looked back at him.

'Oh yeah – and get the boys together for a meet at the Palermo tomorrow morning at eleven. Nice and discreet, no rolling up mob-handed, got it?' she said. 'I'll see you there.'

57

'Basically, Vee, you're just a fucking moron,' Danny was saying.

Vee sat at a different kitchen table this time, in a house that was no better and no worse than the last – in other words, a shit-heap. She was getting very, very tired of shit-heaps. And also of Danny, who did not believe in letting bygones be bygones. He was *still* going on about the fact that she had once – *just once* – left the sodding door unbolted, and the kid had tried to do a runner.

'*Look*,' she said suddenly, losing it. 'She didn't get out.'

'Yeah, but if she had—'

'If she *had*, that would be a different matter, wouldn't it? But she didn't. So can you please now for fuck's sake let it *drop*?'

'Why do I always have to work with fucking

fools?' asked Danny morosely, downing another can of beer.

'Hey, don't include me in this,' said Phil Fibbert, who was also sitting there and who was also getting pretty damned tired of the way Danny kept carping on about ancient history, about things that nearly happened, but didn't.

'And you can shut the fuck up too,' said Danny.

Vita looked at Phil. Phil was built like a brick shithouse and Danny shouldn't keep talking to him like that, or one of these fine days he might just get his teeth back in an ashtray. Right now Vita was looking forward to the day when Phil finally snapped. Phil winked at her and she half smiled back.

Actually, she was sort of beginning to like Phil.

Sure, they'd had their moments, but this was a tense situation. They were all on edge. And Danny didn't help. She wished he'd stop it with the drink. He was a tetchy bastard anyway, but when he had a few pints down his neck, he was like a bear with a sore head.

Vita looked at Phil. She liked his dark good looks and his muscular physique. She didn't notice that he hadn't really defended her, he had only defended himself.

'Ain't it time you checked on the kid?' Danny said to Vita, while eyeing them both with a critical eye.

Vita stood up. 'I'll be so glad when all this is

over,' she groaned, reaching for the hood and pulling it on, tucking her blonde hair up under it. 'You really think she's gonna play it straight now?'

'What else can she do? It's all going good.' Danny downed the dregs of the beer and crushed the can in his fist and grinned. Then he frowned.

That was Danny – happy to crazy mad in a single bound. Vita had long ago got used to his sudden switches of mood.

'And this time, lock the fucking door, okay?' said Danny sharply.

Boy, could her brother hold a grudge.

But then – so could she.

58

When Annie came downstairs next morning, thinking, *Oh fuck, it's Tuesday already*, a stony-faced Ross handed her a slip of paper.

'What's this?' she asked.

He shrugged, uninterested. 'Chap just handed it to me. Said it was a "pizzi", or something. For Mrs Carter.'

Annie felt her heart thud sickly in her chest. The last unexpected delivery here had been Layla's severed finger. She didn't want any more surprises.

'Thanks, Ross,' she said, and took it through to the empty kitchen and spread it out on the table. It was a *pizzino* from Constantine, using Caesar's code. She quickly deciphered the line of numbers. The note read: *Sorry. C.*

Annie stared at it in bewilderment. She thought of their last meeting, when she had behaved like a vestal virgin being propositioned outside the temple. She groaned aloud. Christ, what a fool she'd made of herself. Turned him right off the whole idea; ruined everything. But now this. *Sorry.* Meaning what? Meaning that there still might be a chance he'd go ahead with it, that she could still, somehow, get Layla out of this?

Dolly came in, clipping on discreet diamond stud earrings. She looked at Annie.

'Any news yet?' she asked, indicating the note.

Annie shook her head and folded the piece of paper.

Dolly's face was grave. 'They're phoning back this Friday, ain't that right?' she said.

'I don't need reminding, Doll,' said Annie, the panic eating at her. Time was running out fast now – it was all but gone. And so far she'd achieved nothing. Not a damned thing.

'I thought you were going to get a loan off the Barolli mob?'

'I was. Um . . . there were strings attached.'

'What sort of strings?'

Annie got up and closed the door into the hall. She turned and looked at Dolly.

'Constantine Barolli wanted to sleep with me,' she said.

'And?' Dolly looked at her blankly.

Annie returned her stare. 'What do you mean, *and?* He wanted to *sleep* with me, Doll, and then and only then would he hand over the money.'

Dolly leaned back against the worktop and studied Annie closely. 'Sorry. You've lost me. Barolli wanted to sleep with you . . . ?'

'Yeah, that's what I said.'

'For half a million quid.'

'Yeah.'

'Then what the fuck are you waiting for: hell to freeze over? Why ain't you done it?'

'Jesus, Doll, I was going to.' Annie clutched her head in her hands as her mind replayed the whole embarrassing experience in detail. 'I offered myself on a plate. Which was what he wanted. And then he changed his damned mind.'

Dolly nodded at the note on the table. 'That's from him?'

'Yeah.'

'Saying . . . ?'

'Saying sorry.'

Now Dolly looked bewildered too. 'Sorry for what?'

'I don't know. How the hell should I know? Sorry for changing his mind, I suppose.'

'Look,' said Dolly reasonably, 'if he's saying sorry, then at least he's still talking to you, so maybe it's not too late. You could still get over there, do the deed, get the money, get Layla back.'

'I don't know,' said Annie, her mind in turmoil. The thought of going through that again was humiliating, but she'd do it for Layla.

420

'It's a bit of business, that's all.'

'*What?*' Annie let out a mirthless laugh. 'It might be a bit of business to *you*, Doll, but not to me. I'm a married woman.'

'You're a *widow.*'

'You want me to go and shag some – some *stranger?* For money? You think that's easy?'

'Got it in one,' said Dolly, filling the kettle. 'And no, I don't think it's easy, but tough. Do it.'

'Look, you may have some experience of selling your body like a farmer sells his pigs in a market, but I don't,' snapped Annie.

Dolly's face was suddenly a picture of hurt. 'Oh, and you think I enjoyed being a brass? You think I *liked* being a brass? You know damned well that I was only on the game because of what happened to me at home. I went out on the streets when I was fifteen, and it was only Celia being so kind and giving me a roof over my head that saved me from those filthy rotten pimps out there. You *also* know that I jumped at the chance to stop all that, to become a Madam. You know it.'

Annie took a deep breath. 'I'm sorry, Doll,' she said, contrite. 'It's just . . . it's a really sore subject. Fact is, I tried. I really did. I bottled it, turned him off the idea. I just couldn't do it.'

Dolly switched the kettle on and eyed her friend. 'Oh don't be bloody daft. It's a business fuck, that's all. Have a brandy, take the plunge.'

'Don't drink,' said Annie.

'You know what I mean. Christ, it's not as if he's flipping ugly. *I* wouldn't kick him out of bed, that's for sure.'

Annie eyed her in disbelief. So far as she knew, Dolly had no one in her bed and that had been the case for a very long time. She didn't know what the fuck she was talking about.

'One little indiscretion – just one; and if he's like most men I know, it'll be two minutes then out the door – and then you get the money, and Layla's safe,' Dolly rolled on.

One little indiscretion.

Annie stared at the floor. Angry words, spiteful words poured into her brain.

Words like, *And who are you to tell me about my love life? You ain't got one.*

She swallowed the words whole. Getting arsy with Dolly wasn't going to help anyone.

'Or am I missing something here?' asked Dolly, taking down the teapot and fishing out the tea caddy.

'Meaning what?' Annie looked up at her.

'Meaning – I dunno – maybe you think it wouldn't end there? Meaning, maybe you might actually *like* it, and how would you square that with your conscience about Max?'

Annie looked at the floor again.

'That's it,' said Dolly in triumph. 'I *knew* it.'

'That is *not* it,' said Annie.

'The fuck it ain't. You fancy Constantine Barolli, *that's* the problem. You're terrified you might actually enjoy it.'

'You're off your head, Doll,' said Annie.

'There's nothing wrong with calling a spade a spade,' said Dolly, pouring boiling water into the pot. She stopped pouring and looked up at Annie. 'Come on, Annie love. Get a fucking grip. Max is gone. Layla's life's is at stake here. You got no choice.'

'No?' said Annie stubbornly.

'Nope. Not as I see it. You were ready to go ahead and do it last time, but you put him off by having a fit of the vapours, you idiot. But he's still interested, or else why the note? So you can do it again – and this time for fuck's sake be a little more damned *inviting*, eh?'

The phone was ringing in the hall. Ross picked up and poked his head around the kitchen door.

'For you,' he said to Annie.

Annie went out into the hall and picked up the phone. 'Hello?'

'What have you said to him?' Kath's voice shrieked at her. 'What have you *done?*'

'What?' Annie frowned. 'Kath? That you? Calm down, for God's sake.'

'How can I calm down? He's taken them away. He's *taken them away!*'

'Kath, I don't know what you're talking about. Slow down. What's happened?'

'Jimmy's taken the kids away from me, you cow. It's all your fault, he's *taken my kids away.*'

59

Annie got over to Kath's pronto. She felt like shit. All the way there in the back of the car she thought about her meet with Jimmy yesterday, and how mad he'd been. She'd thought she had the upper hand, but she'd been wrong. Jimmy Bond was sticking two fingers up at her yet again.

Jimmy Bond, her main man.

Who should be her friend, her supporter. Her cousin's husband. Her *kin*, by marriage.

That *bastard*.

By the time she got to Kath's, she was fuming. Kath was in a terrible state, wandering around her tip of a home, crying, saying she'd kill him, she'd kill him.

'He just took 'em,' she said between sobs. 'Came in here bold as brass with that horrible little fucker Jackie Tulliver, and between them they took all the kids' stuff, and the kids too. Didn't even tell me where they were going! *My* kids. I'm still breast-feeding the baby, and I said that to him, begged him not to take little Mo as well as Jimmy Junior, and do you know what the rotten git said? He said she'd have to get used to the bottle. Can you believe he'd do that? Can you?'

Annie thought Jimmy Bond was quite capable of doing it. And she had a fair idea of where they'd be, too.

'I'll have a word,' said Annie.

'Oh for fuck's sake. And what difference is that going to make? He won't listen to you. He only ever listened to Max or Jonjo, and they're bloody gone. It's no use, he's taken them and I can't do a fucking thing about it.'

Kath started sobbing again and pulling her hair, beside herself with grief.

'I'll have a word with him,' Annie said again.

'Yeah. Right,' said Kath.

Sick at heart, Annie left her there and went back out to the car.

Tony handed her a note. 'Some bloke just gave me this,' he said. 'Said it was a pizzi-something for Mrs Carter.' Tony frowned. 'It's just a few numbers on a sheet of paper.'

Another note.

Annie sat in the back and quickly read it, deciphering the simple code as she went. It read: *News. C.*

Annie looked at her watch. It was ten o'clock, and she was going to meet the boys at the Palermo at eleven. She had time.

'Take me over to Constantine Barolli's place, Tone,' she said, her stomach in knots.

Constantine was in the dining room this time, seated at the head of a grand twelve-seater table and finishing breakfast with his sons Lucco and Alberto and the elegant dark-haired woman with the down-turned mouth and unfriendly eyes. The doorman showed Annie straight in, saying that Mr Barolli wanted to talk to her as a matter of urgency.

'Mrs Carter.' Constantine stood up, came around the table, wiping his fingers on a white napkin. 'Thanks for coming. Had breakfast?'

Annie nodded. She'd eaten something about two hours ago, but she didn't know what. Maybe some toast, a bit of egg. Food made her gag, ever since Layla had gone she was living on her nerves, running on empty.

'Right, let's go into the study. You've met Lucco?'

Annie looked at the smooth, dark-haired youth. Beautiful and poisonous. Lucco stared back at her with blank dislike.

'Yeah. We've met,' she said.

'And Alberto?'

The blond one gazed at her with narrowed blue

eyes. He was spookily like his father. Bloody gorgeous, in other words, but half formed, gangly, not yet the man he would become. He nodded.

'Mrs Carter,' he said.

'Hello, Alberto.'

'And this is my sister Gina,' said Constantine, and the woman pinched her lips and gave a nod.

Looks like she's got a bad smell under her nose, thought Annie. *And guess what? It's me.*

Annie nodded back.

'Come on,' said Constantine, and led the way out into the hall, shutting the dining-room door behind them.

They crossed the big empty hall and went into the study. Constantine closed the door behind them, and crossed to the desk. He sat down behind it and indicated a chair to Annie. He was all business today, and she was very glad of that. Their last meeting had been cringingly embarrassing, and she didn't want to be reminded of it. Nevertheless, she remembered it. Vividly. She also remembered what Dolly had said and felt colour start to rise into her cheeks. Was that the real truth? Did she really want Constantine Barolli, just as he wanted her? But he'd changed his mind. And then he'd sent her a note saying sorry. Now what the fuck was *that* all about?

'You said you've got news,' said Annie, cutting across her own tumbling thoughts.

Constantine kicked back his chair and looked at her.

'Do you know a Jeanette Byrne?' he asked.

Annie looked at him in surprise.

'I know a Jeanette, I don't know her last name,' said Annie.

'This Jeanette was a dancer in one of the Carter clubs.'

'A stripper. Yeah, I know her. Blonde.'

'That's right. My people tell me she's involved with one of yours. Jimmy Bond. He's set her up in a house.'

'That's right.'

'He must be creaming a good bit off the business, to afford to run two houses,' said Constantine.

'You think he's cheating the firm? So do I. I think he's been dipping into the takings.'

'And what are you going to do about that?'

'I've no idea, yet. I looked at the books but there's nothing obvious there. But then, I don't *know* the clubs like Max did. I don't know what the takings would normally be. Jimmy does the books.'

'So you have access to them?'

Annie gave a bitter smile.

'Oh yeah. And I've looked at them. I haven't *understood* them, but I've looked at them.'

'I could have our *consigliere* check them over for you,' he said.

'What's that, like an accountant?'

'An accountant, a lawyer, a counsellor. A good, solid man,' Constantine nodded.

A good solid man in the pay of the Mafia. Annie looked at him and wondered yet again what the hell she was doing here.

'So you think this man is robbing you, and setting himself up as . . . what? As a rival for the Carter manor?'

Annie shook her head in irritation. 'Look. Who cares? All that matters is *my daughter*. Once I've got her back, I can sort Jimmy.'

'You remember you told me about the kidnapping? That Jeanette was conscious throughout?'

Annie nodded.

'My sources tell me that Vita Byrne – Jeanette's sister – was shopping in Palma the day before the kidnapping took place.'

Annie swallowed, heartbeat accelerating.

'Only, I think that could be significant – don't you?'

Annie thought about that, frowning. The one thing that characterized Jeanette most strongly was her inability to keep her fat mouth shut. If she'd known her sister was on the island, she would have blabbed all about it to Annie. Wouldn't she?

She remembered now that Jeanette had borrowed Rufio's car the day before the hit and taken off to Palma, alone. She hadn't talked about it when she got back to the villa, except to say that she'd been shopping. Solitary trips did seem out of character for Jeanette, but at the time Annie had been so delighted to get rid of her for a day that she hadn't given it a second thought. If Jeanette had gone into Palma to meet up with her sister, if it was all completely innocent, then why hadn't she told Annie about it?

'You said you thought the line was being tapped, when you were in the villa after it happened?' asked Constantine.

Annie nodded. Even thinking about the aftermath of the hit made her break out in a sweat.

Then he was silent, staring at her face.

'Look, you've got something on Jeanette, what is it?' prompted Annie anxiously. 'Is it to do with this sister of hers?'

'Do you know Jeanette's family?' he asked.

Annie shook her head. But knowing Jonjo's taste in women, she wasn't expecting them to be the Windsors of Buck House.

'She's got two sisters and a brother. The sisters have both done time – petty stuff – and the brother has a record for smash and grab, drug use, demanding money with menaces. You really don't know the family?'

She shook her head again.

'Oh, but I think you do,' said Constantine. 'The brother's called Danny.'

'No, I don't know him.'

'One of the sisters is called Vita.'

'Nope. Doesn't ring a bell.'

'What about the other sister then? She works at Dolly Farrell's massage parlour. Where you're living right now. Her name's Una.'

60

By the time she got to the Palermo at ten past eleven, Annie felt as if her brain had been plugged into the mains and fried.

Una.

Jeanette and Una were *sisters*.

Jeanette, Una, and Vita. Plus Danny, the brother.

There were similarities. The girls had the same broad faces, the same slight overbite. The same big tits too. Una was the taller, but Jeanette was tall too, as tall as Annie.

It was no surprise to her that Una had done time. Una was a hard, vicious bitch, and Annie didn't think for a minute that she would be above a bit of petty larceny. Well, fair enough. She'd done the crime and done the time and that was an end to it.

But was it?

What about the *other* sister, the one called Vita? This one she knew absolutely nothing about. And motor mouth Jeanette hadn't ever mentioned her sisters or her brother Danny, not once. In all the times that they had lounged about together, her and Annie, side by side under the warming Majorcan sun, Jeanette – who could shoot the breeze for England – had *not once* mentioned her family, or that her sister Vita was on Majorca too.

Tony parked the car near the club and she sat in the back and looked at the seedy frontage. No one had the keys now except her, so she expected to see the boys loitering about outside.

But no.

But *then*, maybe they were doing the same as her, sitting in their cars waiting for *her* to emerge. The weather was cold and wet: who wanted to stand shivering their balls off in a doorway? And she had said no group arrivals, keep it discreet. Well, they were only taking her at her word.

At a quarter past eleven she got out of the car. She crossed the road with Tony and unlocked the door to the club and they went in.

The club was silent.

No strippers parading their wares around the stage. No weary, scruffy punters giving the poor long-suffering hostesses a furtive feel.

Annie walked down the stairs into the empty club, her steps echoing. She stood in front of the stage, looking up at the faded red velvet curtains, at the big linked gold MC at the highest point,

where the drapes met. Tony stayed up at the top
of the stairs to greet the boys while she looked
around her. The club was more than silent, it was
dead. An air of sadness, of better days long gone,
permeated the place.

Maybe she'd been wrong to close it, but seeing
the pest-hole it had become had damned near
broken her heart. She remembered the great acts
Max had hired to perform here, Tony Bennett and
Johnnie Ray and Billy Fury – all those solid gold
acts that in the end had become too expensive.

She had closed the clubs on instinct, on impulse.
Put people out of work. Dried up a good source
of income. Pissed off Jimmy Bond.

She sat down at one of the little circular tables,
and waited.

At twelve o'clock Tony came downstairs,
looking unhappy.

'Don't look like they're coming, Boss,' he said.

'No,' said Annie, although she wasn't surprised.
And the irony of Tony calling her 'Boss' for the
very first time didn't pass her by, either.

Some 'Boss'.

Jimmy Bond had put his cards on the table, had
called her bluff. Had taken the kids off Kath. Had
sent Annie Carter a message, loud and clear.

He was the boss of the boys and the manor
now, not her.

She went back up the stairs and out the door

with Tony, locking it behind her. The light was going, the grey weather was turning day into night. People were turning on their car headlights. In the distance, a woman walked away, a woman with a blonde Afro hairstyle. Could be Jeanette. Vita's sister. Una's sister. Danny's sister. And why not? She lived just round the corner, in her little love nest with Jimmy. All very cosy, one big happy family plus Jimmy Bond.

It was all starting to add up.

And what it was starting to add up to was igniting a cold fire of fury in her belly, a stark and sickening realization in her mind. She had believed Jimmy's attitude toward her to be nothing more than male posturing; she'd been sure he was acting up because she'd put his nose out of joint by coming back to rule the roost.

But now there were all these new connections.

Jimmy. Jeanette. Vita. Una. Danny.

The fury consumed her now, leaving a cold and deadly purpose in its wake and a hard single fact in her mind: she had been misled into believing that Jimmy Bond was her friend.

But he wasn't.

He was her *enemy*.

61

'So what do you think?' Chris asked.

Chris was getting to be a regular visitor at Dolly's place. He liked a chinwag with Ross, and having a bite to eat with Aretha and the other working girls. It was about two o'clock on Tuesday, and he'd caught Annie on the stairs when she'd come in and headed straight up them, not wanting to chat, needing to be alone, to think all this through.

'What?' Annie paused on the bottom stair.

Ross was off somewhere, probably on a fag break. Tony was out in the car. Chris and Annie were alone in the hallway.

'About the . . . *you know*,' said Chris pointedly. 'The money.'

He meant the job at his depot. The money. The huge stash of money that could have saved Layla's life. *Could have*, but now wouldn't.

Annie shook her head. 'No, it's off.'

'Why?'

'Can't get the muscle.' She wasn't about to tell him that the boys had just given her a resounding vote of no confidence. It stung too much. She had thought she was gaining ground with them, but now she knew exactly where she stood, and it wasn't in a good place.

'Yeah, but you got the Carter boys,' said Chris, twisting the knife deeper.

'No, Chris. It's off.' She started walking off upstairs. Didn't want to hear any more about it.

'If the boys don't want to get involved, I can maybe get some people together.'

Annie paused, shook her head in irritation. 'Come on, Chris. Be reasonable. There ain't time to set up a decent heist. And you don't want to get into the heavy game. Think about it. We'd have to get you out and away somewhere; you wouldn't be able to get in touch with your family or friends again; it wouldn't be safe. Do you *really* want to go that far, just to please Aretha?'

'We could do it,' said Chris obstinately.

'Oh sure. We could. Forget extra muscle, we could do it ourselves. You and me, Dolly and poor bloody Darren, Ellie and Aretha, all dolled up in balaclavas and packing shotguns. Get real, for fuck's sake. Now drop it, okay? It's *off*.'

She went upstairs. She had decided what she

was going to do now. She sat on the bed, still wearing her coat, and her mind was suddenly clear and sharp. Jimmy had called her bluff, but he was mistaken if he thought she wouldn't send that straight back at him. She sat there, breathing deeply, listening to the sounds of sex coming from the other rooms. Una drifted past the half-open door in a black leather basque and fishnet stockings. She looked in, her eyes cold, her face still bruised from the pounding she'd got off Annie. Then she looked away.

Watching me, thought Annie. *She's been watching me all the fucking time.*

Annie listened to Una's footfalls as she went down the stairs. Annie wanted to run after her, grab her by her scrawny, drugged-up head and give her a harder pounding than last time, but she fought back the urge. No, she had to think. No good going off half-cocked, not with Layla's life still swinging in the balance.

Ecstatic moans were coming from Aretha's room at the front of the house. Now there was a liberal marriage and no mistake. Chris was downstairs sipping tea; Aretha was upstairs shagging the clientele.

Aretha and Una, both mistresses of the dominatrix trade – but there was a difference. Aretha enjoyed enslaving her willing victims, got a sensual buzz from chastising and humiliating them, but there was a line she wouldn't cross. Una was another thing entirely. Una adored shouting and screaming at her victims, relished inflicting pain on them, loved to grind them, squirming in agony, beneath her booted heels.

Max would rip my head off if I went on the game, she thought.

But then, Max was gone. She was alone.

And she wasn't sure about Chris and Aretha. She wasn't convinced that Chris was cool about Aretha coming back on the game. Maybe Chris was fed up with working nights, with the pitiful pay he got as a security guard; maybe he was edgy about Aretha's return to the massage parlour.

Maybe Chris felt Aretha was undermining his position as breadwinner by coming back to work; maybe Aretha was even doing it intentionally, saying: *Look, you can't keep me as I wish to be kept, so I'm going back to humping strangers for money, how's that with you, honey?*

Marriages!

Annie's face clouded. Well, she didn't have any of *that* any more. No more jealousy, no more tiptoeing around the male ego. She had nothing at all.

The phone was ringing in the hall. She heard Dolly pick up. Then Dolly's voice, taut with urgency, was calling up the stairs.

'Annie! You there?'

Annie went out on to the landing and peered over. Dolly, white-faced, was holding the phone aloft to her.

'It's him,' she hissed. 'It's the fucking *kidnapper*.'

Annie wasn't even aware of going down the stairs. Suddenly she was down there in the hall, grasping the phone. Una was gone, thank Christ. She could hear Chris in the kitchen, talking in low tones to Ellie. Dolly stood there beside her, watching her face, wanting to help but unable to.

'Hello?' said Annie.

'Ah, Mrs Annie Carter,' said the Irish man.

Annie's heartbeat picked up. What the fuck was going on? It wasn't Friday yet. She still had some time. Was he going to tell her they wanted the money now, right now? Oh Jesus God – if that was it, then she was well and truly stuffed.

'What do you want?' she asked stiffly.

'Well *that* ain't very friendly, now is it?'

She could hear the smile in his voice – the loathsome piece of scum. She said nothing.

'Just a social call, Mrs Carter,' he went on. 'Just checking you've got the money ready, that's all.'

That's all.

And she didn't have it. Not a fucking penny.

'Yeah,' she lied. 'I've got it.'

'Good. Now I suppose you want to speak to your baby girl, Mrs Carter?'

Layla.

Annie closed her eyes, holding back the hot, sickening flood of hysteria. Dolly put an arm round her shoulders. She opened her eyes. Braced herself.

'Can I? Can I speak to her?' Her voice cracked on the last word.

There was a pause.

'Nah,' he said. 'Not yet. When Friday comes, when I get the money, Mrs Carter, *then* you can speak to little Layla, how's that?'

'You fucking bastard,' said Annie, unable to hold it back.

She had no way of knowing if Layla was alive or dead. Just to hear her voice would be so wonderful, so unbelievably sweet. He was playing with her, enjoying watching her writhing like a fish on a hook.

'Yeah, and I'm the fucking bastard who's got your girl, Mrs Carter, so you just remember that, you remember to keep a civil tongue in your head when you speak to me. Got it? Or maybe I'll let you have a word now. What do you think?'

Annie was swallowing bile, locked in this mad cycle of fury and loathing, feeling powerless and defeated.

'Please – let me speak to her,' she managed to get out.

There was rustling at the other end of the phone. And then Layla said: 'Mummy?'

Annie let out a scream. Couldn't help it. She'd been sure Layla was dead; she *knew* they'd tortured her, cut off her finger, and she sounded so sleepy . . . was she drugged, was that it?

'Now,' said the man's voice after a few seconds. 'You've got the cash, right? I'm just checking, because if you ain't got it, if you're *lying* or some damned thing – then, Mrs Carter, your little girl is dead.'

'Let me speak to her again, you scumbag!' yelled Annie into the phone.

'No. No more talking. Just answer the question, you got my money?'

Annie drew in a breath. Layla was alive. She was *alive*.

'I've got it,' she said.

'Good. Nice to know we understand one another. Speak to you again on Friday. Twelve noon.'

62

Her life was in bits but she still had things to do, places to go. Tony drove her to the place she told him, and when they got there he looked at her and his eyes said, *I don't fucking well believe this*.

They were outside a breaker's yard in Battersea. It was rumoured to be the same yard where Jack 'The Hat' McVitie's car was crushed after he'd been done by the Krays. Forever after, the car had been known on the streets as 'the Oxo', because all that had been left of it was a tiny cube of mangled metal.

'It's okay, Tone,' she reassured him. 'Wait here, yeah?' she said as they got out of the car and stood in front of the gates.

The yard was completely fenced off with tall, thick wire panels. Tony looked at the security guard approaching with a black-faced Alsatian, snarling and yanking at its choke chain. At the back of the yard, piled high with the rusting hulks of dead cars, they could just glimpse the edge of a static caravan that served as an office.

'No, Boss, I'm coming in with you,' said Tony.

The dog was going mad. The guard snapped a command at it, jerked the chain. The dog fell silent.

Annie nodded acceptance of what Tony had said. Easier than arguing. Now she'd braced herself to do this, she hadn't the energy for a fucking debate. Best to get it over with, get it done.

The guard looked them over. And suddenly the one man became, as if by magic, *three* men. Big, hard, flint-eyed men who gathered around the other side of the fence and stared at them with extreme suspicion.

One of them was Charlie 'The Dip' Foster, the Delaneys' number one man. He stared at Annie as if he'd like to slit her open like a rotten fruit. She looked down at his hands; one was bandaged. Annie didn't feel sorry, not any more – even though she knew she'd made a huge mistake over the Delaney involvement in Layla's kidnapping. Charlie was a bastard; she was *surrounded* by bastards. If he had to refine his dipping technique to cope with his new disability, so what? Fuck him.

'I've come to see Redmond,' said Annie.

'Maybe he don't want to see you,' said Charlie.

'Just tell him I'm here,' said Annie, hard-faced even though inside she was quaking.

They all stood there looking at her sceptically. Charlie went away.

He came back inside five minutes. He looked at the guard and nodded. Annie and Tony were ushered inside the yard.

'Open the coat,' said Charlie to Annie.

'Hey!' said Tony.

'It's okay,' Annie told him, and unbuttoned her coat and held it open.

Charlie watched as one of the other men searched her pockets and then frisked her with leisurely relish. By the time his pal had finished, Annie felt completely fine about the damage she'd done to Charlie Foster.

Tony looked like thunder as the man repeated the exercise on him. Neither of them carrying, they had nothing to hide. Tony kept sending Annie looks that said, *What the fuck are we doing here?*

'Okay, come on,' said Charlie, and led the way.

Inside the static, Redmond and Orla Delaney were sitting at a desk. They stared at her steadily as she came up the steps and walked in. It was basic in here – a desk, three chairs, a lamp, a kettle and tea tray, some filing cabinets. Nothing fancy.

The twins said nothing. One man, one woman, with the same thick red hair, white skin, pale green eyes. Both tall, both thin. *Book ends*, thought Annie. A perfectly matched pair of beauties: cold as ice and twice as nasty.

Finally, Redmond spoke.

'Mrs Carter,' he said cordially. The faint Irish lilt was there in his voice. Southern Irish, like the voice on the phone. But Redmond's voice wasn't harsh, it was low and well educated. Totally deceptive, as she knew only too well. This effete and perfect specimen of manhood had ordered Billy murdered with as much compunction as he would swat a gnat.

Annie stepped forward. She felt nauseous and her hands were clammy with sweat. Her heart was pumping madly.

'Hello Redmond,' she said coolly. 'Hello Orla.'

'Annie,' acknowledged Orla.

'Can we do something for you?' asked Redmond.

Yeah, you can drop dead, the pair of you, she thought furiously.

But Annie remained outwardly calm. 'I've come here to set the record straight over a few things.'

The twins stared at her flatly.

Then Orla said: 'What do you mean?'

'I've come to say that what you did to Billy was beyond the pale. He didn't deserve it.'

Redmond shrugged his shoulders. 'We discussed this before, Mrs Carter. It was business. Nothing personal.'

'It was personal to me,' said Annie.

Again the shrug. He didn't give a fuck, she could see that. 'And was there anything else?'

447

'Yeah,' said Annie. 'Plenty. Max is dead. So's Jonjo.'

They were silent, staring. Brains whirring like calculators, if she was any judge.

'They were hit in Majorca,' she went on. 'They're gone.'

'I see,' said Redmond slowly.

'Yeah, I bet you do. But what you *don't* see yet – and I'm going to fill you in on this, stay with me – what you *don't* see is that I'm taking over here. Now we were friends once, and because of that I'm telling you all this, just marking your card before you decide to do anything foolish.' She could feel sweat trickling down her back. 'All the shit stops here. I run the Carter patch now. It belongs to me, and that's the way it's gonna stay. Max is gone. Jonjo's gone too. But I ain't. So, before you get any ideas about taking over or anything rash like that, think again. I've got muscle, and no one is taking anything away from the Carters.'

When she finished speaking, they were silent, taking it all in.

'You're still in Limehouse,' said Redmond at last.

'Not for much longer.'

'Good.'

'I appreciate you letting me stay there,' said Annie, although it nearly choked her. 'It's temporary, as I said. But Dolly Farrell's my friend and I'd

like to call on her in the future if I can. I appreciate it's your patch and I respect that. But I'd like
to be able to call in there. Just occasionally.'

Redmond shrugged again. 'I don't see why you
shouldn't. You see, Mrs Carter, I'm not an un-
reasonable man. Now if that's all . . . ?'

'Yeah,' said Annie. 'That's all.'

She turned and walked out of the little office,
back down the steps. She crossed the yard with
Tony, and the guard let them out, the Alsatian
emitting a low, threatening growl throughout.
Charlie Foster and his co-workers watched them
blankly as they got back into the Jag.

'Jesus,' said Tony.

Annie sat back, feeling on the point of nervous
collapse. She closed her eyes.

'Amen,' she said faintly.

63

'Hot candle wax,' Aretha was saying to Annie and the others later in the day when Annie got back. They were all sitting around the kitchen table. 'Can you believe that?'

'I can believe *anything*,' said Darren, sipping tea and shivering.

'But don't it hurt?' asked Dolly.

'That's the buzz, I guess,' said Aretha with a shrug.

'What a bloody pervert,' said Ellie, dipping into the biscuit tin.

'Hey, whatever gets you through the night,' said Aretha. 'That's what massa wanted, that's what massa got. So there I was, dripping *hot candle wax* on to his balls, and you know what? He seemed to like it.'

'Takes all sorts,' said Darren.

'But when he said he wanted me to pass the

flame over his *cojones*, I drew the line. Think that's more Una's bag than mine. She enjoys beating the living crap out of men, after all. Has a fucking *orgasm* when she hurts people. Burning their balls has just *got* to be a major turn-on for that bitch.'

Annie took off her coat and sat down. Dolly pushed a mug towards her and poured the tea. Annie thought that marriage had softened Aretha, just the same as it had softened her. Which could be a bad thing, and she knew it. She wanted to tell Aretha, to warn her not to let her guard down too far, but she kept quiet and drank her tea. Tried, for five blissful minutes, not to think of the complete mess her life had become. Then Ross came in, and gave her a note.

A *pizzino*, he said coldly. For Mrs Carter.

'What's it say?' asked Dolly eagerly as Annie unfolded it. 'Hey, that's all numbers.'

'It's code,' said Annie, and quickly deciphered it.

It said: *Come Friday morning. Early. C.*

'Is that from Constantine Barolli?' asked Dolly. 'He's keen.'

'He's persistent, for sure,' said Annie. She thought about Constantine: handsome as the devil and just as alluring. She still didn't know if she could trust him. She didn't know *who* she could trust any more. She looked across at Ellie, who was watching her. Redmond must know that she had been in talks with the Mafia boss, because Ellie knew and Ellie was the Delaneys' insider. Nothing happened here that the Delaneys didn't know about.

Ellie blushed as she saw Annie returning her gaze.

'It's okay,' she said sulkily. 'I don't grass to the Delaneys no more.'

Dolly gave her a stern look.

'Yeah, we had a talk about that, didn't we?' Dolly looked at Ellie then at Annie. 'After we had all that trouble with Ellie after Pat Delaney popped off, I took her back in but there were terms. And those terms were, no grassing us up to the Delaneys. What happens inside these four walls – or even outside them if it concerns any of us – *don't* get told to them. That was the deal, and I think Ellie's stuck to it.'

'Course I have,' said Ellie uncomfortably.

'You'd bloody better have, if you know what's good for you.'

'I *have*,' Ellie insisted.

Annie looked at Ellie. She hoped Dolly was right.

'Everyone deserves a second chance,' said Dolly with a shrug.

Annie wasn't sure that she would have been so generous.

'Where's Una?' she asked, thinking of what Constantine had said to her about the woman's family link to Jeanette – and of what she would have to do about all that as soon as she got her chance to act.

She ached to batter Una, very soon. But for now, she knew she didn't dare. If she so much as mentioned the Byrne family to Una, word would without doubt shoot straight back to them that she was sniffing around, getting clever.

No – it was safer to keep quiet. Safer for Layla. For now she would have to hold back. But later, she promised herself, they were going to pay for what they'd done, every one of them.

Annie squirmed with thwarted rage as she thought of the harm the Byrnes had inflicted on her family. For now they had her right where they wanted her. Right where they could keep an eye on her. Right where she could not even think of retaliating.

Una. That bitch. And silly, chatty Jeanette. Vita, the unknown sister. Danny – what about this Danny, was it him who had lopped off Layla's finger, was it him she spoke to on the phone? And Jimmy! Jimmy *had* to be involved, and for that she was going to have his guts.

But not yet.

'Una's out,' said Dolly, pulling a face. '*And* she ain't signed the bloody book again. Thinks rules are for other people, that one.'

I can't do a damned thing to her anyway, thought Annie. *My hands are tied. I'm in chains.*

But Layla was alive, she knew that now. And Constantine might be pissed off with her, but he was still there, still on her side. She hoped.

Ross put his head around the kitchen door. 'Client,' he said. 'For Aretha.'

Aretha hauled herself to her feet.

'A woman's work is just *never* done,' she complained with a grin, and went off into the hall.

64

Annie went and sat upstairs on the bed to think. She got out Max's ring and held it in her hand; it gave her some comfort. In the other one she had the *pizzino* from Constantine Barolli.

Come Friday morning. Early. C.

She closed her eyes and let it all wash over her: the rage, the grief, the guilt, the fear. Max was gone for ever, and she had to accept that. *Had* to. She could hear Norman Greenbaum's *Spirit in the Sky* drifting out from Ellie's room. Lyrics all about death.

But accepting Max's death was hard, almost too hard to bear. He was dead, and she was still alive, and she almost wished their positions were reversed. But Max wouldn't allow his feelings to stand in the way of what he needed to do, and neither must she.

She had to be strong.

Dig deep and stand alone.

She'd lived by that creed all her life, clinging to it when the going got hard. It had sustained her, allowed her to always find a way through.

Would she find a way through this time?

She had to.

Annie turned her face into the pillow and gritted her teeth and *willed* herself to be strong enough to go on with this.

She had to find a way through the obstacles, to get Layla back.

Yes, Max was gone.

And there was something else she had to privately admit to – that there was a strong tug of attraction between her and Constantine Barolli, and that it was mutual. She thought of Barolli, suave bloody American, handsome, authoritative, sitting over there in Holland Park with everything nicely under control.

She thought of his family – his exquisite yet sour-faced sister Gina, the angelic Alberto, and slimy, dark-eyed Lucco, who had seen that there was a spark there, and warned her off. She thought of Constantine's wife, Maria, dead five long years. He'd been through what Annie was going through now. He knew how it felt.

How it felt was *bad*.

She clutched Max's ring harder, felt the metal digging into her palm and welcomed the pain of it.

It was no use, though – whatever she did, however she felt, there was no way to summon him back to her side, no way now to make it all right again.

Max was *gone*.

And she was still here.

And so – for now at least – was Layla. She had to cling on to that.

So she was going to have to go to Constantine's early on Friday, and this time she was going to make sure that things went smoothly between them. He would provide the cash as soon as she fell into line, so she would do it.

Friday morning, early.

This time, she was *determined* to do it.

Until then, all she could do was wait.

Oh yeah – and *pray*.

65

It was an attack designed to evoke panic.

They broke down the door of the little house near the Albert Docks at one o'clock in the morning, storming in, shouting and screaming and brandishing weapons. They ran down the hall into the kitchen, kicking open doors into the lounge, the cellar, what had once been a dining room. They ran up the stairs, kicking open more doors, bounding into rooms, intent on mayhem, on sudden surprise, on making anyone in there freeze with fear and not have time to try to harm the girl or use her as a shield.

The one in charge stood up there in the empty bedroom, looking around him in disgust. Nothing. No one.

Fuck it.

One of the boys came up the stairs behind him.

'They haven't been gone long. Trash in the bin. Stove's been used.'

A miss is as good as a mile, thought the one in charge.

'You want us to do door-to-door round the area?

'Yeah,' he sighed. 'Do it.'

66

'Two days and we'll be out of here,' said Danny confidently.

They were in a scruffy family safe house near Epping Forest. Vita sat at the kitchen table with her watercolours. Phil was leaning against the worktop, sipping tea. They said nothing.

'We're nearly home and dry.'

There was no response.

'We get the money, drop the kid off, smooth as silk. Well, ain't you got nothing to say about it?' Danny asked Vita, nudging her shoulder.

Vita pulled a face. 'Just that I'll be fucking glad when all this is over,' she said.

'*Now* what's bit you up the arse?' hollered Danny. 'Christ, you're a moody cow.'

'I hate this place. I've hated all the places we've been in, they're pigsties.'

'They *got* to be, Dumbo. What, you think we

should stay in some posh neighbourhood where people would say, who the hell are they, mooching about? And tell the fuzz all about it? It's quiet here, out in the sticks, it's ideal.'

'I just want it all over,' said Vita, dabbing at a duck's wing with a little turquoise paint.

Amen to that, thought Phil. The pair of them were arguing again. They were always arguing. Nutters, both of them. Talk about bad blood. Vita was half-simple but Danny was *seriously* demented. Killing that couple on the island, that had been bad. And harming the kid had been worse. He hadn't signed up for anything like that. He looked at Danny and thought, *Mad bastard.*

'You got something to say?' Danny asked Phil with a challenging grin.

Phil shrugged. 'Not a thing,' he said.

'Well, good,' said Danny, and poured himself some tea, thinking that really everything was working out just fine.

By Friday he would have more money than he'd ever had before, and that felt good. He might give Vita a small share, but he wasn't planning on letting Phil have any. In fact, he was planning on giving Phil a very nasty surprise, a *terminal* sort of surprise, poor old Phil. And of course, he wasn't going to hand over the kid. It was a pity, but after all, it made perfect sense. She had seen his face. And he couldn't have that.

67

Constantine got the call at dawn on Friday morning. He was an early riser – most of the family were – so he was already up and in the study, talking to Lucco, when the conversation with his son was interrupted by the phone. Lucco listened to his father speaking and his lips grew tight. He was getting everyone working hard to help the Carter woman. Lucco knew why. Lucco had seen her and, more important, he had seen the two of them together.

'What you got?' Constantine asked the man on the phone.

'We got an address. A Byrne cousin's got a house out in the wilds near Epping. We got it staked out, from a safe distance.' He gave Constantine the address. 'I've seen two guys going in and out, no one else. What you want us to do?'

'Hold back. Keep watch. I'm coming.'

Constantine put the phone down and stood up. 'Got to go, Lucco,' he said. 'Business.'

Lucco nodded. 'For the Carter woman, yes?'

'For Mrs Carter.' Constantine looked at Lucco, sitting there, pouting like a truculent five year old. 'You got a problem?'

Lucco shrugged and stood up. 'No, not at all,' he lied. 'I'll leave you to it.'

Constantine watched his son leave the room. Lucco. Dark and deep, just like Maria, his mother, had been. He had loved that trait in Maria, loved her mystery, her sensuality. Annie Carter had that quality too. You never knew which way she was going to jump, you only knew that her direction would surprise you. He liked that. He liked *her*.

But shit – he'd blown his chances with her, big time.

And anyway, for today, the girl must be his priority.

68

Annie, Dolly, Aretha, Darren, and Ellie were having breakfast. Annie was sunk in gloom. Today was *it*. At midday the kidnapper would phone her.

Within the next hour she had to get her arse over to Constantine's and do the deed. Last chance. Get the cash from him. Christ knew he could spare it; he was loaded. Save Layla. Or, if not, lose Layla for good.

Dolly was moaning on about Una not showing up for work again.

'Friday's party day. I've told her time and again, we need to get everything in place ready for the party, no hanging around in bed and no going out on the piss on Thursday nights with your druggie mates, but does she listen? Does she fuck as like.'

'Hey, no sweat, I can fill in,' said Aretha, glancing at Annie with a sigh.

Ross stuck his head round the kitchen door. He was holding out a note and he looked narked.

'Another one of these bloody things just came. For you again.' He held it out to Annie.

What the fuck now? she wondered, taking it. Another fifteen minutes and she'd have been on the road to Constantine's place, all primed and ready to do the deed and bag the money. *Now* what?

'What's it say?' asked Darren.

Annie looked up at him briefly.

Poor bloody Darren. His eyes looked sunken. His hair, once so lustrous, was dry. He coughed all the time now – a dry, hacking cough. No clients now. He wasn't up to that; didn't even look good enough to attempt it any more.

Her eyes drifted on to meet Aretha's, and she saw her own concern for Darren reflected there. And on to Ellie. Ellie the traitor, given another chance by Dolly, who was so kind, the best friend any woman could ever have; and look at the shit Annie had brought to her door, and yet still, *still*, Dolly hadn't turned her away.

She looked at the note from Constantine. Spread it out on the table. She was now so panicked, so completely driven by dread, that she found it hard to break the code. Possibly because he was saying something different this time. *Oh sure*, she thought. Like, *Your arse is mine*. But then, she knew that already.

She had to force herself to concentrate, to break the very simple code. A was four, B was five. She read it, very slowly, struggling with the numbers and the words this time because she was in a dark place in which her baby could die unless she complied with Constantine's demands.

Well, she had already decided that she was going to do it. She had a second bite of the cherry, and she had to take it. She knew that.

She would read this note, and then she would go over to Holland Park, get it over with. Get the money. Get Layla. Please God, let her get Layla.

'Come on, Annie, don't keep us in suspense, what's it say?' demanded Dolly, craning over to get a look.

Annie's jaw had slowly dropped as she deciphered Constantine's latest *pizzino*.

'Annie?' Ellie was staring at her. 'What is it, what's wrong?'

'Come on, girl,' urged Aretha, eyes wide with worry. 'Tell us, for fuck's sake. What is it? Is it . . . is it bad . . . ?'

Annie looked up and her eyes were full of shock.

The kitchen was silent.

'He's found them,' she said numbly. 'He's only gone and fucking found them. The address is right here.'

And the kitchen erupted in yells and screams, such a frenzy of delight that Ross came charging in and asked what the *fuck* had happened now? But they only laughed. All except Annie, whose shock had deepened to nothing less than abject fear.

What if Layla was dead already?

Yes, she had spoken to her on the phone, but they could have done it straight afterwards. Killed her. Too much trouble to let her live, to deliver her back to her mother. They'd already hurt her. They were animals. Scum. Pond life.

She looked at the note again while all the others whooped and leapt around the kitchen in a mad cacophony of joy.

'I've got to get there,' she said dazedly, clinging on to the merest chance that Layla might still be in the land of the living. She stood up, shaking, and went into the hall to get her coat.

'Wait a sodding minute,' said Dolly. 'If you're going, we're coming with you.'

'Yeah,' said Ellie and Darren together.

'Damn sure,' nodded Aretha.

'No,' said Annie, already in the hall, shrugging on her coat, Ross standing there looking at them all as if they'd finally flipped.

'Yes,' said Dolly.

Annie didn't have time to argue the toss. She hesitated, then said: 'Wait.'

She tore up the stairs and into Dolly's room. Flung open the knicker drawer, took out the Smith

& Wesson, checked it was properly loaded, checked the safety was on, shoved it in her coat pocket. Then she ran back down the stairs and straight out of the front door.

They all ran after her. They barrelled up to the Jag, parked at the pavement with Tony sitting there, reading his paper behind the wheel.

Annie piled in the front, Dolly and her workers jumped in the back.

'What the f—?' asked Tony, dropping his paper.

Annie told him where they were going, and why.

'Fucking hell,' said Tony. He gunned the engine and shot out into the traffic with the Jag's wheels screaming in protest. He didn't even apologize for the language.

69

Danny was going to make the call at twelve noon, tell the Carter woman where to drop off the money, and no funny business or else she wouldn't get her daughter back, alive or dead.

Now it was nearly eleven, and he was getting sort of nervous.

After all, it wasn't every day you took possession of half a million pounds.

He sat there at the kitchen table and daydreamed pleasurably about what he would do with it. Jimmy would take his share and Vita would get a small cut: that was okay. But he'd need the rest, get a nice place abroad in the sun, get a car, get all the pussy he could *eat*, it would be fucking amazing.

'Today's the day then, yeah?' Vita said behind him, washing up dishes, making all that bloody noise, clattering stuff about. Jesus, she was a pain in the arse.

'Yeah,' he grunted, looking at the pistol in front of him on the table, its clip already loaded, ready for action.

'I'll be glad when it's all over,' said Vita for about the zillionth time.

'Yeah,' said Danny.

'It's been hard,' said Vita. 'And, let's face it, you ain't made it any easier.'

Why doesn't she ever just shut the fuck up? wondered Danny.

'You got to admit that's the truth, Dan,' she went on.

Danny imagined picking the pistol up, half turning in his seat, and blowing Vita's tiny, troublesome pea brain straight out of that window over the sink. Now he remembered why he'd left home so early. Their mum had been a nag too. In fact, all the women in his family seemed to have a talent for mindless high-pitched chatter – except Una, who was so spaced out of her head most of the time that she said very little.

Jeanette was nearly unbearable, gabbling on yack-yack-yack all day and night. She might have a good body but, let's face it, her brain was screwed.

His poor old dad. A nag for a wife, and three stupid daughters, and just the one son, the one boy he could rely on.

Danny sat there feeling good about himself, even though reliability had never been his strong suit.

He didn't know how his father had ever stood it, but then Dad had been in and out of the nick for most of his life, mercifully, and his stays at home had usually been brief. His father had died inside, heart attack. Well, that wasn't going to happen to *him*, thought Danny. He was going to finish this one big job, then take the money and run as far and as fast as it would take him. Which was pretty fucking far, he believed.

'Dan? You're not saying much,' said Vita, turning away from the sink to look at him.

'That's because I never get a fucking *chance*,' said Danny. 'How's anyone supposed to get a word in edgeways with you always carping on?'

'Hey – it wasn't *my* idea to get into all this,' said Vita hotly. 'And it wasn't *my* idea to start cutting bits off the fucking kid either. I tell you straight, Dan, I don't like that one bit.'

'Will you for once let that fucking rest?' Danny stood up and loomed over his sister, his finger poking the air for emphasis. 'If you remember clearly, Vee, it was *you* who nearly lost the kid altogether; it was you who was fucking *stupid* enough to let her see your face – and mine, incidentally, and do you think *I'm* about to throw a party over that? You've got no right to stand there telling me what you *do* and what you *don't like!*'

'Well, there's no need to fucking shout at me like that,' yelled Vita.

'There's *every* need, Vee,' roared back Danny. 'You know what Mum ought to have called you? Eh, Vita? She should have called you fucking *Titanic*, because you're a bloody disaster.'

'Well, fuck you,' screamed Vita, hurling a plate into the sink where it smashed loudly. 'You think I ever wanted to be part of this crazy scheme? You think I was pleased when you and Jeanette cooked this up with her fucking boyfriend, that fly bastard Jimmy Bond?'

'Well, you were keen enough to join in when you thought about the money!' *And that's kind of funny, because you ain't seeing a penny of it now, you mouthy cow*, he thought.

'I signed up for the money, sure. But not for torturing innocent people. Not for cutting kids about. Not for that.'

Phil Fibbert had come soft-footed into the room, and here they were again. Shouting and screaming. Fighting. He reckoned they'd been doing it since the cradle, and would be doing it right up until they were tucked into their respective graves. Christ, he was so *sick* of hearing them ranting at each other.

This time he didn't hesitate.

He picked up the pistol from the table and with calm consideration he shot Danny through the back of the head. Danny's dead body shot forward against his sister, who started screaming in earnest, so Phil took aim and shot her too, straight between the eyes.

Silence fell.

Blissful, wonderful silence.

Phil liked silence.

He looked at the bodies, slumped on the floor. He frowned. He hadn't intended to *kill* them, but they'd been shouting and screaming and it was all like being small again, like being the small help-less boy he had once been, watching his mum and his dad, coming back roaring drunk from the pub and tearing lumps out of each other. He had cringed on the stairs as a child, watching, fearful, unable to sleep, unable to move, afraid they would kill each other – but at least, he had started to think, if they *did*, then it would be quiet.

It was certainly quiet now.

He loved the quiet.

He looked again at the bodies, piled up there by the sink. Looked at Vita's half finished painting of the Mandarin ducks on the table, her brush still standing in the sludge-coloured cup of water. She'd never finish it now.

A sound made him turn, look towards the door into the hall.

Layla was standing there, looking at the bodies. Her dark hair was tousled, and her bandaged hand was at her mouth. She looked very small. Her eyes, huge and dark green, met his.

Phil sighed.

He wasn't wearing his hood.

That *stupid* bloody Vita had left the kid's door unbolted again.

Oh *fuck*.

Now he was going to have to do it for real. He was going to make the call to the Carter woman instead of Danny, that was not a problem, but first he was going to have to kill the child. And then he'd have to get rid of the bodies, Vita's and Danny's – and now Layla's too, which was a damned shame, but there it was. Bury them all out in the woods somewhere: that was the thing to do.

He turned the pistol in her direction.

But she was quick.

Layla saw the gun swinging her way, and she ran.

70

Phil was getting impatient.

He had dashed out looking along the hallway, but he hadn't been quick enough; it was empty. The girl had gone. He checked the lounge, kicking over furniture. She was small, she could hide away, tuck herself into some little corner and he would *never* find her. But he had to find her. It was a quarter to twelve, he had to make the call in fifteen minutes, sort out the drop for the money; he had to keep his mind on that, and he had to find the bloody kid.

He looked upstairs, throwing open wardrobe doors, looking under beds, everywhere.

He couldn't find her.

Fuck it.

'Layla!' he bellowed.

No answer.

Only silence, and this time the silence wasn't

475

comforting. It was unnerving. Because he had to get this sorted, and quick. He glanced anxiously at his watch. Ten minutes to go and he had to call the Carter woman, get the money in place.

He went back down the stairs, *ran*, slipping and sliding, wondering where the hell she could be hiding. The outer doors were locked and they were too high for a kid not quite four years old to reach. She was still in here, somewhere.

It was then that he saw the cellar door was slightly ajar.

Smiling, he walked towards it.

He nudged the door open with his foot. The light at the top of the cellar steps was on. Low enough for her to reach, she'd fled down into the cellar, but the dark had spooked her and she'd put the light on and given the game away. She was down there.

'Oh, Layla!' he called, making his voice as friendly as he could. 'Come on sweetie.' Then he had a thought. Layla loved chocolate. 'Come on darlin', got some chocolate for you. It's okay, the nasty people are gone now. Come and have some of this chocolate, okay?'

He waited.

'Or else I'll just have to eat it myself,' Phil elaborated, walking softly down the steps. 'Layla?'

His eyes searched the gloom down there. The place was whitewashed and full of the usual household junk. The air smelled damp, fetid. A whiff of rat urine caught his nostrils and he winced. *Shit*. He hated rats.

'Come on, Layla, come and get the chocolate,' he cooed.

And Layla stepped out of the shadows and looked at him as he reached the bottom of the stairs.

He smiled.

Then a voice behind him said: 'Don't move, arsehole,' and the smile froze on his lips.

'You'd better put that fucking gun down. Right now,' said the voice behind Phil.

It was over, then. Fuck it. Phil thought of all they had gone through to get this far. All that time, trouble, and planning. Snatching the girl, kicking the mob boss off down the mountainside, shooting the brother right there by the pool, and then the hiding, the sneaking around and trying to keep it all under wraps while he'd been closeted with those two fruit-loop Byrnes. But now they were gone, and he was in charge and he had thought, he had really *believed*, that he could hack this. Polish off the kid, make the call, collect the money, and vamoose. But now there was someone behind him on the stairs, trying to put a stop to all that, and he wouldn't finish what they had begun in Majorca.

Phil just hated not to finish a thing once he'd started.

He'd always been the same. Liked things done *right*. Done *just so*. His dad had always said to him: 'Son, you start a job, you finish it.'

He would have finished this one a rich man.

Maybe he still could.

Looking down into the cellar, he could see that Layla had scooted off into the darker shadows again. Bloody kid, nothing but trouble. But he'd sort her out later. First . . .

He turned on the steps, as fast as he could. Fast as one of those gunslingers in those old Westerns his dad had loved to watch on the telly. But his dad had been a loser, and Phil was a winner. He saw the figure standing above him, outlined against the light at the top of the stairs, a clear target. Pale hair, a flowery shirt, flared cords. He took aim at the torso and fired. Up in the house somewhere, a woman screamed.

71

Constantine was out on the road near the house, three meaty henchmen at his side. He didn't look pleased to see Annie.

'What the fuck you doing here?' he asked her, as she and her mates swarmed out of the Jag.

He didn't *sound* very pleased, either. But fuck him. Layla was her daughter. She couldn't just stay away and do nothing.

'I've come for Layla,' said Annie.

'I think you should go home,' said Constantine.

'And *I* think you should forget it,' said Annie.

'I don't want you messing this up.'

'Look, if anyone's going to mess this up it's you, standing here having a fucking debate when my little girl's in there with those bastards.'

'Mrs Carter . . .'

'No. Don't even think about it. I'm staying put.'

Constantine looked at Annie, then at Dolly

standing there, all bubble-perm blonde and neatly suited, as much use on a day like this as a French poodle – but standing there anyway, obstinately, at Annie Carter's shoulder. He looked at Aretha looming behind her, her face black thunder. Tony was standing at the back of the group, like a brick wall.

'Where's Darren got to?' Dolly was looking around. 'And where the fuck's Ellie?'

'I don't think—' Constantine started.

That was when they heard the shots, and a woman screaming.

'*Jesus*,' said Annie, her face draining of colour.

'Gene, Michael, round the back,' said Constantine quickly, and two of the heavies shot off like well-trained attack hounds.

Annie stood there, frozen with fear for her little girl, swamped by dread but unable to act, terrified of what even moving could bring.

Dolly put an arm around her shoulders. Tried to give her comfort. Annie shrugged her off. She was totally strung out, all her attention focused on this remote, neglected house and what could be happening to Layla inside there *right now.*

Constantine and the other heavy ran up the path and the man crashed his shoulder into the door. It gave instantly, and he piled into the hallway, Constantine right behind him. Annie somehow got her legs moving and followed with Dolly.

The first thing they saw was Ellie cringing against the wall at the top of the cellar steps, and the cellar door standing wide open.

Tears were flooding down her face.

She looked at the men and then her eyes fastened on Annie.

'We went round the back. Darren got through the open window over the sink,' she sobbed. 'He's so skinny, you know how skinny he is, and he opened the door round there for me, and he heard the man down in the cellar talking to Layla, and he went down there and saw the gun in that man's hand and he just bluffed him, just said, put the gun down . . .' Her voice tailed off as she sobbed harder.

They didn't need to ask her to elaborate further. The man had shot Darren. Annie, Aretha, and Dolly stood there open-mouthed, aghast with horror.

'I saw her down there. I saw the little girl, I saw Layla,' Ellie cried.

One of the men barrelled past Ellie, who was being pulled into Dolly's comforting arms, and aimed a gun down the cellar steps. Annie surged forward, but Constantine held her back. The kitchen door was open and Annie stared at the bloodied corpses on the floor beside the sink.

One male, one female.

Jeanette's brother and sister, she guessed.

The one down in the cellar killed his partners in crime. He'd shot Darren, and God knew how badly he was hurt. Thwarted, he might now shoot Layla. Perhaps he had hold of her right now. Perhaps, right this instant, he was putting the muzzle of the gun to her head.

Annie shuddered.

The fact that he was trapped would make him even more dangerous and desperate. He knew the game was up, that there would be no payout, no good ending to this mad scheme. And, knowing that, he might decide what the hell? That he would thwart Annie Carter anyway, pay her back for breaking the rules, for having the temerity to come looking when they had told her no. He might even now kill Layla, out of spite.

Constantine's henchman was looking down the cellar steps. He looked briefly back at Constantine, held up one finger, then passed the finger across his throat.

One down.

Darren, thought Annie painfully. Poor brave bloody stupid Darren.

Then Constantine's man was gone, moving fast down the cellar steps. Another shot rang out, a ricochet, and a shout.

Oh Jesus, thought Annie. *Not Layla. Please, not Layla.*

72

Constantine's other boy was now at the top of the stairs, peering around the edge of the wall, very cautious. Shooters were being used; he was right to be bloody cautious. As Constantine and the women watched, he started off down the cellar steps.

'Take Ellie in there,' Annie hissed to Dolly, and Dolly nodded grimly and led the devastated girl into a shabby old lounge.

Annie exchanged a tense glance with Aretha. 'Go with them,' she said.

'No, girl.'

'Yes, Aretha,' said Annie firmly. 'I've got one friend down there who could be dead already, I don't want to have to worry about you too.'

Aretha reluctantly nodded and went into the lounge with Dolly and Ellie, pulling the door closed behind them.

Tony stood there at Annie's side. He looked at Constantine.

'What you want me to do?' he asked.

Fuck it, shouldn't he be asking me that? thought Annie angrily. She was the boss, not Constantine. It was *her* daughter these freaks had got hold of.

'Watch that she stays safe,' said Constantine, indicating Annie. He threw his coat aside, pulled out a pistol, and started to head towards the cellar steps.

Annie felt a new thrill of fear.

Not for her daughter.

Not for Darren.

Not for herself.

For *Constantine*. Because he was actually going to do it. He was going to lay his life on the line for her and for Layla.

'No, don't go down there,' she said.

Constantine stopped moving. He looked at her. Leaned in close, just for a fleeting moment. Kissed her lips.

Panic gripped her. She'd already lost Max. She could still lose Layla. She was shocked to find that she didn't want to lose Constantine, too.

What the hell is going on here? she wondered wildly.

He went over to the cellar door, and vanished down the steps.

'I'm going too,' said Annie, starting forward.

'No, Boss. No way,' said Tony, blocking her progress.

'Then you go. Go and help him, for God's sake!' Frantic, Annie drew out Max's revolver. His faithful old Smith & Wesson. 'It's a hair trigger, Tone. Be careful.' She handed him the gun.

Tony weighed it thoughtfully in his hand. 'You stay up here, okay, Boss? You stay up here where it's safe. We don't need too many down there, you got me?'

In other words, you're a woman, and a woman has no place in a situation like this.

It rankled with Annie, but she knew it made sense. 'I'll stay here,' she promised.

Tony gave her a cheery grin. 'We'll get Layla back, Boss. Don't you worry.'

And Tony too vanished into the cellar's maw, and she wondered if she was going to see any of them again.

Suddenly she was alone in the hallway. The cellar was quiet. She hugged herself hard and screwed her eyes tight shut. Horrible images crowded into her brain, of Layla scared, hurt, and alone. If ever there was a time when she had to dig deep, it was now.

She opened her eyes and they fastened on the nightmare just visible through the half-open kitchen door.

Two people, brother and sister, lying dead in a pool of blood.

She knew their names now. Vita and Danny Byrne.

She thought with vicious hatred of Jeanette, their sister, once Jonjo's bit of fluff and now the mistress of that traitorous bastard Jimmy Bond. Jeanette, with her motor mouth and her silly prancing ways: she had fooled them all. She had been the viper in the Carter nest, the insider, ready to turn against her hosts at a moment's notice, the greedy, treacherous cow. Annie promised herself that she wasn't even *started* with Jeanette and Jimmy yet, not by a long shot.

She froze as she saw the back door start to swing inward and she held her breath when she saw who was standing there.

'Vee? Dan?' Una called softly.

Una. Una really was in on it too.

Annie felt sick and dizzy with rage.

Una had watched her suffer, had enjoyed her suffering. All that smirking and stalking about the place, and all the time she had *known*; the bitch had known that Layla was being held hostage by her brother and sister. The whole Byrne family were due to profit from Annie and Layla's misery and distress, and from Max's and Jonjo's untimely deaths.

Bastards!

Una paused in the doorway, looking left and right. Her eyes fell upon the two bodies and her mouth dropped open. She fell to her knees beside them, muttering *no no no*, checking for pulses, her movements jerky with shock and horror.

Waste of fucking time.

Annie felt a shudder of grim satisfaction as she watched Una's frantic efforts to rouse her siblings.

No pulses there, not a hint of a breath.

Her brother and sister were dead.

Good riddance to bad rubbish, thought Annie.

For Una, reality sank in slowly. There were even a few tears squeezed out by that cold, hard, hateful bitch. Annie saw them fall on to the broken bodies lying there, heard the guttural sounds of grief emanating from her.

She had made those noises too. She recognized them. They were old friends, those noises of pain and anguish and unbearable loss. Her husband had died. Her daughter had been snatched and subjected to mutilation and incarceration and maybe even worse, how the hell would she know?

So Annie felt no sympathy for Una. None whatsoever. She stood there like a stone, watching as Una realized that her loved ones were gone. Then the blonde Amazon half turned towards the open hall door, and her eyes met Annie's.

Annie was smiling.

With maniacal speed, Una came screeching down the corridor towards her.

73

Layla huddled in a dark corner with her eyes closed. She felt safe that way. In fact, it was the only time she actually felt even a little bit safe, when her eyes were closed, because then she couldn't see anything bad, and if she couldn't see it, then it wasn't there.

Now she heard movement very near to her. Layla opened her eyes. It might be a rat. She had seen a rat down here just now. She didn't mind rats. They were like big mice.

But it wasn't a rat. It wasn't the man with the dark eyes and hair either. It was a big, bald-headed man wearing golden earrings with tiny crucifixes dangling from the small gold hoops. The man held a finger to his lips as their eyes met in the half-gloom. His lips moved.

Shh, Layla. Keep quiet.

Layla stared at the man. He was ugly but he had nice eyes, kind eyes. Probably, Layla decided, he wasn't a man at all. He was probably an angel, Mummy had told her that she had a guardian angel and that the angel looked after her. Layla had begun to doubt that, just a little. But here the angel was, shushing her. Saying that everything would be all right.

The angel was coming closer.

But what if he *wasn't* an angel?

What if he was a bad person, like those other bad people?

She opened her mouth; she was going to scream.

The angel put his hand over her mouth, shook his head.

No, Layla, keep quiet, it's all right, it's all going to be okay, he mouthed.

And then there were more loud noises, bangs and things, and that funny smell that guns made when they went off, and Layla buried her face in the big man's neck and tried not to cry. When she dared to look up, she could see someone moving behind him, someone approaching fast. Someone big and dark and strong. Her eyes widened in alarm but she couldn't tell the man, because his hand was still over her mouth. She couldn't tell him there was danger.

74

Una came at Annie like a thing possessed. Annie just had time to fish in her pocket and to think, *Oh fuck, I ain't got the kiyoga,* when Una crashed into her like a ton of bricks, punching, kicking and biting.

Annie fell back, arms up, blows raining down on her from all directions.

Una was bigger and stronger than her and she was enraged. Annie was driven back against the hall wall. A stunning blow caught her on the side of the head and she saw stars. She lost her footing and slid down the wall, dazed, disorientated. She saw Una looming over her, saw Una's booted foot coming in, swinging in slow motion towards her stomach, and she tried to double over, to protect herself from the blow, but still there was terrible pain, it exploded hotly in her midriff and she screwed her face up in agony.

Rib, thought Annie, nausea flooding into her throat. *Has she broken my fucking rib?*

Una was coming in for a second kick.

Fuck it, thought Annie. She knew that Una's boot had only to catch her in the wrong spot and she could bleed internally, bleed to death, in less time than it took to say knife.

Knife.

In the kitchen, there would be knives. If only she could reach the kitchen

Which she couldn't.

Annie tried to stand up but wobbled on her feet like a newborn lamb.

Una's kick landed on her shin.

Bitch.

Annie fell to her knees, turning her body into the wall to shield it from Una's punches and kicks.

Una was screaming, calling her a *bitch*, a murdering fucking *bitch*.

I'm dead, thought Annie. *This is it, I'm dead.*

Una pulled her leg back.

Annie sagged there and watched her do it.

Should have listened to Dolly, she thought dimly. *Una's not the sort to let a grudge go.*

She braced herself for the next kick. There was nothing else left to do.

75

Tony saw Layla's eyes widen, saw her staring over his shoulder, knew someone was coming up fast behind him. He half turned, raising the gun, trying to shield her small body with his own much larger one, and found himself staring into the black muzzle of a pistol with a strong steady arm and menacing dark eyes behind it.

'Drop the gun,' whispered the man.

Tony put the gun down. From up there in the hall he could hear a commotion, a woman screaming and swearing hysterically. The Boss was in trouble up there and, fuck it, now he was in trouble down *here*; his brains were about to paint this gloomy sodding hole in the ground, and the kid was going to die too.

'Put the kid down,' said the man.

Tony lowered Layla lightly to the ground.

'Come here, kid,' said Phil.

Layla bolted.

The man let out a shout and in the same instant there was a deafening noise and the gun spun away.

'*Shit!*' he roared, clutching at his bloody right hand.

Two of his fingers were gone, and Tony couldn't have given a flying fuck for the man's pain.

Constantine stepped out of the shadows, holding a smoking gun.

'Watch it!' yelled Tony, as Phil Fibbert pulled out a knife.

76

Annie was waiting for the next kick. It was going to hurt like crazy, and she was bracing herself to take it, or maybe to catch Una's foot if she could, hold it, tip the crazy, despicable bitch off balance. That was her plan.

It wasn't much of a plan, she knew that.

She felt very weak and her stomach was throbbing. Una had already done some damage. She braced herself, waiting for the kick.

It didn't come.

Una let out a shriek of rage.

Annie looked up and saw that Aretha, six feet of solid black muscle, had come out of the lounge on hearing all the noise Una was making, and she had grabbed Una's leg on the backswing and held it. Una was left hopping there, off balance, peering back in rage and hate at the woman now standing behind her.

'Hey, stupid – why don't you just pick on someone your *own* size?' Aretha demanded, and gave Una's leg a heavy sideways shove.

Una went flying and ended up in a tangle of arms and legs beside the kitchen door. But instead of coming back at Aretha straight away, she turned and ran into the kitchen.

Ellie and Dolly crowded out through the open lounge door. Ellie screamed when she saw what was going on in the hall. Dolly fell to her knees beside Annie, fearing she was seriously hurt.

'Watch out, Aretha!' yelled Annie, who was still watching Una.

But Aretha was on it. Years of beating up on willing clients had given her strength and speed, and the physique of a honed athlete. She tore after Una, and caught her before she got to the knife drawer beside the sink, bringing her down with a flying tackle.

Una was tough. She wriggled sideways, and booted Aretha in what should have been her face, but Aretha saw it coming and turned aside at the last moment so that it only caught her shoulder. Even so, it was painful. Aretha winced and let out a shout of protest. Then she clawed her way up Una's squirming body and socked her squarely on the jaw.

Una's head thudded back on to the hard tiled floor. '*Bitch*,' she gasped out, and stuck her foot in Aretha's midriff and hauled her up so that she went flying over her head.

Aretha hit the floor hard, all the wind knocked out of her. She lay there for seconds, unable to do a thing. Una grabbed her chance to scramble up on to hands and knees and come at her again. Una belted Aretha on the jaw, but Aretha shot straight up after that and hit Una between the eyes.

Ellie came flying into the kitchen, trying to pull Una off Aretha, but Una turned and whacked her hard across the face, knocking her aside. Then she turned and socked Aretha again. This time the blow really connected. Aretha's head spun. She fell back on to the floor and lay there, dazed.

Una saw her moment. She struck Aretha savagely again, then scrabbled above her to open the sink drawer and reach the knives inside. They were right beside the two dead bodies of Una's brother and sister. Aretha's leg brushed against one of them and she felt a chill as the skin on the corpse was already cooling. Hell, *she'd* be cooling too, if she didn't stop the bitch getting a fucking carving knife out of that damned drawer . . .

Una's hand fastened over a tin-opener and she brought it down viciously towards Aretha's forehead. Aretha rolled, and the tin-opener speared her dreadlocks, pinning one to the floor. Aretha tugged, but she was nailed there. Panicking, she saw Una going for the drawer again, unable to see what she was reaching for, but scrabbling around in there, looking for something, anything, to finish this.

Aretha grabbed Una's arm, but her hand was slippery from the blood off the corpses. She could dimly hear Ellie screaming at Una to *stop, for God's sake stop*, and Dolly was shouting at Ellie to fucking well *do* something. She saw the knife in Una's hand, saw her start with the upswing, and thought, *oh shit*

Tried to get her head free again.

Couldn't do it.

The knife was coming down.

77

Phil Fibbert lunged forward.

'Christ!' yelled Tony, grabbing Layla and shielding her with his own body.

But Constantine's men were on it. Phil went down in a devastating hail of bullets, the knife still clutched in his hand. He crumpled into a heap and lay there, twitching and bloody on the cold concrete floor.

There was a sudden silence.

Constantine was the first to move, gathering Layla up, pulling her in tight against him so that she couldn't see the mess that was all that was left of her kidnapper.

From above them, up in the main body of the house, they could hear women screaming and shouting.

'Jeez,' said Tony, and pushed past Constantine and his two helpers, tore up the stairs two at a time past the fallen body of Darren and barrelled out into the hall.

Annie was crouching there, clutching her side. Dolly was there too, kneeling beside her, sobbing and pointing towards the kitchen. 'Aretha!' she screamed at him.

Tony dashed into the kitchen, slipping and nearly going down on to the cheap tatty lino in his haste.

He saw Aretha pinned down and Una straddling her with a knife in her hand, drawing back her arm to stab Aretha.

He saw Ellie there, trying to hold Una's arm back and failing.

In one movement he pushed Ellie aside and caught Una's arm and pulled back. The woman gave a shriek of protest, and Tony punched her hard in the face. She fell back onto the bodies of her brother and sister, groaning.

Aretha lay there, stunned, breathing hard, vaguely surprised to still be alive.

'You okay?' asked Tony, ripping the tin-opener out of the lino to free her dreads.

Aretha sat up, nodding shakily.

'Mad *bitch*,' she muttered, looking sideways at Una, who was now weeping over the bodies, clutching at her sister's limp hand, smoothing her brother's lifeless torso.

'She's finished,' said Tony. Una looked up and

her eyes were full of hatred as she stared at him. Tony stood up and grabbed her arm, hauling her to her feet. He shook her like a dog shakes a rat.

But Una wasn't finished yet. She swung round fast and stabbed her fingers at Tony's eyes. He fell back with a shout, tumbling over the corpses, losing his grip on her.

'Crazy *bitch*,' he muttered, scrambling back to his feet, but Una was out through the back door at a run.

'Shit,' said Tony, and launched himself after her.

'Tone!' shouted Annie from the hall.

Tony stopped in the doorway. Looked back at Annie.

'Let her go,' said Annie. 'For now.'

'Fuck it all,' said Aretha painfully. She sat up, wincing. Then her brow creased with worry as she looked at Tony. 'You got the kid? You got Layla?'

'She's fine. Look.' He indicated the open door into the hallway.

Aretha looked, and started to smile through her pain.

Constantine had emerged from the cellar carrying Layla.

Incredulously, Annie stumbled to her feet.

'Layla? Baby?' she whispered, hardly able to believe it.

Layla looked at her mother crossly. 'Mummy, where have you *been*?' she demanded.

A wild laugh escaped Annie. *In hell,* she thought. *I've been in hell and now I'm out of it.*

Layla held out her arms to Annie.

Annie took her daughter in her arms, not caring that it hurt her ribs, and hugged her tight, and kissed her.

'You're squeezing me too hard, Mummy,' objected Layla.

'Sorry, sweetheart,' mumbled Annie against Layla's neck.

She caught Layla's hand, looked at the bandage there, where her daughter's tiny finger should be. Her face clouded.

'Oh, my poor sweet baby. Does it hurt?' she moaned, wishing she could have spared Layla this.

Layla shook her head. 'No, it itches.'

'That means it's getting better,' said Dolly, smiling shakily at the little girl.

'I don't like those people,' said Layla. 'They're nasty.'

Annie looked at Constantine over Layla's silky dark head.

'Thank you,' she said.

'We'll get her checked over,' he said. 'But she looks fine. You okay?'

Annie nodded. Her ribs hurt but she didn't give a fuck. She had Layla back.

'I owe you,' she said. *And I didn't believe in you, not for an instant.*

She felt bad about that now. Worse than bad.

She had thought that Constantine was stringing her along, intent only on using her as a sex object, uncaring of her daughter's plight.

She'd been wrong. She could see that now.

All the time, while she'd been stumbling around trying to find answers, feeling desperate, bewildered, barely able to function, Constantine had had his people working steadily toward this moment, when she would be reunited with Layla, her beloved daughter, her little star.

Layla was peering over her shoulder at Constantine, her eyes bright with interest.

'You're pretty,' she told him.

Annie laughed and hugged her hard.

'Well, at least I've found favour with *one* of the Carter women,' said Constantine with a wry smile, picking up his coat and dusting it off.

'Where's Daddy?' asked Layla.

The laughter died in Annie's throat. She didn't answer. She couldn't. She looked at Constantine. His smile was gone. He pulled on his coat, saying nothing.

Ellie had moved to the top of the cellar steps and was looking down, her face a picture of misery.

'Oh God, Darren . . .' she muttered, and went back down the steps.

Dolly followed, and Aretha.

Annie stood there looking anxiously after them,

holding Layla. She looked at Constantine. He shook his head and held open his arms.

'I'll take her,' he said.

'Mummy . . .' whined Layla as Annie made to hand her over.

'It's okay, sweetheart, stay with the nice man just for a moment while Mummy does something important,' said Annie.

Layla allowed herself to be transferred into the stronger, surer arms of Constantine Barolli.

With a new dread in her heart, Annie followed Dolly and Aretha. Constantine's men were still down in the cellar, tidying up the remains of Phil Fibbert. Ellie was a quarter of the way down the cellar steps, kneeling beside the crumpled form of Darren. She looked up, face streaked with tears, as the three other women came down.

'He looked back at me when he was coming down here,' she said to them all. 'He had a look on his face . . . like he was saying, "Oh well, may as well go out with a bang . . ." Oh Darren, you bloody fool.'

She started to sob.

Dolly looked hopelessly at Annie. They all clustered around him. He was still breathing, but weakly. His torso was a bloody, mangled mess.

'We'll get an ambulance . . .' said Aretha.

'Don't you fucking dare,' whispered Darren.

They all fell silent.

His eyes flickered open. He looked up at Dolly, Aretha, Annie, and at Ellie who was in floods of tears.

'Don't c-cry you daft mare,' he said faintly. 'Better this way.'

Darren knew he was dying. They'd all known that the wasting disease was going to take him one day, and it would be a long, slow, painful process – much worse than this.

Annie thought that Darren was right. It really was better this way. He'd done this reckless, heroic thing and they all had to be proud of him for it. He'd charged in to save Layla, knowing that his own life might be the forfeit. It was better to go for it than to just hang around, waiting for death to sneak up on you.

But still, Annie felt the grief cutting into her like a razor-edged knife.

Darren had been a good friend: the best. They had been through so much together, all five of them. And now it was time to say goodbye.

She leaned in close to him, knowing that this was all down to her; that Darren was dying because of her, because of Layla.

'Is there anything I can do for you?' she asked him.

'Can't think of a damned thing,' he said, and gave a weak ghost of his usual cheery smile. Then the smile faded and he winced and coughed. Blood sprang to his lips. Ellie wiped it away with a corner of her cardigan.

'Don't try to talk,' said Dolly, distraught.

'Won't have the . . . chance much longer,' he said, grimacing.

'It's okay,' said Dolly, her voice cracking with emotion. 'Just rest, just try and rest . . .'

'Yeah, what made you think you could charge in here and act the bloody hero anyway?' asked Aretha, but the harsh words were softened by a tone of love. There were tears on her cheeks. She was going to miss him like crazy. They all were.

'You're only jealous . . . because you didn't get the . . . chance to do it,' whispered Darren, and started coughing again. He closed his eyes.

'Shh,' said Dolly soothingly.

Darren's blue eyes opened. They looked around vaguely, as if he couldn't see too well. They fastened on Annie's face.

'There is something,' he mumbled.

'Name it,' said Annie. 'Anything.'

Darren told her. Annie nodded, and tried to smile at him. 'It's done,' she assured him.

'And so am I, my darlings . . .' sighed Darren, closing his eyes again.

'You're such a fucking drama queen,' cried Aretha.

'Yeah, that's me . . .' He coughed again, wincing with pain. 'Oh . . . fuck . . .'

'Shh,' said Dolly, her face fraught as she smoothed his brow with her hand, giving him whatever comfort she could.

Darren stopped coughing, his breath wheezing out, all the tension seeming to drain out of him.

He didn't breathe in.

They watched him. Nothing.

Annie put her hand to his neck. There was no pulse.

Darren was gone.

78

Tony took the girls back to Limehouse an hour later. They were all subdued. After Constantine made a couple of quick telephone calls he left with Annie and Layla, leaving two of his men to stay there and see to the clearing-up of the kidnappers and to make arrangements for Darren. They would take him to a hospital and leave him there. Nothing else they could do for him right now.

'Go careful with him,' Annie told him.

Constantine's other heavy drove him and Annie and Layla round to Harley Street where a private doctor was waiting to check Layla out.

Annie stayed with Layla while the doctor gave her a thorough examination, assisted by a friendly, professional nurse. They checked over the stump on her hand and replaced the dressings, declaring that it was healing and would cause her no trouble.

Yeah, except she's going to be one finger short for the rest of her life, thought Annie angrily.

They also checked her to be sure that she had not been physically or sexually assaulted, something Annie protested against at first, but she knew it had to be done. To Annie's great relief, Layla was fine. Completely fine. It was Annie who physically shook and felt nauseous and bit her lip throughout the examination, while Layla chatted brightly to the nurse and seemed to be suffering no ill effects whatsoever.

'The problems might manifest themselves later,' said the doctor to Annie, when it was all – thank God – over.

'Meaning?' Annie asked, anxiety flooding through her like a poisonous stream.

'Children sometimes bury things,' he said. 'Painful things. And sometimes these things come out later. Physically she is fine, but mentally there may be scars.'

Annie listened as Layla wittered on to the nurse, seemingly completely okay. But maybe damaged.

Please don't let that be the case, she prayed. *You've brought her home to me, now let that be the end of it.*

Then they checked Annie herself. There was bad bruising over her ribs, and on her legs, but she was tough; she'd survive, she'd heal.

Constantine was in the waiting room. He stood

up when she emerged and Layla dashed straight over to him, smiling. Annie hung back a little, more cautious than her daughter. But didn't they say kids always knew who was basically good and who was bad?

Constantine was a mobster. Annie had no illusions about that. But also . . . also he had moved heaven and earth to help her. Layla already liked him. And she had to confess, if only to herself, that she liked him too.

She liked the way he squatted down to Layla's level and chatted easily to her about how nice the doctor was, and that the nurse was a lovely lady, not as nice as her mummy, but really lovely.

'Well, your mummy's a very special lady,' he told her gravely.

'Yeah, she is. My daddy's nice too.'

Constantine's eyes met Annie's over Layla's head.

Jesus, how was she supposed to break news like that to Layla? wondered Annie hopelessly. How could she possibly tell a girl who was not quite four years old that her father was dead?

'It'll all work out,' Constantine told her when she stood there looking troubled. It was as if he'd read her mind.

Constantine stood up, swinging Layla up into his arms. She laughed at the speed of it, and clung on to him as if she'd always known him, as if none of this nightmare had even happened.

509

Children bury things, Annie recalled the doctor's words. *Problems can come out later.*

'Will it all work out? Really?' Annie fretted, wondering if, after all this, Layla could stand to hear that Max was gone.

'Sure it will,' he told her positively. 'The worst is over. Where to now?'

Annie told him where she wanted to go next. 'But if you're busy, I can call Tony . . .' she said awkwardly.

'I'm not busy,' he said, and a look passed between them over Layla's head. 'Come on, let's go.'

79

Half an hour later Annie was standing on Jeanette's doorstep. The door had been mended. When the blonde opened it in a grubby bathrobe, looking bedraggled, her face formed into a scowl at the sight of Annie.

'Oh, it's you.'

'Yeah. Thanks for the warm welcome.'

If Jeanette had known the state her family were in right now, the welcome would have been even less effusive.

'What, you're not going to bust my door off its hinges this time?' Jeanette demanded irritably. From back in the house there came a wail. 'Oh for fuck's *sake*.' Jeanette closed her eyes as if trying to hold on to the last shreds of her sanity.

Jimmy Junior came toddling out from the kitchen. He looked grubby too. His clothes were dirty and his face was streaked with snot.

'Will you for God's sake stop making all this bloody *noise*,' Jeanette yelled at him.

Annie saw the little boy's grin fade as he shrank back, startled. 'Don't yell at him like that,' she said.

Jimmy Junior's eyes met her and he held out his arms. 'Choc,' he said. 'Choc!'

Annie gave a wry smile. 'Nothing wrong with your memory, is there, little Jim?' She walked past Jeanette and went to the little boy. 'Want to go and get some more chocolate with your Auntie Annie?'

'Yeah!' Jimmy Junior looked delighted.

From the kitchen came a longer, louder wail. The baby was crying, shrieking its head off.

Probably hungry. Or hadn't had her nappy changed in a month of Sundays . . . Annie stalked grimly in there and the smell hit her like a punch in the nose. The baby was lying there in its cot, wet through, bawling its poor little head off.

'Jeanette,' Annie called back over her shoulder, 'when exactly did you last change her?'

'Look, I'm not good with kids,' said Jeanette, hustling into the kitchen behind her and glaring at Annie as if she was in the wrong. 'I've never been good with them, okay? They're messy at both ends and noisy in the middle. I didn't *ask* to be playing bloody surrogate mummy to these two, so *don't* give me any hassle, okay?'

'Where's Jimmy?' asked Annie over little Mo's screaming. Jimmy Junior had fastened himself firmly to her leg and seemed disinclined to let go.

'As if I fucking know,' snapped Jeanette.

'Meaning?' Annie snapped right back.

'Meaning I ain't seen him all week. Meaning he's buggered off somewhere, Christ knows where, and left me in the shit, *really* in the shit, trying to cope with these two brats of his.'

Annie smoothed a hand over Jimmy Junior's silky head. 'Hey, Jim,' she said.

He looked up at her.

'Got someone for you to meet outside. Someone you're going to really love.'

He was staring at her, smiling.

'Your cousin Layla,' said Annie.

Years later she would remember that moment, when she had told Jimmy Junior he had a cousin, and that he was going to love her. She would also remember the look on Jeanette's face, the way the colour drained from it, the expression of guilty surprise.

'She out?' Jimmy Junior pointed with one chubby finger towards the door.

'She's outside, yeah. And she really, really wants to meet you.'

Annie picked up the baby from the cot, took Jimmy Junior's hand and took them both to the door. Constantine's man was there. He silently took the grizzling baby and the small boy from her, and went off down the path to the car.

Annie went back into the kitchen.

'Hey, don't get any ideas,' said Jeanette, rallying bravely, trying to keep her voice level while her eyes, darting frantically and settling on nothing, gave her away. 'I don't want you getting all pally with those kids, Jimmy wouldn't like it.'

'Jimmy's long gone, ain't that sunk in yet?' Annie stared at her. Shit, she really was dense. 'No, I guess not. These kids are my family. They're going back to their mother, right now.'

'Hey, you can't just walk in here and *take* them,' said Jeanette hotly.

Annie stuck her hands in her pockets to keep them from throttling Jeanette.

'I just did. You want to make something of it?' she asked, pushing the anger down. Had to stay calm, rational, even though a killing rage was gripping her. This *bitch*, this treacherous little *cow*, was trying to face her down.

Jeanette looked at Annie's face. She shrugged nervously.

'Hey, I should care,' she said. 'I didn't want the damned kids in the first place. But Jimmy'll be back soon, and then there'll be trouble.'

Now Annie almost felt sorry for her. Almost, but not quite. It was obvious that Jimmy had realized the whole thing was going tits-up. And he'd fucked off without even bothering to tell Jeanette the news.

'Your family been in touch?' Annie asked her.

'What?' Jeanette was pale now; she looked slightly sick.

'You know, the family. Danny. Vita. *Una.* They been in touch with you recently?'

Jeanette shrugged, trying to play it cool. 'Oh! Nah, I hardly ever see them. We're not close.'

Annie nodded slowly, her eyes acute on Jeanette's face.

'Well, that's good,' she said at last. 'Cos I think that Danny and Vita might not be in touch again for . . . oh . . . a very, very long time. I guess it must have been quite convenient, having Una right there on the spot to keep an eye on me.'

Jeanette said nothing. Her eyes on Annie's were suddenly full of fear.

'Did you do it for the money, Jeanette?' asked Annie. 'Every successful hit needs an insider, did you know that? I bet you did. And you were the insider on this one.'

'Hey, wait—'

'Yes, you were. You met Vita in Palma the day before the hit. Did a little girly shopping. Bought some shoes. Bounced a cheque. Had lunch. Oh yeah – and told her the perfect time to strike.'

'I didn't . . . how could . . . ?'

'How could I know about that? Friends in high

places, Jeanette. And low ones too. And think about it. Why did they knock me out while it was all going down, but not you? Why would they do that?'

Jeanette was silent. Her eyes dropped away and she swallowed.

'What, nothing to say?' prompted Annie.

Jeanette's eyes met Annie's. Jeanette's were sick with terror now.

'None of it was my idea,' she said.

Annie nodded.

'Oh, good. That makes me feel a whole lot better about things. About . . . oh, about having my husband and his brother murdered. And my friends murdered. And my child snatched and *mutilated*.'

Jeanette's eyes were desperate now.

'Look, it was *nothing to do with me*. Danny and Jimmy cooked up the whole idea; they roped in Phil to help, and Vee's good with kids so she went along too. I didn't want anything to do with it.' Her eyes fastened again on Annie's face. 'What have you done with them?' she asked, her voice trembling.

'Me?' Her eyes were cold as they rested on Jeanette. 'I've done nothing, Jeanette. I've done nothing and I've seen nobody. Some friends got my child back for me. That's all I know.'

Jeanette blinked and suddenly her eyes filled with tears. '*What have you done with them?*' she shrieked.

Annie's eyes remained on Jeanette. She saw the girl's pain, and she relished it.

'Yeah, it hurts, don't it?' she said softly. 'It hurts to have people you love torn from you. I can see you appreciate that now, Jeanette. It's just a fucking pity you didn't think of that before you and Jimmy fucking Bond and your crooked family started in on all this.'

Jeanette was shaking her head, tears streaming down her face. 'I don't know anything,' she insisted weakly.

'Sure you don't,' said Annie. Her voice hardened. 'You were the insider, Jeanette. You knew when was the best time to strike, and you told them. The day before it happened, you borrowed Rufio's car and went into Palma on your own. You didn't tell anyone you were going until after you were back. You were afraid I might want to go in with you, weren't you? You didn't want me tagging along, because you were going to meet up with your bloody sister and check that everything was in place for the hit the next day, tell them it was good to go. Isn't that how it was?'

Jeanette shook her head wildly.

'Good old Jeanette, always the innocent,' said Annie with a sour smile. 'And Jimmy was in on it too,' said Annie. 'My number one man, Jimmy. *Max*'s number one man. Only that wasn't quite good enough for him, was it? He wanted to have it all.'

517

Jeanette's face crumpled and suddenly she looked years older. 'I thought we really had something good going, me and him . . .'

'Oh? Like you had with Jonjo?'

'I'm not sorry about Jonjo,' she said, her expression fearful but surly. 'He knocked me about. He was nasty to me.'

And Jimmy would have been just the same, given time, thought Annie.

'A bullet through the brain's a bit of an extreme punishment for that, wouldn't you say?' Annie looked at the woman in disgust. 'Come off it, Jeanette. Jimmy's no better than Jonjo, in fact he's a fucking sight worse. Say what you like about Jonjo, but at least he was always loyal. But not Jimmy. Oh no. He wanted the Carter manor for himself. I suppose you all met in the pub for a pint and started talking, saying about how much money Max and Jonjo had made over the years, and maybe thinking that you didn't have the fucking *rent* money, let alone money to spare for fancy villas in sunny Spain, and everyone got a touch resentful, is that how it started? And once it started, I suppose it was easy to see how everything could fall into place. Working as a team, you could all have what you craved. Danny and Vita and this Phil character could have money to burn. You could have money, plus Jimmy. And Jimmy could have money, and more important the manor could be his and his alone, once Max and Jonjo were history.'

Jeanette said nothing. Her silence was more telling than all her previous protestations of innocence.

'But it's all gone wrong, hasn't it?' Annie shook her head sadly. 'Such a good plan and such a bad result. Deary deary me. No money. No manor. No fuck-all, in fact. Jimmy's legged it while he's still got legs to do it with, *Really* smart move, but it won't do him any good because I'll find him. I swear to God I'll find him. And as for your brother and your sisters . . . well, it don't look good. It looks sort of fatal, Jeanette, if you want the truth. And that just leaves little you. Which is pretty fitting, don't you think, since it just *started* with little you. What, did you just happen to get the stripping job at the club and meet Jonjo there? Or did you get the stripping job there because you knew you could wheedle your way into his bed? Poor old Jonjo and his weakness for blondes. Looks like it's a weakness that finally killed him.'

Jeanette was hugging herself and shaking now.

'Look, I didn't set him up. He came on to me, I just went out with him, that's all.'

'Until you met Jimmy and he started whispering in your ear about how he could take over the manor, get the Carters out of the way and make a good bit of money out of them in the process?'

'I didn't do nothing wrong,' insisted Jeanette.

'No, sure you didn't. You know, it puzzled me why your brother Danny – the kidnapper – knew no one would pay to get me back. That's what he said when I offered to exchange me for Layla. How could he have known that? Let me guess. Jimmy told you. And *you* told Vita and Vita told Danny. You told them when we were at our most vulnerable. All you did was give them the key to the door, Jeanette. You went into Palma the day before the hit, you met up with your family and you said, tomorrow's the day, go for it. You know, you should get a fucking Oscar for the performance you gave in the villa after the hit. Straight up, you should. You even made as if to phone the Guardia Civil – and congratulations on that, it made your act look *really* good – because you knew I'd stop you going through with it.'

'I didn't do nothing,' said Jeanette, more weakly this time.

'No? You wrecked my life, Jeanette. You wrecked it, stamped on it, ground it into the dust. My husband died. My brother-in-law died. My friends died too. And your hoodlum *fucking* family took my baby girl and hurt her while I was left tearing my hair out, trying any way I knew how to get the money to pay them for her safe return. All the while not knowing whether I would ever get her back. No, you didn't do a damned thing wrong, Jeanette. You're a sodding saint, that's what you are.'

'What . . . what are you going to do to me?' whispered Jeanette, white-faced.

'Me? You know, I've thought about that. Dreamed about it, even. About what I would do to the people who caused all this when I caught up with them. And now I have. I've caught up with you, Jeanette. I've got you in my sights, right now.'

Jeanette gulped 'But I—'

Annie lifted a finger, silencing her. 'I've got just one last question, Jeanette,' she said.

'Wh-what?' Jeanette was pale and sweating.

'Did you try to run me over?'

'*What?*'

'You heard. A car came at me and if Tony hadn't seen it coming, I'd be dead. What I'm thinking is, a friend of mine, a really good friend who's rarely wrong about things like this, she thought Jimmy fancied his chance with me. So what happened, Jeanette? Did the jealousy outweigh the greed? Did you think to yourself, stuff the money, what if I can't trust Jimmy? What if he's planning to change horses in midstream, set himself up with Annie Carter instead of me? Is that what happened? Did you suddenly see red, lose it, want to take me out?'

'No . . .' Jeanette's eyes slid away from Annie's. 'I didn't do it. It wasn't me. I don't know *nothing* about that.'

Annie stared at her. 'You're lying,' she said.

'You've got to believe me,' pleaded Jeanette with a desperate movement towards her. She started to cry. 'You've got to . . .'

But Annie didn't. Jeanette was guilty as sin. The crazy bitch had tried to kill her. And if she'd succeeded, what would Jimmy and her family have done to Layla then, with no prospect of payment, no devoted mother to target?

They'd have killed her too.

Annie straightened. 'Goodbye, Jeanette,' she said, and walked out of the kitchen and to the front door.

Constantine's man was there.

The kids were in the car, with Constantine.

Annie looked at the man, looked back along the hall.

'Do it,' she said.

80

Annie knew she would never forget the expression on Kath's face when she knocked on her door with little Mo in her arms and Jimmy Junior at her side. Kath burst into tears at the sight of her children, taking the baby tenderly into her arms after hugging little Jim until he protested and ran off inside.

Seeing the three of them reunited, Annie knew she couldn't doubt the depth of Kath's love for her kids. Now that Jimmy Bond was off the scene, Annie hoped that Kath would find the strength to get a grip. She was going to help Kath any way she could, she promised herself that. For a start she was going to get Ellie back to help out.

'I don't know what to say. After everything that's gone on between us, and you do this for me?' Kath said, tears spilling down over her chubby cheeks, her eyes sparkling with happiness as she looked at Annie over the baby's head.

Jessie Keane

Then her eyes clouded. 'He'll take them away again. He'll come back and take them off me again . . .' she wailed.

'Jimmy's gone, Kath. He won't be back.'

Unless it's in a box, she thought grimly.

'What about Layla? What happened about Layla?' asked Kath a little more calmly.

Annie looked into Kath's eyes and wondered – just for a second – if Kath could have known anything about the hit. But no. Kath might carp at her, might call her a tart and a treacherous bitch, but what Kath would *never* do was betray her family.

'I've got her back,' said Annie.

'She okay?' Kath's eyes were anxious.

'She's fine.'

'I'm glad,' said Kath. 'Come on, got something to show you.'

Still hugging the baby close, and with Jimmy Junior trotting at her heels, Kath showed Annie upstairs to where Jimmy had kept his stash under the loose floorboard beside the bed. When they lifted the board out, the space underneath was empty. Jimmy had obviously cleared out any cash before he left.

'He used to keep loads of money in there. Hundreds. *Thousands.*'

Yeah, thought Annie. *The firm's money. My money.*

524

This explained a lot. No wonder Jimmy hit the roof when Ellie arrived on the scene. No wonder Kath had panicked and kicked Ellie out when she had said she was going to start on the upstairs rooms. If Ellie had found the hiding place, and reported back to Annie, the shit would have hit the fan in a big way.

Just keep running, Jimmy Bond, thought Annie as she left Kath there with her kids and went back outside into the refreshing spring rain. *Keep running you bastard – but I'm going to find you.*

But Kath came running after her and stopped her at the door. She was holding out a piece of paper.

Annie paused, and took it. Kath was still beaming, incandescent with joy, flushed with it. Annie saw in her face a glimmer of the girl she had once been – funny, friendly, confident. She wanted to see that girl again, but this time as a woman, the woman Kath *should* have become.

'What is it?' Annie asked her curiously.

'Ruthie's phone number,' said Kath with a grin.

81

Two weeks later, Annie granted Darren his dying wish. A gleaming pair of black horses pulled a glass-sided hearse bearing his flower-strewn coffin through the streets of the East End. The funeral director stepped gravely ahead of the horses, his highly polished black top hat tucked neatly beneath his arm as he walked at a stately pace ahead of the cortège.

The pavements on either side of the roads down which the funeral procession passed were packed with silent, respectful mourners and, as the hearse passed by, everyone bowed their heads. The word had gone out: Annie had squared it with Redmond Delaney. Even though it was taking place on Delaney turf, this was a Carter funeral; the man they were burying today was a friend of Annie Carter's, and respect was due.

Dressed head to toe in black, Annie Carter

walked with Dolly, Ellie, Aretha, Chris, and Ross behind the hearse. She'd left Layla with Kath, and she was pleased to see that already Kath was making changes, tidying up, taking more pride in her appearance.

Darren had no family, or at least no family that he had ever cared to acknowledge – although Dolly had contacted his parents and told them the funeral was today, they hadn't shown up. So for today he belonged to the Carter family, he was one of their own, and Annie was proud to give him the send-off he deserved.

Darren would have loved this, she thought.

Thinking of Darren choked her up, but there was love and humour there along with the sadness. She felt such admiration for the way he had risked himself to save Layla, such gratitude for the sacrifice he had made, and overwhelming anger at those bastards who had taken him away from them.

But he had been dying, she told herself. Darren had chosen his route out of this world, and truthfully they all knew it was a better route than the one that would have awaited him if nature had been allowed to take its course.

So for today she had to be at peace with this. And today she felt, as the sun broke through the clouds and shone down upon the procession as it wound its way into the churchyard, that she was burying more than Darren. She felt that today she was also saying goodbye to Rufio, and Inez, and even to loutish Jonjo and – yes – even to Max.

She felt that she had come a long way and gone through fire and fury to get to this place. And now it was time to say goodbye. Time to let it all go, and move on with her life.

All through the service she thought about what that might mean. So much crap had gone down recently and it had taken time for it all to settle. But settle it had. Kath was one hundred per cent better off without that toerag Jimmy. Annie knew that for a fact. She still had scores to settle with him, but that would come. Constantine had put the word out that Jimmy was to be found. Jimmy Bond was toast. He just didn't know it yet.

So everything was working out. There was sadness today, but there was also pride and joy. At last the service came to an end and the pall-bearers, led by the vicar, carried Darren's coffin out into the brilliant sunshine outside the church.

The friends stood around the grave and saw Darren buried there with full honours – buried as a hero, a Carter boy, a beloved companion. Annie felt the pangs of soul-eating sadness, but she remained dry-eyed and straight-backed, because everyone from Carter soil was clustered into the graveyard and their eyes were upon her, the boss of the manor, and she was expected to set an example, to behave with dignity and grace.

She threw one single dark-red rose down on to the coffin, along with a silent blessing, then she walked away, out of the graveyard and into the sunshine, and got into Max's big black Jag – now hers – and told Tony what she had never wanted to tell him. It was time.

There was no way to dress it up. She sat in the back of the car with him in the front and she said: 'Tone . . . Max is dead.'

He was silent, watching her in the mirror.

'Jonjo too,' she went on. 'They were hit in Majorca when the Byrne clan snatched Layla. Jimmy Bond was behind the whole thing. He wanted to take over here.'

Tony looked down. Then his eyes lifted and met hers again.

'I could see it was bad,' he said. 'But not as bad as that. I'm sorry, Mrs Carter. Max Carter was the best.'

'Yeah,' said Annie with a gulp. 'He was. Now, the question I have to ask you, Tone, is are you with me? Or are you bailing out?'

Tony stared at her steadily. 'I'm insulted you gotta ask me that, Mrs Carter.'

Annie smiled a little at that. 'You're with me, then?'

'Yeah. One hundred per cent.'

'Okay.' She let out a sigh. 'Let's get over to Queenie's, then. Time to tell the boys.'

82

The boys were waiting for her. As she came up the stairs and entered the room with the big table and the chairs all around it, they all got to their feet. *Her* boys. Jackie Tulliver, rat-faced little Jackie with a cigar clutched in his nicotine-stained hand, had let them in and followed her and Tony up here.

Annie went to the head of the table – Max's place, now hers – and looked around at them all. At lanky Gary Tooley, solid, muscular Steve Taylor, Deaf Derek and Benny and the others. All snappy dressers, the Carter boys. Max and his brother Jonjo had set the style of the gang. Immaculate. Dark. Fucking scary.

'Sit down, boys,' she said, and took off her black coat.

They sat down, looking expectantly at her. Tony remained standing behind Annie's chair, arms folded, face grim. She had told him what she was going to do, and he knew there could be trouble.

'We was wondering where Jimmy's got to,' said Steve, looking hard-eyed at her.

'And when Jonjo'll be coming back,' said Gary, eyes sharp as a shit-house rat's as he stared at her.

Annie took a breath. 'Jonjo won't be coming back,' she said flatly. She looked down at her hands, clasped together on the tabletop. 'Neither will Max.'

She looked up at their frozen faces. 'There was a hit in Majorca. Max and Jonjo were taken out. Jimmy Bond was behind it. He was in with the Byrne family, they did the hit and snatched our daughter and they wanted me to pay half a million quid to get her back.'

Jackie Tulliver let out a low whistle.

'Holy *fuck*,' muttered Benny.

There was a thick silence.

Then Steve said: 'Did you pay it?'

'I didn't have it; how the fuck could I pay it? I didn't know where Max stashed his cash and Jimmy had all but cleaned the firm out by the time I got back here.'

'You didn't say a fucking word about this,' said Gary.

'I didn't dare. They had Layla. I had to find a big source of money, fast. And that was Constantine Barolli.'

'Jesus H Christ in a sidecar,' breathed Gary, exchanging a look with Steve. 'Sure, the firm's done a bit of legit business with him up West and that's okay, but taking money off the guy? He's fucking Mafia, you crazy?'

'I thought so, but then I was desperate enough to risk it. And Jimmy thought so too, but only because he was getting worried because I was calling in the big guns. The first time I asked him to contact Barolli's mob, he didn't do it. He said they'd try to take over the manor, but really he was shit-scared they'd mess up his grand plan. I think Jimmy believed I would know where Max kept a large stash of money. I didn't. I still don't.'

'What was his plan?' asked Deaf Derek with a frown. 'Jimmy, I mean.'

'Have the manor all to himself. No Jonjo, no Max. Just him.'

Silence fell in the room.

'Fuck's sake,' said Steve, shaking his dark head. 'Max *dead?*'

'Yeah,' said Annie. 'I know.'

'Fucking Jonjo too. But they didn't kill *you*,' said Jackie, eyeing her with a flicker of suspicion.

'Only because I was more use to them alive. I was the one to provide the money in exchange for my little girl. But I didn't know where Max's money was, so I had to go elsewhere to get it, and that's where their plan started to unravel.'

'So what the fuck now?' asked Steve.

Annie took a breath. Her heart was hammering. Her palms were damp with nervous sweat.

'What the fuck now is this.' Annie stood up, planted her fists on the table, and looked around at them all. 'Constantine Barolli's got the word out for Jimmy. He knows I want him found, so Jimmy's on borrowed time. I'm taking over here, just as I said. I meant it. So here's the deal. If you're with me, that's fine. That's good. If you're not, if you've got any doubts about this, or you're not willing to take orders from a woman, then that's good too. You can fuck off out of it. Now. This minute. I can get others to take your place.'

Which wasn't really true, especially not of Gary and Steve. These were staunch, reliable men, and she believed them to be unflinchingly loyal to the firm. She needed them.

'So.' She stared around at them. Tony stepped forward and stood at her shoulder, a solid wall of menacing muscle. 'Who's with me, and who's for walking out that fucking door?' she asked.

Dead silence.

Then finally Gary said, 'If this is true, all this stuff about Jimmy doing Max and Jonjo, we want to deal with him.'

There were nods and murmurs of agreement from around the table.

'We will deal with him,' Annie promised. 'You

think I ain't got the bottle for that or something? He had my husband killed and my daughter kidnapped. We'll deal with him all right.'

Gary and Steve exchanged another look.

'Then . . . I reckon we're with you,' said Steve.

'Yeah,' said Jackie. 'Me too.'

'And me,' said Derek.

'Yeah,' said Benny.

Thank fuck for that, thought Annie.

83

When she got back to Limehouse they were holding a party for Darren; he'd told them straight – no wakes. And so a bloody party was what they were having. All their best clients were in, enjoying themselves in a strictly non-sexual way – this wasn't *that* sort of party – swigging champagne and eating nibbles, dancing like nutters to the England World Cup squad singing *Back Home*.

At the end of the evening, Dolly got up and a hush fell over the room. Annie sat on the couch with Layla dozing on her lap. Aretha and Ellie were standing by the door, their faces solemn. Aretha patted Ellie on the back. Ellie – poor, two-faced Ellie – would miss Darren the most.

'Ladies and gentlemen, you all knew Darren,' said Dolly into the sudden sober silence. 'He was kind, and gentle, and funny. He was also – and none of us knew this about him until right at the

end of his short life – bloody brave. He was trying
to save the life of this little girl right here.' Dolly
indicated Layla. 'Our Darren had the heart of a
lion. So let's drink a toast to him now. To our dear
friend who is now at peace – to Darren.'

A roar of approval went up around the room.
Ellie burst into tears, and Aretha hugged her. Dolly
swiped away a tear or two.

God bless you, Darren, thought Annie, hugging
Layla's warm little body closely to hers.

'Now come on – who wants more champers
. . . ?' And Dolly was off around the room again,
and the music restarted – the Stones doing
Honky Tonk Woman – and suddenly the party
was back on.

Just as Darren would have wanted.

Later that night, after Annie had tucked Layla up
in Dolly's bed, she took out the scrap of paper
Kath had given her and looked at it.

Ruthie's number.

The number of the sister she had betrayed, and
still missed like a part of herself.

She wondered if she dared ring.

Would Ruthie want to talk to her? She wasn't
sure. And she was – all right she could admit it
to herself – terrified of Ruthie rejecting her
all over again. She'd been through all that

already, and to open up that particular wound would be more painful than she could stand right now.

Annie sat on the bed in the darkened room, watching her daughter sleep. She found it hard to take her eyes off Layla, even for a moment. She couldn't believe that she had her back again. It was nothing short of a miracle.

Her nerves felt raw, she had been through too much these last few weeks.

She couldn't take aggro off Ruthie, not right now. She put the paper back in her pocket.

There was a soft tap at the door.

'Who is it?' she hissed.

The door opened a crack and Ross put his head around it. She still wasn't his favourite person, but Layla's presence had thawed him, just a bit. He clearly loved kids.

'Phone for you,' he said.

Annie's heart clenched. It was very late. Was there trouble? Kath . . . ?

She followed Ross downstairs and picked up the receiver. It was Steve Taylor.

'We caught up with the tart,' he said bluntly. *Una.*

'You want to know the details?' he asked.

'No. So long as it's sorted.'

'It's sorted.'

Annie heaved a sigh of deep satisfaction. Una was gone. Thank God.

'It was a piece of piss,' said Steve casually. 'Found her, followed her – and she led us to a little bonus.'

Annie's heart-rate picked up. Her own boys had beaten the Barolli mob to the post and she felt proud. 'Where are you?'

'Queenie's,' said Steve. 'You want to come over?'

'I'll be right there.'

She reluctantly left Layla in Dolly's care. This had to be seen through to the bitter end, and she knew it. Tony drove her over there. He knocked on the door and Jackie Tulliver let them in.

Jimmy Bond was on his knees in the empty front room. All the boys were standing around looking at him, with disgust written clear on their faces. You didn't betray the firm. That just wasn't done. Jimmy was going to learn that the hard way.

He'd obviously put up a fight when they'd caught him. Annie looked at his bruised, swollen, and bloody face as he knelt there, no longer hard or handsome, no longer immaculate, his shirt torn, his trousers muddy. His hands were tied behind his back. When she entered he squinted up at her with eyes that were almost closed, so severe was the beating he'd had.

'Hi, Jimmy,' said Annie, walking forward to stand over him.

'Fucking *bitch*,' said Jimmy, and spat out a tooth.

Annie hauled back and kicked him hard in the balls. He doubled over, wheezing and retching.

'That's for Layla,' she said.

Gary Tooley was leaning his lanky frame against the mantelpiece, watching. 'What you want done?' he asked.

Annie stared down at the wreck in front of her and spoke to Jimmy Bond.

'The only reason you ain't dead already is because you're the father of Kath's kids, you know that?'

Jimmy gulped and coughed, his eyes on the floor. He nodded.

'If it was up to me I'd stick you on a meat hook. You had Max and Jonjo killed and my Layla kidnapped. You ain't anywhere near paying for all that yet.'

Gary was still looking at her; all the boys were. Asking the question. What *did* she want done?

Annie's eyes lifted from Jimmy and she looked around at them – her boys, there to do her bidding.

'You know what?' she said at last. 'I'll leave it to you, boys. *You* choose. But I want no comebacks, you got that? No comebacks.'

They nodded. Jimmy Bond was to vanish off the face of the earth. She'd just signed his death warrant, but her hands were clean.

She walked out of there, knowing that finally, *finally*, she had taken her revenge, and that the thing was finished.

When they got back to Limehouse, the phone was ringing again. Ross answered, and handed it to her with his usual scowl.

'Hello?' said Annie, unbuttoning her coat with one hand and holding the receiver with the other.

Ross went off into the kitchen.

Her sister's voice said: 'Annie? Is that you? Are you okay?'

Ruthie.

For a moment Annie couldn't say a word. Her eyes were full of tears and she couldn't utter a sound through a huge lump in her throat.

'Fuck it all, Ruthie,' she gasped.

How could she begin to tell her all that had happened? That she'd been through hell, that Max was gone?

'Annie, are you all right?' asked the kind, concerned voice of her sister. 'Kath phoned and said you'd had trouble. I just wanted to check you're okay.'

Annie blinked and clutched hard at the receiver. She swallowed and dragged her hands through her hair, but somehow managed to force out a laugh.

'I am now,' she said, and it was true.

She sat down on the bottom stair and told Ruthie everything.

84

Annie had an attack of nerves next day when she had to leave Layla again.

'Fuck me,' said Dolly in exasperation. 'She's got me here with her, and Aretha, and Ellie adores her – and Ross is her very own personal bodyguard. He's soft as butter with kids, though he tries to hide it. Get your arse off out of it, she'll be fine.'

But Annie had to really brace herself to do it, to kiss her daughter goodbye and go and pay her dues.

'Are you coming back soon, Mummy?' asked Layla, wrenching at Annie's heart.

'A couple of hours and I'll be back with you,' Annie promised, hastily scribbling a note. 'Mummy has to do a bit of business, that's all, and she'll be right back.'

Unlike Daddy, thought Annie as she walked out the door. She hadn't addressed that problem with

Layla yet. How to tell her that Max was dead? She didn't know how she'd face giving Layla that sort of pain to deal with. Layla was a daddy's girl. Max was the moon and the stars to her: he was everything.

But Annie comforted herself with the fact that her daughter was a tough little thing. She'd withstood all this – she would deal with that, too. It would hurt her. It would hurt her horribly. But she would get through it, Annie would make sure of that. She would dedicate the rest of her life to keeping her daughter – *Max's* daughter – safe. She owed him that.

The pain hit her again as she went out to the car and climbed in the back.

It always surprised her, how *physical* the pain of his loss could be. It hit her right in the gut again, made her gasp. But she had accepted it now. She knew he was gone. She had made her peace with that.

'Where to?' asked Tony, folding up his paper and half turning in his seat to look at her. 'You okay, Boss?'

'I'm fine, Tone. Couldn't be better. Holland Park. Mr Barolli's place.'

Tony nodded, gunned the engine into life, and eased the big car out into the traffic. They were silent all the way over to Constantine's house, but it was an easy, companionable silence. No words needed to be spoken. Annie sat back and relaxed. Relaxed completely, as she hadn't for weeks.

In her mind she bid them all goodbye. Max. She had slipped his ring on to her thumb this morning, it felt right there somehow. She was comfortable with it and with what it represented. She looked down at it, blue and gold. *Oh, Max, how I loved you.* And there was Jonjo. A pain in the arse, but her brother-in-law, to be accorded respect. Dear, sweet Billy Black. She wished him the sleep of the just. And Darren, the unlikely hero, the golden boy of Limehouse. *God bless you, Darren.*

She was half dozing by the time the Jag pulled up outside Constantine's place.

'Won't be long, Tone,' she said, and jumped out of the car and ran up the steps, feeling light, feeling free and airy all at once.

Everything was ahead of her now. She might reopen the clubs, but as what? She still wasn't sure about that. Raymond's Revue Bar was raking in plenty of dosh in Soho, but did she really want to go that route? Jonjo had made the clubs tacky and seedy; she wanted to bring the tone back up. But how to do that, and which market to tap into, was as yet unclear.

She might do anything – there were no limits, no obstacles. She smiled as she thought of her breakfast chat with Dolly. Even Dolly was catching the bug of ambition from Annie: she was talking about expanding into the escort business.

Humming to herself, Annie lifted the heavy brass knocker. A middle-aged woman wearing a maid's uniform and sensible shoes opened the door.

So where are the big ugly heavies? wondered Annie vaguely.

'I want to see Mr Constantine Barolli,' she said.

'Mr Barolli not here,' said the woman in a Spanish accent, and made as if to shut the door.

Annie stuck her foot in the gap.

'Hold on,' she said. 'What do you mean, *not here?*'

The woman looked at Annie's foot. Annie kept her foot right where it was. The woman's dark eyes rose and rested on Annie's face.

'He gone airport.'

'*What?*'

'He gone airport.'

'*Which* airport?'

'Heathrow.'

'Not Gatwick? Not City?'

The woman shook her head.

'I tell you – Heathrow.'

'Is he going back to New York?'

'*Sí*, New York.'

And without a fucking word to me, thought Annie, feeling deflated, irritated, disappointed to her bones.

He was going, and he hadn't told her.

'And the rest of the family?' she asked.

'They go days ago,' said the woman.

Lucco would have been sorry to have missed another opportunity to snipe at her, that was for sure. Annie glanced at her Rolex. 'Has he been gone long? What time's his flight due to leave?'

The woman told her.

Fucking *hell*.

Annie skidded back down the steps, wrenched open the back door of the Jag and threw herself in.

'Heathrow, Tone. Step on it, will you?'

Epilogue

Constantine was just about to go through passport control at Heathrow to board his private Gulfstream 111 jet when he heard a shout. He turned – and so did the meaty mound of black-suited muscle beside him. They saw Annie Carter running full-pelt towards him. She was all in black, dark hair flying out behind her as she ran. Actually *ran*.

Constantine stepped out of the queue.

Annie skidded to a halt in front of him, looking breathless, venomous, disbelieving.

'You *bastard*,' she said when she could get her breath. She glared at him standing there, looking annoyingly good as usual. Immaculate suit, thick silver hair. Dark tan, startling blue eyes.

Bastard.

Constantine gave the heavy a 'give us a minute' look, and the man walked several paces away. He kept watching his boss with a protective eye.

'That's some greeting, Mrs Carter,' said Constantine. 'Care to try again?'

'Oh don't give me all that smooth stuff, I'm not impressed,' snapped Annie, shooting a glare at two women who turned and looked at them. 'I can't believe that you were just going to fuck off and not even say goodbye, you bastard.'

'I'm going home to do some business, catch up with family. We'll be landing at Teterboro. On the way, we'll stop in Goosebay – that's Newfoundland – to refuel. Is there anything else you'd like to know?'

'No,' she said, feeling unreasonably rattled by all this. 'I can't believe you were going to do that, just clear off out of it without a word.'

'Well I can't believe how *upset* you are about it, Mrs Carter.' Constantine looked at her and then grimaced. 'For fuck's sake, I can't have endeared myself to you by what I've done.'

'And *stop* calling me that. Can't you call me Annie, for God's sake? Everyone calls me Annie, why don't *you*? And what do you mean by that? You helped me get Layla back. Ain't that what matters?'

Constantine looked down at the floor and back up at her face.

'Mrs Carter – okay, *Annie* – you and I both know what my motivation was for helping you get Layla back. And you'd have every right to despise me for it. Christ knows I made my intentions plain enough.'

Annie was silent, staring at his face.

'I want to ask you a question,' he said, staring right back at her.

'What?'

'Have you ever wanted something so much that you tried to grab it and then you held it too hard and crushed it?'

Annie thought of Max and of her ruined relationship with Ruthie.

'Yeah,' she said slowly. 'I suppose I have.'

Constantine heaved a sigh. 'Look, I'm used to getting what I want,' he said. 'No one says no to me. Ever. So all right, hands up: I mishandled things. I got right to the wire, knowing what I wanted, but suddenly I couldn't do it. You were in a corner. You'd lost your husband and you were in danger of losing your daughter too. I wanted you so much I thought I was willing to exploit that. Turned out I wasn't. But I knew you'd hate my guts for what I put you through.'

Annie took a breath. So he hadn't been turned off by her frigid behaviour. She thought back to the time when she'd wondered if she should appeal to his better nature. She'd decided that he didn't have one. But she'd been wrong. He *did*.

'I don't hate your guts,' said Annie, frowning. 'But what was that note all about then? The one

that said, *Come Friday, early.* I thought you meant
. . .' She faltered to a halt.

'I *meant* I had the money waiting there for you,
no strings attached,' said Constantine. 'What, you
think I meant come and I'll jump on your bones
and then maybe I'll hand over the money? You
thought that? Not that I *didn't* want to jump on
your bones. I did. I still do. But if you thought
that, if you thought I was *still* going down that
path, trying to force you into things you didn't
want to do, for fuck's sake – I was an idiot, I
know it – then you really ought to hate my guts.'

'So sue me. I don't. You know what?' Annie
looked at him consideringly. 'Underneath all that
scary stuff, I think you could actually be a really
nice man. Are you coming back?'

'I'm coming back. And I'm *not* a nice man. If I
was a nice man I'd have bought you roses and taken
you out to dinner and given you the cash without
a murmur: *that's* what a nice man would do.'

'Well,' said Annie slowly, 'there's still time for
all that.'

She looked at his face, looked into his eyes.
She felt her heart lift and her stomach drop at
one and the same moment. Elation and terror
grabbed her and held on. Something very serious
was happening here. She had let Max go, with
huge regret and heartache – and now once again
her heart was her own.

Only maybe it wasn't.

She gazed at Constantine, and knew that this could have a future. What that future would be, she had no idea. But it might be exciting, finding out.

Constantine took her wrist and pulled her in close against him. His eyes played with hers. 'So, now we're clear that you don't hate my guts and that you think I could be a nice man – a mistake, by the way, I'm not nice at all – are you going to kiss me, or what?'

Annie stood on tiptoe and kissed his lips. Constantine leaned into the kiss, put his arms around her, held her close against him. They stayed like that for several minutes, and then Annie pulled back.

'How long?' she asked.

'Soon.'

Annie smiled into his eyes.

'I wrote you a note,' she said, slipping the piece of paper out of her pocket and into his hand. 'Read it on the plane, okay?'

'Okay. See you,' he said, and kissed her again, very briefly, very lightly.

'Soon,' said Annie.

'Yeah,' said Constantine.

Somehow, Constantine had got under her guard, under her skin. She was sad to see him go, but she was thinking, *He'll be back.*

'Is Layla okay?' he asked.

'She's wonderful.'

'I'll see you soon – Annie.'

'See you, Constantine.'

Annie turned away. He watched her walk off across the bustling terminal, then he and his minder rejoined the small queue at passport control.

When he was through security and on board his jet, with the pilot running through the safety checks ready for take off, he spread out her *pizzino* and looked at it. Caesar's code, the one he always used. Very simple, very effective. He deciphered the numbers quickly, and smiled. The note said *Call me. A.*

'Where to, Boss?' Tony said, when Annie got back to the car.

Where to?

Annie wondered about that.

She thought of all she'd been through, of the deep, gut-wrenching sadness of losing Max. She'd loved him so much. And now there was Constantine. Would she always be drawn to these bad boys? But then, the two were very different. Max had been a rough diamond; Constantine was smooth, intriguing, fascinating.

Yeah, where to?

She had no idea what the future might hold, or if a suave American mafioso could be a part of it.

Who knew? For now she was going to look forward to seeing him again, and in the meantime she was going to get on with her life. She had her little girl back: that was what counted.

'Back to Dolly's, we'll pick up Layla,' she told Tone, and he gunned the Jag's engine into life and pulled out into the traffic flow.

Yeah, she had lost Max.

But she had Layla back.

After that, everything else was a bonus.

As good as Martina Cole – or your money back!

We're so sure that you're going to love Jessie Keane's *Black Widow* as much as Martina Cole's books, that if you don't enjoy it, we'll give you your money back.

All you have to do is send us back the book, along with a copy of the sales receipt and a letter outlining your reasons for returning it to:

Jessie Keane Moneyback Offer
Fiction Marketing
HarperCollins*Publishers*
77–85 Fulham Palace Road
London
W6 8JB

We'll refund you the price you paid for the book, plus £1.00 to cover your postage costs.